HITLER'S ZEITMASCHINE

HITLER'S ZEITMASCHINE

The untold story behind the historical record

BRIAN FARBER

A CIP catalogue record for this book is available
from the Australian National Library

Self published by Brian Farber
Book & cover design by Wordzworth
Cover imagery by Kelepics

ISBN:
978-0-646-98538-1 (paperback)
978-0-648-31220-8 (ebook)

The moving finger writes; and, having writ,
Moves on: nor all thy Piety nor Wit
Shall lure it back to cancel half a Line,
Nor all thy Tears wash out a Word of it.

– OMAR KHAYYAM –

ACKNOWLEDGEMENTS

Thanks go to my son Jess and wife Marguerita for their helpful insights, to fellow author Alicia Hope for her generous mentoring and guidance, to Stefan Keller of Kellepics for providing some of the extraordinary imagery on the book cover, and especially to the main protagonist in this epic tale, Morgen Schreiber, for allowing me to tell her story.

PROLOGUE

Where, or perhaps I should ask, *when* is Karl Hartmann?

I think of little else these days, struck as I am by the irony of my present circumstances.

In my former career as editor of Die Welt newspaper, I had what might have been considered an open door policy for those of our senior citizens who wished to free their minds from the phantoms of their past. Quite early in this editorial role I advised my secretary that, should any of these elderly folk call into our offices claiming to possess important information as yet unknown to the general public, then providing I wasn't particularly busy and their story sounded extraordinary, or at least most unusual, she could send them into my office for a quick interview. Usually, those who made it through this process felt their tale might be of sufficient interest to make our paper's Sunday editions, and some of them actually did end up appearing in the paper's feature pages. But the folk I was really keen to interview were those who wanted to right a past injustice or lay before me the true, as-yet undisclosed facts behind a scandal or conspiracy that had managed to elude public scrutiny. The interviewees in these instances were generally motivated by a desire to ease their conscience before their looming demise and therefore, no longer fearing possible consequences to themselves, sometimes revealed incredible truths that, had they been much younger, they might very well have been at great pains to conceal.

The paper's readership would probably be quite surprised to learn that over previous years some of its top news scoops have been initiated by the chance disclosures revealed in these interviews which, when followed up by the paper's assiduous journalists, unveiled corruption and unravelled political intrigues that, without those earlier revelations, would have remained unknown forever.

The irony I spoke of earlier arises from the most curious twist of fate that, having patiently listened to other peoples' stories for so many years, now that I myself am old and in similar circumstances to my erstwhile elderly informants, with the most incredible story to tell, I am unable to convince any of my associates in the media that my tale warning of the direst consequences to humankind is actually true and should be taken seriously. This then has been my motivation for presenting it instead in the form of the fictional novel you are about to read.

By these means, I fervently hope and pray that at least one of my readers who possesses sufficient influence in government circles will believe my tale and petition legislators to pass laws to thwart the greatest danger civilised society has ever known.

For if this evil invention should ever reappear on this planet, the orderly nature of society – the very essence of our civilization – would rapidly descend into total and absolute chaos.

CHAPTER 1

I had just finished off a backlog of paperwork and glancing up at the office clock, was advised by that unwavering custodian of my daily routine that I was due to take part in our weekly staff luncheon meeting in another half hour. At that very moment my secretary buzzed on the phone to advise that *another old gentleman,* as Freda called them, was in the outer office with a most unusual tale he wished to share with me. I checked the clock again, and figuring I had just enough time for a quick interview, agreed to see him before leaving for my appointment.

The man she ushered into my office immediately gained my interest and for the moment dispelled thoughts of lunch. Although judging by his general appearance he must have been in his eighties, he neither stooped nor showed any sign of the infirmities one expects to see at that age. He strode into my office in a manner suggesting previous military training in an earlier life, and his pale blue eyes fixed mine with a fire of intensity we rarely see in the elderly. However, upon seeing me, his stern expression melted into the smile of one who has just been re-united with a long lost friend.

"Ahh. At last, after all these years, we meet again Morgen Schreiber."

He searched my face for a reciprocal sign of recognition, but not receiving the acknowledgement he sought, his smile quickly changed to a puzzled frown.

I, on the other hand, was a little affronted by his familiarity and taken aback by his greeting. Rummaging through my memory trying to place where I might have seen him previously proved fruitless and in the end I gave up in the belief he was mistaken.

I invited him to take a seat, indicating the usual visitor's chair. He looked down at it, then up at Freda standing near the door, and making no movement, turned to me with face rigidly set.

"Perhaps you will allow me a private interview?"

I thanked Freda, nodding toward the door, which she shut on her way out. I turned back to my visitor, still standing to rigid attention, and repeated my invitation.

He examined the back of the chair, took hold of the top rail and adjusted the chair's position somewhat so it ended up exactly opposite and the same distance from the desk as was mine. Two strides took him to the front where he paused, surveying the seat as if debating whether to sit or not. Then he lowered into it, changing posture from ramrod standing to ramrod sitting in one swift movement.

He searched my face for a few seconds, after which his gaze swept the office as would a searchlight looking for hidden dangers, before once again fixing on me with that same intense look. He cleared his throat.

"My name is Karl Hartmann. I was Adolf Hitler's chief personal aide toward the end of the Second World War, and I was the last person to see him alive in those fateful hours that marked the final collapse of the Third Reich."

I stiffened, startled by this extraordinary claim, his words crisp and clear cast at me as darts to a dartboard, and I chuckled inwardly. This, I thought, whether true or false, was certain to be a most interesting interview.

He gazed at me intently searching my face for any sign which might have indicated a negative response to his claim, but although momentarily speechless, I managed to maintain a strict poker face. As previously mentioned, my office had hosted many interviews with senior citizens seeking to tell their story. Through this process I learned from hard experience that the flow of information could be seriously disrupted if I displayed surprise or any other emotion evoked by the story teller's tale, regardless of how absurd or outrageous it might have sounded at first. Wearing nothing but an encouraging smile had always been my policy in these circumstances, and this proved once again to be the correct approach, as a look of satisfaction crept over Hartmann's face and he visibly relaxed a little.

For a few seconds we contemplated each other, he, shifting and settling into his chair, whilst I, elbows on desk, fingers arching, tips touching under my chin, waited patiently for him to continue.

"I have a story to tell Frau Schreiber that you will probably find totally unbelievable at first, but it is nevertheless true in its every detail."

Everything I had discerned since he first strode into my office informed me that regardless of what he might say, I was about to hear something quite different from the usual old gentleman's tale.

"Please go ahead with your story, Herr Hartmann. You have my full attention."

Karl Hartmann nodded.

"Thank you. But before telling you about my relationship with Hitler, I would first like to briefly tell you something of myself."

He leaned forward in his chair.

"After the surrender of Germany at the end of the War, I was interred for many weeks in a Russian encampment for disarmed enemy forces. Having been Hitler's personal assistant would have landed me in a heap of trouble had my captors been aware of my true identity. However, a day before capture I had been given the false identity of *Oberschütze* – just a common foot soldier – and I was thus able to avoid the fate suffered by those close to the Nazi leadership. After my escape from that nightmare camp, I wandered around my devastated country, homeless and friendless, always hungry and without protection from the weather, in possession of a secret so strange, so incredibly important in determining future events, that at times the burden of my knowledge almost drove me insane. I desperately wanted to share this privileged knowledge with the authorities, but because I had given my oath to certain persons …"

He paused here and gave me a very strange look before continuing.

"… ah yes … an oath to certain persons, that I would not reveal my secret to anyone except to you on this day, I managed to hold on to my sanity, and my tongue …"

I couldn't contain my scepticism at this juncture and before he could carry on with his story, held up my hands to interrupt the narrative.

"Whoa! Hold it right there. Tell me, how could you know you would be granted this interview with me today, when you made that oath some sixty years ago? That, Herr Hartmann surely would indicate an incredible degree of foresight, would it not?"

He nodded acknowledgement and paused to formulate an answer whilst closely scrutinizing my face.

"Yes it would Frau Schreiber, but I ask you be patient with me. I will explain this unusual knowledge later in my story, but for the moment, please bear with me until I am done."

I waved a hand to indicate acceptance, but felt a little uneasy about where this man's story might be heading after such an extraordinarily improbable statement.

"At first, I was engaged in menial tasks – clearing rubble from the streets and filling in bomb craters. But as we both well know Frau Schreiber, Germany slowly recovered from the devastation suffered during the War, and along with so many of my fellow countrymen, I was swept forward on the wave of progress which carried our country from poverty to prosperity. I went from job to job, always improving my circumstances, and as I and the society around me prospered, I thought less frequently about the secret that was known to none other than myself.

"I married. My wife was a beautiful woman. A wonderful woman, Frau Schreiber, and I loved her very dearly. We had a good life together and had children, all successful in their lives, and now I have many grandchildren. I was most distressed when she passed away a few years ago, and am afraid I became a bit of a recluse, concentrating only on my work. To this day I miss my wife so very much."

Hartmann clasped his hands together and looked down fixedly at his shoes for a moment whilst I waited rather impatiently for him to return to his narrative. When he looked up again his eyes glistened with incipient tears, but he quickly regained his composure, and clearing his throat again, resumed his story.

"For many years that secret knowledge lay in the backwaters of my mind. After all, I had commitments to family, and my work so fully occupied my days and nights that I had little time to dwell on matters of the past. But in recent years, with my wife no longer beside me and my children having families of their own making demands on their time, I was often left alone to reflect, and increasingly became concerned that what had happened in the past would have a profoundly disturbing influence on my children and their families in the future."

His eyes roamed around the office for a second or two.

"The promise I made in 1944," – and he gave me that strange look again – "has kept me silent about my secret for many years, but the person to whom I gave my oath informed me that in the future, when certain information was revealed, I was to visit Die Welt offices in order to tell you my story, and that my failure to do so would plunge the world once more into darkness. I am well advanced in years as you can see Frau Schreiber, and know my time will be coming soon enough, but I am not a madman," … He paused here and looking at me thoughtfully added, … "although when I begin to tell you my story, you will probably think I am."

"However, I must press on because I am the holder of information so vital to the future of humankind that not to reveal it now would dramatically change the course of history – to humanity's detriment."

At this point I shifted uneasily in my chair. Hartmann's narrative had begun to sound a little too messianic for my liking; too much indeed like the words of the messiahs and prophets who preached their messages of Armageddon in the corridors of mental institutions.

I stared at Karl Hartmann with a mixture of – well, I guess, disappointment, pity and disbelief, my earlier poker face an interviewer's device no longer. As my thoughts returned to my luncheon meeting, I snatched another quick glance at the office clock whilst pondering how to terminate this interview diplomatically without overly hurting Hartmann's feelings. He followed my glance at the clock before turning to face me with what appeared an amused, wry smile.

"I see you have the feeling that here before you sits another raving lunatic, out to change the world, and I'm not overly surprised. But I have with me substantial proof with which to corroborate my story."

He reached into his vest pocket and withdrew a large envelope which he laid on the desk in front of me.

"When my story is finished, you will find in this envelope proof in the form of an article from your very own newspaper together with other documents which will finally convince you of the importance of what I know to be true."

I eyed the envelope, my curiosity in deep conflict with my scepticism, and lifting my gaze saw he was observing me closely with a shrewd foxy smile.

"Of course, should you not be prepared to hear my story, I shall go to another newspaper, and another and another, until my story is believed and told. The world will then be alerted to the great danger I know of, and you will have missed out on the biggest news scoop of all time."

The man who sat on the other side of my desk just didn't fit the mould of a would-be saviour of humankind. There was something compelling about his posture, his demeanour and his earnestness that tugged at my curiosity. He seemed supremely confident the secret he claimed to have carried since the War was of the greatest importance, and to bait an old newspaper hack like me with the hook about missing out on a scoop demonstrated a wit that foretold a good story at least.

I eyed the envelope and looked from Hartmann to the phone on my desk, and although still highly sceptical, debated – lunch meeting or possibility of gleaning something newsworthy from this man's story.

My hand hovered over the phone for just an instant whilst I measured up Hartmann and contemplated his narrative. He was watching intently, and although he was tightly gripping the chair's arm rests, he nevertheless managed to return an air of confidence with a smile and general demeanour indicating assurance I would decide in his favour. I gave his envelope one last glance and picking up the phone, excused myself from the luncheon meeting.

Karl Hartmann relaxed his grip on the arm rests and with an audible sigh of satisfaction – or was it relief – he settled more comfortably into his chair.

I gave him a reassuring smile.

"When you are ready, Herr Hartmann, please tell me your story."

CHAPTER 2

Adolf Hitler dropped the phone back onto its cradle and strolled across to the window-less frame in the Great Room of the Berghof. The huge panelled window had been lowered into the basement to allow a cool breeze to waft into the room, and he contemplated the majestic snow covered Bavarian mountain peaks in the distance.

The War was going far from well. July 1944 had seen Western allied forces fanning out into occupied France from their beach head in Normandy, whilst allied forces were steadily pushing Northward through Mussolini's Italy. To the East, the Russians were also gaining ground in their Westward push toward Poland.

But despite the constancy of bad news from the front, the message he had just received lightened his spirit and he was smiling to himself for the first time in days.

Hitler turned from the panorama outside as Karl Hartmann entered the room from the doorway opposite and descended a short flight of stairs. He marched across the room, came within a respectful two metres from the Führer and, standing stiffly to attention, gave his leader a Hitlergruiß Nazi salute.

Hitler inspected the youthful officer standing before him, his stern countenance masking the pleasure he felt that here to do his bidding was the one person he knew could be trusted absolutely in the execution of his plan. He had been personally instrumental in mentoring Hartmann's career ever since his attention had been drawn to this tall, fair-haired, blue-eyed youth at a *Hitlerjugend* training camp, and he had been kept posted on Hartmann's career as the young man rose rapidly through the ranks of the *Schutzstaffel* to the rank of *Obersturmführer*. Reports from Hartmann's superiors consistently identified him as intelligent, imaginative, loyal to the Reich beyond the call of duty, and a stickler for following orders to the letter, no matter what the task. He was to Hitler the personification of the Aryan ideal with which he had hoped to purify the German race, and he was more than just a little pleased, and perhaps more than a little instrumental, in having Hartmann seconded to his personal staff.

"The Führer has requested my presence?"

"You may rest easy, Hartmann."

Despite Hitler's invitation, Hartmann showed little relaxation. Hitler indicated two chairs at a nearby coffee table and taking up one of them, requested Hartmann be seated. Once settled, he paused briefly to measure up the young Obersturmführer sitting stiffly to attention, before taking him into his confidence.

"As you are no doubt aware Hartmann, in January 1942 our Propaganda Ministry announced Germany's *Uranverein* atomic weapons development project was to be abandoned. This was however, disinformation Minister Joseph Goebbels proclaimed, to mislead the foreign press. In fact, the Uranverein project suffered nothing of the kind but instead went underground. It has been progressing steadily and satisfactorily ever since in secret laboratories with the objective of creating atomic bombs, each of which I have been assured by our scientists, would have the capacity to destroy an entire city. It was envisaged once we deployed these weapons, our enemies would be brought to their knees in surrender before they were able to make any further advances on the battlefront, and with the military advantage at last firmly in our hands, we would finally achieve victory for the Reich.

"However, it soon became apparent that more time was required to complete research and development of such weapons, and we therefore faced the prospect of the War being lost before the Uranverein Project was able to produce bombs sufficiently advanced to achieve our objective. This then was the catalyst for initiating a parallel research project which would provide the additional months of developmental time required by the atomic scientists. To this end, for the last two years a top secret team has been working on what has been dubbed the *Time Extension Project*. Its aim, Hartmann, has been to produce a device that could distort time, and in so doing, allow our scientists to visit the future, confer with scientists who had already unlocked the secrets of the atom, and then return to the present armed with the knowledge necessary to complete our production of these weapons."

Hitler paused, studying Hartmann to ensure his young aide had followed the narrative so far. Then he smacked fist into palm and exalted.

"And they've done it, Hartmann! They've succeeded! The Time Extension Project has achieved what the scientific community previously regarded as a fantasy – an impossible quest. I have been informed moments ago that our scientists have successfully completed testing a machine which will enable us to access future knowhow. A giant leap forward has been made this day Hartmann, and Germany shall finally triumph over its enemies. The time transcending device they've devised has been assembled right here in the Berghof's bunkers and at this very moment awaits our inspection."

Hitler rubbed his hands together relishing his moment of triumph whilst Hartmann puzzled that a person of his lowly rank should be taken into the Führer's confidence regarding matters of such importance and secrecy. Hitler rose abruptly and Hartmann followed suit, snapping to attention.

"I want you to accompany me during inspection of this machine, to ensure we are both completely satisfied with its capabilities. You, Hartmann, shall be playing a most important and pivotal role in my scheme.

"Come!"

Sentries stiffened to attention ahead of them as Hartmann followed Hitler to a doorway in the retaining wall in the rear court of the Berghof. A long flight of stairs led down into the bowels of the Berghof's bunker complex where an adjutant stood waiting to guide the Führer to a doorway flanked by two troopers. On instruction, the troopers pushed aside the heavy steel door and as it swung open, a short tunnel ending in a secondary doorway was revealed. Beyond, it appeared to widen out into a brightly lit space from which emerged loud, excited voices. As they entered, the troopers guarding the door behind them shut it with a loud metallic clang which had the immediate effect of reducing the loud chatter ahead to furtive, hurried whispers.

The second doorway opened into a large chamber with a vaulted ceiling, higher than the corridor leading to it, spanning a circular space of some twelve metres in diameter. On the far side, an array of electrical cabinets decked with coloured winking lights, toggle switches and meters lined the rear wall, whilst toward the centre of the room a large, bizarre-looking object dominating much of the central space sat on one of two identical steel framed cradles on wheels. The object, illuminated by festoons of lamps hanging near the opposite wall, had the shape of an egg which had been cut in half crosswise, with its flat base now resting on one of the cradles. The egg was about three metres high and two metres in diameter, with a mirror-like surface that sent lamplight dancing around the room whenever the festoons were inadvertently disturbed.

The chamber was currently occupied by three men in white laboratory coats who had been conferring with one another in a huddle as Hitler and Hartmann entered, but now sprang to attention and sang '*Sieg Heil*' in unison as they delivered their Hitlergruiß salutes.

Two of the scientists, a tall bespectacled giant with humourless countenance, and his edgy younger assistant, detached themselves from the huddle and hurried over to the electrical cabinets whilst the third scientist, a bearded balding bear of a man, strode over to welcome Hitler to his laboratory.

"So Fuchs, I have received word of your reported success in trialling this so-called *Zeitmaschine*. Can I take it travel to the future is not merely a possibility, but is now a proven fact?"

Fuchs looked uncertainly from Hitler to Hartmann with a frown and nodded toward the young Schutzstaffel officer.

"You may speak freely in Hartmann's presence Fuchs. He is the one I have chosen to navigate this machine of yours on its first mission to the future."

Fuchs' face brightened, his excitement far too difficult to hide.

"You are entirely correct *Mein Führer*. I am pleased to announce you have arrived at exactly the right moment to witness an extraordinary demonstration of this Zeitmaschine's ability to transcend time. Please allow me to explain.

"Over the past week we have experimented with this machine, at first setting the controls to travel forward by one hour into the future and then remain there. The air around the Zeitmaschine shimmered and it disappeared in a haze, leaving the support cradle on which it had stood empty. We recorded its time of departure and exactly one hour later, the Zeitmaschine rematerialized out of thin air seating itself back on the vacated cradle. This simple experiment confirmed it had indeed travelled through time.

"The next step then, was to determine whether a living creature could travel through time without suffering ill effects. To this end we placed a caged laboratory rat inside the Zeitmaschine and repeated the experiment, this time setting the controls to travel forward by one hour into the future, remain there for an hour, and then return to its time of departure. As before, the air shimmered and the machine disappeared momentarily, before re-solidifying on its cradle.

"Now, there is a most important detail which must be observed in the execution of time travel, and this refers to the simple indisputable fact that two solid objects cannot occupy the same location in space at the same time.

"After the Zeitmaschine had returned from the future, if we had just left it sitting on its cradle, then after another hour had elapsed it would still be sitting there, is this not so?"

Fuchs paused to ensure he had the full attention of his audience before proceeding to expand on a concept he suspected his visitors might find difficult to grasp.

"However, after that hour had passed, the Zeitmaschine we had sent into the future an hour earlier would also be arriving from the past and would be attempting to seat itself on the very same cradle. The two versions of the same machine would fight with each other for space on the same cradle and would consequently be destroyed in the ensuing catastrophic collision.

"We overcame this technical difficulty by the simple solution of providing the two support cradles you see before you. By moving aside the one on which the Zeitmaschine sits after returning from its journey and locating the empty cradle in its place, we would then have an empty cradle ready to accommodate the Zeitmaschine when it arrived from the past in an hour's time, thus avoiding the collision between the two machines.

"Now, after the Zeitmaschine had returned from the future, we removed the rat and examined it thoroughly to ensure there had been no detrimental changes to its usual patterns of behaviour, and just as was expected, whilst examining the rat, exactly one hour after having removed it from the Zeitmaschine, the machine arriving from the past materialised onto the vacant cradle alongside the Zeitmaschine we had moved to the side to avoid a collision.

"Although its arrival had been anticipated, we nevertheless marvelled to see the two identical machines standing side by side on their cradles, each one being the only one of its kind ever built. We were also able to see the rat in the machine that had arrived from the past when the very same rat was also there under investigation on the examination table.

"We made no move to interfere with the Zeitmaschine arriving from the past and after an hour, as had been programmed, it dematerialised carrying the rat back to the past where we had removed it from its cage an hour earlier."

Fuchs' enthusiasm for his experimental methodology was unfortunately not shared by the Führer whose countenance had shown complete boredom during Fuchs' lengthy discourse. Noting his leader's increasing disinterest, marked by Hitler's gathering frown, and realising the very real danger of invoking his displeasure, Fuchs glanced at his watch and made good on his earlier promise.

"And now, Mein Führer, we are most pleased to demonstrate in the next few minutes, that a human being can also successfully travel to the future and back without suffering harmful consequences to their body or mental faculties."

Fuchs called across the chamber, requesting young assistant scientist Jung to join them, before turning back to Hitler.

"Yesterday the cradle locations were exchanged as was done in the rat experiment for similar reasons. Now, Jung here will explain what has previously transpired in this chamber."

Jung joined the assemblage at the door and looked uncomfortably from Fuchs to Hitler before continuing the narrative.

"I realise at this very moment you will not agree with me Mein Führer, but I met and saluted you briefly yesterday. You will no doubt believe this not to be the case, but soon something quite amazing will happen to show what I have said was, and still is, in fact true."

Hitler frowned, his annoyance somewhat tempered by curiosity. He had definitely not been saluted by, or even been in this man's presence the previous day, having spent most of it in the Great

Room finalising next week's propaganda offensive with Goebbels. What on earth was this babbling fool of a scientist talking about?

Fuchs, who had meanwhile been nodding affirmation of Jung's clumsy exposé, came to his colleague's rescue by looking at his watch again and declaring the time for their promised demonstration was near at hand.

"Jung, you will stand here beside the Führer in order that he may understand all that is about to happen. Now, please everyone, stand exactly where you are, do not move and keep your eyes fixed on the two cradles."

As they re-focussed their attention on the Zeitmaschine and the vacant cradle alongside, the silence falling over the onlookers was broken by Kluge, the scientist who had remained by the electrical consoles, who was now gazing fixedly at a hand held chronometer.

"The time is near. On the count of ten the machine from the past will be arriving."

There ensued a lengthy pause during which all eyes kept a keen watch on the cradle in eager anticipation of what might follow.

Suddenly, Kluge began to count in a steady monotone.

"One … Two … Three … Four … Five … Six … Seven … Eight … Nine … Ten."

On his utterance of the word *ten*, the air shimmered in front of the parked Zeitmaschine and another Zeitmaschine, an exact duplicate, materialised on the second cradle. Hitler was startled and took a backward step, whilst Hartmann moved forward instinctively, hand unbuttoning his pistol holster, preparing to protect the Führer from possible danger.

Fuchs hurried to face the onlookers and reassured them with upraised palms.

"Please. Please. There is no cause for alarm. Be assured we are all perfectly safe. But keep your eyes on this second Zeitmaschine and watch what happens next – you will be truly amazed."

He stepped back so as not to obscure Hitler's view, and now that assurance had been given, Hartmann also quietly retreated from his forward position.

Hitler glanced to either side at his neighbours. Fuchs was beaming and rubbing his hands together in anticipation of what was to come; Jung was wide-eyed and perspiring, whilst Hartmann's gaze was riveted on the machine, hand on holster, ready to take action if deemed necessary.

A glass panel in the wall of the newly arrived machine slid to the side and a figure dressed in standard issue white laboratory coat climbed out of the Zeitmaschine, straightened and looked around the chamber in apparent confusion.

The man who had emerged was an exact duplicate of Jung.

Hitler snatched a quick glance to his right, half expecting to find Jung had quietly parted company from the cluster of onlookers, and had somehow managed to slip around to the machine that had just materialised on the cradle.

But Jung was still there at his side.

After vaguely surveying his surroundings, the Jung at the Zeitmaschine finally focussed on the assemblage near the chamber entrance. Seeing an exact duplicate of himself standing alongside the Führer obviously unnerved him as he propped an outstretched hand against the side of the Zeitmaschine for support. Then, managing to overcome his disquiet, he walked unsteadily toward the astonished visitors and stopping a short distance in front of Hitler, gave the Führer a Hitlergruiß salute.

The Jung standing at Hitler's side silently mouthed the words '*I have come from…*' whilst the Jung in front of him spoke the very same words in an obviously well-rehearsed statement.

"I have come from yesterday Mein Führer, to demonstrate the gift of time travel which this Zeitmaschine now presents to the Reich."

The newly arrived Jung paused whilst Hitler and Hartmann stared back speechless.

"And now, with your permission I must return to my own time."

Duplicate Jung swung around, returned to the Zeitmaschine from which he had emerged, climbed aboard and slid the door panel closed behind him. As they watched, the machine seemed to dissolve in a blurring of the air and then it was gone, leaving empty the cradle on which it had stood.

Hitler and Hartmann stared in wonder at the vacant cradle, whilst Fuchs came forward, exultant.

"Please let me explain what we have just experienced here, Mein Führer."

Fuchs dropped a hand on Jung's shoulder and gave him a vigorous shake.

"Yesterday, Jung here volunteered to be the first man in history to travel forward through time, and we planned this venture to coincide exactly with your scheduled visit to our laboratory today. Before your visit, we swapped cradle locations in order that the Zeitmaschine arriving from yesterday would land on the empty cradle and not collide with the machine already sitting there.

"One might be troubled by the appearance of two Jungs in the chamber at the same time, but this can be explained quite simply. If one considers the past, present and future form a straight line in the continuum of existence, then given the Zeitmaschine's ability to distort time, it should not be difficult to see the line can be bent so much that, like the legs of a hairpin, the past and present are able to come ever closer toward each other, and ultimately even overlap, resulting in yesterday's object and today's object appearing together in the same location."

Hitler contemplated the excited, exuberant scientist and his face again gathered in a frown of annoyance. He had not come here for long-winded explanations regarding the intricacies of time travel – the machine worked and that was all he needed to know. There was much work to be done now it had proved itself operational, and owing to the criticality of time constraints, he had to move quickly to fulfil the promise of the Uranverein project. Satisfied with the demonstration, he turned to leave.

Realising Hitler's intention, Fuchs spoke hurriedly.

"Excuse me, Mein Führer, but there is another important detail about time-travel about which I believe you should be aware."

Hitler turned to him impatiently.

"Well, then?"

"The past is the past, Mein Führer, and cannot be changed. We also explored this avenue of research by sending Jung to the day before yesterday. His mission involved taking with him an object to leave on the floor of the chamber before he returned to the present, the idea being that if the object suddenly appeared on the floor in the present it would demonstrate the past could be changed to yield different outcomes in the future. However, the Zeitmaschine would not return Jung to the present time until he collected the object and took it back to the future with him.

We attempted several similar experiments, but no matter what we tried, found we were unable to alter prevailing circumstances in the present by changing things in the past. I mention this important aspect of time travel because if the Führer had intentions of re-visiting the past to correct previous tactical decisions that had failed to produce desired results, he would find such remedies impossible."

Hitler fumed with suppressed anger at the implied suggestion that he, the Führer, might have made such errors. He made a mental note to deal with this presumptuous upstart scientist at a later date for his impertinence. However for the moment, Fuchs still had an important role to play, and the scientist's ill-considered remark could await a reckoning. The Zeitmaschine worked, Hartmann was ready to fulfil his mission, and this was all that mattered at this point in time.

CHAPTER 3

If the walls enclosing the Great Room of the Berghof could have spoken, they would have told of momentous decisions of global consequence that had taken place within their confines. Here in this stately room the highest ranks of the Nazi regime had met with their generals to plan the subjugation of Europe. In this very room Hitler had entertained ambassadors and presidents from around the globe. However, on this particular day, no-one in the Reich, or in fact the world at large, could have been of more importance to Hitler in his quest for world domination than Karl Hartmann, whom he bade be seated in the lounge chair opposite.

Hartmann too had been present in this stately room on a number of occasions, attending to the minutiae raised during those important meetings, and to the present time had never thought to be the sole focus of the Führer's attention.

"Hartmann, I have chosen you for this mission because of your intelligence, your unswerving loyalty to our cause and an attention to detail few of my other aides are able to equal. You are to perform a critically important assignment which will determine the outcome of the War and consequently, the fate of the Third Reich."

He paused and Hartmann responded with pride and enthusiasm.

"I am ready to serve my Führer in whatever task he may care to entrust me."

"Excellent! You have witnessed for yourself today, and are now familiar with the capabilities of this Zeitmaschine. The scientists whom you met earlier are at this very moment preparing it to transport you sixty years into the future. Your objective when you reach your destination will be to identify the specialists at the forefront of atomic research, and upon informing them of your purpose, prepare them for a meeting with atom scientists from our own time. To this end, on your arrival you will discuss your objectives with Reich officials who will assist you in your quest following orders that shall accompany you in the form of documents personally signed by myself."

Hitler paused, leaned back in his armchair and surveyed his aide.

"That, Hartmann, is the essence of your assignment. Do you have any questions?"

Hartmann responded without hesitation.

"A very obvious one Mein Führer – why send me? Why can't your atomic scientists be sent on this mission at the very outset without my having to become involved? Surely doing this would speed up the process of bringing back the knowledge you require from the future?"

Hitler paused to consider his reply.

"An intelligent and thoughtful response, Hartmann. In answer to your question, it all comes down to a matter of trust. Put yourself in the shoes of one of the scientists you would have me send to the future. On your arrival there, you would find the problems currently confounding today's scientific community largely resolved. Instead of struggling with laborious experimentation, you would have unfettered access to an abundance of new knowledge with which to further your career. Additionally Hartmann, you would have ownership of my Zeitmaschine to buy yourself a position of high standing in that future society, and you would also be leaving a country suffering the privations of war to arrive in a Germany, triumphant, rich and powerful – a land of plenty where opportunities unparalleled in our present circumstances now abounded. The temptation for such a scientist to remain in the future and not complete his mission by returning to the past would be great. With the outcome of the War increasingly dependent on the success of this project, I cannot afford to risk losing my one and only Zeitmaschine by gambling it away on people I don't trust.

"I have complete faith in your integrity and loyalty to our cause Hartmann, and this is why you above all men have been chosen for this venture. Upon your return, you will accompany a group of our atom scientists to the future. You will be suitably armed and in possession of every authorisation you require to ensure they perform their function as directed, after which you will ensure they return with the necessary knowledge to bring our Uranverein project to a successful conclusion."

Hitler rose from his chair and Hartmann followed suit, his heart bursting with pride in having the Führer's confidence and being allowed this opportunity to serve the Fatherland in such a pivotal role.

"Mein Führer, you have bestowed upon me a great honour. I therefore pledge my solemn oath that your confidence in me shall be rewarded by the success I shall deliver to this assignment."

Hitler beamed with pleasure, pleased and vindicated in his decision to choose Hartmann.

"The scientists you met in the Zeitmaschine chamber earlier today are at this very moment finalising preparations for your imminent departure. You shall return immediately to receive their instruction. After your return you will not divulge any of the information you have gathered from the future, but shall bring your report directly to me."

Hartmann stood stiffly to attention and clicked his boot heels.

"It shall be as the Führer has commanded."

After Hartmann had given his salute and left the room, Hitler strolled over to the great window frame, relishing the thought of final victory over his adversaries. He stood for a while, hands loosely clasped behind his back, contemplating the vista of green valleys and hills rolling off into the distance to the foot of the snow-capped mountains. A cool zephyr blew in through the opening, ruffling maps and papers on a nearby table. Hitler shivered and reached for the button at the side of the frame to start the great window's ascent from its repository in the basement.

CHAPTER 4

On Hartmann's return to the chamber he found the three scientists busily conducting final checks on the Zeitmaschine. Fuchs looked up from unplugging the power cord at the rear of the machine and struggling to his feet, ambled over to greet Hartmann, his face aglow with eagerness and anticipation. He extended a hand to give the young Obersturmführer a congratulatory shake, but Hartmann, who felt more comfortable with Hitlergruiß salutes, looked down condescendingly on the scientist's proffered hand before reluctantly extending his own, allowing it to be shaken, albeit rather stiffly.

"You are about to make a most historic journey Obersturmführer Hartmann, but first we must educate you in the operation of the Zeitmaschine. Yes?"

Hartmann acknowledged the scientist's enquiring glance with a perfunctory nod, and leading him to the time machine, Fuchs slid the access panel aside to reveal the machine's interior, whilst Jung and Kluge at the instrument panels laid down their clipboards and, with arms folded, leaned back against the consoles to watch.

Hartmann had recently enjoyed the opportunity of inspecting the cockpit of a Messerschmitt fighter at a military airfield in Munich and recalled how impressed he had been by the array of dials and controls surrounding the pilot's seat. By comparison, the cabin of the Zeitmaschine proved to be a spectacularly disappointing affair. The surprisingly austere layout was far more basic than Hartmann could ever have imagined for such a technological triumph. He ran his eye over the cabin's internal structure wherein a semi-circular bench capable of seating six or possibly more occupants, ran around the internal wall, broken only by the gap where intending time travellers gained access. In the centre of the cabin between opposite benches stood an oval console, the top of which housed a small grouping of meters, a large red lever and two mushroom buttons encased in glass housings, these devices apparently being the total extent of the machine's instrumentation.

Fuchs, indicated the seat adjacent to the controls.

"Please enter and be seated over there Obersturmführer Hartmann."

Hartmann boarded the machine and slid across the bench followed by the scientist who clambered in after him, puffing with the effort. Outside, Jung and Kluge abandoned their stance at the cabinets and strolling over to the Zeitmaschine, peered in through the access doorway to observe Hartmann's instruction.

Fuchs waved a hand over the instrument panel.

"We have kept the machine's controls as simple as possible as the persons operating this Zeitmaschine will not necessarily have the intelligence of scientists."

Hartmann frowned at the implied insult and the note of scornful smugness in Fuchs' voice, but refrained from responding with the reproachful comment which came to mind.

"As you can see, ranged along the top of the control panel there are six circular meters, each with an accompanying control knob underneath. These are what we term the *time duration dials*. Their needle pointers can be set to show however far into the future or the past the occupants wish to travel by adjusting the control knobs below them. The first meter dial on the left is, you will note, marked with the numbers zero, one and two, whilst the dial beside it is marked with the numbers zero to nine. These two dials are grouped together and their settings can be adjusted to show any number of hours from one to twenty four. The next dial to their right reads zero to seven and indicates the number of days the operator wishes to travel. To its right, the next two dials are again paired, the first showing the numbers zero to five, the second showing the numbers zero to nine. These, when read together, indicate duration in weeks. And finally on this sixth dial, which you will note is considerably larger than the previous five, are shown the number of years to be travelled. We experienced some difficulty in marking this last dial as we were unsure how far into the future the Führer intended sending you, so in the end we gave it a logarithmic scale which as you can see, results in the divisions between the numbers growing smaller as the numbers grow larger. We have marked this dial with the numbers from zero to seventy, but beyond seventy we weren't able to continue marking numbers with any accuracy due to the crowding which occurs as the values increase toward the top of the scale.

"The operator can therefore select to the hour with absolute precise certainty, how far he wishes to travel through time up to an upper limit of seventy years, by simply adjusting the knobs below the dials. Beyond seventy however, we could not guarantee how far one would travel as the end point of their journey would not be precisely defined."

Fuchs reached across in front of Hartmann and rotated each of the knobs, altering their corresponding meter settings whilst Hartmann looked on.

"There, observe! I have set the dials to read one, two, three, four, five and six reading from left to right. On this setting the Zeitmaschine would travel a total of twelve hours, three days, forty five weeks and six years into the past or the future, depending on which direction the operator wished to travel. Agreed?"

Fuchs gave him a sidelong glance and Hartmann nodded his understanding. Fuchs grunted grudging approval and pointed to the large red handled lever on the right hand side of the year duration meter.

"This control lever determines whether you go forward or backward in time. Push away from the operator to travel forward to the future and back toward the operator to travel to the past. When not in use, the lever locks into the central neutral position to avoid accidental movement.

"Closer to you on the panel, you will see there are two large buttons encased in glass housings. When you have set the duration on the dials and have made your selection with the red lever, you must raise the glass cover over this enclosure, and press the red button inside to commence your time journey. The Zeitmaschine will then go forward or backward in time, whichever you have selected, by the amount you have shown on the duration dials.

"When you wish to return to the time from which your journey originally began, you need only press the green button in the second glass compartment. This will automatically return you to a fraction of a second after the moment you departed.

"If on the other hand you wished to travel to a different time location rather than return to the time from which your journey began, you would have to reset the duration dials to your preferred temporal destination, select the desired red lever position and depress the red button once again."

Fuchs peered closely into Hartmann's face.

"All the controls are clearly labelled so there will be no mistakes. Yes?"

Hartmann nodded again, resentful of this arrogant scientist's impertinent insinuation that he might have difficulties with such simple controls. A young child could operate this machine.

Fuchs again grunted satisfaction with Hartmann's training so far.

"And finally, this last dial here to the left of the green button compartment is what we term the *time speed meter*. Similar in function to the speedometer of your car, it shows how fast one is travelling through time. Just as in a car when one depresses the accelerator pedal, the vehicle moves forward with gathering speed, so too does the Zeitmaschine. It starts to travel through time slowly at first when one presses the red button, and then accelerates. As the machine approaches its time destination it starts to decelerate, finally slowing to a halt when it reaches the dialled target time. Unfortunately, we have not had sufficient time to calibrate this dial to tell the operator exactly how fast he is travelling through time, so the meter is indicative only."

Turning to the cabin wall behind them, Fuchs drew Hartmann's attention to a large toggle switch mounted above head level.

"This is the main power switch. It draws the energy the apparatus requires from on-board batteries in the base of the machine, and also switches on the overhead cabin lamp. The meter directly below it indicates level of charge in the batteries. It is a most important requirement that one keeps the batteries as fully charged as possible before setting off on a time journey because if they fail, the traveller might end up stranded in another time not of his choosing, or worse still, he might become trapped in a void between two alternative times. You will find a port in the machine's rear which allows the batteries to be connected to a standard power supply for a recharge. However, and we found this most surprising, our test trials revealed time travel consumes very little energy and the batteries should therefore be good for quite a considerable number of hours before requiring a top up. The electronic cabinets you've no doubt observed against the rear wall of the laboratory were only used during development of the Zeitmaschine and for final calibration and testing. They have fully charged the batteries and the machine is now a totally independent entity ready to transport you to the future.

"However, before you venture forth, there are two extremely important cautions I must impress upon you.

"Firstly, as was explained during our earlier briefing, you must always be aware of the possibility of the Zeitmaschine colliding with another version of itself at the conclusion of a time journey. For instance, if after spending time in the future you were to return to a moment *before* you had actually departed, the machine in which you were travelling would crash into the machine still lying in its cradle being readied for departure. The two machines would be destroyed in the ensuing collision, and you of course would be killed.

"Secondly, it is imperative that you keep the access glass door closed at all times whilst time travelling. Under no circumstances are you permitted to leave it open, let alone project your arm or any other part of your body outside. We have not had sufficient time to conduct experiments in order to see exactly what would happen, but I believe if you were to reach out of the Zeitmaschine, your arm would be sheared off and fragments of your flesh would materialise out of nowhere throughout the times you had been passing through. To warn of this potentially dangerous situation we have installed a red warning lamp to the side of the time speed meter. Whilst the power switch is turned on, the lamp will flash continuously until the door panel is firmly shut. On completion of a time journey one must always check the time speed meter to ensure it has come to a complete standstill, marked by the small green indicator globe on the dial lighting up when it's safe to open the door and disembark.

"This completes your instruction and is all you need to know in order to operate the Zeitmaschine. Do you have any questions?"

Hartmann shook his head.

"It is all perfectly clear and straight forward."

Kluge and Jung stepped back to make way as Fuchs extricated his bulk from the machine and turned, waiting for Hartmann to follow. The four men walked over to the entry door where two large baskets had been deposited inside the chamber by a Berghof adjutant whilst they had been occupied in the Zeitmaschine. Reaching into the nearest basket Fuchs picked up an army water canteen lying on top of the other contents and turned to Hartmann.

"Here we have some things you will require on reaching your destination."

He shook the canteen, nodded satisfaction and handed it to Hartmann who, not condescending to show any interest in it at all, passed it on to Kluge.

Fuchs directed Jung to upend the basket and whilst its contents spilled onto the floor, he pointed to the second basket.

"It will be early summer at your destination as it is here at present – warm, pleasant and comfortable. In the second basket we have provided you with a hiking outfit, as military uniforms and everyday civilian clothing will have undergone substantial fashion changes over the coming years, whereas hiking attire has changed little over time and will make you a little less conspicuous amongst the people you'll meet initially in the future before being able to make contact with Reich officials."

From the pile on the floor, Fuchs picked up a cardboard box containing a parcel wrapped in brown paper and neatly tied with string.

"This is a lunch package we had freshly prepared for you this morning, to sustain you just in case you experience problems in obtaining food."

Hartmann sniffed at the wrapping and nodding approval, passed the parcel to Kluge who had picked up a rucksack from the pile on the floor in anticipation, and proceeded to pack canteen and food inside it.

"And here, Obersturmführer Hartmann, this is a most important item."

Fuchs picked up a large, stiff official-looking envelope and handed it to Hartmann for inspection.

"In this envelope you will find credentials and authorisations personally signed and sealed by the Führer himself in order to impress upon the staff of the future Berghof your importance and the criticality of your mission. These documents will enable you to enlist from them all the assistance you require."

Hartmann took the envelope Fuchs proffered, turned it over, inspected the seal on the rear side and handed it to Jung.

Whilst he was doing this, Fuchs picked up and opened a leather pouch from which he extracted a cloth-wrapped bundle.

"You might also find some of the items in this small package necessary in marshalling the resources you require."

As he peeled back the last layer of cloth, a generous collection of diamonds and gold coins came into view, glittering and gleaming under the glare of the festoon lights.

"You might require money in the future, but due to inflation and social change, the currency in use today will most probably be archaic in sixty years' time and would therefore not be acceptable. However, these gemstones and coins will always have value and you should be able to trade them for the currency of the day, should the need arise."

Hartmann took possession of the bundle and after briefly studying its contents, carefully re-wrapped them and inserted the package back into its pouch whilst Fuchs looked on closely.

"The selection you have in your hand should be exchangeable for money at a jeweller or perhaps a pawnbroker. Take good care of them, they have considerable value. The remaining items on the floor are what one might be expected to carry on any hiking holiday – matches, torch, binoculars, pocket knife, a diary and pen, compass, map of the *Obersalzberg*, raincoat, some toiletries and a few other essentials."

Whilst Fuchs set Jung the task of gathering the remaining articles off the floor and packing them in the rucksack, Hartmann picked up a pair of hiking boots from the second basket and inspecting them closely noted they were his preferred style and exact size. Everything seemed to have been very well thought out in preparation for his journey, and attention down to this level of detail reassured him all measures necessary to bring about a successful conclusion to his mission had been put in place.

Jung passed the rest of the hiking apparel to Hartmann who, after inspecting the outfit with considerable distaste, carried it to the rear of the Zeitmaschine where a little privacy would be possible whilst changing into attire he would have rather thrown into the garbage bin.

After changing, he placed his neatly folded uniform on top of the electrical cabinet panels with his peaked hat perched squarely on top and walking around to the front of the machine found Fuchs seated behind the controls in the Zeitmaschine's cabin. The scientist looked up as he peered in at the access opening.

"I have set the controls to transport you exactly sixty years into the future as commanded by the Führer. The Zeitmaschine I now hand over to you, Obersturmführer Hartmann. God speed and good luck."

Fuchs manoeuvred his substantial bulk out of the narrow opening whilst Hartmann retrieved the bulging rucksack from Jung and heaved it onto the bench opposite the control station. He cast a last backward glance around the chamber before climbing into the seat behind the controls, and double checked to ensure Fuchs had set up the dials correctly.

The time duration dials were set at sixty years and the red lever was in the forward position. The main switch was on, confirmed by the interior lamp brightly lighting up the cabin, whilst the red warning light flashed constantly to remind him the door panel was yet to be closed. The meter needle on the wall behind him indicated one hundred per cent battery charge and, satisfied all was in order, Hartmann slid the access panel door shut, took up a position squarely behind the controls and lifted the clear glass cover above the red button. He looked through the portal window to give the three scientists standing in line outside one last contemptuous glance, and as his fist came down on the red button inside the glass enclosure, observed them raising their arms in a parting Hitlergruiß salute.

Then the view outside disintegrated into a bright grey blur.

He glanced at the speed meter. It had started rotating slowly and was gathering speed as he watched. The grey blur outside persisted for only a few seconds, when it was suddenly supplanted by total darkness. Concerned something might be amiss, Hartmann inspected the speed meter again and was much relieved to see its needle was now racing around the dial at high speed.

He sat stiffly upright with his back pressed hard against the wall of the cabin. There was no sensation of movement nor could he hear any sound. He had expected time travel would be accompanied by a modicum of vibration and noise, but instead his senses were only conscious of a disturbing calm and silence. Indeed, the only clue to indicate the Zeitmaschine was actually performing its intended function was to be found within the small speed meter where the pointer needle continued to race around the dial at a frantic rate. Hartmann relaxed a little and considered his intended course of action once the Zeitmaschine arrived in the future.

He would return down the tunnel to the Berghof, present his credentials and authorisations and query resident officials with a view to determining the best method of researching developments in atomic weapons.

Once again checking the speed meter he noted the needle's gyrations were slowing and returning his gaze through the glass door panel, waited expectantly for the light outside to reappear. But to his annoyance the darkness outside shrouding the chamber persisted.

Hartmann mentally shrugged and waited impatiently as the speed meter needle crawled its way around the dial for a few more seconds, before coming to a standstill. He peered into the gloom and figuring the lights in the chamber may have been switched off for some reason, opened the rucksack, and rummaging through its contents, withdrew the torch. Climbing out through the portal he found, as expected, that the Zeitmaschine was still in exactly the same position it had occupied upon boarding, but he was astonished to discover an exact duplicate of his machine parked on the formerly empty cradle beside it. Hartmann paced around the second machine and shone his torch through the access door panel. This Zeitmaschine was identical in every respect, inside and out, to the one in which he had just arrived, and he wondered how it came to be there. The scientists had assured him his machine was the prototype and therefore the only one of its kind in existence, a fact reinforced by Hitler's observation about scientists sent to the future not returning with his *one and only* machine. Finally dismissing pointless conjecture, he resolved to take up the matter with the scientists on his return to 1944.

At the rear of the second machine he discovered its battery charging port was connected by cable to a small engine with an integral fuel tank that smelled of petrol and was fitted with an industrial hose connecting its exhaust to a ventilation panel in the ceiling. This was obviously some sort of generator which had been rigged up to recharge the Zeitmaschine's batteries, but Hartmann marvelled at how compact it seemed compared with the bulky diesel units the Wehrmacht deployed on the battle front.

He turned his attention to the Zeitmaschine's surroundings, and his torch revealed a very different picture from the chamber he had left in 1944. A pile of empty, heavily-rusted metal boxes bearing the insignia of the Schutzstaffel lay on the floor next to the Zeitmaschine, and the electrical cabinets along the rear wall were now dead and silent, their lamps extinguished and covered in dust. Dust on the floor bore footprints leading from the second Zeitmaschine to a steel door in the North wall – a door which hadn't existed there in 1944. He swept his torch around to the other side of the chamber to examine the door leading back to the Berghof and was puzzled to see that a large pile of sandbags had been heaped to one side of it. Hartmann walked over to the door noting that it was already ajar and pulled at the handle. The hinges creaked and the door moved another inch or two. He tugged at it harder and it opened a little more with a groan.

Hartmann shone his torch into the blackness behind the door and gasped. The corridor beyond was filled from floor to roof with rubble and it was immediately apparent that return to the Berghof via this tunnel was out of the question. He turned his back on the Berghof door and strode across the chamber to the door in the North wall. Turning its handle, he gave it a mighty tug expecting similar resistance, but it swung open so easily and violently that it nearly knocked him to the ground. Beyond the door, a tunnel stretched further into the gloom than he was able to discern by the beam of his small torch.

Retrieving his rucksack from the Zeitmaschine, he ventured cautiously along the new tunnel and found it to be a good deal longer than the one leading back to the Berghof. There were changes in direction and quite a few steps upward, which seemed to indicate he was heading up the mountain behind and away from the Berghof. The tunnel ended abruptly in a narrow steel door which Hartmann tested and discovered it too opened easily. Passing through, he found himself in a small cave lit by shafts of sunlight penetrating through an entrance overgrown with foliage. On inspecting the door he had just passed through, he found its external face had been covered in a camouflaging layer of rocks cemented onto the metal surface so skilfully and blending so well with the surrounding wall, that Hartmann immediately realised he would experience great difficulty in finding the door catch again unless he now committed its location to memory.

He brushed aside the foliage overhanging the cave entrance and scrambled out into bright sunshine to find he was surrounded by a forest of trees which hadn't existed in the immediate vicinity back in 1944. A narrow track wound through the ferny under-growth between the trees leading away from the cave and on following it, the timber soon thinned out sufficiently for him to see more of the surrounding countryside. Further down the slope where the Berghof should have been, there was nothing to suggest a building had ever existed there, and instead, the site was now covered in a scattering of trees. The Hotel *Zum Türken*, which had been to the left and somewhat up the slope from the Berghof was still there, but it had obviously been completely renovated, boasting features and paintwork in stark contrast to the drab building in which he was currently billeted back in his own time. In the location in which he now stood there was not a trace of the barracks that had housed hundreds of service personnel and officials during the War, and beyond the Zum Türken, higher up the mountain side he searched in vain for Bormann's and Göring's chalets, but they too had disappeared.

Hartmann was puzzled by these unexpected changes in his surroundings, but seeing the Zum Türken was the only building in the immediate vicinity, he decided to start his enquiries there, and hefting the rucksack a little higher on his shoulder, struck out across the meadow.

CHAPTER 5

In the Zum Türken's carpark Hartmann stopped to admire some of the hotel guests' shiny vehicles. He marvelled at their futuristic, sleek streamlined shapes and luxurious styling which, though radically different from those to which he was accustomed, were nevertheless very pleasing to the eye. An inspection through the cars' side windows revealed the necessary fixtures with which he was familiar accompanied by other features which proved a complete mystery. Hartmann made a mental note to prepare for the many strange innovations he was likely to encounter in this future world, and braced himself to expect the unexpected before approaching the hotel entrance.

However, on entering the lobby he felt a great sense of relief. Whilst crossing the meadow and on seeing the Berghof and surrounding buildings wiped out of existence, he had fought against misgivings that perhaps Germany might not have done so well in the War. But now, seeing the expensive looking cars in the parking lot, the Zum Türken's new facelift and the carefree relaxed nature of the hotel's smartly dressed inhabitants, he felt reassured his country must surely have triumphed after all.

Hartmann made his way to the reception desk and tapped the plunger of a small bell on the counter. Its shrill ring summoned the desk clerk sorting mail in an adjacent cubicle. The young man was suitably attired in a tie and black satin waistcoat, but Hartmann frowned with disapproval at his coiffure, tied up in a long pony tail. He asked to speak to the manager.

Casting an eye over the stranger's odd-looking hiking attire reminded him of clothing his grandfather used to wear, and observing Hartmann's stern countenance, the clerk guessed this stranger might present a problem in which he'd rather not become too involved. With a '*One moment, Sir,*' he asked Hartmann to wait whilst he attended to his request.

The clerk withdrew to a glass windowed office behind the counter, and through the panes Hartmann could see him pointing toward the desk as he spoke to a portly moustached gentleman dressed in a navy blue suit that sported a white carnation in the lapel. The man, presumably the manager, looked up at Hartmann through the window glass, reluctantly slapped down his newspaper, hauled himself out of the sofa and ambled out to the reception desk. Placing his two pudgy palms flat on the surface he leaned forward across the counter looking Hartmann up and down. His rather indifferent expression turned to a look of incredulity as he stared into Hartmann's face. It was a countenance he remembered only too well, having seen it previously on several separate occasions in the past under circumstances he would never forget.

The first time had been when as a child he had run his scooter into the leg of a man with exactly the same features, and who had even been wearing the same hiking clothes. He remembered the incident vividly because his mother, who was the hotel's manageress at the time, had given him a good hiding as a consequence of his misdeed.

The second occurrence was when as a young counter clerk he had reserved rooms for a person, again with identical features, who had occasioned the hotel several times whilst in the company of a rather attractive young woman.

And now here standing in front of him, thirty five years later, was this person who looked like, and even dressed exactly like, the one he remembered from so very long ago. The similarities in every one of these appearances spanning so many years was inexplicable and the manager shook his head at what he imagined must have been an extraordinarily uncanny example of the *Déjà vu* experience. How very, very strange. Disregarding for the moment these bizarre and somewhat disturbing memories, the manager raised a bushy enquiring eyebrow.

"Yes, Mein Herr, I am Herman Wirth, manager of the Zum Türken, at your service. How may I be of assistance?"

Hartmann had been concocting a strategy as he strode up the hill to the Türken in order to keep his identity under wraps until he could arrange a meeting with Reich officials.

"I am conducting research for publication of a travel guide to the Berchtesgaden locality with special reference to the Obersalzberg, which of course includes the area in which your hotel is located. I thought perhaps you might be able to assist me in my research."

On being acquainted with Hartmann's purpose, the manager dismissed his troublesome memories, and breaking into a broad smile, welcomed the opportunity to gain publicity for the hotel.

"Then you have come to the right place, Mein Herr. I have lived in Berchtesgaden and the Obersalzberg my entire life and can offer you much information with regard to its peoples, its geography and its history. In addition to this, the hotel also boasts a fine internet café where you might wish to conduct further research on your own if my knowledge happens to fall short on any subject … or perhaps you would rather begin in there first, gathering some basic ideas before we have our discussion?"

"Internet café?"

"Yes, Mein Herr. If you will just follow me, I would be delighted to show you the very modern facility we have recently installed here in the Zum Türken, and of which I am extremely proud."

The manager led Hartmann across the lobby to an office located to the right of the staircase, and ushered him through the door. On their left, a comfortable settee pressed against the wall was separated from two easy chairs by a coffee table. Beyond them, in the far corner on top of a walnut dresser an urn issued a wisp of steam, and beside it a small basket full of tiny packages was accompanied by a cluster of cups on saucers. The manager followed Hartmann's gaze and nodded toward the urn.

"There is of course a very reasonable charge for use of our internet facility, but coffee and tea are available free for patrons of the café."

Along the right hand wall from one side of the room to the other ran a built-in desk on which were positioned five unremarkable looking black rectangular boxes. Each box was connected by cables to a screen on which a large multi-coloured ball appeared to bounce slowly back and forth between its borders. In front of the screens lay an unusually flat and oddly configured typewriter keyboard, and a stylish office chair, presumably meant for the typist, completed the inventory for each work station. Between two of the black boxes stood a larger, featureless white box with nothing more to identify its purpose than a raised lid on top and a wide slot in front from which projected an empty tray.

Hartmann looked despairingly at the machines on the bench and tried to hide his ignorance regarding these unfamiliar contrivances.

"I am not overly familiar with this equipment. Perhaps you would care to demonstrate how they work?"

The manager gave him a quizzical look, wondering what they taught journalists in school these days, but nevertheless acquiesced diplomatically.

"It will be my pleasure."

His curiosity regarding the young man's strange lack of information technology skills was, fortunately for Hartmann's subterfuge, surpassed only by his eagerness to show this potential publicist that the Türken had been keeping up with the times, and he strolled over to one of the black boxes on the desk. Before taking a seat, he turned to Hartmann, giving him a knowing wink accompanied by a finger tap to the nose.

"Of course if the hotel offered you the use of this equipment for a very modest discounted fee, one might expect a favourable mention of one's establishment in your final report?"

"That is very generous of you, Herr Wirth. I will undertake to make your fine hotel a stand-out feature in the next issue of our travel guide."

The manager expressed satisfaction with this and sitting down, commenced tapping some keys on the typewriter whilst Hartmann looked on over his shoulder, fascinated. At the manager's first keystroke the coloured ball moving across the screen had vanished and was replaced by a brightly coloured background on which appeared the word '*Google*' in colourful letters complemented by a blank rectangular space below it.

The manager swivelled around in his chair.

"This is all you need to get you going. Just type some relevant keywords into the box on the screen and Herr Google will oblige with information on any subject in which you might have an interest."

On noting Hartmann's look of bewilderment, he swivelled back to the screen.

"Here, I'll show you, using as an example the area in which the Zum Türken is located."

He tapped out '*Obersalzberg*' on the keyboard and as he did so, the letters he typed appeared miraculously in the rectangular box, which in turn, had jumped to the top of the screen. Under it, a list of titles in blue lettering appeared, each accompanied by a brief descriptive paragraph and a scattering of photographs.

Hartmann was horrified to see that one of the titles read '*Obersalzberg/Berghof – Third Reich in Ruins.*'

Although beset by a feeling of dread, he managed to control his emotions sufficiently enough to point to the title on the screen without sounding too over-excited.

"There! That one there. I wish to see how one finds out more information about such a title."

"Not a problem. I take it you know how to use the mouse?"

Hartmann scrutinised the desktop suspiciously looking for evidence of the rodent which had so suddenly and surprisingly entered the conversation. Puzzled, he put on a brave face and again managed to hide the depth of his ignorance.

"Show me."

The manager was only too pleased to flaunt his knowledge and to Hartmann's wonder and immense relief, spent a few moments demonstrating the intricacies of the mouse, whilst seeming not to be overly troubled by the fact he was hosting a travel writer who had no computer skills whatsoever. Finally, the manager stood and indicating the chair he had just vacated, invited Hartmann to take a seat.

"If you will now excuse me, I have some accounts requiring my attention. You should be able to find what you are looking for by yourself, but please give me a call if I can be of further assistance."

As the manager turned to leave, Hartmann caught hold of his sleeve.

"Before you go, do you have some means here of recording the things I have seen on this screen? Perhaps a camera?"

The manager gave him another look of absolute astonishment and pointed to the white featureless box.

"All the computers are connected to the printer. Just hit '*print*'."

So saying, the manager headed for the door muttering to himself and shaking his head, but reflecting on the puzzled expression on the face of this poor excuse for a journalist, he stopped at the door to give Hartmann a last piece of guidance.

"Just left click the mouse on the print button at the top of the screen and your document will print out."

Then he left, closing the door behind him.

Hartmann watched through the window until the manager had disappeared from view. Then swiftly returning to the computer he retyped '*Obersalzberg*' into the Google rectangle just as the manager had done, bringing the title '*Obersalzberg/Berghof – Third Reich in Ruins*' once again onto the screen.

He clicked on the title and scrolled through the pages that rolled out across the screen. Hartmann's heart sank as horrific narratives and photographs followed one after another, revealing the extensive destruction of buildings and infrastructure on the mountainside in the wake of British bomber raids, and his dismay quickly turned to outrage on seeing images of American and French troops raising their flags over the ruins. He backed out of this distressing account, and fished about with key words desperately seeking confirmation that the devastation he was witnessing was confined to the Obersalzberg and that Germany had in fact triumphed in the War after all. However, the emerging picture proved too much for Hartmann and as the bitter truth revealed itself in painful detail, he buried his face in his sleeve and wept silently for all the leaders whom he had so respected and admired. To a man their lives had ended under the most ignominious of circumstances – hanged; suiciding; sentenced to rot in prison for war crimes, and worst of all, facing humiliating defeat, the Führer had suicided with Eva Braun in the Berlin Führerbunker.

Hartmann's heart ached at what he was reading, but with the last remaining vestiges of optimism, he was struck by the thought that perhaps the images Google presented were a pack of lies. A malicious fabrication in fact. Was it possible these electronic machines didn't always tell the truth? With lingering hope he challenged the computer, keying in historical detail remembered from his earlier education at the Academy. But over and over again he found the information with which Google responded aligned exactly with what he knew to be true, and finally with heavy heart, he was forced to the realisation that what he was reading about the War's outcome must also be the historical truth.

Abandoning his futile search for something of a positive nature to report, Hartmann turned to the task with which he had been charged – to source the information required by the scientists to further their Uranverein atomic weapons project – even though he now realised this to be a pointless exercise. He was astonished to discover that not only had the Uranverein project finally been abandoned soon after his return from the future, but atomic, or *nuclear* weapons as they were now called, had become the preserve of all Germany's enemies – England, France, America and Russia.

In so many ways what he was learning about the Third Reich's future and its atomic weaponry ambitions – and consequently what he would have to report to the Führer – was devastatingly opposed to what he and the Führer had expected.

And yet … and yet inside and outside the Zum Türken at this very moment, everything he had witnessed to date seemed to be so very much at odds with what one might expect of a nation so overwhelmingly defeated in war – the flashy vehicles in the car park; the prosperous looking patrons of the Zum Türken and the hotel's handsome facelift. He returned to the keyboard and applied himself with zeal to learn more about the Germany which now existed beyond the immediate environs of the Obersalzberg.

In response to Hartmann's typed-in key words, Google rolled out the most incredible images across the screen. Tall majestic buildings sheathed in sunlit glass facades rose up in the midst of the capital's historic landmarks and in multi-storied shopping complexes, myriad boutiques boasted the most exotic of wares to tempt smartly dressed customers who swarmed around the goods on display like bees around a hive. High-speed trains hurtled across the countryside, whilst expensive looking cars sped along eight-lane autobahns and enormous silver aircraft flew high overhead above them all.

Hartmann shook his head in near disbelief. After enduring many years suffering the privations of war, he found difficulty in fathoming how Germany could have risen from the ashes of the past to present such a wondrous picture of prosperity. Cheered somewhat by the glowing future these images presented, he was glad to have at least some good news with which to temper the distressing content of his report, although knowing only too well no amount of good news would be enough to lessen the Führer's outrage on being presented with his shocking findings. He could only hope the Führer would consider Hartmann's own past devotion to the cause and not, as previous messengers bearing bad news had experienced, be condemned to face the Russian onslaught at the Eastern front – or worse – as a consequence of his adverse report.

Hartmann spent the next few hours sifting through a number of Google sites, selecting information pertinent to his briefing, interlacing them wherever possible with details of the glorious future lying ahead for his country, a future so temptingly prosperous that thousands of migrants and refugees were now flooding into the country seeking a better life. The printer clattered away with barely a pause as he despatched document after document to be copied, but he doggedly battled on despite many frustrating stumbles due to unfamiliarity with the mouse and keyboard, and repeatedly cursed the copier for its insistence on printing out voluminous documents in their entirety when only one or two pages had been required. He was on a number of occasions, tempted to call Manager Wirth for assistance, but sensibly reconsidered on reflecting that the subject matter of his print-outs did not fit very well with his fictitious guide book story.

Hartmann glanced up at the clock. It was late in the after-noon – hotel patrons would soon be returning for drinks and dinner after their hiking tours. Thinking they might enter the internet café and begin asking awkward questions about his work at the machines, he gathered together the stack of printouts and packed them into a few large envelopes he found on a shelf under the bench. He glanced unhappily at the waste paper bins overflowing with his discarded printing errors and considered the bulging envelopes under his arm. Manager Wirth had indicated a charge would be levied for use of this facility and in addition, coming from a country embroiled in war where paper of this quality was expensive, Hartmann guessed a tidy sum might be requested to cover the reams of paper he had either used or wasted in printing his report. He rummaged through his ruck-sack and withdrawing the bundle of valuables, contemplated its contents. Though unfamiliar with the cost of fine jewellery, he instinctively knew diamonds were far too valuable to offer as payment in such a situation. Even the gold coins might raise the manager's eyebrow, but seeing no alternative, he slipped a couple of them into his pocket to accommodate whatever the charge might finally come to, and re-wrapped the rest.

The desk clerk was busy filling out a registration form for another guest, but the manager, who had resumed his comfort-able seat on the sofa in the glass walled office, looked up to see Hartmann waiting for attention at the counter, and heaving his portly frame out of the couch once again, ambled out of the office to assist him. He cast an eye over the thick wad of envelopes under Hartmann's arm.

"You have been in the café a long time, Mein Herr and have no doubt gathered much useful information?"

"Yes, I found Herr Google very helpful and printed out a great quantity of worthwhile material for my report, but unfortunately I've wasted much paper in the process. Of course I will pay for this as well as the usual fee for the internet café. However I am now much embarrassed to discover I have left my wallet in Berchtesgaden, and wonder if some valuable coins I was intending to sell in town would suffice to cover my expenses."

Hartmann withdrew the coins from his pocket and laid them on the counter. The manager scrutinized them suspiciously and looked up at him with a pained expression.

"I'm afraid I don't have the expertise to determine whether your coins are valuable or not and cannot put a price on them. Do you not have a credit card or cash in your bag?"

There was movement as the guest behind Hartmann completed his transaction with the clerk and turned to join them in conversation.

"Pardon me, but I couldn't help overhearing your difficulty in settling the hotel account, and believe I might be able to assist. I'm an auctioneer and am often called upon to value rare coins. With your permission perhaps I could inspect what you have there?"

Hartmann acceded to his request and looked on as the auctioneer polished one of the coins on his sleeve, weighed it in his hand, inspected it closely and after turning it over a few times handed it back.

"You have there two of the finest Prussian twenty Mark pieces I've ever seen. If you are intent on selling them, I would be prepared to offer you two hundred Euros for the pair. Mind you, I don't have that amount of cash on me at the moment, but if you're staying in the hotel tonight I could pay you tomorrow morning on my return from a business trip to town."

Hartmann had no idea what a Euro might be worth in relation to the Reich mark, the prevailing currency back in 1944, but he knew the coins were indeed valuable. He enquired after the cost of bed and breakfast and the fee for the internet café, to which the manager responded that fifty Euros would be quite sufficient to cover all charges.

Feeling relief at the promise of delayed cash compensation rather than having a dispute with this strange travel writer, the manager also advised Hartmann he would be only too happy to await payment until the following day. Relieved on hearing this, Hartmann accepted the auctioneer's offer and shaking hands on the deal, thanked him for his assistance. Hartmann had assessed the situation in which he now found himself and had come to the conclusion that overnighting in the hotel wouldn't be a problem at all. His stay would make no difference to the time spent away from his duties in 1944 as he only need press the green button on the Zeitmaschine's control panel *whenever* he happened to be and it would carry him back to a fraction of a second after he had departed from 1944 that morning – regardless of how long he might stay in the hotel.

What made the thought even more appealing was that for at least one night he could enjoy a comfortable bed with fresh clean sheets instead of the hard bunk and rough linen of his billet in the wartime version of the Türken. He also relished the thought of enjoying fresh sausage and eggs for breakfast the following morning and real coffee rather than the disappointing ersatz substitute they dished up in the billet canteen.

That night Hartmann lay between sheets of the softest cotton on an unbelievably comfortable bed and despite his concern regarding the dismal tidings he would have to report to the Führer on his return, he slept more soundly than he had done for a long, long time. Here in this future world, for just one day at least, he had no War to worry about, no one to give him orders and no unpleasant duties to which he was obliged to attend.

CHAPTER 6

In the morning Hartmann enjoyed a hearty breakfast and delighted in consuming several cups of the best coffee he had ever tasted. Afterwards, he retired to the lobby to await the auctioneer's return, taking the opportunity to delve through the hotel's newspapers and magazines, finding fascination in the technical advances which were commonplace in this world of the future, and which of course would be awaiting him in his own future once he returned to the past.

The auctioneer returned just before noon. Hartmann traded his two gold coins for a sheaf of twenty denomination Euros and the pair shook hands again, very pleased with what each had gained out of the deal. After settling the hotel's account, Hartmann slipped the remaining Euros into his rucksack and hoisting it onto his shoulder, marched out of the hotel. His overnight stay and breakfast in the Türken had raised his spirits immensely, despite the worrisome problem of reporting adverse findings to the Führer. On his way to the track across the meadow he passed a group of chattering British tourists alighting from a bus in the carpark, and snorting disapproval, the thought passed through his mind that back in 1944 these enemy aliens would have been immediately incarcerated in concentration camps if they had dared do such a thing. He clucked his tongue and softly whistled his favourite marching song '*Erika*' all the way back to the secret cave.

Sweeping the ferns aside, and in the narrow confines of the cave, he once again marvelled at how well the door to the tunnel had been camouflaged when it took him longer than he had anticipated to find the catch necessary to open it.

Inside the chamber he surveyed the room's contents with the sweep of his torch. The Zeitmaschine stood silently next to its companion machine, ready to transfer him from this peaceful world of the future back to the 1944 world of war and destruction. He sat down on the pile of sandbags and opening the rucksack, withdrew the food parcel Jung had packed inside. Peeling back the wrappings he selected a thick dark rye sandwich bulging with *Braunschweiger*, mustard, pickles and onion – his favourite – and chuckled at the thought that Hitler's security staff knew so much about his personal affairs even down to this, his singular preference.

For a few seconds as he munched, the idea of not returning to 1944 drifted into his consciousness. He had in the rucksack the bundle containing the diamonds and gold coins and considering the worth of its valuables against the relatively meagre amount it had cost to enjoy a night in the Zum Türken, they would surely be sufficient to start a new life in this world of the future.

But as quickly as the thought had come to mind, he dismissed it at once. The Führer had entrusted him with this critical mission and even though it had ended in failure and his own future after delivering the report seemed grim, the very idea of not completing his assignment was simply beyond comprehension.

He repacked, and feeling much better after the sandwich, strode across to the Zeitmaschine to stow the envelopes and rucksack onto the bench opposite the control station. Before climbing aboard however, a disturbing thought came to mind, compelling him to take a second look at the blocked off tunnel to the Berghof. He crossed the chamber to re-examine the confusion lying beyond the door and once again brought his flashlight to bear on the rock fall inside the tunnel.

'*When would this have occurred?*' he puzzled.

The tunnel had of course been entirely accessible when he had left the chamber in 1944 and the door in the North wall was at that time, non-existent. The changes to these avenues of access must have occurred well after he left for the future. Surely there could be no other cause for the tunnel collapse than its having occurred during the British bombing raids he had read about in the internet café. This would in turn, imply the new door in the North wall and the tunnel beyond it were built to access the chamber well after the bombing raids. But for what purpose and by whom? With the tunnel between the Berghof and the chamber destroyed, how would the American invaders arriving in this area have known of the secret that existed down here behind a rubble filled tunnel? And even if they managed to learn of the chamber's existence by questioning captured defenders, why would they then build such a long and well-constructed tunnel to get to it when they could have more easily built a provisional stair well straight down to the chamber? And why, he wondered, would the Americans hide the new tunnel behind such a well camouflaged door, tucked away inside a secluded cave?

It certainly was a mystery.

Inside the Zeitmaschine, he found the needle on the battery meter had scarcely moved after his journey to the future, indicating they were still near-fully charged and ready to power the machine back to 1944. He opened the glass cover over the green return button and hesitated, his palm poised above it whilst he reflected on the Führer's most likely reaction to his report. Hitler didn't deal very well with bad news, and in many instances, messengers bearing tidings not to his liking invariably found themselves in the most appalling conditions, facing the might of the Russian army on the Eastern front. He stiffened with resolve – he would not waver from his duty, come what may – he would present his report to the Führer in person and face his leader's anticipated wrath with the equanimity and discipline becoming of an Obersturmführer of the SS. However, he concluded gloomily, his journey to the past would almost certainly condemn him to a future in which he had no future.

'*Duty*', he counselled himself, and his palm came down firmly on the green button.

Without a sound emanating from the Zeitmaschine, the needle on the speed meter started rotating slowly in the opposite direction to its earlier forward travel and picking up speed was soon rotating rapidly as the Zeitmaschine catapulted him back to 1944.

It remained pitch black outside for the passing minutes until darkness finally gave way to the return of the bright grey light as the speed dial needle completed its rapid phase and began slowing down. It crawled to a standstill, and just as the blur outside coalesced into a solid picture, Hartmann glanced through the access portal to see the three scientists outside, their arms dropping from the Hitlergruiß salute they had been giving him on his departure.

He slid the door aside and climbed out into the chamber. The three scientists gathered around him their eyes roaming over his face, torso and limbs, examining him minutely with the curious expectancy they might have bestowed on a test rat after it had run the gamut of a complex experimental maze.

Fuchs broke the silence.

"We saw the Zeitmaschine blur and become transparent for an instant, before it re-solidified. What happened Obersturmführer Hartmann? Were you successful in your voyage to the future?"

"I was. I travelled sixty years into the future as instructed and the fate of the Reich was revealed to me."

The scientists cast glances at each other and nodded in a knowing hush for a second or two before exploding with joy, laughing, shaking hands and playfully punching each other's shoulders, whilst Hartmann eyed their histrionics in stony silence.

Fuchs turned to him beaming.

"What was it like, Obersturmführer Hartmann? Please, tell us everything you saw in the future."

Hartmann scrutinized each of their faces in turn and frowned.

"I will report first to the Führer and he alone will decide on which facts may be revealed."

He reached into the Zeitmaschine and pulling out the rucksack, handed it to Kluge.

"The torch was useful and very necessary. I recommend you also provide a spare and extra batteries. I used some of the valuables, but the rest are safely secured inside the rucksack. You shall lock it, together with its contents in one of your cabinets and hand me the key."

Kluge took the rucksack and opening one of the cabinet doors, brushed some drawings and journals aside to allow space for the rucksack, before locking the cabinet door after it.

Whilst he was thus occupied, Hartmann turned to Fuchs.

"How many Zeitmaschines have you created altogether?"

Fuchs was startled by the question.

"Why, only this one, Obersturmführer Hartmann. The machine we have here is the prototype – the only one of its kind in existence. Why do you ask?"

Hartmann searched the scientist's face.

"Never mind. Confirmation of this fact is all I require at the moment."

After Kluge handed him the cabinet key, Hartmann walked over to his neatly piled clothing sitting on top of the cabinets and with some relief, changed back into his uniform. He locked his discarded hiking attire in the cubicle beside the rucksack, and returning to the Zeitmaschine, withdrew the envelopes containing his report, and with them under his arm, he gave the scientists a last scornful glance before marching out of the chamber.

CHAPTER 7

The secretary in the outer office put down the phone and looking up at Hartmann with a recently acquired look of respect, nodded toward the inner office door.

"The Führer will see you immediately."

He jumped to his feet and opened the door ahead of Hartmann, closing it behind him.

Hitler was standing in front of the office window with hands on hips, feet astride, his back to the door, taking in the view outside. On Hartmann's entry, he wheeled around and examined his aide from top to toe as if to ensure Hartmann's journey to the future had not affected him physically in any way. He glanced inquisitively at the bulging envelopes under Hartmann's arm.

"So! You have successfully negotiated your mission to the future and are now ready to report?"

"I am, Mein Führer."

Hitler strode across the room to an armchair and sitting, waved a hand toward the chair on the other side of the small table between them.

"Your report if you please, Hartmann."

Hartmann settled uncomfortably into his chair.

"I had no need to approach Reich officials for information about scientists working in the field of atomic research, Mein Führer. Instead, I discovered the citizens of the future possess extraordinary electronic machines which allow one to access the total accumulated knowledge possessed of all humankind. There are typewriter keyboards attached to these machines which enable one to enquire about any subject at all by typing in pertinent key words. The machines instantly react by posting their response on a screen facing the typist and what one sees on the screen can be transmitted to another machine which prints out the required information. Due to the convenience of these facilities, some of which were available in the nearby Zum Türken, I found it unnecessary to visit any other sources of information. I double checked the material I gathered using facts already known to me, and found these machine's responses were one hundred percent accurate in every detail they dispensed. I have therefore included in these envelopes the information they provided regarding atomic weaponry, the outcome of the War, and the economic and societal future awaiting Germany sixty years from the present time."

Hartmann drew the envelopes from under his arm and carefully deposited them on the table. He looked down despairingly at the stack of documents for a moment before looking up, only to observe Hitler frowning, closely scrutinizing his face.

"I regret to inform Mein Führer the information contained in this report is not at all what we might have wished for, and I hope you will forgive me for presenting you with such regrettable and shocking findings."

Hitler stared darkly at the young Obersturmführer for a few seconds before leaning forward, picking up the top envelope, and withdrawing its contents. He slowly turned the pages, his face at first showing a dismay that quickly turned to horror.

Hartmann had wisely arranged the pages to start with the least troublesome news – the destruction of the Berghof and the surrounding buildings, which one might have expected as a consequence of the Allied bombing campaign, but the information they contained quickly progressed to the worst news of all – the Führer's demise in the Berlin bunker.

Hitler slammed the first sheaf of documents down onto the table and snatched up the second envelope, his face reddening with anger.

Amongst the copious photographs and reports describing the destruction of Germany's infrastructure and armed forces, Hartmann had included details of Germany's final surrender and its failure to develop atomic weapons, incidentally noting they had in fact been deployed by the Americans in a bid to end the War in the Pacific.

Hitler scrunched the page he had just finished reading in a clenched fist, and cast the crumpled document aside.

"Enough!"

He erupted from his seat, overturning chair and table, sending documents and envelopes flying across the floor. Ignoring Hartmann who had immediately jumped to his feet and was now standing stiffly to attention, he paced the length of the office fuming. He stood with his back to Hartmann, fists clenched, for what seemed an eternity, and Hartmann, not daring to move, stood rigidly erect waiting for the forthcoming explosion of rage. Hitler finally whirled around, his face contorted and inflamed with fury, and he screamed at Hartmann.

"I do not accept the contents of this report! … I will not be dictated to by history books."

He thrust a fist high in the air and roared.

"I, Führer of Germany, am the one who dictates history!"

He glared at the documents scattered on the floor and thrusting fist in their direction yelled at them.

"Fuck you!"

Again he shouted at Hartmann as he unlocked fist to point a denouncing forefinger at Hartmann's report, now lying scattered across the carpet.

"That bullshit is someone else's history. It's the history of a traitor to our cause. I do not accept the lies appearing in these documents."

Hitler stamped up and down the room in a fitful rage, swearing and cursing whilst Hartmann endeavoured to remain as silent, still and invisible as possible.

The Führer's tirade gradually lost a bit of its steam, his loud outbursts died down into incoherent muttering, and he was finally able to regain a little of his former composure. He stomped over to where Hartmann stood silent and erect, staring fixedly at the opposite wall. Hitler scrutinized his aide's face at disturbingly close quarters, and Hartmann felt a slight trickle of sweat running under his collar.

"Come, Hartmann! You shall show me this future world from which you have collected this outrageous misinformation."

Hitler marched to the door and flung it open, slamming it into the wall with a shattering crash. The secretary outside who had heard his loud outbursts through the closed door, sank low in his chair as the Führer strode past, closely followed by a much cowed Hartmann.

They made their way out of the Berghof and through the bunkers to the secret chamber where the three scientists were still at work. Hitler ignored them completely as they sprang to attention offering their salutes. He strode up to the Zeitmaschine and walked around it, inspecting the machine distrustfully. On finishing his circumspection, he peered through the open sliding panel and turned to Hartmann.

"You are competent and confident in navigating this machine?"

"I am, Mein Führer. The controls are not at all complicated and having travelled in it previously, I would have no problem in guiding the Zeitmaschine to any destination the Führer might care to nominate."

"Then you will take me immediately to the time in the future you visited earlier today."

Hitler boarded the machine, taking up a position on the bench opposite the control station, and sat stony faced, drumming his fingers on the control console, waiting impatiently for Hartmann to climb aboard. Hartmann paused to consider the situation ahead of them at their destination, and hurried over to Fuchs who, having gauged Hitler's foul mood, was standing with the others, well clear of the Zeitmaschine.

"Quickly, do you have torches more powerful than the one you packed in my rucksack?"

Fuchs nodded and made for a rack on the far wall, talking to Hartmann over his shoulder as he released two torches from their holding clips.

"We keep these ones here on the wall for emergencies in case of blackouts."

Hartmann hurried back to the Zeitmaschine and stowed the torches on the bench alongside the Führer. Then claiming the bench opposite, he inspected the controls. They hadn't been touched since returning from the future, and the time duration dials still read the same – sixty years. The red lever was still in the forward 'future' position and everything appeared ready to take them to the very same day he had previously visited, albeit a few hours later, allowing for the time taken to make his report to Hitler.

Fortunately for their survival, Hartmann's mind was in a high state of alert and recalling Fuchs' warning about the Zeitmaschine colliding with future versions of itself, he quickly assessed the situation they would be encountering on arrival. A shiver ran through his body. He had spent the afternoon and night in the future on his previous visit. If he now left the duration dials on their current setting, the Zeitmaschine in which they were about to travel would collide with the machine he had left parked in the chamber whilst he was residing in the Türken – and he and the Führer would perish in the resultant clash. To avoid this potentially calamitous situation, he advanced the duration dials by a further two days to keep the two Zeitmaschines well separated in time, reckoning this would not affect the overall situation the Führer would be experiencing once they reached their destination.

Hitler watched him like a hawk, following Hartmann's every move as he readjusted the dial and slid the access panel door shut. Fuchs had topped up the Zeitmaschine's batteries during his absence and the dial under the main switch again indicated the batteries were once again fully charged and ready to power them to the future. Hartmann glanced through the access panel glass. There was no sign of the three scientists. Fuchs had warned the others of the Führer's dark disposition and the three of them were keeping a discrete, precautionary distance out of sight on the far side of the Zeitmaschine.

He raised the red button's glass cover and announced the Zeitmaschine was ready, at which Hitler scowled, folded his arms, pressed his back against the wall and nodded. Hartmann pushed down on the button and the view outside the window disintegrated into a blur.

As they travelled forward in time, Hartmann took the opportunity to apprise the Führer of the many things he had observed on his previous journey – the grey blur of light outside that would soon succumb to a darkness which would prevail until journey's end: the changed condition of the chamber once they reached their destination: the rock fall in the old Berghof passage, and the new passage to the outside world. He also told of finding a second Zeitmaschine parked alongside him on arrival in the future, a conundrum exacerbated by the scientists' claim that only one Zeitmaschine had ever made.

When the speed meter needle finally came to a standstill, Hartmann slid the door aside and picking up the two torches, climbed out. He switched them on lighting the area immediately around the access door, and handed one to Hitler as he emerged.

They stood in silence sweeping the chamber with their torch beams. Just as Hartmann had done previously, Hitler walked around the second Zeitmaschine examining it closely by the light of his torch. He returned to Hartmann shaking his head.

"This is indeed a mystery, Hartmann. We shall discuss this intriguing turn of events with the scientists on our return."

Turning his back on the machine he strode over to the Berghof tunnel's access door which stood ajar as Hartmann had left it, and shone his torch into the cavity behind. The rock fall was just as Hartmann had described. He shook his head again and returned to where his aide stood waiting.

Hartmann directed his torch beam to the door in the North wall indicating the way out and Hitler followed in thoughtful silence as they passed through the doorway and tramped up the narrow passage. Hartmann flung open the camouflaged door at the tunnel exit and brushing aside the foliage at the entrance, led the way through the thicket of trees surrounding the small clearing. After following the path for a minute or two, the woodlands thinned out sufficiently for Hitler to recognise exactly where he was. He and Eva Braun had on several occasions strolled from the Berghof through this meadow to the Zum Türken to enjoy informal get-togethers with Reich officials and visiting dignitaries. But his beloved Berghof was nowhere to be seen. Gone! Surveying the slopes beyond the Zum Türken he was unable to detect any evidence to suggest that Göring and Bormann's chalets had once dominated these hills, nor in the immediate vicinity was there any sign of the barracks which in 1944 had housed hundreds of troops, officers and officials.

Hitler sat down on an outcrop of rock and contemplated the situation in the light of these changed surroundings. He trusted his young Obersturmführer aide unreservedly and yet still couldn't bring himself to accept the content of Hartmann's report. The disappearance of the Berghof and the other chalets would appear to corroborate the report's findings, but the critical importance of having atom bombs as a means of winning the War demanded he at least explore this future world to the maximum extent possible before deciding whether to abandon the Uranverein project.

Hitler rose from his seat.

"We shall press on to the Zum Türken, Hartmann."

Hartmann was instantly alarmed at the reaction the Führer's distinctive clothing and general appearance might provoke amongst the staff and guests at the Türken, let alone the additional effect his own Obersturmführer uniform might have. But considering Hitler's current mood, he considered it prudent at this juncture to hold back on his counsel, and later manage any difficulties which might arise.

They struck out across the meadow and on arrival in the hotel's carpark, Hitler, just as Hartmann had done two days previously, was attracted by the streamlined shiny vehicles there. He was engrossed in inspecting the plush interior of a very expensive looking Mercedes through its side window, with Hartmann standing at his side, nervously on the lookout for passers-by, when a nearby car door opened. Its occupant, dressed in a navy blue blazer, tan trousers and white shirt topped by a rather garish orange tie, alighted from the vehicle. After pausing to look them up and down, he strolled over to where they were standing. Hartmann placed a warning hand on Hitler's sleeve and as the Führer turned and straightened at his touch, he nodded in the stranger's direction.

The stranger stopped a few paces from them and after pausing to scrutinize the pair in the awkward silence which followed, his face broke into a broad grin. He greeted them in halting German, delivered with a distinctly American accent.

"Hey, incredibly realistic outfits you guys have got there. You sure as hell look like the real thing. Is there some sorta masquerade going down at the Türken tonight?"

Hartmann's mind raced and quickly deciding there could be no better way of handling the present tricky confrontation, he agreed with the stranger.

"Yes. My friend and I have put a lot of work into our costumes over the last few days, but now that we're here, I'm not so sure we'll be very well received."

The stranger shook his head.

"Damned tootin' right you are, pal"

Hitler bristled as the stranger stepped closer to run a critical eye over his uniform and peering closely at it, fingered one of his jacket's brass buttons. However he managed to contain his outrage at the stranger's disrespect and silently played along with Hartmann's stratagem.

The stranger snorted approval and turned to Hartmann.

"You and your buddy look great – just like the real thing. You've got a few details wrong with the uniforms, but the folk attending tonight's shindig aren't likely to be as fussy as myself about historic detail."

He turned to Hitler.

"That is, of course, providing they even let you in through the front door. I'm surprised you guys have the nerve to front up to a public event dressed in Nazi outfits. Surely you're aware that doppelgangers of Hitler are just about always banned from masquerades. I've been stationed here in Germany for the last two years and find folks hereabouts get kinda touchy and pretty hostile when anyone's dumb enough to remind them they were coerced into an unwinnable war by Hitler and his rotten gang of Nazis … and then had to suffer the consequences of losing it."

Hitler and Hartmann were incensed at the American's remarks, but before they could respond in any meaningful way, the stranger turned on his heel and left them to stride up the path to the hotel entrance.

As he disappeared out of earshot, Hartmann apologised to Hitler for his response to the stranger, feeling perhaps he had been somewhat disrespectful to the Führer in what had just transpired.

"I deeply regret my impertinence to you Mein Führer, but we found ourselves in a very difficult situation, and I had to make sense of our appearance in front of the American."

Hartmann was relieved to see the Führer's angry frown had been supplanted by an amused smile.

"You handled a critical situation very well Hartmann. Dressed as we are at present, entering the Türken to investigate further is quite obviously out of the question – therefore we return forthwith to the Zeitmaschine. However, I have taken note of the stranger's comments which do indeed appear to corroborate your report, although I still have doubts about the certainty of its content. But just in case there is truth in it, and as a matter of insurance, I will necessarily review my plans and reconsider how this Zeitmaschine might be otherwise deployed to avoid the fate the historical record seems to have proscribed for me, and yet still allow us to achieve greatness for the Reich."

At that moment, a car rounded the corner of the road leading into the carpark and being in full view of the vehicle's occupants, Hartmann suggested a hasty retreat back to the Zeitmaschine might be in order before its passengers took advantage of the opportunity to question them about their appearance.

In their retreat across the meadow Hartmann cast cautious glances behind them at the man and woman who had alighted from the vehicle and were now standing on the carpark curbing, staring in their direction. Hitler on the other hand was deep in thought all the way to the cave. Hartmann trailed a little way behind him, anxious to keep his distance lest the Führer's currently agreeable mood prove transient and he relapse into another torrent of his former outrage. However, to Hartmann's surprise, Hitler appeared quite coolly composed as he entered the chamber, and turning to him, made known his deliberations.

"I have been reflecting on a number of matters Hartmann. Your report; the changes we've observed inside the secret chamber; the destruction of our facilities here on the Obersalzberg and the comments made by that American in the Türken's carpark. When we return to our own time, I intend making a more comprehensive examination of the documents you provided in your report, in order to build on some rather interesting ideas that have come to mind. I don't believe your report provides the whole story regarding the future, and have been asking myself, what if the scientists are wrong about the past. Could it be possible, Hartmann, that past events are not quite as unalterable as they have claimed? … And would it perhaps be possible, using the powers of the Zeitmaschine, to avoid the fate the history books insist upon?"

He climbed into the Zeitmaschine with renewed and surprising vigour.

"Come Hartmann. There is much work to be done and *time is of the essence.*"

Hitler evinced the trace of a smile at this witticism as he took his seat and Hartmann, studying his face, wondered briefly whether the shock of witnessing the destruction of his beloved Berghof and losing the War might have unhinged his grip on reality.

Hitler guffawed at the look on his aide's countenance.

"The past is the stuff of history books Hartmann, but the future is mine to grasp now that I have the Zeitmaschine at my disposal. Do not delay. We must move quickly to ensure my future and that of the Reich."

Hartmann closed the entry panel, slid across the seat to the control station and lifted the glass cover over the green return button. He looked up to Hitler who nodded approval, and brought his hand down. Once again, the speed meter needle performed its rapid rotation backwards around the dial. The bright light emerged out of the darkness as the needle slowed, and the chamber came into sharp focus as the Zeitmaschine came to a temporal standstill.

Hitler climbed out of the cabin first and turned to his aide as he exited.

"Hartmann, access to this chamber shall be denied to all persons ..."

Hitler indicated the three white-coated figures standing nervously to attention beside the electrical panels,

"... including these damned scientists!"

"Additionally, the entry door from the Berghof shall be kept locked, with you and myself the only ones to possess keys. It shall be guarded by troopers on an around-the-clock basis to ensure no-one enters until I give further instruction. I will summon you when I have finalised my plans, but for now you will carry out my orders."

Hartmann snapped to attention, clicking boot heels, responding that he would see to it at once, to which Hitler gave a cursory nod, wheeled around and strode out of the chamber. Hartmann turned to the three scientists.

"You heard what the Führer said."

He pointed to the door.

"Out!"

Fuchs looked at him in bewildered dismay and protested.

"But we have important unfinished testing which must be completed before we leave the chamber today, Obersturmführer Hartmann."

Hartmann scowled at the scientist and to lay emphasis on his instruction, meaningfully brought his right hand down to unbutton his pistol holster.

"I said, out!"

The three scientists reluctantly gathered up their files and a few papers lying on the electrical cabinets, and grumbling amongst themselves, shuffled out of the chamber with Hartmann driving their white forms before him, with all the determination of a sheepdog herding rebellious sheep.

At the head of the passage he locked the door and gave the two troopers posted there brief instructions before returning to the Berghof to pass Hitler's orders on to their commanding officer.

With his duties completed for the time being, Hartmann left the Berghof and marched up the hill to his billet in the Zum Türken. As he crossed the meadow, dominated by barracks, ancillary buildings and quadrangles where troops were drilling in formation, he compared the scene around him with the one he had just witnessed sixty years hence. He slowed his pace to consider this vast military complex that history decreed should be wiped from the face of the earth over the coming years, and shook his head as he wondered what the Führer might have had in mind.

Hitler had signalled his intention to defy the past, but what could one possibly do to change eventualities that were already recorded in the history books of the future? Hartmann attempted to grapple with the problematical intricacies of time travel but the complexities arising out of his deliberations led him nowhere and in the end he gave up content that, due to the plan Hitler appeared to be hatching, he had probably been saved from being sent to fight and die on the Eastern front.

On reaching the Zum Türken he strode straight through the lobby and ascending the staircase leading up to his room, cast a reflective eye to the right at the darkened store room which, in sixty years' time from now, was destined to become an internet café.

In the quiet solitude of his room, he stripped off his boots and jacket, and lay down on the bed to get some rest while he waited for the Führer's anticipated summons.

CHAPTER 8

Hartmann interrupted his narrative to ask for a glass of water. I indicated the water cooler in the corner and he strolled over to fill a paper cup.

"Your story, as you yourself have admitted Herr Hartmann, is quite unbelievable, but nevertheless I have found it strangely compelling. I take it from the fact you are still alive and here talking to me today that whatever Hitler had in mind saved you from being punished for delivering that unfavourable report. But surely he must have realised his fate was sealed, as was clearly indicated in those documents?"

Hartmann shook his head and emptied his cup in two quick gulps.

"It was a close thing. My life hung balanced on the razor's edge that day. And no, the history books don't tell the whole story."

He refilled his cup and strolled back to resume his seat.

"Well Herr Hartmann, your story certainly is a twist on what we have all read in the historical record, and no doubt your version of events leading to Hitler's demise will provide us with some fresh insights?

"My tale has hardly begun, Frau Schreiber. Please bear with me. There is so much more to be told, and when my story is done, we will examine the contents of the envelope on your desk – documents which will conclusively prove the Zeitmaschine is not just a figment of my imagination."

I raised an eyebrow. What kind of evidence did Hartmann think would ever convince me such a blatantly impossible tale could ever be taken seriously?

I glanced up at the office clock. It was mid-afternoon and I was beginning to feel the consequences of my missed luncheon appointment. I reached for the phone and buzzing Freda, asked her to have an assortment of sandwiches sent up.

As I hung up, I turned to Hartmann.

"I regret our canteen doesn't do rye sandwiches with Braunschweiger, mustard, pickles and onion. Will *butterbrot* and *aufschnitt* be acceptable?"

Hartmann smiled fleetingly at my attempt at humour and nodded.

"Well Herr Hartmann although I must admit to finding your story patently unbelievable I am still intrigued by the way you have woven your personal tale into the historical record and would certainly like to hear where your story takes us next."

"I can well understand your sceptical standpoint, Frau Schreiber …"

He leaned forward in his chair.

"… and now that I have seen you again, I am reassured you will hear me out. I can promise when I am done, you will be absolutely convinced."

There it was – that word '*again*'. Several times during Hartmann's narrative I had scrutinized his face trying to figure out where I might have encountered him previously, but still to no avail. He paused to finish off the contents of his cup, and I invited him to return to his story when he was ready. He thanked me, leaned forward in his chair to place the cup on the edge of my desk before gathering his thoughts, and returned to his story.

CHAPTER 9

Toward evening an adjutant knocked on Hartmann's door to inform him of Hitler's summons. He rose sluggishly from fitful slumber and sat on the side of his bed, head bowed, combing fingers back through his hair whilst abstractedly contemplating stain patterns in the threadbare carpet.

Finally managing to shrug off his torpor, he pulled on boots, stood to attention, buttoned up his jacket, and reaching for his peaked cap on the dresser, inspected his image in the mirror as he pulled it firmly onto his head.

The hotel lobby was throbbing with life as the change of shift marked the return of Schutzstaffel officers and Reich officials from their duties in the Berghof, the barracks and the other chalets. He strode past them all as they relaxed in easy chairs, smoking cigarettes, poring through newspapers or gathering in small groups in the bar area to share a stein of pilsner. Stars were beginning to appear in the fading twilight outside, but there was still sufficient visibility for Hartmann to quite easily make out the well-trodden path down to the Berghof.

Hitler's secretary looked up as he entered the outer office, and Hartmann enquired about the Führer's mood.

"Much better than earlier on, thank God. Much, much better!"

The relief in the secretary's reply was almost tangible, as he bade Hartmann enter the office directly. However, still obviously apprehensive about the Führer's disposition, he didn't volunteer to open the door ahead of him on this occasion. Hitler was seated at his desk writing notes in a journal. He looked up as Hartmann entered and waving a hand toward a nearby chair, resumed his preoccupation with the journal. Then, finishing his writing with a flourish, he rose from the desk and strolled over toward Hartmann, hands clasped lightly behind his back. Rather than immediately taking a seat in the other chair, Hitler walked past his aide, and close to the door paused, as if to inspect an interesting detail he had noticed on the wall. He turned about and for a moment, studied the young Obersturmführer sitting rigidly upright in his chair, gazing at nothing but the air in front of his face.

Hitler strode back to the chair opposite and sat down.

"Hartmann, I have devised a way of cheating the fate the historical record has prescribed for me. However, I cannot achieve my objectives alone and am forced to rely on someone in whom I have complete trust and confidence to attend to the details inherent in my plan.

"I intend to travel to, and live in the world of the future. It's there I shall forge ahead with our goal of world domination and once again lead the German people in becoming the master race we have all believed is its rightful destiny. You, Hartmann, are the person I have chosen to assist me in this glorious quest. I therefore require your complete attention and concentration on what I am about to reveal because from this moment forward, I will be requiring you to carry out my orders to the letter without question. I trust I can count on your unqualified support in this venture?"

Hartmann responded without a moment's hesitation.

"I am very much honoured by the role Mein Führer has suggested, and he can be confident of my absolute commitment to his plans."

"Excellent."

Hitler leaned back in his chair and thoughtfully studied Hartmann for a moment before again leaning forward.

"While we were returning from the Türken's carpark, I was struck by the thought that, when our enemies finally do sweep through this area at the end of the War as your report would have it, they will no doubt discover and destroy the extensive bunker system we have built linking all the buildings on the Obersalzberg.

"Why then Hartmann, when we arrived in the future, did we find the Zeitmaschine chamber still intact and not demolished as were the rest of the buildings and bunkers?

"The answer of course seems quite obvious. The tunnel from the Berghof leading to the secret chamber was completely blocked off by a rock fall, and at its far end the new access tunnel leading to the chamber was concealed behind a camou-flaged door in a small well-hidden cave. The chamber therefore remained undiscovered for sixty years after the War. But who then, would have been responsible for creating these artifices which have so successfully concealed the chamber and its con-tents for so long?"

Hartmann contemplated the question, but before he could respond, Hitler thumped the table with his fist, his face glowing with a look of triumph.

"The answer to the riddle lies in the fact that our ability to travel safely to the future – as you and I have already done – would be seriously compromised should the Zeitmaschine's present hiding place ever be discovered. If solid objects were placed on the support cradles or the cradles were moved during the Zeitmaschine's absence, the machine might well be damaged or destroyed when it re-materialised in the future and smashed into these things. At this point in time, we cannot transfer the Zeitmaschine to a more secure hiding place because it's too large to transport through the existing access passage, and we must therefore take steps to keep it well hidden in its present location to avoid discovery. To this end Hartmann, it is we ourselves – *we ourselves Hartmann* – who must arrange for the complete blockage of the tunnel leading to it from the Berghof, whilst at the same time constructing a new access tunnel with its entry point camouflaged, in order to prevent discovery of the chamber and consequently, possible tampering with the cradles in the years to come."

The Führer's reasoning made sense and all at once Hartmann could see every piece of the puzzle falling into place. Hitler nodded satisfaction as the dawn of understanding crossed his aide's countenance.

"Your first task, Hartmann, will be to locate the cave in which the rock faced door is to be installed. After you have found it, you shall organise construction of the tunnel linking the cave to the Zeitmaschine chamber. To preserve the ultimate secrecy of this project you shall ensure that all of those involved in its construction will not be in a position on conclusion of the works to share their knowledge of the project with others. After the new access tunnel has been completed, the existing tunnel between the chamber and the Berghof shall be destroyed. You Hartmann, will be responsible for arranging every part of this construction and demolition work.

"Next, we must reflect on my future and the fate of the Reich itself, and in this regard I will give you a brief outline of what I have in mind.

"After examining your report thoroughly and in particular, references to conditions prevailing in Germany in sixty years' time, I considered the opportunities which would avail themselves to a person such as myself with the power of the Zeitmaschine at his disposal.

"Sixty years from now Germany, though prosperous, will nevertheless still be plagued by political unrest. Although your report indicates the country will rise to become the economic powerhouse of Europe, its path to European domination appears to be hindered by the petty dictates of its neighbours in this so-called European Union. I also believe a majority of our people born after the War will be seeking vengeance for the humiliation to which their forebears were subject during occupation by foreign forces, and am convinced they will rise, Hartmann, in support of a leader of conviction, strength and vision such as myself, who is prepared to fight for German dignity and its rightful leadership of Europe. Our countrymen of the future are confronted daily by a rising tide of immigrant workers and refugees from the wars in the Middle East. This flood of worthless scum will no doubt be creating unrest and loathing as they steal the jobs of honest German workers, and pollute our age old culture with their alien traditions. In other words, I put it to you Hartmann the situation in sixty years' time could very well be equated in many respects to the situation prevailing in this country prior to the War. Such conditions will prove the necessary breeding ground for the discontent I shall build upon to prepare our people once more for the conquest of Europe.

"But Hartmann, how would a relative unknown such as myself gain political control in a country where good governance is constrained by party politics, factional splits and coalitions rather than being guided by the strong leadership that I have been able to deliver? My charisma and oratory skills would simply not be enough to enable me to attain the powerful position to which I aspire. What other important ingredient do you imagine a political unknown such as myself would require in the Germany of tomorrow in order to gain the support of his people?"

Hitler searched his aide's face and not finding there the answer he sought, smashed fist into palm.

"Money, Hartmann. Money! Money can buy a world of political influence if one has enough of the stuff. Do you follow me?"

Hartmann nodded, but didn't understand where all this was leading. The amount of money required to launch the Führer – a would-be political unknown in the world of the future – into the prominence and leadership he was suggesting, would be astronomical and clearly defied comprehension.

But Hitler pressed home with his argument.

"Imagine Hartmann, we load the Zeitmaschine with gold and valuables, a fortune which, I might add, is presently available for my discretionary use, and which could be cobbled together within a couple of weeks. Surely this would be sufficient to allow my entry into the millionaires' club, would it not?"

Hitler observed the dubious expression on Hartmann's face.

"But as you are no doubt thinking, this would still fall far short of the vast resources I would require to achieve my goal of leadership, is that not so?"

Hartmann again nodded.

"However, if I invested this wealth I carried with me in stock market bonds and shares knowing with absolute certainty which of them would be rising dramatically in value over the following days, what then? What happens when one knows which horse to back because one has visited the future and has already viewed the race results? Or perhaps which numbers to select in a lottery because one has prior knowledge of the winning numbers after having visited the future?

"By repeatedly travelling back and forth through time in this manner I shall gain these insights and then by backtracking the necessary days or weeks in the Zeitmaschine, I can invest in certainties that are guaranteed to yield massive increases in my capital. In fact, by these means I could easily become the richest man to have ever lived and would therefore certainly have the funding necessary to ensure my political success."

Hartmann at last understood and he regarded the Führer with renewed awe and admiration. Noting Hartmann's unspoken concurrence, Hitler continued to unroll his plan.

"I shall requisition a portion of the treasure the Gestapo has confiscated from the countries we now have under our control, and have it brought here for temporary storage in a suitable bunker cubicle, ready to be loaded into the Zeitmaschine prior to my departure.

"Now, regarding the Uranverein atomic program, once I have departed in the Zeitmaschine, its time transcending powers will no longer be available to assist scientists in gaining atomic weaponry know-how from the future, and consequently they will be unable to develop and deploy atomic bombs in time to alter the outcome of the War – as has been foretold in your report. Persisting with the Uranverein project therefore becomes a pointless distraction serving only to divert valuable resources from Germany's war effort.

"However, atom scientists stripped of their work and privileges could be troublesome – some may flee to work with our enemies abroad. You shall ensure all persons working on the Uranverein project are arrested and incarcerated in *Konzentrationslager Flossenbürg* to prevent this unwelcome possibility."

Hitler rose from his chair and Hartmann followed suit.

"I will provide you with all the necessary authorizations you require for these undertakings. That will be all for the time being, Hartmann. Please give these tasks your immediate and urgent attention."

CHAPTER 10

Over the next few days, Hartmann enthusiastically dedicated his energies to carrying out the Führer's instructions. On the very same day Hitler gave him his orders, Hartmann held discussions with the Gestapo to initiate the arrest of the Uranverein project scientists. Despite their best efforts to keep the lid on the forthcoming purge, no sooner had the first scientists been arrested then word quickly spread, warning the others of their intended fate. Although the majority of those involved in the project were eventually rounded up and incarcerated, a few managed to evade the Gestapo net and escaped to the United States, whilst others made their way to Russia, where they contributed to the eventual success of those countries' nuclear programs.

While Hartmann was working on his allotted tasks, Hitler allocated one of the vacant cubicles in the bunker complex to house the amassed treasure trove destined to accompany him to the future. The room he selected was located behind a heavy steel door which could be securely sealed and locked by shot bolts which slid into recesses in the floor and ceiling, to be secured thereafter by heavy padlocks. Only two sets of keys were made available. One was secreted in the safe in Hitler's office whilst the other was held secure in the buttoned leather pouch hanging from Hartmann's uniform belt.

After leaving the roundup of the scientists in the hands of the Gestapo, Hartmann initiated work on the tunnelling project by commandeering a surveyor from the Wehrmacht Heer Engineering Corps, who was given express orders by his superiors to give every assistance to Hartmann on a top secret mission in the bunkers. Hartmann led the man to the Zeitmaschine chamber where, following his instructions, the surveyor loaded his equipment inside the machine's cabin and climbing aboard, sat expectantly, eyeing Hartmann with curiosity as the Schutzstaffel officer reset the time duration dials and depressed the red button to take them one year into the future. Hartmann paid no heed to the surveyor's consternation as the chamber lights dissolved in a haze and were in turn supplanted by the darkness that enveloped their machine.

The circumstances in the chamber on arrival in the future were exactly as Hartmann had expected, but to the surveyor's amazement it had undergone the most incredible transformation. The festoon lamps which had earlier lit the chamber were now extinguished and instead, the torch Hartmann handed him revealed a nearby heap of metal boxes that hadn't been lying there on the floor when they had first entered the room. Across the dusty floor a stack of sandbags stood to one side of the door leading back to the Berghof, but most astonishingly of all, the Schutzstaffel officer led him to a steel door in the North wall which certainly hadn't been there when they had first entered the chamber. Hartmann ignored the surveyor's excited commentary regarding the chamber's mysterious transformation and instead, ushered him through the door, commanding silence and advising him to keep his mind on the job in hand. Hartmann then set the surveyor to work with compass and theodolite, taking down the directional coordinates defining the tunnel route from the doorway in the North wall to the camouflaged door in the cave at its far end.

With an accurate map of the tunnel's coordinates now in his possession, Hartmann led the surveyor back to the Zeitmaschine where, deploying the green button, he returned them back to the present time. The surveyor was once again amazed to find that the North door through which he had just passed minutes earlier had disappeared, leaving not a trace of its former existence in the brickwork. Hartmann again dismissed the surveyor's incredulity with a sharp rebuke and led him upstairs to trace out a path across the meadow using the coordinates they had gathered from their work in the tunnel below. On reaching their objective as defined by his map, Hartmann immediately realised the impossibility of ever having found the cave without the survey. It was located at the end of a rocky ravine, its entrance hidden behind a gigantic monolithic slab that would require removal using heavy craneage to gain access. Hartmann dismissed the surveyor, and to preserve the ongoing secrecy of his project made immediate arrangements to have the man transferred to the Eastern front with orders to his commanding officers noting he was 'expendable'.

Hartmann now turned his attention to the tunnel construction works that lay ahead. He tasked the Berchtesgaden metal works with the manufacture of the two steel doors required – one for the chamber exit in the North wall and the other, a narrower, smaller door for the tunnel exit into the cave, both based on dimensions of the doors he had carefully measured whilst in the tunnel with the surveyor. Temporary partitioning panels were installed around the Zeitmaschine to conceal it from the tradesmen who were brought into the chamber to cut out brickwork for the doorway in the North wall, and satisfied with progress once work was under way, Hartmann turned to the major task of constructing the tunnel itself. His requisition to the Wehrmacht Heer for the surveyor had been accompanied by a request for an engineer with expertise in bunker and tunnel construction, and the next day Hartmann sat at his desk scrutinizing the man they had sent in response.

"So, Ober leutnant Engel. Your papers indicate you have had extensive experience in bunker construction?"

"That is the case, Obersturmführer Hartmann. I've supervised many of the tunnelling projects on this mountain, and because I have the necessary expertise and live nearby in Berchtesgaden with my wife and young daughter, I'm usually the one called upon when it comes to supervising repairs and extensions."

Hartmann nodded satisfaction and, unfolding the survey map indicating the proposed tunnel route, pointed to the chamber's location.

"We are at present installing a doorway in this wall to access the tunnel you will be constructing. However, construction traffic through it will not be permitted – the door will remain locked throughout the tunnelling works. At the other end, the exit will be located within the confines of a small cave which must retain its present size and appearance and is not to be disturbed. Consequently, you will be required to employ other means of accessing the tunnel works during construction."

With access through the chamber and cave thus denied, Engel elected to excavate a large well down to the centre of the new tunnel route, where craneage could be employed to hoist out excavated spoil and lower in personnel, concrete and bricks to build the tunnel floor, roof and walls.

The doorway in the North wall was completed within three days of Hartmann receiving Hitler's instructions, and the new steel door from the metal works was installed in the wall on the same afternoon. Hartmann inspected the completed work and after satisfying himself the door could now be relied upon to separate future tunnel works from the chamber, he locked it and pocketed the key. Construction machinery was already arriving on site in the meadow and by the time the door was fitted, work had already commenced on the well to access the tunnel works.

Hartmann ensured the supervisors under Engel's direction were drafted from the Wehrmacht Heer's Engineering Corps, whilst slave labourers were drawn from the nearest Konzentrationslager. To further preserve the secrecy of the tunnelling project, on its completion, Engel and his team would be sent to join the fight on the Eastern front where they would face little hope of survival, whilst the labourers would be returned to the Konzentrationslager for subsequent elimination.

Over the next two weeks, Hartmann rendezvoused with an armoured car that drew up in the Berghof's car park at ten each morning. On its arrival, two armed Schutzstaffel officers disembarked from the vehicle to retrieve a heavy steel box the size of a twenty litre gasoline jerry can from the locked luggage compartment in the rear. They carried the box between them to where Hartmann stood waiting on the pavement, and after presenting his credentials, laid it at his feet. The box lids were securely padlocked and bore the circular *SS-Runen* insignia of the Schutzstaffel. Not a word was spoken during each of these exchanges. Hartmann signed consignment papers; the couriers handed him the key to the padlock, and on completion of the transfer, they took a pace backward, raised their right arms in a Hitlergruiß salute and snapped '*sieg heil*' in unison.

As they drove off, the two Oberschütze riflemen accompanying Hartmann picked up the box and carried it to the cubicle in the bunker complex where he unlocked the steel door ahead of them. After each delivery was safely secreted amongst the growing stack of treasure boxes, Hartmann slammed the door shut, rammed home the shot bolts, locked up the cubicle and pocketed the key.

On the occasion of his next visit to the Berghof, Hitler joined Hartmann in the carpark to witness the delivery of one of the boxes. As they followed the riflemen carrying it back to the cubicle, Hitler slowed their pace a little in order to distance themselves from the men in front.

"At this point in time Hartmann, you are the only person who knows of my plans. I have let it be known that Fräulein Braun and I will soon be taking a short private holiday in order not to be missed during the first few days following my departure. I have also drawn up documents to be released five days after I have left, nominating my successor and giving final instructions to the Generals. I trust there will not be overly-much disruption to the war effort arising out of my departure."

Hartmann glanced unhappily at the Führer striding at his side.

"Your departure from this present time Mein Führer will be a great loss for the generation of Germans to which I belong."

He paused reflecting, and with a grim smile added as an afterthought.

"But your reappearance in the Germany of the future will no doubt bring great joy to our descendants."

CHAPTER 11

There was a knock on the door. It opened and Freda wheeled in a tea trolley bearing an assortment of food and drink laid out on a white cloth.

"They had your favourite, *leberkäse* in the canteen today and of course the usual selection of butterbrot. There's iced water in the carafe, but I thought your guest might enjoy a bottle of *apfelwein.*"

She turned to Hartmann and with an inviting gesture indicated a selection of small bottles nestling in a bowl of ice.

Hartmann smiled appreciation in return and I thanked her.

Freda tapped her watch and glanced at me enquiringly.

"Our guest might be with us a little longer, Freda. Would you please reschedule my appointments for another day?"

She nodded, and gave Hartmann a friendly smile on the way out.

I rose from my chair and walked around the desk to inspect the tea trolley. Hartmann also rose and as I deposited leberkäse and some butterbrot on my plate, he picked up the carafe and poured himself a glass of water.

"Please help yourself to food and perhaps some apfelwein, Herr Hartmann."

"Maybe a little later. My appetite might return once I have finished my story and unburdened my mind."

He returned to his seat while I carried my plate and a drink back around the desk. Hartmann took a swallow from his glass.

"With your permission, I'll continue with my tale while you eat?"

He raised an enquiring eyebrow and I nodded consent, picking up a butterbrot topped with cheese and herbs from my plate.

CHAPTER 12

On Hitler's next visit to the Berghof he gave vent to growing impatience as they watched a load of bricks being lowered through the well into the tunnel.

"You have done well with the tasks of closing down the Uranverein project, receipt of valuables and locating the secret cave Hartmann, but building this new tunnel is taking far too long. You must drive the project harder. Push the labourers to the very limit of endurance. If necessary, have some of them shot for malingering – that will keep the others on their toes. As soon as I receive word that the new tunnel has been completed, it will take me less than two days to arrange for transfer of command to my Generals, after which I shall immediately leave for the future."

Hartmann smarted at the Führer's censure and as a consequence, spent long hours scrutinizing the tunnelling works, looking for ways to improve upon progress. He railed bitterly and repeatedly at the project's supervisors, accusing them of not attaining the maximum output the labourers were capable of, and threatened that if increased productivity wasn't forthcoming, he would have the supervisors incarcerated in the

Konzentrationslager along with the slave workers on project completion.

After giving them yet another tongue lashing, Hartmann, frustrated and infuriated on being unable to move the project along any faster, retired to the only place he knew of where he neither had to give nor take orders; where he could sit undisturbed in peace and quiet, smoke a cigarette and have a nip of schnapps from his hip flask in order to relieve the stress under which he was now labouring.

He hailed the guards at the Berghof end of the tunnel as he passed through the first steel door and once inside the chamber, shut and locked the second door behind him.

Hartmann shook the last cigarette from its packet whilst he contemplated the Zeitmaschine from his stance at the door. In its mirror-like panels he caught a glimpse of his reflection, grossly distorted by the machine's curved surface and intrigued, he strolled over to take a closer look. With a forefinger he traced a line around the exaggerated image of his face before taking a stroll around the machine, deep in thought. Whilst doing so, he accidentally brushed against one of the dangling festoon lamps, sending reflections from the Zeitmaschine's shining panels dancing around the chamber. He sat on a pile of sandbags brought in for the next phase of the project, lit his cigarette and drawing upon it, quietly contemplated the gleaming machine sitting on its cradle, whilst the reflections on the chamber walls gradually settled down. Its batteries had been fully charged and it now stood silently waiting to transport the Führer to the future.

'Waiting to transport the Führer to the future.

Waiting to transport ...

... Hartmann to the future?

'*No! Impossible!*' His mind rebelled at the notion and he shook his head.

But the thought persisted.

The Zeitmaschine stood there waiting, waiting, shining in the glare of the festoons, its access door panel open; so very inviting and seeming almost to beckon him to come closer and climb inside.

He glanced uncomfortably around the chamber, struggling with the thought worming its way through his mind, eating away at his steadfast devotion to duty. He took stock of circumstances inside and outside the silent, brightly lit room – both doors, the one leading back to the Berghof and the other in the North wall leading to the tunnel construction works, were locked, removing any possibility of his being observed or interrupted in what he might do next. He glanced instinctively at his watch.

Ten thirty.

Ever since his first journey in the Zeitmaschine, Hartmann had experienced an inappropriate but nevertheless overwhelming desire to experience a little more of the good life which had apparently arisen out of the War. If he was to climb aboard the Zeitmaschine and travel to the future this very minute, all he need do after spending a short spell in the pleasant post-war future, away from the demands of this frustrating, seemingly endless struggle for victory, would be to press the Zeitmaschine's green button – a simple enough action which would return him to the present time a fraction of a second after his erstwhile departure.

Even if he spent a couple of days treating himself to a relaxing sojourn in the future, in effect, once he returned to the present time he would have only been away for a split second, the consequence of this being his absence would never be realised by anyone outside the chamber.

He recalled the softness of the bed and the splendid taste of coffee he had enjoyed in the Türken on his earlier foray, and the more he thought about it, the more he was able to convince himself that, having faithfully fulfilled every undertaking the Führer had set for him, surely a small reward was due – a short relaxing break from his duties for a day or two. He knew only too well that once the Führer departed, taking this machine with him to the future, the chance to enjoy the opportunity the Zeitmaschine presently offered would be lost to him forever.

And besides, if he was to do such a thing, who would it disadvantage?

Hartmann rose from the sandbags with resolve, flicked his cigarette to the floor, and strode over to the electrical cabinets to retrieve his rucksack and hiking clothes. He decided to leave straight away for a short excursion whilst there were no immediate demands requiring his attention. As an afterthought, he reminded himself that even if a matter of importance did arise, he would be returning an instant after he left to give it his immediate attention.

He paused whilst changing clothes to consider the optimum number of years to be travelled. If he ventured too far, he would be assailed by complicated things like the Zum Türken's computers which had caused him so much grief in printing out his report. He had no stomach for a future that was most likely to prove challenging and bewildering. And yet, if he didn't venture far enough from the present time, he would be exposed to the devastation he knew would exist immediately after the War. He finally decided that fifteen years into the future would be far enough, and a safe compromise to start with, comforted by the thought that if he found the year 1959 unsatisfactory, he could always travel forward a little further in time to a temporal destination more to his liking.

Hartmann, once again attired in his hiking outfit, placed his neatly folded uniform on the electrical cabinets and striding back to the Zeitmaschine, tossed the rucksack onto the bench opposite the controller's station. After a final sweeping glance around the chamber to ascertain all was in order, he climbed into the cabin, slid the access panel shut and turned his attention to the controls. He set the duration dials, pushed the red lever forward, lifted the glass cover and without further hesitation, depressed the red button.

When the time speed meter needle finally came to a standstill, he slid the access panel door open and climbed out. Hartmann swept the chamber with his torch and was satisfied to find its overall appearance remained similar in most respects to the situation he had faced on his earlier journey sixty years into the future. However, on this occasion, there was neither Zeitmaschine on the second cradle nor the strange looking compact generator that had been in the chamber on his two previous visits. Hoisting the rucksack over his shoulder he strolled across to the new exit door in the North wall, stopping a few paces short of it to stare at a sign fastened to its upper panel. It read:

Rocks have been placed in the cave entrance
to assist in hiding its presence.
Simply push out to exit.
Best wishes,
Hartmann.

Hartmann puzzled over the message for a few seconds. He had not planned to follow up with any such notice once Hitler had departed, but on seeing it now, it struck him as a very good idea which could be easily implemented on his return, and which would assist in concealing the cave against future accidental discovery.

Passing through the doorway, he made his way along the tunnel to the cave. Rocks had indeed been placed in the opening to the outer world. He pushed them outward with ease to reveal the curtain of foliage that had successfully hidden the cave from passers-by during the intervening years.

CHAPTER 13

Hartmann drew aside the ferns, stepped over the fallen rocks, and found himself once again in the small clearing outside the cave. Its immediate surroundings in 1944 had been devoid of trees, and in another forty five years' would be surrounded by a dense forest of aspen and lindens, but now in 1959 the area was covered by a grove of spindly saplings. After trampling a pathway through the ferns growing lush between the trees, the woods finally thinned out to an extent allowing him to view the landscape further down the slope to his left, where he saw that the Berghof now lay in ruins. As he watched, two men were occupied in demolishing a section of stone and brickwork still standing amongst the above-ground remains of the building, whilst a third man wheeled a barrow load of materials the others had removed towards a small lorry parked close by.

Across the meadow, the Zum Türken had survived the ravages of war intact, and although it still looked a little shabby, it had obviously resumed operating as a hotel, evidenced by the vehicles in the car park and a small group of guests dressed in civilian clothes drinking beer and chatting under the sunshades sheltering the building's veranda. The meadow occupying the space between the edge of the woods and the Türken was littered with the crumbling remains of the old barracks buildings, and beyond the Türken, Bormann's and Göring's chalets had been reduced to piles of rubble.

Hartmann hoisted the rucksack a little higher on his back and trekked across the meadow to the Türken. On arrival at the car park, he stopped momentarily by the curb-side to watch a young boy of about ten years enthusiastically racing his scooter around a circular track he had marked out in chalk on the pavement. The youngster's face reminded him of someone he had spoken to quite recently, but at that particular moment he couldn't place who, where or when. Hartmann, his curiosity aroused, stepped out onto the bitumen, held up his hand in the way of a police-man stopping traffic, and brought the boy and his scooter to a halt in front of him. Summoning his most charming manner he asked the boy's name.

"Herman Wirth, Sir,"

Herman Wirth! Hartmann was fascinated. At this very moment he was engaged in conversation with the boy who would one day become manager of the Zum Türken. The youngster was looking up at him expectantly and Hartmann couldn't resist asking him about his future prospects.

"When you grow up young man, would you like to become manager of the Zum Türken hotel?"

The youngster regarded him with a very serious expression.

"Oh yes, indeed Sir. Our family has owned the Türken for many years, except during the War when it was requisitioned as a billet to accommodate soldiers. My mother is the manageress and our hotel is now always full of interesting people. Are you perhaps one of our guests?"

"No, not yet, but I was hoping to stay in the hotel for at least one night."

The boy shook his head.

"No, I don't think that would be possible, Sir. The hotel is fully booked out at the moment, so much so in fact, that I have been forced to share a bedroom with my two sisters."

He finished off the sentence with a look of disgust which made Hartmann laugh out loud on observing the expression on the boy's face.

"Well in that case young man, I think I might hike down to Berchtesgaden and look around there for accommodation."

The boy shook his head again.

"It's even worse down there in the village. The inns are all crammed full with American soldiers."

Having delivered his final verdict on the possibility of finding accommodation, the boy re-mounted his scooter and dodging around Hartmann's legs, whisked off for another circuit around the car park.

Hartmann chuckled and headed off down the road leading to the small town in the valley below. His walk, being downhill practically all the way, was pleasant and easy. The sun shone warmly and Hartmann luxuriated in the peace and serenity of the countryside. He stopped at a babbling brook along the way to top up his water canteen and further along, cheerfully returned the wave of some farm hands tossing hay onto a stack in an adjacent field. Eventually the steeper grades flattened out and soon the pastures began to merge with the township fringes. The light scattering of houses grew closer together, and before long Hartmann was in the centre of town surrounded by shops, taverns and parks bordering a large plaza.

He stopped at a bench on the footpath, opened his rucksack, and withdrawing one of the twenty Euro notes received from the auctioneer in forty five years' time, headed for a kiosk across the plaza to purchase a pack of cigarettes.

Inside the cubicle, surrounded by racks of colourful magazines and newspapers, the elderly vendor picked up the note Hartmann laid on the counter and after examining it suspiciously, handed it back to him.

"Sorry Sir, we don't take foreign currency here."

Foreign currency? Hartmann stared at him perplexed and annoyed at the vendor's rebuff until it dawned on him the Euros he had obtained from the auctioneer were from the future. The stash of notes he had in his rucksack would not be acceptable currency for several decades to come and were invalid and useless in this present time. He cursed under his breath, and retrieving the note, mumbled an apology, promising to return with local money. Hartmann wandered up the street and again laying down his rucksack, withdrew the cloth wrapped bundle from its pouch. Looking about to ensure no one was watching, he picked out one of the larger diamonds, slipped it into his pocket and after re-wrapping the rest of the valuables, headed for a small jewellers he had noticed tucked away in a huddle of shops on the far side of the plaza.

The tinkle of the bell attached to the front door heralded his entry, and the young shop assistant facing away from him climbed down backwards off a step-up, and laying down her feather duster, turned to greet Hartmann with a delightful smile, full of warmth and welcome.

"Good morning Mein Herr, isn't it a beautiful day outside? I see you have been hiking, but I haven't seen you before in Berchtesgaden. Do you not love our beautiful little town?"

Hartmann was captivated by the warmth of her greeting, her shining wavy chestnut hair and a pretty face framing a pair of hazel eyes that sparkled like the diamond he carried in his pocket. He was momentarily struck by a strange and strong emotion he had not experienced before.

The shop assistant was staring at him expectantly and he snapped out of his reverie on finally realising some sort of response was required.

"Yes, er … well, yes. I have actually spent a lot of time in this area many years ago constructing tunnels in these mountains, but in those days I just passed through Berchtesgaden on my way to my work. I have not actually stopped to look around your town until now."

She smiled at this tall handsome man's apparent nervousness, and again he was lost for words as he became captive to a pair of eyes that shone and sang to him.

"Perhaps I can help you with something?"

"Er … yes. Oh, yes. I find I am in need of lodgings in Berchtesgaden but my money is all spent. However, I do have here in my pocket a diamond that belonged to my mother, and which I am willing to sell. Could you please give me some idea of its value?"

Hartmann reached into his pocket, withdrew the diamond and passed it over the counter to the shop assistant. For the brief moment as their hands touched, he felt something akin to a slight electric tingling and his heart raced a little.

The young woman smiled and held the gem up to the light.

"I am not at all expert in valuing precious stones, but if it is a real diamond, I think it might possibly have a value comparable to some of the gems under the counter here."

She directed his attention to an attractive array of glittering stones under the plate glass top, and passed the diamond back to Hartmann. He peered through the counter noting the gemstones she had indicated ranged in price from 1,500 to 2,200 Deutschmarks.

The shop assistant was considering him thoughtfully when he looked up.

"Of course, those are the prices Herr Kaufmann puts on the jewellery he sells, but when he buys from the public he usually offers a sum well below half the selling price. However …"

She looked over her shoulder to a doorway in the rear of the shop, and leaning forward across the counter, whispered conspiratoriously with a mischievous grin.

"… as he would be offering you much less than half, if you really want to get the most out of the transaction, you must hold out for more."

Hartmann was enchanted by her manner and was again momentarily lost for words. She searched his face waiting for a response, but not receiving one, turned from the counter and retreated to the rear doorway, calling over her shoulder.

"Please wait there – I will ask Herr Kaufmann to attend you."

His eyes followed her attractive, slim figure until she disappeared between the folds of a curtained partition through which he now became aware of the sound of a brass band playing marching songs on a radio. There ensued a muffled conversation behind the curtains and a minute later she reappeared following an elderly gentleman who shuffled into the shop in dressing gown and slippers. He looked Hartmann up and down, cleared his throat and grunted.

"My assistant informs me you have an article of jewellery to sell?"

Hartmann held out the diamond. Kaufmann took hold of it between thumb and forefinger, and bending down with an effort, retrieved a small balance scale from under the counter with which he weighed it. Next, he put a jeweller's magnifying loupe to his eye and carefully studied the stone from various angles. At last he sat it down on a small velvet cushion on the counter, and clearing his throat again, searched Hartmann's face.

"Your mother had extremely good taste in jewellery young man. This stone is of such exceptional quality, I'm prepared to offer you a generous six hundred Marks for it."

Hartmann's attention was drawn to the young shop assistant standing behind Kaufmann. She was shaking her head and, frowning at him, was pointing her extended forefinger vigorously up and down toward the ceiling.

"I have been told it is worth much more than that. If what you have offered is the best you can do, perhaps I might take it to another jeweller for appraisal."

He made to retrieve the diamond but Kaufmann held up his hand and grumbling, gave Hartmann a look of near despair.

"You and your mother's diamond will be the undoing of me young man. The very best I can offer is seven hundred and fifty Marks, take it or leave it."

The shop assistant was smiling and nodding her head in affirmation behind Kaufmann, and acting upon her apparent approval, Hartmann agreed to the sum on offer.

"Unfortunately, I don't have sufficient cash on hand to pay you right now, but if you are in a hurry young man, I can make arrangements with the bank to have the requisite amount ready to be picked up tomorrow morning. Would that be satisfactory?"

Hartmann eagerly agreed to his proposal and promised to return the next morning at nine. The old jeweller acknowledged their agreement with a grunt and a curt nod, and as Hartmann watched him shuffling back toward the rear doorway, the young assistant stepped forward, picked up the diamond and popped it into a small velvet pouch. With outstretched hand she dangled it above the counter and gave Hartmann an impish grin. Again his awkwardness beset him and not knowing how to appropriately show his thanks for her intervention, he reached for the pouch and stuffing it into his trouser pocket, blurted out appreciation.

"Thank you. Yes, thank you for your help. You were very helpful."

The shop assistant looked at him expectantly, but to her surprise, Hartmann snatched up his rucksack and without another word, hurried from the shop, embarrassingly aware of his nervous-driven social ineptitude.

Once outside on the footpath he cursed himself for not making a better impression on the attractive young woman inside. Things were so simple in the Wehrmacht Heer he reflected. In the army it was different – there were rules, and discipline and orders to be obeyed. But in the very few dealings he had experienced with women, he discovered there were no such guidelines to give him desperately needed advice, and it always seemed to end up like this.

He wandered aimlessly down the road, avoiding the cigarette kiosk, still without the wherewithal to purchase a packet. He passed four American soldiers smoking cigarettes as they lounged against their Willys Jeep, and contemplated how strange it seemed coming from a time when these men were his mortal enemies to now find them in this peaceful town, seemingly fitting in as a totally acceptable and normal feature of the local landscape.

He walked through a small park where elderly men looked up as he passed, before resuming their games of chess on purpose-built tables whilst nearby, matrons in long black skirts strolled the pathways wheeling their charges in prams. He enquired at three inns and a guest house in his search for accommodation but found them all totally booked out with billeted American soldiers. He looked through shop windows and marvelled at how abundant were life's little luxuries which in 1944 could only be purchased if one had coupons and permissions.

But no matter what diversions he came upon as he walked the street, his thoughts kept straying back to the jewellery shop and the pretty young female assistant with her bewitching smile and delightfully precocious manner.

Hartmann paused in mid-stride to survey the road ahead of him – a road which now seemed to be leading nowhere that might deserve his interest. Instead, he turned to gaze back in the direction of the jewellery shop.

'*Go back, go back*' a voice inside his head exhorted. He stood undecided for a few seconds, until indecision finally gave way to a strong sense of determination, and he retraced his steps back to the shop with a growing feeling of purpose.

The bell on the door once again announced his entry and the pretty female assistant looked up from the brass barometer she was polishing. She smiled when she saw that it was Hartmann.

"What time do you finish work in this shop?"

She laid aside the barometer and studied the young man's face before replying to his question, somewhat bemused by the rather surprising transformation from his earlier nervousness to his present brashness.

"Herr Kaufmann usually lets me go at six."

She frowned a little and searching Hartmann's face added, "But if I ask him, I think he would let me leave a little earlier."

"Then I will be waiting for you outside the shop. I would like to take you to a tavern for some supper and refreshments to repay you for the help and kindness you have shown me today. I hope you will find my proposal agreeable?"

"Yes, that would be really lovely. I should be able to finish my work sometime around five."

She paused, waiting for a response, but all Hartmann could manage was a quick nod before his awkwardness with women made him feel foolish again, and hefting his rucksack higher, he turned and hurried from the shop before his uneasiness again became overly apparent.

Outside, walking the cobbles, there was now intent in his stride and Hartmann allotted himself the task of discovering the most intimate of taverns in Berchtesgaden. There were several to choose from but he finally settled on the *Gasthof Neuhaus* for its old world charm. His stomach growled a protest to remind him he hadn't eaten since very early that morning, and suddenly with dismay he was also reminded that, until tomorrow morning, he wouldn't have any of the local currency to buy coffee, let alone some nice accompaniments to assist in impressing the pretty shop assistant.

He couldn't possibly ask her to pay for him, and because of the high value of each of the treasures in his cloth bundle, he knew that trading any more of them for anything like their real value would not yield him cash until the following Monday, whereas trying to offload them at too low a price to passers-by in the street would invoke the suspicion he was attempting to sell illegal black market goods, thus risking a possible confrontation with the police. He pondered over the list of items the scientists had packed in his rucksack, wondering whether any of them could be traded quickly to provide the requisite cash, and again laying it down on a park bench, he rifled through to pull out the binoculars, compass and pocket knife. All three had been withdrawn from stores by the scientists in preparation for his time journey and were in pristine, as-new condition. He repacked them on top of the other articles in the rucksack and hurried back to the centre of town. The first person he asked was able to direct him to a rather decrepit-looking pawn brokerage in a side street. The proprietor, a middle aged war veteran with a missing ear and livid scar across his cheek, gazed down at the three items Hartmann laid on his counter, looked up to search Hartmann's face and then down at the three items again, muttering more to himself than to Hartmann.

"Genuine military issue items, but in such top condition. The last time I saw such things was in the officers' mess when I served with the Wehrmacht."

He looked up again at Hartmann.

"Where did you get these things?"

Following the destruction of all weaponry after Germany's surrender, wartime paraphernalia in such excellent condition was rare and much sought after, and Hartmann, who was becoming rather adept at fashioning stories to explain his anomalous circumstances, responded they had belonged to his father, an officer in the Wehrmacht, killed in a bombing raid before he had a chance to use them. His mother kept them locked away for many years until recently passing them down. The pawnbroker shook his head and again scrutinised the items lying on the counter.

"As new condition and very collectable. I can offer you eighteen Marks for the three."

Hartmann, recalling his successful bargaining in the jewellery shop, protested.

"Surely you can give me a better price for such well-presented items?"

The pawnbroker clucked his tongue.

"Well, they are indeed rare in such good condition, and there is much demand for World War Two militaria these days. Perhaps I can let you have twenty Marks, but no more."

Hartmann had studied food prices whilst peering through Berchtesgaden's shop windows, and calculating the amount on offer should be more than sufficient to pay for food and drink at the Gasthof Neuhaus, he readily agreed.

The pawnbroker lifted the lid off an ancient rusty biscuit tin and fished around inside for the requisite banknotes, which he then carefully counted out across the counter. Hartmann thanked him, pocketed the notes and shouldering his lightened rucksack, hurried from the shop.

Outside, he glanced at his watch. Three o'clock. Two long hours to wait. He wandered back through the streets to the cigarette kiosk and purchasing a packet of *Lucky Strikes*, retired to a park bench to enjoy a smoke. He inspected his watch at frequent intervals and agonised over how slowly the hands crept around the dial. At quarter to five he couldn't stand the wait any longer and walked briskly back to the jewellery shop where he feigned interest in a shop window two doors down the road. Five o'clock came and went and as the minutes dragged by, Hartmann fought against a rising tide of disillusionment.

Then the bell on the jewellery shop door made him look up and there she was, standing on the threshold, casting her eyes up and down the street. Seeing him close by, she closed the door behind her and hurried over, giving Hartmann a look of delight that made his spirits soar.

"I'm so glad you returned after your first visit to the jewellery shop."

"I was foolish not to ask you the first time I was in there, after you had so kindly given me your valuable assistance."

Not being able to immediately come up with words to dismiss the overly long pause that followed, Hartmann snapped to rigid attention and saluted.

"Karl Hartmann at your service."

She giggled and proffered her hand and as he held it, appreciating its warmth and satin softness, she gave him a coquettish smile and bobbed in a slight curtsy.

"Linde Engel, Herr Hartmann. I'm delighted to make your acquaintance."

He paused momentarily taking in her glowing face and savouring the fragrance of her cologne.

"I have done my research well this afternoon Fräulein Engel, and believe, unless you have no better place in mind, the Gasthof Neuhaus would be an excellent place in which to have some refreshments to show my gratitude for your assistance today …"

He hesitated looking uncertainly into her eyes.

"… and perhaps avail myself of the opportunity to get to know you better?"

"That would be lovely Herr Hartmann, thank you."

A puzzled look crossed her face.

"But didn't you say in the shop that you had spent all your money? Perhaps I can help out until Herr Kaufmann pays you tomorrow?"

"You are very kind, but that won't be necessary. Fortunately, I had some military artefacts in my rucksack which happened to be of sufficient interest to a pawnbroker here in your town, and I believe I now have enough money for both of us to have a fine time this evening."

The Gasthof Neuhaus proved to be much larger and more barn-like than Hartmann had at first determined, but he managed to find a table in a small alcove which gave them a little privacy. Hartmann ordered a platter of *brühwurst, pretzels, salat* and steins of *weissbier* and proffered the pack of Lucky Strikes to Fräulein Engel who shook her head, but encouraged him to have a smoke if he wished.

She studied him thoughtfully as he lit up a cigarette.

"What kind of man goes hiking through the Bavarian Alps without any money, a rucksack full of military hardware and a diamond in his pocket?"

Hartmann chuckled at the image she conjured of him.

"It is a very complicated story and one even I find difficult to comprehend at times, let alone find easy to explain. Please, can we talk instead about yourself first and perhaps later on I will attempt to enlighten you as to my circumstances."

She studied his face for a moment and gave a wistful sigh.

"Well, Herr Hartmann, my story must be exactly opposite to your mysterious situation. It is indeed so simple and straight forward, I'm afraid in its telling you will fall asleep from sheer boredom."

He smiled.

"I'll try my hardest to stay awake. Please tell me."

"Well, I have lived in Berchtesgaden practically all my life, except for the two years when I studied History at university in Munich. My father served with the Wehrmacht in the Engineering Corps during the War, but was killed in the *Valley of death* at Dukla Pass, Poland. I was only nine years old at the time and have only a few, but nevertheless very special memories of him. My mother, to whom I was very much devoted, fell ill while I was away in Munich, so I abandoned my studies and returned to Berchtesgaden to look after her. Her condition deteriorated over the following year, but I nursed her constantly until she passed away three years ago. I was left with very little by way of support, but Herr Kaufmann who had been a very good friend of my father, kindly offered me a job in his jewellery shop and I've worked there ever since."

"Your story is certainly filled with much sadness, and yet you strike me as one of the happiest persons I've ever known. How is this possible?"

"It's because of the sadness that I am happy. I have since learned that life is so very short and because tragedy can strike at any moment, there is no time to waste in feeling miserable. Don't you agree that we should all seize whatever happiness we can glean out of every passing moment? I believe this way of thinking is best described by the expression *'Carpe diem'.*"

The waiter arrived and laid out their food and drink on the table. On his departure, Hartmann seized his stein of weissbier and raised it high in front of Fräulein Engel, as in a toast.

"I wish to officially thank you for your kindness and assistance today. This is yet another of your '*passing moments*' that we shall fill with happiness."

So saying, he raised the stein a little higher and repeating her words '*Carpe diem*' lowered it to his lips and swallowed a heavy draught. She laughed at his mock gallantry and in response, raising her glass not quite as vigorously, also repeated '*Carpe diem*' before following suit.

They ate and drank whilst Fräulein Engel chatted with enthusiasm about her life, hopes and dreams. Hartmann listened, hanging on to her every word, enchanted by her earnestness, cheerfulness and above all, her soft sweet voice which to his ears hardened by the commands and harshness of war, bubbled like a brook and sang like a symphony.

Halfway through torte and coffee, Fräulein Engel's expression changed to take on a more serious aspect and she sliced the air between them with her palm.

"But enough of me, Herr Mystery Man, it's time for you to reveal the secret life of Karl Hartmann."

Hartmann gazed into her searching eyes and knew she was hungry to know everything about him. His heart would not allow him to deceive this lovely woman, but how could he disclose to Fräulein Engel the truth regarding his circumstances without frightening her away with a tale that could only have been concocted by a madman?

"Tomorrow is Sunday and the jewellery shop will be closed for business, is that not so?"

She nodded.

"I would like to take you to a place not too far from here where I will be able to reveal my closely guarded secret – a secret which will explain all you wish to know about me. Please tell me you will come, because without seeing what I have to show you, you cannot even begin to understand the Karl Hartmann who sits here before you at this table."

"Herr Mystery Man becomes more mysterious by the minute. Can't you assuage my curiosity just a teensy little bit right here and now?"

He shook his head.

She tried another tack.

"Where is this place you want to take me then?"

"Do you know of the hotel Zum Türken?"

"Yes, it's up in the hills only a few kilometres from Berchtesgaden. My parents took me there for picnics when I was a child – the surrounding countryside is so beautiful – is that where your secret lies?"

"What I wish to show you is close by. Please say you'll come, and if I might add a little sweetener, we could also have a very fine lunch at the Türken with the money I receive from Herr Kaufmann tomorrow."

Fräulein Engel pouted.

"I'm not going to learn any more about you tonight, am I?"

"No."

She gave a deep sigh.

"My mother warned me about going to remote places with strangers I'd only just met ..."

She paused for effect, frowning mischievously.

"… but I was never able to resist a good mystery and would love to accompany you."

"Thank you Fräulein Engel. You will not regret your decision and I can promise you a story like no other you've ever heard before."

He looked around the inn noting the supper crowd had diminished somewhat.

"Perhaps we'd better leave soon. I've yet to find a place to stay for the night and have already asked at several hotels without success – the lodgings always seem to be full of American soldiers."

"Then let us try Frau *Krüger* at my boarding house. I'll introduce you as my cousin from Berlin, and although I believe all the rooms are taken up, I'm sure she will be able to squeeze you in somewhere as long as you wave some Deutschemarks under her avaricious nose."

Hartmann paid for the meal and they strolled back to Linde's *gästehaus* where, true to form, at the offer of two Marks for one night's stay, Frau *Krüger* cleared some chattels out of a storage annexe and laid out an old mattress on the floor, topping it with an ancient faded eiderdown. The gnarled old woman retreated to her own room, muttering about the inconvenience of accommodating latecomer transients, as she stuffed his Deutschemarks in her apron pocket.

Fräulein Engel turned from watching Frau *Krüger* as she disappeared down the corridor and looked dubiously at the tattered mattress in Hartmann's allocated sleeping quarters.

"I do hope you will be comfortable, Herr Hartmann."

He gave her a reassuring grin in return.

"I've slept on a lot worse."

He moved closer and taking her hand, gazed into Fräulein Engel's eyes until she blushed.

"I have had a lovely evening Herr Hartmann, and am so very much looking forward to our outing tomorrow."

"So too am I, Fräulein Engel."

He hesitated, unsure, not knowing what to do next and finally, reluctantly, let go of her hand. She looked up into his face, searching his eyes, wanting to say more, but only managed to wish Hartmann a good night's rest before turning and making her way to her room. His eyes followed her departure and held her form captive until she disappeared around the corner at the end of the hallway.

Sleep evaded Hartmann for a long time as he lay on the uncomfortable, lumpy mattress staring at spider webs on the cracked, stained ceiling of the store room, wondering how Fräulein Engel would react when he introduced her to the Zeitmaschine. He finally succumbed to a fitful slumber, where half asleep, half awake, he experienced visions of her standing outside the entrance to the secret cave, arms folded across her chest, obstinately refusing to accompany him into the dark passage leading to the secret chamber.

CHAPTER 14

The next morning Hartmann awoke to the sound of gentle knocking on the store room door.

"Are you awake Herr Hartmann?"

He pushed the eiderdown aside.

"One moment if you please, Fräulein Engel."

He had slept fully clothed apart from his hiking boots which he quickly laced up, and hurried to the door, combing his hair back between his fingers. She was waiting for him smiling, her gloved hands folded in front of her, looking pretty as a picture in a colourful floral frock.

"I gave Frau *Krüger* a little extra money this morning so that we could have a nice breakfast together before we see Herr Kaufmann. The bathroom is just up the passage over there and when you're finished you'll find me in the dining room at the front of the house."

Hartmann thanked her and shortly after joined Fräulein Engel at table to enjoy a hearty breakfast of crusty *brötchen*, boiled eggs, sausage and coffee.

She made several attempts to persuade Hartmann to relent and tell her something of his closely guarded secret life, but he was adamant, and in the end she resigned herself to chatting about her work and the people she met whilst working in Kaufmann's jewellery shop.

At nine o'clock, Fräulein Engel waited a discreet distance from the shop whilst Hartmann marched inside. Herr Kaufmann shuffled out of the room behind the curtained partition on hearing the doorbell ring, and their transaction proceeded smoothly and quickly. Hartmann stuffed the parcel of bank notes he received into his rucksack's pocket and came out of the shop grinning.

"Now Fräulein Engel, let's see if we can find a bus that can get us up to the Zum Türken."

"I know something which might get us there quicker than waiting around for a bus, Herr Hartmann. If you would just accompany me down this street, there's a good chance we could be lucky."

She led him to the place where yesterday Hartmann had observed the four American soldiers lounging against their Jeep. Today there was only one soldier – a young GI topped with the seemingly ubiquitous crew-cut favoured by the American troops. He was champing on an unlit cigar butt and wore a furrowed brow of concentration as he bent over the kerbside mudguard of the vehicle, engrossed in painting a scantily clad lady on the metal surface.

Fräulein Engel stood on tiptoe behind the soldier peeking over his shoulder, studying his artwork for a few seconds. Then with a wink, she signalled Hartmann with a forefinger to her lips, before addressing the man from behind.

"Good morning, Hank."

Hank straightened and whirled around, his paintbrush only missing her dress by a fraction, and he beamed with pleasure when he saw who it was.

"Howdy missy Linde, you sure as hell look good today. Where are you all off to in that nice outfit?"

Hartmann stiffened with concern at the American's familiarity toward Fräulein Engel, but relaxed a little on noticing she didn't seem to be offended by it.

"My friend and I are hoping to go up into the mountains today to have lunch at the Zum Türken hotel. Do you know the place?"

"Yeah, yeah, sure. That's the old hotel just up the hill from the ruins of Hitler's Berghof. My buddies and I go up there some days on furlough breaks to take in the scenery and have a beer or two in the bar."

"We were going to take the bus, but …"

Fräulein Engel heaved a dramatic sigh and gave a theatrical glance at her watch before searching Hank's face with a look of grave concern.

"… I fear we might have just missed it, and believe the next bus would be getting us there far too late for lunch."

"Hey, not a problem Linde. It's Sunday, right? – My day off, and the Türken's only a few miles up the road. Why don't I run you and your buddy up there? I can finish my artwork later when I return to town."

"That would be very kind of you Hank, but are you sure you won't get into trouble for using your army services vehicle to take us up there?"

"Nahh! Uncle Sam will never know, and anyway United States policy is all about winning over the *hearts and minds* of the German people, right?"

He cast a quick sidelong glance at Hartmann before turning back to Fräulein Engel with a look of earnest yearning.

"Maybe if I work hard at it, I can win *your* heart and mind someday?"

She laughed.

"Perhaps."

Hank put away his paints, and ushered them into the Jeep, seating Fräulein Engel in front beside him whilst Hartmann was left to push aside some heavy bundles of military hardware before squeezing into the rear seat. Fräulein Engel chatted easily with the American soldier all the way up to the Türken's car park, turning at every opportunity to translate and include Hartmann in the conversation. Hartmann, who only had a rudimentary knowledge of English was impressed by her command of the language and although he realised she was using her acquaintanceship with the American for his benefit as well as her own, he was disturbed by her easy informality with Hank, and struggled with an unaccountable feeling of jealousy.

In the hotel carpark they clambered out and after a round of thanks and handshakes, Hank climbed back into the vehicle and with a crunch of gears, a beep of the horn and a cheery thumbs-up, he left them, waving goodbye as he drove off.

Fräulein Engel turned to Hartmann.

"Well Herr Hartmann, if you don't reveal your secret very soon, I fear I shall either burst from pent-up anticipation or die of unrequited curiosity."

"Very well Fräulein Engel. But first, why don't we have a quiet coffee in the Türken."

They entered the hotel where, in crossing the lobby, Hartmann was almost run off his feet by young Herman Wirth racing around the room on his scooter. The boy fell sprawling to the floor in front of Hartmann and all three of them jerked their heads around toward reception as the boy's mother bellowed out at Herman from behind the desk.

Frau Wirth, a hefty framed, buxom, middle-aged woman, lifted the hinged counter and muttering angrily, bustled across to the cowering boy, lifted him off the floor by his ear and vigorously spanked his behind. Still firmly in charge of his ear, she turned to Hartmann.

"I am the manageress of this hotel, and the mother of this wretched, stupid boy. I hope he has done you no harm Sir."

Hartmann laughed and told her indeed no damage had been done. But as Frau Wirth strode away pulling along the unfortunate Herman by his ear, Hartmann turned to Fräulein Engel.

"Take note of the boy's face and commit it to your memory, Fräulein Engel. There is something I wish to show you a little later that requires you do this."

She glanced enquiringly at Hartmann, not understanding, but finding no explanation in his countenance, she complied with his odd request, turning back to scrutinize the boy's face before following Hartmann into the bar.

Later, on their way out of the hotel, Hartmann picked up a copy of the Sunday paper from a lounge table, and folded it under his arm without appearing to give it any further interest.

"It's now time to reveal my secret. What I wish to show you is not here in the hotel but out there on the other side of the meadow."

Hartmann shouldered his rucksack and led Fräulein Engel to the secret cave. He swept aside the ferns at the entrance and switched on his torch.

"Please trust me and don't be afraid. We need to pass through an old war-time bunker tunnel to an underground chamber where you'll learn everything there is to know about me."

Fräulein Engel hesitated. For the briefest moment she wondered whether it was wise to enter such a dark place with this strange young man about whom she knew so little, but reflecting on her first good feelings for him, decided to be guided by instinct rather than her good sense.

Inside the narrow cave, Hartmann opened the camouflaged door in the rock wall and assisted Fräulein Engel in entering the tunnel.

"How did you manage to discover such a well-hidden passage?"

"A good question Fräulein Engel, and one I hope to answer after you've witnessed what is at the other end."

At the far end of the tunnel Hartmann opened the steel door to the chamber and ushering her through, directed the beam of his torch at the Zeitmaschine. Its shiny steel panels reflected the light, and ghostly outlines of heaped sandbags, empty boxes and electrical cabinets moved in and out of the shadows as the reflections skipped around the room. But Fräulein Engel's gaze was riveted on the machine captured in the stream of light, standing on its cradle, dominating the centre of the chamber.

"What is *that?*"

Hartmann advanced in quick strides to the machine's access portal and reaching inside, turned on the main switch. The interior lamp lit up the cabin and the Zeitmaschine's immediate surrounds, whilst the flickering red warning light created an eerie disturbing stroboscopic effect in the shadowy recesses of the chamber, startling and unnerving Fräulein Engel.

"This is the time machine that brought me to 1959 to finally meet you."

"*Time machine?*"

She cast a nervous look at him and took a backward step.

Fully aware of her mounting concern, Hartmann made an attempt to dispel her unease.

"No doubt you are wondering whether you have been lured down to this chamber by a madman and are now considering whether you might be in danger, and I would not blame you for thinking such things. But I assure you Fräulein Engel you are not in any peril at all and if you will only please trust me a little longer, I will show you I am not crazy and mean you no harm."

He smiled reassuringly and climbing into the Zeitmaschine, sat down behind the controls.

"Come Fräulein Engel. Please sit here on the bench opposite and you will soon witness the truth for yourself."

She hesitated again, until finally deciding she would be in no greater danger sitting across from this strange man in the machine's cabin, safely separated from him by the solid console between them, than remaining standing outside, alone and exposed in the dark chamber. She climbed aboard whilst continuing to watch him anxiously as she took her seat.

Hartmann set the dials to carry them forward by ten years into the future and looked up to see Fräulein Engel studying him anxiously.

He explained what he had just done in setting the controls and she stared back at him, her look of concern deepening, her eyes not leaving his face for an instant.

He slid the door panel closed and pressed the red mushroom button while she looked on expectantly.

"Well? What happens now?"

"We are at this very moment travelling forward in time Fräulein Engel. The Zeitmaschine in which we sit makes no sound or vibration when it operates, and the only indication to show it is actually travelling through time can be seen here on this small speed dial."

She glanced where he pointed to the rapidly rotating indicator needle and then, studying his face closely as if for the first time, began to feel perhaps her first good impressions of this man may have been more than a little misguided.

Hartmann realised her patience was wearing extremely thin and hurried to reassure her.

"We should arrive in another few seconds, and then you will see. Look, the needle is already slowing down."

She looked, and the needle's rotation around the dial was indeed slowing, and for some inexplicable reason the gyrations of this tiny strip of metal did seem in her mind to add a minute amount of credence to Hartmann's outrageous claim. The needle finally came to a standstill and sliding the access panel aside, Hartmann suggested Fräulein Engel might like to alight from the cabin. She disembarked but turned to face him as he climbed out of the cabin, very much annoyed rather than frightened, and overwhelmed by a feeling of betrayal. With hands on hips, she let fly with her feelings of frustration and disappointment.

"Well Herr Hartmann, your little demonstration has not been particularly enlightening. You must admit that sitting in the cabin of a strange machine with an even stranger man, watching a needle spin around a meter dial would do very little to convince any reasonably minded person they had just travelled through time. But more to the point, you promised to tell me all about yourself, and up to the present moment I haven't learned anything new about you at all."

"You have indeed been remarkably patient with me Fräulein Engel and have my thanks for that. But I beg you be patient just a fraction longer. All will be revealed when we leave this chamber and return to the Zum Türken."

Hartmann led her through the tunnel back to a world that had grown older by ten years. As they exited the cave, he indicated the surrounding forest with a sweep of his hand.

"Do you notice anything different about the trees?"

Fräulein Engel scrutinized the woodland around her and did indeed notice a difference.

"They seem to have grown taller since we first entered the cave."

As they approached the Türken across the meadow she was startled to see the entire building had been renovated and repainted, and large brightly coloured shades now replaced the smaller drab umbrellas previously sheltering the veranda tables. It just wasn't possible that such an extensive amount of renewal work could have been performed within the short space of time they had been away, and Linde Engel now realised something inexplicably bizarre must have taken place during the preceding minutes. However, an even greater surprise lay ahead when they entered the hotel and made their way to the Türken's reception desk. Behind the counter stood Herman Wirth, the boy who had run his scooter into Hartmann's leg earlier that morning. But he was no longer a boy. He was a handsome looking youth in a waistcoat and bow tie, busy in conversation with a hotel guest.

Fräulein Engel spun around in shock to see Hartmann nodding and grinning at her.

"I have another equally startling piece of evidence Fräulein Engel, to finally convince you we have indeed travelled forward in time."

He led her into the lobby and requesting she hold the news-paper he had picked up earlier, retrieved another paper from a nearby table and handed it to her for inspection.

"Please compare the dates of the two papers, Fräulein Engel."

She looked at him quizzically, but did as was asked.

"They are not the same. The one you just picked up off the table is dated ten years into the future."

"No, that's not quite correct Fräulein Engel, the one from the table is not from the future, it's today's paper and the one I gave you first is ten years old. In the world where we now find ourselves, it is a relic from the past. I hope this last demonstration will finally convince you we have travelled forward in time by ten years."

She stared at him too stunned to respond and Hartmann, realising Fräulein Engel needed time to digest what she was now experiencing, suggested they take a seat in the lounge and have another quiet coffee together. She nodded agreement and he left her, poring over the newspapers of this future world, to order their beverages and some pastries at the bar.

On his return, Fräulein Engel looked up from the newspaper she was reading, her face flushed with excitement.

"Herr Hartmann, the papers are so full of the most extraor-dinary stories. I have just been reading the headline article in this newspaper claiming the Americans have landed a man called Armstrong on the moon and then they managed to bring him back to earth – alive! Isn't that absolutely amazing! And that's not all – there are so many other fascinating discoveries and innovations which have occurred over the previous ten years since Hank drove us up to the Türken that I still find it hard to believe we have actually time-travelled, and keep thinking I will soon wake up to find I have been dreaming."

Hartmann sat down on the couch beside her.

"Yes, I can understand how you must be feeling, but I assure you this is no dream Fräulein Engel. Before I embarked on my voyages in the time machine I never imagined for a moment that the world of technology could be progressing at such a rapid rate. In my previous journeys I travelled much further into the future than we have just now done, and read about the many incredible discoveries and inventions which will bring about the complete transformation of human society."

He paused to search her eyes.

"Will you now believe when I tell you that I had travelled from the past prior to entering Kaufmann's shop, and that we have just now travelled a further ten years into the future?"

"Yes. Yes."

Fräulein Engel was thrilled with everything she was experiencing, but was more delighted still by the fact she no longer need doubt the sanity or good intentions of this handsome mysterious man sitting by her side.

"Will you now please, please tell me about yourself? I want to know everything about you."

A waiter arrived at their table and laid out coffee and pastries before returning to the bar. Hartmann related his story, carefully avoiding mention of his relationship with Adolph Hitler and the intended purpose of the Zeitmaschine, lest the knowledge of his mission and the fact he was an aide to the Führer, adversely affect Linde Engel's regard for him.

She listened eagerly, interrupting his narrative with many questions, one of which he noted with some amusement was a subtle, shy enquiry asking whether he had a wife and children back in 1944.

But her final question was something he had not considered up till the present moment.

"When do you plan to return to your own time?"

Hartmann contemplated the question, taking a sip of his coffee, noting with satisfaction that its delicious flavour and aroma had not changed since he had first enjoyed coffee at the Türken thirty five years into the future.

"Well Fräulein Engel, I have been so enjoying my time with you in this world of the future that I really haven't given the matter very much thought at all. I could stay here with you in the present time for as long as I wished, or perhaps spend some time with you ten years ago in your own time and still, by adjusting the dials in the Zeitmaschine accordingly, return to my own time a fraction of a second after I originally departed back in 1944."

Fräulein Engel didn't quite appreciate how any of this could be accomplished, but her face brightened on hearing his response because a wonderful idea had just taken hold in her mind.

"If that's indeed the case, Herr Hartmann, would it not be possible for the two of us to spend a few days together here in this future world where we now find ourselves? A little break from my daily routine would be ever so enjoyable before I had to return to a life which, although pleasurable, is nevertheless without excitement. If you were to take me back to Sunday ten years ago after our lunch here, I would be left with nothing to cherish but the memory of this all-too-brief outing with you, whereas a few days together in our future would truly be a holiday to remember."

Hartmann gazed into her pretty face glowing with hopeful petition and considered her proposal. Of course, he could at any time at all return Fräulein Engel to her own time, by merely depressing the green button in the Zeitmaschine, and afterwards by resetting the dials and pressing the red button, return to the beginning of his own foray into the future. Why then should he not spend a few days with this delightful maiden to whom he found himself so very much attracted?

His response was swift.

"What an incredibly good idea you have there, you clever girl. Perhaps I could make a start by arranging rooms for each of us here at the Türken, if you are agreeable that this would be a good way to begin our holiday together?"

Fräulein Engel responded enthusiastically, and finishing their coffee, they made their way to the reception desk where Herman Wirth was sorting travel brochures and laying them out across the counter.

He looked up at them pleasantly for only an instant before his face clouded and his brow knitted into a frown. The couple who stood before him bore a striking resemblance to a man and woman vaguely remembered from an episode back in his child-hood, a recollection which he now struggled to dredge out of the backwaters of his memory. His face brightened as he recalled the occasion.

"Pardon me for asking Sir, but didn't I see you and the Fräulein in this hotel about ten years ago when I was a young-ster? I remember you both very well because my mother gave me a good hiding for running into your leg with my scooter."

Hartmann turned to Fräulein Engel and winked before feigning surprise at Wirth's observation. He peered closely into Wirth's face with pretended interest.

"Yes, now I remember. Your mother dragged you away by your ear."

Herman Wirth blushed slightly and Fräulein Engel put her hand to her mouth to stifle a giggle.

"We were wondering if you might have two adjoining rooms available for the next few days."

Herman Wirth overcame his embarrassment to page through the guest register. After a cursory search he looked up at Hartmann shaking his head.

"I'm afraid we're solidly booked out with a large tour group this week, and only have rooms becoming available the following Monday."

Hartmann glanced toward Fräulein Engel at the end of the counter and noted her look of disappointment.

"Then we shall book two adjoining rooms for four days commencing next Monday week when rooms have become available."

Fräulein Engel was shaking her head in consternation, but he responded with a reassuring smile and a fingertip to his lips. After registration and payment in advance, Hartmann led her into the lobby where, out of earshot and seated on a secluded sofa, she anxiously questioned him about what he might have in mind.

"Where are we to stay for the next week whilst we wait for our booking to come around? Won't I have to return to the shop in the intervening period, and where will you be staying?"

Hartmann dismissed her concern with a chuckle.

"You have forgotten what we are capable of achieving with the Zeitmaschine, Fräulein Engel. All we need do now is return to the chamber, go forward in time by another eight days and then take up the rooms which I have only just now booked."

Fräulein Engel stared at him incredulously and laughed at the absurdity of it all.

"I can see this time travelling business might take some time to get used to."

Hartmann agreed, adding he too was only just beginning to get his head around the possibilities.

They left the Zum Türken, and strolling across the meadow toward the secret cave, laughed and delighted in discussing the possibilities which lay before them during their next few days together.

CHAPTER 15

On returning to the chamber, Fräulein Engel demonstrated a greater interest in her surroundings than she had shown on her first visit. Whilst Hartmann busied himself at the Zeitmaschine's controls, she wandered around the chamber examining its contents with his torch. She peeked behind the steel door on the other side of the chamber and, just as he had described, found the tunnel beyond completely blocked by rubble. The electrical cabinets against the far wall boasted a variety of dusty dials, levers, switches and unlit lamps that yielded not the slightest clue as to their purpose, whilst the only other items of marginal interest in the chamber amounted to a pile of sandbags whose contents were beginning to spill out of age-rotted holes in the fabric, and a heap of empty steel boxes which bore a vaguely familiar insignia, and were beginning to show signs of rust.

Hartmann leaned out of the cabin to call her to the machine. Hurrying back, she clambered onto the bench and wiggled along until she was pressed against his side. His skin tingled as they touched and as he gazed into her eyes, he again felt that strange intense emotion as she coyly looked up at him. A hot flush spread across his face and fearing it might appear as an unmanly blush, he sought to distract her attention by pointing to the time dials and the adjustment he had made to take them forward by a week and a day.

He stared fixedly at the dials so that finally she too felt compelled to look down upon them, not at all out of interest but more to suppress her feeling of disappointment at this unfulfilled '*passing moment*'.

Hartmann depressed the red button and the speed meter needle commenced its journey around the dial, hardly reaching moderate speed before it began to slow down.

On its coming to a standstill Hartmann invited Fräulein Engel to open the access panel and exit the machine. She did as suggested, but hesitated a couple of paces from the portal, arrested by the red warning light flashes that stabbed the darkness of the chamber. Turning with determination, she stood resolute to face Hartmann as he clambered out of the cabin. With little room to move between Fräulein Engel and the Zeitmaschine, she answered his look of surprise by raising herself on tiptoes, cupping his face in her hands and kissing Hartmann lightly on the lips. She dropped down, but in an instant his arms enveloped her, nearly lifting Fräulein Engel off the floor, and he kissed her ardently while their bodies remained locked together. Breathing heavily, he lowered her gently to her feet, and for a few seconds they stood searching each other's eyes. Hartmann had, as far as he could remember, never allowed his emotions to take control of any situation he had faced in his past, and he consequently felt some sort of explanation was owing to explain his undisciplined eruption of passion.

"I passed straight from *Hitlerjugend* youth to the Junkerschule Academy and from there into the ranks of the Schutzstaffel and have not had very much experience with women …"

She raised a hand and crossed his lips with a forefinger.

"Don't speak another word. Your kiss tells me all I need to know."

She took a step forward and as their bodies met again, he gently enveloped her in his arms. She raised a hand to his face and caressed his cheek, studying his shining eyes before plunging into another long, lingering kiss.

As their lips parted, Hartmann softly confessed.

"I felt an excitement I had never known the very first moment I saw you in the jewellery shop Fräulein Engel, and I knew even then that somehow my life wouldn't be worth living unless you were part of it."

She gently disengaged from his embrace and holding his hands in hers, stepped back a pace to examine his glowing face, reflecting shyly.

"I also thought you were someone very special when you first came into Kaufmann's shop.

"Please call me by my first name, '*Linde*'."

"Only if you will call me *Karl*."

"Yes, I would like that very much."

Hartmann gave Linde another lingering kiss, before releasing her.

"Come! We must take up our booking at the Türken and whilst we are having our lunch, we can plan the adventures we are going to have over the next few days."

They returned to the hotel to find Herman Wirth once again at the reception counter. He looked up from the desk as they approached.

"Ahh, Herr Hartmann, we are so happy to see you and Fräulein Engel back in the hotel once more. Your adjoining rooms are ready for occupation and a very nice buffet lunch will be served in the dining room in another hour or so … and if I may suggest, try our *dampfnudel* – it's the chef's speciality. Do you wish me to call the porter to carry your bags upstairs?"

"No, that won't be necessary. We've left the rest of our belongings in Berchtesgaden and all we have with us at present is my rucksack."

Hartmann shot a glance to the end of the counter where Linde was idly flipping through some of the Türken's travel brochures. She looked up at him with a shy smile and he considered their needs over the coming days. They had no toiletries or spare clothing and were certainly going to require rather more than what they were currently wearing if their holiday was to be an affair to remember.

"On second thoughts, perhaps we might return to town to pick up a few things that we've left behind. Does the Zum Türken have transport to get us back to town?"

"Certainly, Herr Hartmann. The hotel's shuttle bus leaves for Berchtesgaden after lunch each day. It remains at the station for four hours in order to meet the train from Munich, before returning to the hotel at around five in the afternoon. Do you wish to reserve seats?"

Linde looked up from the brochures nodding vigorously, and Hartmann responded promptly by purchasing tickets. They made their way upstairs and before entering their separate rooms, glanced cautiously down the corridor to ensure they wouldn't be disturbed before stealing a parting kiss. Hartmann cast his rucksack onto a bed which, by comparison with Frau *Krüger*'s mattress was, he thought, fit for a king.

There was a light tap on the door and Linde entered at his invitation.

"This is so lovely Karl – everything is perfect. I am so happy, and want to thank you for agreeing to return to town to pick up some of my clothing."

"We had to go back. If I wore these hiking clothes for the next few days and had nothing to shave with, I have no doubt your affection for me would be very short-lived indeed."

Linde laughed.

"I was thinking the very same thing myself. Shall we go down now for lunch?"

"Only if you will allow me another of your kisses here and now as entrée."

"Only one kiss? I fear you are losing your appetite, Herr Hartmann."

They embraced and he tenderly kissed her lips, finishing with a final peck to the tip of her nose, which made her giggle with delight.

"My cravings for entrée are satisfied, and now my dear Fräulein Engel, my stomach demands we go downstairs for lunch."

As they sat at table and ate, Linde produced some of the brochures she had collected from the reception desk, passing one of them across the tablecloth to Hartmann.

"Some time during our stay here, I'd really love to visit this picturesque little spot if that would be agreeable to you, Karl."

He picked up the brochure and read aloud:

"Enjoy the pristine beauty of Lake Königssee, located eight Kilometres south of the idyllic village of Berchtesgaden, between the majestic Watzmann and Gotzenberg mountains ..."

The description was accompanied by photographs of small boats, colourful sails set against a background of deep blue lake waters, rustic taverns clustered around a small plaza and an attractive white plaster daubed church on a grassy promontory. He looked up to see Linde looking at him anxiously, hoping for a positive response.

"It's such a beautiful place. Before the War when I was still a child, my parents sometimes took me there for picnic outings. Papa made a seat for me behind the saddle of his bicycle and Mama carried a special picnic lunch in the basket attached to her handle bars. It was the happiest time of my life. Oh, do say we can go there, Karl. They also have ferries that leave from the jetty to take tourists across the lake to the beautiful little Church of St. Bartholomew you can see pictured there in the brochure."

Hartmann looked down again to examine the photos.

"It looks very scenic and would certainly make a most agreeable change from the state of affairs I've left behind in 1944. After we've finished lunch I'll make some enquiries about the Königssee and also see if the hotel has bicycles for hire."

They ate at their leisure before strolling down to the carpark to board the hotel's courtesy bus for the trip into town. It left punctually at one thirty, and ten minutes later arrived with a squeal of brakes at the depot opposite Berchtesgaden railway station.

As they walked out of the bus terminal, Hartmann reminded Linde that they were now ten years into her future and therefore they couldn't be certain whether her future self still occupied the room she had rented in Frau *Krüger*'s gästehaus back in 1959. To avoid a potentially awkward meeting with her landlady or indeed, the likelihood of a difficult encounter with her future self, Hartmann suggested that rather than returning to pick up some of her clothing, they could instead purchase new clothes for Linde to wear, using the generous supply of Deutschemarks he had received from Herr Kaufmann. He also cautioned Linde about the possibility of other unexpected changes they might strike after their leap into the future.

Despite his warning, Linde was shocked to discover the shop in which Kaufmann had conducted his jewellery business now housed an electrical appliances store. They stopped in front of the building where Hartmann was immediately drawn to the shop's window to gaze at the popular crime show '*Der Kommisar*' showing on a black and white television cabinet facing the street. Linde eschewed all interest in the novelty of television, and instead peered anxiously through the window pane, looking for clues inside the dim interior which might have shed light on the fate of her employer.

"What do you think became of Herr Kaufmann and his jewellery business, Karl?"

Hartmann shrugged and shook his head, still absorbed in the drama being played out on the screen.

"Well, I'm going inside to find out what could have persuaded him to abandon the business he loved so dearly."

Hartmann nodded absently as Linde disappeared inside the shop.

She reappeared a few minutes later, very much shaken and upset.

"The proprietor inside told me he began trading here in Berchtesgaden after relocating from Munich ten years ago. He said that before he moved in, Herr Kaufmann had a young lady assisting him in the shop, but she had left town in a hurry under the most mysterious of circumstances. Due to the old man's advanced years and infirmities, Kaufmann soon discovered he wasn't able to satisfy the needs of his customers on his own, and when he couldn't find a suitable replacement for his young assistant, he decided to close down his jewellery business and retire."

Linde beseeched Hartmann with a look of anguish and was on the verge of tears.

"That young lady must have been me, Karl. Why did I … I mean, why *will I* be leaving town? I don't understand – I've always loved living here in Berchtesgaden. What happened to me? … that is … Oh dear, this is all very confronting and confusing. What I really want to know is what's going to become of me when I finally return to my own time after our holiday at the Türken?"

Hartmann wrapped his arms around Linde, and gave her a reassuring hug.

"Please don't fret Linde. The ability the Zeitmaschine affords us in foretelling the future can no doubt be a curse as well as a blessing. If we hadn't travelled forward in time, you would be blissfully unaware of your impending decision to move on – knowledge which now causes you so much distress. I'm sure there'll be a very good reason for you wanting to leave Berchtesgaden – perhaps the insights you'll have gained from travelling around in the future will lead you to an exciting new life which awaits you somewhere else."

She looked up to him hopefully.

"Do you really think so?"

He smiled encouragingly.

"I am sure of it. Please don't upset yourself by worrying about the future – remember what you yourself have taught me – *Carpe diem.*"

Hartmann raised her chin with a forefinger, looking into her troubled eyes.

"Come now, we must hurry. We have many purchases to make and not much time before the bus returns to the Türken. First of all, we must buy you some clothes. I have plenty of money now, so please choose all the garments you think you might need to tide you over the next few days."

"There's a dress shop just down the road from here where I've bought clothes in the past – I hope the lady who owned it hasn't closed down her business as well."

The dress shop was still there after the passage of ten years and looked exactly the same as it had looked when Linde visited it ten years and a few weeks ago, apart from the latest fashions now adorning the mannequins in the display window.

Inside the shop, the manageress was attending to another customer, and whilst Hartmann took a seat on a chaise longue near the entrance to flip through a magazine, Linde wandered among the clothes racks. After a couple of minutes, the cash register gave a loud ring and moments later, the manageress made her way over to assist Linde as the other customer left the shop.

Her eyes opened wide with surprise.

"Why, Fräulein Engel. We haven't seen you in Berchtesgaden for such a long time. What brings you back to our little town? And, my, my, how young you are looking. Have you perhaps discovered the fabled *Fountain of Youth*?"

She took hold of Linde's hands, held her at arm's length, and leaning backward looked her up and down with a touch of envy.

"You must tell me your secret."

Linde laughed, and quipped mischievously.

"I think it all depends on how one passes one's time.

"We've been holidaying in the area around Berchtesgaden and after discovering I hadn't packed sufficient clothing for the trip, remembered your dress shop from ten years ago. Would you help me choose some outfits to see me through the rest of our holiday?"

Two hours later, Hartmann accompanied Linde out onto the street carrying a clutch of parcels containing more new clothes than she had been able to afford during the previous three years. They made their way to a nearby shop selling men's apparel where Linde assisted Hartmann in choosing suitable clothing because at this point in time, being twenty five years into his future and having not worn civilian clothes for a number of years previously, he had not the slightest idea regarding prevailing men's fashions.

Shopping for clothes was followed by a quick buying spree for incidentals and toiletries in a small emporium before they hurried back to the terminal in time to catch the Türken's shuttle bus for its return run to the hotel.

CHAPTER 16

Hartmann indulged himself in a relaxing hot bath and dressed in one of the smart outfits they had purchased that afternoon. Satisfied with his appearance on inspecting himself in the mirror, and whilst Linde was still in her room dressing for dinner, he seized the opportunity to wander downstairs to the dining room. The Maître d'hôtel, a kindly gentleman with a penchant for encouraging young lovers, wouldn't for a moment entertain Hartmann's offer of generous reward in return for special attention. Instead, he promised to reserve for them an intimate table with the assurance Hartmann and Fräulein Engel would be accorded the best service the hotel had to offer. Hartmann returned upstairs feeling very pleased with himself and knocked lightly on Linde's door.

"Just a moment Karl. I'll be ready in another five minutes."

He returned to his room and, sitting on the edge of his bed, abstractedly studied patterns in the rich Persian carpet whilst mulling over thoughts alternating between his growing attraction to Linde and his oath of loyalty to Hitler and the Reich. Eventually tiring in his attempt to resolve inner conflict, he left the room and paced restlessly up and down the corridor outside Linde's door, impatiently waiting for the minutes to pass.

At last, and after a good deal more than five minutes, Linde's door opened and she stood before him looking radiant.

Hartmann caught his breath. She looked stunning. Linde's lithe, attractive figure was accentuated by the line of her new dress, and a blush of rouge, bright red lips and sparkling long lashed eyes blended into a face unmatched by any portrait he had ever seen.

"You look wonderful, Linde."

She took a step forward and gazed up into his face as she straightened his tie.

"You look pretty handsome yourself, Herr Hartmann."

Time stood still as they silently admired each other, hardly daring to breathe lest the magic of this *passing moment* be broken, until finally, the voices and sounds of the hotel forced themselves onto Hartmann's consciousness, and as the world around them came rushing back into being, he gently took hold of Linde's hand and led her down the staircase to the dining room.

Hartmann couldn't remember a meal he had enjoyed more. The wine and food were excellent, Linde's chatter was as music to his ears and true to the Maître d's promise, the table service was impeccable.

Later, outside on the veranda, under a cloudless star studded sky, Linde held Hartmann's hands in her own and looked down on them in thoughtful silence before looking up into his eyes.

"I know I have only known you for the shortest possible time Karl, but I do believe I am falling in love with you. I've experienced some disappointing liaisons in the past, so I'm hopeful you will be kind and understanding with me."

"I too have similar feelings for you Linde and have never known such happiness in the company of another person. I will approach our developing relationship as gradually and gently as you wish without regard to expectations, and we'll see what happens."

He kissed Linde tenderly and hand in hand they gazed in silence across the valley to the distant moon-lit mountain peaks, each deep in thought, wondering what might lie ahead for two lovers coming together in this world of the future from two entirely different pasts.

They parted company after an embrace and a good night kiss at Linde's door, and that night, Hartmann lay awake on his bed for a long time gazing at the decorative ceiling, wondering how he could possibly reconcile his growing love for Linde against his duty to the Fatherland and his oath of allegiance to the Führer.

CHAPTER 17

The next day after breakfast Linde approached the Maître d' with a request for a picnic lunch, whilst Hartmann sought out the desk clerk to arrange the hire of bicycles. The Maître d' tried to persuade her an excellent lunch could be had at any one of a number of fine restaurants and cafés bordering the Königssee, but Linde was determined to relive the joyous picnics of her childhood. Having earlier instructed Hartmann to ensure her bicycle was fitted with a carry basket, she would not be swayed and was unshakeable in persisting with the picnic option.

They cycled from the Türken down to the small lakeside village comprised of a compact cluster of neatly laid out chalets, taverns, shops and a plaza bordering the lake. At the wharf where colourful boats and ferries bobbed gently alongside, they parked their bicycles and walked out to the end of the pier to admire the view across an expanse of sparkling deep blue lake waters stretching far away to the south, bounded on either side by towering craggy mountains.

"My mother couldn't swim and because she was afraid to go out in the boats here at the wharf, my father opted to have our picnics in the village park. But I'm not afraid of the water Karl, and have always longed to be taken out to the beautiful little church of Saint Bartholomew that I showed you in the brochures yesterday."

"Then I shall purchase ferry tickets straight away, Linde."

Hartmann gave her a fleeting kiss on the cheek, and hurried off to obtain tickets from the gaily decorated kiosk they had passed on entry to the pier.

On his return, they clambered aboard a sleek white ferry already nearly filled with noisy excited tourists whilst the crew were making her ready to sail. Hartmann and Linde settled into seats that would give them an excellent view of the scenic mountain vistas through the large picture windows lining either side of the cabin, and soon the boat was slipping away from the pier, the sound of its electric motor nearly imperceptible against the swish of water against the hull. Linde marvelled at the depth of colour in the placid lake waters whilst Hartmann, fresh from the theatre of war, was captivated by the serenity of his surroundings.

On the way to their destination, the ferry's steward produced a Flügelhorn and entertained the passengers by training it on a particular cliff which, he informed them, was known as 'echo wall' to the local villagers. Giving a few short blasts on his instrument, the passengers were delighted to hear the ensuing rush of echoed notes that returned. After the steward had laid down his instrument, Hartmann, not able to resist a sudden impulse, rose to the occasion by giving a few short yodels which also rebounded off echo wall, causing Linde to laugh whilst eliciting a patter of congratulatory applause from some of the other passengers.

The Church of Saint Bartholomew was located on a flat grassy promontory surrounded by tall rugged mountains, and could only be accessed by crossing the lake as they had just done in the ferry. Linde and Hartmann strolled the neatly manicured pathways past the hunting lodge into which most of the other tourists had disappeared for lunch. They inspected the austere, simple interior of the quaint, white plaster daubed church with its curious but distinctive onion domes, before selecting a shady spot for their picnic lunch under the boughs of a nearby ancient spreading linden. Linde knelt down on the grass to inspect the contents of their picnic basket, whilst Hartmann stood gazing out across the lake, taking in great lungsful of fresh mountain air and basking in the tranquillity of this little Garden of Eden. As she laid out the food and drink Linde looked up at Hartmann and her eyes sparkled with delight.

"I have so longed to come out to this oasis of peace and serenity ever since my parents first showed me the brochure of the Königssee, and now you have fulfilled my childhood dream. Thank you, Karl. Thank you."

He smiled indulgently and kneeling beside her, lightly pinched her cheek and kissed her forehead.

After they had eaten, Linde sat with her back against the massive bole of the linden whilst Hartmann lay outstretched with head resting on her lap. A light breeze rustled the leaves above them and Hartmann closed his eyes in rapture as Linde combed her fingers through his long curly hair whilst softly crooning a love song she had learned listening to her radio. He had never felt happier.

The day's outing ended with their having to walk a good deal of the way back to the Türken because of the hotel's elevation above the valley floor and the difficulty they experienced in pedalling uphill. As they puffed their way up one of the steeper grades wheeling their bicycles, Hartmann observed to Linde's great amusement that he preferred travelling in the Zeitmaschine where the only climbing involved was in and out of the machine's cabin.

That evening after another enjoyable dinner, they again strolled out onto the Türken's veranda to enjoy the freshness of the air outside.

Linde pressed forward against the veranda railing, lifting her face to bathe in a cool mountain breeze, and gazed at the distant ghostly outline of mountain peaks against a darkening azure sky.

"I'm so enjoying my time together with you Karl that I never want this holiday to end."

Hartmann glanced sideways to admire her profile against the moonlit background before joining her in gazing into the distance. A troubled frown clouded his face as he recalled his thoughts in bed on the previous night.

"I too have never experienced such happiness before, Linde but …"

She turned and gave him a quizzical glance as he paused.

"… we both know our holiday here is an escape from reality. I come from a world at war where nations are tearing each other apart, whilst you come from a world of peace where the very same nations are united in repairing the wounds of the past. I could never ask you to return to my world. But I'm a professional soldier Linde, with responsibilities and duties to perform. Where would you find a place for such a man in your world?"

Linde pouted and Hartmann could see she was once again on the verge of tears.

"This is certainly *not* an escape from reality Karl!"

She swept the air around her with outstretched hands to emphasise the point.

"This! All of this. *This* is reality.

"You and me and everything we are experiencing together … and our love for each other. Are all of these things not a reality?"

And she burst into tears.

Hartmann wrapped his arms around Linde's quivering shoulders and murmured soothing words of love in her ear as he tried to console her.

"It's all right Linde. It's all right. Let's not talk about the future whilst we are here at the Türken. I promise you nothing but happiness in the few days we have together and afterwards we will see what can be done about our situation."

Linde raised her tear-stained face to look into his eyes.

"Thank you Karl, thank you."

They remained on the veranda for a long, long time locked in each other's embrace, whilst dark clouds gathered and drifted across the moon, creating a moving theatre of shadows around them.

CHAPTER 18

Linde leaned forward across the breakfast table, her face aglow. "I've just had another wonderful idea, Karl."

Hartmann laid down his stein of weißbier, wiped his lips, and smiled at her expectantly.

"Why don't we go to Munich and take part in the Oktoberfest?"

It was early August. Oktoberfest wouldn't be starting for another six weeks or so and he looked at her blankly, puzzled by the suggestion, not at all comprehending what she might have in mind.

Linde giggled at the perplexity clearly written across his face.

"The Zeitmaschine, Karl. We can travel forward to the exact time of the beer festival and join in the fun. And whilst we are there in Munich, I can also show you around the beautiful Ludwig Maximilians University where I studied History before having to return home to look after my mother."

Hartmann slapped his forehead, astonished that he had not immediately recognised in Linde's suggestion the opportunity the Zeitmaschine afforded them.

"Of course we can, Linde. You are so clever to think of this. Although I have experienced a number of Oktoberfest celebrations previously in Berlin, it has always been a rather drunken affair with my comrades in the barracks. It would be another thing altogether to take part in the festival surrounded by local Bavarians celebrating in the streets and taverns."

Hartmann cradled his chin between thumb and forefinger and frowned down at the tablecloth, whilst Linde waited in anticipation for him to work out a plan.

A few seconds later he thumped the table and looked up in triumph.

"This morning, we shall return to the Zeitmaschine where I'll set the controls to take us to the time of Oktoberfest. After our time journey, we'll return back here to the Türken, purchase tickets for the shuttle bus, and in Berchtesgaden we'll take the train to Munich. There we'll stay overnight in an inn and on the following day we'll enjoy every bit of fun the festival has to offer. The next morning we'll return by train and bus to the Türken. But before entering the hotel, we'll return to the Zeitmaschine where, by depressing the green button, we will be carried back to a fraction of a second after we departed two days earlier, which of course will be today – this morning in fact, just after we had finished the breakfast which presently sits before us here on this table."

Hartmann leaned back in his chair and gave Linde a look of accomplishment, whilst she in turn responded with a soundless handclap and a look of pleasure.

They quickly finished off their meal and shortly afterwards were on the track across the meadow heading for the chamber. Hartmann, having found out all he needed to know about the

Oktoberfest from brochures on the Türken's reception desk, set the Zeitmaschine's controls to take them to the last week in September, and after their brief trip through time they returned to the Türken to purchase tickets for the shuttle bus.

Herman Wirth looked up and gave them a welcoming smile as they approached the desk.

"Ahh, Herr Hartmann and Fräulein Engel. It's so good to see you back again after only a few weeks. Will you be requiring two adjoining rooms once again?"

"No thank you, not today Herr Wirth. We have organised accommodation elsewhere – but we do wish to purchase tickets on this afternoon's shuttle bus run down to Berchtesgaden, returning the day after tomorrow."

In Berchtesgaden they boarded the train to Munich, taking with them food, drink and magazines from which they would learn more of this world of their future, on a journey which would take a few hours with a possible change of trains before arriving at their destination.

Overcome by a wave of nostalgia on being back in the city of her student years, Linde begged Hartmann to first of all take her to the University where, strolling through its hallowed hallways, she delighted in pointing out its inspired architecture and the intricate wood panelling in the halls, library and lecture theatres in which she had once studied.

As they passed, a door to one of the theatres burst open and a cohort of bright-eyed chattering students came streaming out.

"Many of my lectures were held in that room, Karl. The seats and fittings are centuries old and are so very interesting. Let's just wait a minute until the students have left and we'll take a peek inside."

After the last of the students exited, Linde led Hartmann into the theatre. The lecturer was still at the rostrum busily shuffling her notes into a briefcase and looking up, stared at Linde for a few seconds, her eyes widening.

"I don't believe it! Linde Engel! Is it really you?"

"Mitzi? Mitzi Bayer?"

The two women rushed to each other and embraced. Both had tears streaming down their cheeks when they finally separated. Linde turned to a puzzled Hartmann who had joined them, and wiping away a tear explained their relationship.

"Mitzi and I were in the same History classes and shared a room in the students' college for two years. We did absolutely everything together and had so much fun here in Munich, didn't we Mitzi?"

Mitzi nodded enthusiastically and proffered her hand when Linde introduced Hartmann as her best friend.

They shook hands warmly.

"Please call me Mitzi."

She turned to Linde to inspect her friend's face.

"You look so young Linde. You haven't changed a bit in all these years. It's uncanny."

Linde acknowledged the fact but deciding against trying to explain, quickly changed the subject.

"Tell us Mitzi, what are you doing here at the University?"

"Well, after I gained my degree in History, the University granted me a position as tutor, and by accumulating some additional qualifications over the years, I ended up here as lecturer in History.

"And you, Linde. We lost contact with each other. I remember you had to leave because your mother was ill. Is she well now?"

"No, I'm afraid she passed away a year after I left Munich and afterwards I wasn't able to return because I couldn't meet the expense of completing my studies."

The two women hugged each other again.

"Karl and I arrived here in Munich this afternoon and intend spending tomorrow enjoying the Oktoberfest celebrations before returning to Berchtesgaden, but I brought him straight here to see the University first before we start looking for a place to stay tonight."

"Then I insist you stay with us. We've plenty of room in our apartment and Gunther – he also lectures here at the University – always enjoys a vigorous discussion with the guests I bring home, especially if they show an interest in German history …" She glanced at Hartmann, "… or perhaps philosophy. Do you think you could keep him occupied with some interesting discourse, Karl, whilst Linde and I catch up with each other about the good old days?"

Hartmann hesitated, filled with doubt at the suggestion.

He had transcended time in the Zeitmaschine. He knew so very much about the future which lay ahead of them all – a world where computers could dispense more historical knowledge than Mitzi could ever learn in a thousand lifetimes. His country was at war with the rest of the world. He was Hitler's personal aide and was going to assist the Führer in defying the historical record by escaping to the future.

But could he discuss such things with a stranger?

Nevertheless, he responded with as much enthusiasm as could be mustered, declaring it would be his pleasure to engage in discussions with Gunther to the extent he was able. Mitzi thanked him and shutting her briefcase, suggested they retire to a nearby *Kaffeehaus* where she was due to meet Gunther within the hour.

They settled at a sunny outdoor table and after Hartmann left to order coffee and pastries at the service counter, Mitzi turned to Linde accusingly.

"You naughty little cradle snatcher, Linde."

"Why, whatever do you mean, Mitzi?"

"Well, you may look younger than you really are, but don't forget, I know you were twenty years old when I last saw you fourteen years ago. That puts you around thirty four, whereas that boy, handsome as he is, can't be much older than you were when you left Munich."

Linde stared at her in surprise until Mitzi's logic sank in, and smiling at how their situation must have been perceived by her friend, decided to go along with Mitzi's mistaken belief.

"He too is a little older than he looks, but yes, I guess I am a bit of a cradle snatcher. But Mitzi, we get on so well together – it's unbelievable. We love each other very much."

Hartmann returned from placing their orders and finding the two women totally engrossed in conversation about their student past, quietly took a seat and listened with interest to their conversation until Gunther arrived a little later.

In the evening the foursome made their way to the *Theresienwiese* in the centre of Munich where masses of revelling citizens and foreign tourists had gathered to enjoy the entertainments on offer. In the *Augustiner* tent they found seats at a table in the midst of a rowdy throng of wassailing Bavarians, and Hartmann, having just come from wartime Germany where good food was hard to come by, was soon to be dazzled by buxom waitresses bustling past clutching more steins of beer in each hand than he could ever have thought possible, whilst others whisked past bearing platters piled high and near-overflowing with *hendl, schweinebraten, steckerlfisch,* and *knödel.*

Talk at their table followed the usual patter employed by people well-disposed toward one another in order to get to know each other better, and they spoke at first of their various occupations. Mitzi as they had already learned, was a lecturer at the University. Gunther turned out to be professor of History and he and Mitzi gave an account of how they had first met. Linde described how Herr Kaufmann had taken her into his jewellery business, after which she and Hartmann spoke of their instant attraction toward one another the moment he entered the shop, both agreeing and declaring it had been a case of love at first sight. Hartmann told them he was an officer in the German army and was able to respond to the most basic of their questions about the military because he was indeed an officer in Hitler's army, but he skilfully avoided showing ignorance of modern warfare and weaponry by asserting he was bound not to reveal details of his special forces unit and instead deflected the conversation by claiming to be a keen amateur war historian with especial interest in the Second World War. History, being the natural passion of both Mitzi and Gunther, quickly became the topic of conversation and after a while, Hartmann, who was feeling a little more relaxed after having consumed several steins of beer, casually asked Gunther what approach he would take to historical studies if he had a time machine at his disposal. Would he avail himself of the opportunity to study the historical past or would he prefer to look ahead into the future? Linde shot him an anxious look that relaxed into a smile when he winked back at her. Gunther took the question very seriously and stroked his chin, gathering his thoughts before responding.

"We learn from History that humanity never really learns from History. Governments keep making the same mistakes over and over again. I believe humankind is repeating its historical madness in this cold war currently being waged between the United States and Russia, and the proxy war China and America are fighting in Vietnam. With all sides heavily nuclear armed, I would travel to the future to discover whether we are about to repeat our historical insanity by wiping ourselves off the face of the planet, as this would finally spell the end of all human history."

Gunther was talking about matters of which Hartmann had no knowledge whatsoever, but he persisted with the idea of travelling through time.

"Still, if you found yourself alarmed at what you discovered in the future, then on your return to the present time, would you try to urge people to change their ways so that the unwelcome future you had observed would not eventuate after all?"

"The answer to that question Karl, all depends on one's concept of time. To my way of thinking, the future I had observed would be the future which would come to pass no matter what I tried to do to change it. Consequently there would be no point in trying to change things when I returned to the present."

Hartmann was momentarily stunned by this observation and sat back in his chair. Gunther had just echoed the very same sentiments in labelling the future immutable as had scientist Fuchs' expounded regarding the past.

The conversation at the table segued into a related area but whilst the other three were engrossed in the new topic of conversation, Hartmann speculated on how Fuchs' and Gunther's concepts of time might impact on the success of the Führer's plan. Hitler would be travelling to and residing in the future and Hartmann couldn't think of any reason why he shouldn't be successful in achieving this ambition, as it would in no way be tampering with the past, whilst his arrival in the future would simply be another occurrence in the normal course of human affairs. Consequently, he could see no conflict with either of Gunther's or Fuch's dictums. And yet Hartmann still could not reconcile the conundrum of Hitler living in the future whilst the historical record had him dying in the past.

He was roused from his reverie by laughter. The other three were chortling, regarding him with amusement after Gunther had brought Hartmann's daydreaming to the attention of the others. Returned by their cajoling to the present moment and pleased that paradoxical problems attendant to his leader's planned escape were not ones for which he was obliged to find answers, he gave up in his quest to resolve the riddle and re-joined the conversation.

After a thoroughly enjoyable evening they returned to the Bayer's apartment where, true to his word, Hartmann maintained an interesting dialogue with Gunther to give the women the opportunity they craved to reminisce over their early college days. After supper, whilst the men smoked and drank beer in the parlour, Mitzi and Linde retired to the kitchen to tidy away the dishes.

During the ensuing conversation, Mitzi diplomatically enquired about their preferred sleeping arrangements for the night.

Linde blushed.

"Can you find us separate beds? Karl and I are very much in love and though we are romantically involved, our relationship hasn't reached that stage ... yet."

Mitzi smiled sympathetically, but was filled with wonder that her attractive thirty four year old friend had not yet consummated her relationship with this very handsome and intelligent young man.

The next day the foursome again visited the Theresienwiese to witness the traditional Munich procession of marching bands, decorated drays of the Munich breweries, floats displaying typical local traditions, flag-throwers, trumpeters on horseback and the host of performers who followed in their wake. After the parade they strolled through the crowds of sightseers where Mitzi and Gunther, who had experienced the Oktoberfest many times previously, found amusement in their guests' enthusiastic embrace of every little entertainment on offer as well as spur-of-the-moment purchases they made at booths selling everything from hats and pins to lederhosen.

After another pleasant evening at the Bayer's apartment, Linde and Hartmann were farewelled the next morning by their hosts at Munich Main station, and on arrival back in Berchtesgaden, they returned to the Türken's car park on the afternoon bus run. Diverting across the meadow to the secret chamber, they boarded the Zeitmaschine and just as Hartmann had foretold, were able to return to a split second after they had departed two days ago, by depressing the green button.

CHAPTER 19

Just before noon the sky grew overcast and heavy with angry black clouds, and during lunch it began to rain. As they ate, Hartmann and Linde looked out on a landscape obscured by rivulets of water flowing over the window panes.

"This damned rain won't be of much assistance if I'm to keep you happy today Linde."

She smiled and reaching across the table, placed her hand on his.

"I know just the thing we can do on a rainy day, Karl. Why don't we go to the picture theatre in Berchtesgaden and take in a movie? I read in the paper they're screening '*Where Eagles Dare*'. It's a new release and was mainly filmed right here in the Alps, not that far from where we are today. I believe the story is all about the daring rescue of a British brigadier held captive in an impregnable German castle during the Second World War. But there's a lot of intrigue in the plot and it all sounds very exciting. I'm sure you would enjoy it because you must know a lot about such things."

Hartmann scoffed.

"A good war movie is just what I need to remind me of what I have left behind in 1944. I would also assume that, given the movie is a British production and is being shown to an audience largely populated with billeted American soldiers, our brave German soldiers won't be shown in a particularly flattering light …"

Hartmann observed Linde's look of disappointment at his somewhat negative response and he hurriedly recanted mid-sentence.

"… still, I'm sure it would be very interesting to see the War from the perspective of the other side."

At the theatre, whilst Hartmann purchased tickets, Linde waited out of sight in the foyer some distance from the booth lest the man dispensing tickets, whom she had known quite well ten years ago, recognise her and remark on her youthful appearance. When Hartmann re-joined her, she pointed to the poster she had been studying, promoting the movie they were about to see.

"Look Karl, isn't this interesting. '*Where Eagles Dare*' stars two men – Richard Burton and Clint Eastwood – and although I must confess to being a bit of a Hollywood movie buff, I'd never heard of either of them ten years ago. Now, ten years later they are both famous film stars. So much can happen in such a short space of time – I'm finding this whole time travelling business so very fascinating."

The movie was indeed thrilling. Hartmann had his arm wrapped around Linde's shoulder throughout the film and he could feel Linde's excitement as she gripped his other hand tightly during the action scenes.

Predictably, the German soldiers and their commanders as portrayed in the movie proved no match for the allied rescuers in their bravery and cunning, but Hartmann was nevertheless able to disregard his natural bias and in the end, thoroughly enjoyed the film's action and suspense.

On their way out of the theatre, Linde thought she saw the man in the ticket booth glancing at her in an uncomfortably familiar manner, and in order to avoid the possibility of being recognised by other townsfolk she had known ten years ago, they again visited the small emporium where she bought and donned scarf and sunglasses.

In a *teehaus* close to the bus terminal they drank coffee and discussed the film to while away the time before departing for the Türken.

"The castle they featured in the movie, Linde, reminds me of a place I know of right here in the Alps – a place that is just as impregnable and is, incidentally, located not more than a half hour's drive from the Türken. Perhaps you've heard of the *Kehlsteinhaus*? The British called it '*the Eagle's Nest*' during the War and as the name suggests it's rather inaccessible, being perched up high on a mountain top."

"I have heard some mention of it Karl – didn't it have something to do with Hitler?"

"Yes, that's right Linde, indeed it does … *did* … have something to do with him. The lavishly built and furnished chalet was commissioned by Martin Bormann to celebrate Hitler's fiftieth birthday, and offered incredible vistas from every side of the building – from the balcony one could even see as far as Salzburg in Austria. I've visited the place a few times during my tours of duty back in 1944, but I've no idea what became of it during or after the War – perhaps it was destroyed in the British bombing raids over the Obersalzberg."

"It sounds fascinating, Karl. Why don't we see if it survived, and if it did, then perhaps we can find a tour that takes us there."

"It's definitely worth a visit Linde – I'll see if the staff at the Türken can organise something for us."

On the bus, Linde snuggled up against Hartmann and he again wrapped an arm around her shoulder.

"I'm having such a good time, Karl."

She looked up into his face hopefully.

"Do you think the Maître d' would allow us to have a champagne dinner in the privacy of our rooms tonight to celebrate another lovely day together?"

"What a splendid idea, Linde. Yes, I'm sure it can be arranged."

He smiled down at her and after a quick glance around the bus to ensure no one was watching, kissed Linde's upturned lips.

On their arrival back at the hotel, Hartmann discussed their proposed tête-à-tête with the Maître d' who suggested the couple might enjoy a candlelit banquet for two. Hartmann enthusiastically embraced the proposal and next visited the desk clerk to enquire about excursions to the Kehlsteinhaus. He discovered to his delight that not only had the building survived the War intact, but it had also become quite a popular tourist destination, and by good fortune, the hotel's courtesy bus ferried tourists there in the morning before its return to the Türken for the daily afternoon run to Berchtesgaden station. Hartmann promptly purchased tickets for the next day's tour and felt exuberant at the prospect of visiting the Kehlsteinhaus once again.

After a quick bath, Hartmann donned the smartest outfit he could muster from their shopping trip, and was just completing outfitting himself, adjusting his tie in the mirror, when a kitchen hand knocked on the door to set up his room for dinner. After the man had finished, Hartmann ventured out into the corridor and knocked on Linde's door.

"I'm nearly ready, Karl. I'll be with you in another five minutes."

Hartmann returned to his room to survey the dining arrangement with a critical eye. A small table covered by a pale pink linen cloth edged with alpine motifs and flanked by two matching dining chairs had been placed adjacent to the bedroom window. Silver cutlery and pearly white plates gleamed in the light cast by a candelabrum bearing a brace of lit candles. A squat crystal bowl brimming with delicate meadow flowers had been placed to one side, and a magnum of champagne wrapped in a white serviette collar stood upright in an ice bucket alongside the table, awaiting their pleasure.

'*Perfect*,' he thought, entirely satisfied with the setting. Hartmann checked his watch and commenced pacing the floor awaiting Linde's arrival. Twenty minutes later there was a light tap on the door. He hastened to open it and stood in the doorway transfixed. Linde was standing outside in the corridor smiling demurely, her white lace dress cut just low enough to show the gentle swell of her breasts before they plunged under the bodice. Her waist seemed smaller than he remembered, and her face was a radiant portrait framed in cascades of curly locks.

She acknowledged his gaze with a short melodious laugh.

"Well now, Herr Hartmann, are you going to invite me in or am I to spend the rest of the evening eating my dinner in this hallway?"

"I'm so sorry, Linde. Yes, please do come in."

He stood aside, ushering her in.

"Linde, you look absolutely stunning."

"Thank you Karl. I was very much hoping you would agree to having this private dinner so that I might have the opportunity to wear this dress I bought especially for you … and you too look so handsome in your new clothes."

She cast her eye around the room and her gaze fell on the table setting.

"Oh, Karl. How wonderful. Your room looks just like a set from a romantic Hollywood movie."

She whirled around and flinging her arms around his neck, kissed him passionately. Hartmann responded with equal enthusiasm, before finally unwrapping her arms.

"If I don't make a phone call to the dining room requesting our food to be sent up, I'm afraid there'll be nothing to eat, and I'd have naught to sustain me apart from your kisses."

Linde glanced at the champagne nestling in the ice bucket.

"Champagne and kisses – I'm sure I could survive on such a wonderful diet, Karl."

She sighed with mock resignation.

"But if you really must, well, go ahead and order the food."

He did so and as they chatted at the table, smiling waiters were soon bringing them course after course of sumptuous dishes, occasionally unobtrusively topping up their wine glasses when the need arose.

Finally, waiters cleared the table and left them alone for the night with a dessert of *Prinzregententorte*, a pot of coffee and a small flask of *Kirshwasser*.

Linde eyed the torte dubiously.

"It looks so tempting Karl, but I don't think I could manage another thing to eat."

"It does indeed look tempting, Linde. I'm reminded of dinners with my family many years ago when I was a boy. If I told my parents I was full and there still happened to be some of Mutti's cake left on the table, my father would send me out into the front garden to check whether there had been a mail delivery to our letter box. There were, of course, no letters for collection, but the walk outside was supposed to settle my stomach and make room for more food."

Hartmann smiled into the distance on recollection of this fondly held childhood memory.

"Then perhaps a short walk in the moonlight might just rekindle our appetites, Karl?"

They rose from the table, kissed and made their way downstairs. As they passed through the lobby on their way to the veranda, Hartmann waved his appreciation to a grinning waiter in the dining room.

They stood side by side for a while silently gazing out across the meadow. A brief shower had left tiny droplets of rain over the shrubbery and the leaves now sparkled in the light of the moon as if dusted with a sprinkling of a thousand diamonds. Linde leaned back against a veranda post, encircling it behind her with her arms as she looked out on the magical scene before them. Hartmann turned to Linde and cupping her face in his hands, he kissed her long and tenderly. Her breath was warm on his fingers as they traced a line across her lips to her cheeks, then continued slowly on a downward journey that caressed her neck, her shoulders and finally, his hands came to rest over her breasts. Linde relinquished her hold on the post and covering his hands with her own, pressed them firmly against her bosom.

They gazed into each other's eyes in silence until Linde brushed Hartmann's cheek with a kiss, whispering in his ear in a low husky voice.

"It's getting a little chilly out here on the veranda, Karl. Perhaps we should be getting back to your room and the Prinzregententorte dessert?"

Hartmann nodded, and gently taking her by the hand, led her upstairs.

No sooner had the door closed behind them then they were enveloped in a passionate lover's embrace. Linde tore at the buttons of Hartmann's shirt and thrust her hands inside to feel the warmth of his muscular manly chest, whilst he drew down the zipper on the back of her dress. Between urgent kisses and caresses they hurried to strip off their clothing down to the barest of underwear, at which point Hartmann grasped Linde by the hand and pulled her onto his bed.

He reached behind her back, unclipped her brassiere and slowly lifted the garment from her bosom to reveal her firm rounded breasts. Hartmann gazed at them in admiration as they rose and fell rapidly with her excited breathing, and cautiously extended his hand to caress her. As they explored each other's mouths with their tongues, his hand descended to experience the satin smooth softness of her thighs. Feeling her pleasure, he rose from the bed and Linde sobbed with waves of emotion as he gently lowered onto her, and rocking back and forth, plunged himself into the very depths of her being.

* * *

Linde lay on her side propped up on an elbow abstractedly twirling the short curly hairs on Hartmann's chest.

"I feel so good, Karl – so fulfilled. I've wondered for years what it would be like and now I know. It's like … it's like all the good feelings I have ever had all happening at the same time."

Hartmann had one arm crooked behind her neck and gently combed his fingers through her curly locks with his free hand.

"It was the first time for me too, Linde. You know I love you, don't you?"

"Yes, of course I know, silly."

As the sounds of the hotel around them gradually diminished over time and the candles in the candelabrum flickered, sputtered and one by one surrendered to the night, they chattered about the Zeitmaschine, the movie, the church on the Königssee and many other things besides. Hartmann asked if Linde had developed sufficient appetite to attack the Prinzregententorte. She laughed and shaking her head, offered him her share, which he too declined.

They moved closer to make themselves more comfortable on a bed not really intended to accommodate two persons in total comfort, and gradually their conversation trailed off into mumbled whispers and they fell asleep in each other's arms.

Hartmann was the first to wake in the morning. For a few minutes he gazed lovingly at Linde, still lying sleeping at his side, breathing heavily with a slight snoring sound. He carefully slipped his numbed arm from under her neck, but the movement awoke her. She stretched her body languidly and turning to face him, gently traced a path across his cheek with a fingertip whilst looking shyly into his eyes.

They kissed and embraced and made love again.

CHAPTER 20

The next day, on the way to the mountain retreat, Hartmann enthused about the Kehlsteinhaus, describing in great detail its unique and fascinating features.

"From the carpark, one enters via a tunnel which penetrates deep into the side of the mountain, and at its far end, there's an elevator waiting to convey guests way, way up through solid rock into the heart of the Kehlsteinhaus, which itself sits atop the highest ridge. I was so very happy to learn it survived the War intact, and would have been very much saddened had allied bombing raids damaged the building, as the architects and decorators spared no expense in furnishing and fitting it out. The feature I admired most was the large red marble fireplace in the building's reception area, which the Italian dictator, Benito Mussolini, presented to Hitler as a gift from the Italian people. And outside, behind the chalet there's a pathway which, if one has a mind, leads to the very top of the mountain. From there, one can see forevermore."

Linde had been gazing out through the bus window at the passing countryside as he spoke, but now turned an enquiring eye to Hartmann.

"How is it you know so much about this place, Karl?"

He hesitated, fearing she might find his answer disturbing, but determined from this day onward there would be no place for deception in their deeply developing relationship, he glanced nervously around the bus before replying.

"This is very difficult for me to discuss here, Linde, but …"

Linde frowned at his hesitation.

He glanced uneasily around the bus again.

"In the time from which I come, I was … *am* … one of Adolph Hitler's personal assistants and have accompanied his entourage to the Kehlsteinhaus on a number of occasions."

Linde stared at him in disbelief.

"*You*! Is this true? Do you mean to tell me that during the War you were … *are* … actually assistant to this very same monster who was responsible for my father's death at Dukla Pass?"

Hartmann was stung and deeply hurt by her accusation, and again cast a wary eye around the bus before responding.

"Please Linde, try to understand – I come from an entirely different country from the one you know. The majority of Germans in my time think of Hitler not as a monster but as the nation's saviour. I beg you please do not let these matters of politics interfere with the love we share."

Linde stiffened and after scowling at him in sullen silence for a second, turned to watch the passing scenery outside, blurred as it was by the tears welling up in her eyes. Hartmann regarded the back of her head helplessly, not knowing what he could say or do to give her comfort. He loved Linde more than words could say, but his honour and the very essence of all he stood for as a soldier of the Reich would not permit him to disown his allegiance to the Führer. In the end he turned to gaze out of the windows on the other side of the bus, hoping time would weave its magic and bring them together once again under better circumstances.

The Kehlsteinhaus proved to be just as Hartmann had described. Linde gazed unhappily at Mussolini's red marble fireplace, conjuring up a picture of Hartmann standing where she was now standing – admiring it – twenty five years ago.

Carpe diem.

Carpe diem.

Linde's heart was in turmoil. She desperately wanted to reconcile her feelings for Hartmann against what she now knew about his dark past and turned to him, tears streaming down her cheeks.

"I love you so much Karl. I don't want to think about the past or the future. I just want to share every precious moment we have together right here and now in this present time, and let fate do with us what it will later on."

Hartmann enveloped Linde in his arms and gently pulling her to his breast, buried his face in her hair, and they embraced, locked together in silence. The other tourists in their party regarded them with curiosity as they walked by, shaking their heads, pointing and whispering to one another.

After morning tea in the restaurant, during which they picked disinterestedly at their food, Hartmann led Linde to the rear of the chalet where he lifted her chin with a forefinger and studied her troubled face.

"Come with me Linde, there is something you must see before we leave the Kehlsteinhaus."

He led her onto a well-worn path that meandered up the mountain ridge behind the building. As they ascended, the path quickly deteriorated, finally ending up little better than a tortuous rocky goat track. It wound its way ever higher up the ridge, until Linde was forced to use all fours to scramble up onto a prominent rock ledge jutting out from the summit. The landscape fell away steeply on all sides and she cast her eyes nervously around the shelf on which she now stood. Hartmann followed Linde onto the platform and coming up behind her, gripped her shoulders.

"Look up Linde, look up and around you and see where you are."

Linde responded, lifting her gaze.

The works of God were evident all around them, revealed in a panorama unsurpassed by any vista she had ever known. In every direction, at every point leading to the horizon, mountain peak after mountain peak thrust its purple snow-capped majesty skyward as far as the eye could see, all held in mysterious suspension above the mists that swirled and drifted up from the lush green valleys far below. Linde gazed in awe at the magnificence surrounding them and caught her breath with the emotion it evoked. Hartmann stood behind her, his hands still firmly holding Linde's shoulders as she took in this superb spectacle, and she exulted in the feeling that the world spread out before her eyes belonged to the two of them – and to the two of them alone.

She turned to see whether Hartmann was imbued with similar feelings, only to find with concern that his gaze was fixed on the distant horizon in a manner that sent a shiver through her body. It seemed at that particular moment he was totally oblivious to her presence. She waved her hand in front of his face, and he slowly re-focussed his attention on her with troubled, glistening eyes.

"What is it Karl? What's the matter? Is something wrong?"

"No, no, it's nothing, Linde. Nothing. Seeing this grandeur once again makes me feel so very, very small – so insignificant – and reminds me of matters which must yet be dealt with – matters I would rather have forgotten about completely."

Linde scanned his face apprehensively as again his attention began to drift toward the distant horizon. Deciding to allow his disturbing disposition to pass without further remark, she brought Hartmann out of his reverie by reminding him that backtracking downhill over the rocks wouldn't be easy, and the tour bus would be leaving soon.

He nodded absently and followed after Linde as she scrambled down the rocky track back to the Kehlsteinhaus to finally re-join the band of tourists gathered around the doors of the elevator, awaiting the return of the tour guide who had been searching the building for them.

That evening at the dinner table, Linde could see Hartmann was still troubled.

"Is it because we are going home tomorrow?"

"Yes, Linde, we cannot stay here in the future forever – I must return you to your time in 1959 and I too have commitments back in my own time which are yet to be dealt with. But I'll continue to search for some way of using the Zeitmaschine to allow our love for each other to be fulfilled – there simply must be a favourable answer to our predicament."

He paused, taking in her look of concern and smiled reassuringly despite the troubling uncertainty gnawing at his heart.

"Let's not think about tomorrow, but instead continue to enjoy the time we have together in the present. Remember what you yourself told me, Linde, on our first outing together – to glean whatever happiness we can out of every passing moment."

That night, they slept together again and Hartmann made love to Linde in a far gentler and more enduring way than had been the case on the two previous occasions when passion and urgency had dictated their congress.

CHAPTER 21

The next morning as Hartmann paid the hotel's account, Herman Wirth enquired whether they had enjoyed their stay and whether they might visit the hotel again.

"Another time perhaps."

As an afterthought, a wry smile crossing his lips, he added.

"Yes, another time. I can say without a doubt I will definitely be visiting the hotel again in the future."

"And will you be requiring tickets for today's courtesy bus run to Berchtesgaden?"

Hartmann shook his head. '*Yes*', he thought. Of course they would be requiring a ticket, but he would be purchasing it ten years ago. In response to Wirth's enquiry he politely declined, informing him they had other means of transport.

Hartmann re-joined Linde waiting for him in the lobby with their bundles of clothing and rucksack, and they made their way across the meadow to the secret cave.

Hartmann loaded their luggage onto the bench opposite the Zeitmaschine's control station and climbed aboard. He reached for Linde, taking her hand, and she slid across the bench seat to link her arm in his, pressing against his side. She searched his eyes for reassurance but his heart was filled with sorrow as he contemplated the decision he had been forced to make that morning. He avoided her gaze on finding himself unable to respond with the words of comfort she so desperately sought. Instead, he turned his attention to the duration dials to consider the settings required to take them back to Linde's time. He calculated they had initially travelled forward by ten years, followed by another eight day voyage to take up their booking at the Türken, and finally, they had spent four nights in their stay at the hotel. He reset the time duration dials to arrive a couple of hours after they had departed on the day when Hank, the American GI, had given them a lift to the Türken, once again subtracting extra hours from the total to ensure against the Zeitmaschine colliding with itself by arriving before it left. He pulled on the red lever, depressed the red button and the time speed needle commenced its backward rotation. They watched in silence as the tiny strip of metal accelerated and spun around the dial before slowing and coming to rest again. As they exited from the machine Hartmann tried to cheer Linde.

"You are now safely home again in your own time, Linde. It's just past noon on Sunday, a few hours after we departed for the future four days ago."

But there was something in his voice which heightened her unease rather than giving her the relief she had hoped would accompany their return. They gathered their belongings together and exited the cave into the open air and bright sunshine, where Linde observed the trees around the clearing had returned to their former sapling size.

Hartmann laid down his load and indicating a nearby rock ledge, asked Linde to take a seat.

"I have a most distressing matter to discuss with you, Linde."

She sat down apprehensively, hoping against hope he would not be announcing the very thing she most feared.

"I have told you that in my own time I am an aide to Hitler, Linde. But my role in determining the future of the Reich and therefore the destiny of humankind is far greater than being a mere assistant in executing his plan. I have a key role to play in a grand strategy which will see him travelling to the future to once again stamp Germany's dominance across the face of Europe. Believe me, I have struggled hard to find some way of resolving the conflict between my one true desire to remain here with you and the commitment I pledged on oath to Hitler, but regrettably I have not been able to find a solution that favours our being able to stay together. It grieves me to say that I feel duty bound to leave you and return to my own time in order to honour my obligation to the Führer and the Reich."

Linde looked up at Hartmann and implored him to see reason.

"Please, please listen to me Karl. If you return to assist Hitler and he then uses the Zeitmaschine to travel to the distant future, you will be left without any means of returning to me in my own time. I will then have lost you forever."

Hartmann knelt in front of Linde and took hold of her hand, gazing sorrowfully into her eyes, seeking her understanding.

"I realise this would be so Linde and believe me, the decision I have been forced to make is breaking my heart, but I have sworn an oath and now, to preserve my honour, I must keep my promise."

Linde shook her head and begged Hartmann to consider the absurdity of his decision.

"But Karl, you yourself have witnessed the future. You know from what you have seen on the computer screen in the future Türken that Hitler committed suicide in Berlin at the end of the War. What good can come of your pledge now, when the certainty of the past informs us of Hitler's fate? If escaping to the future was indeed to be the answer to his salvation, then his plan must surely have been doomed to failure from its very inception."

"Ahh, but you are forgetting what can be achieved using the Zeitmaschine, Linde. Hitler will defy the past by travelling to and living in the future. Once this has been achieved, how could it be possible for him to die in the past? It is of the greatest misfortune for us that to achieve his goal he will be taking the one and only Zeitmaschine with him to the future, but I made the pledge and am now duty bound to return his machine to him without questioning the soundness of his plan."

"I don't care about Hitler, or his plans. I just care about us. What about the love we share for each other Karl? Do our feelings mean nothing to you at all?"

"How can you ask that of me Linde? No man has ever loved a woman as much as I love you, and I'm tormented by the decision I have had to make. But when a man must choose between two mutually exclusive and conflicting options, does he have the right to favour his own personal happiness over the course he knows will re-write the destiny of all humankind? I do not feel I have the right to choose what I personally want most of all."

At these words, Linde burst into uncontrolled sobbing and buried her face in her hands. Hartmann sat down beside her and tried to wrap an arm around her shoulder, but she shook him off angrily.

Suddenly, a shout came from the path between the trees.

"Hartmann!"

Hartmann's head whirled around at the sound of his sharply spoken name and as he looked up, a figure who had emerged from the forest was now swiftly striding toward them.

Hartmann stared in disbelief.

The approaching figure was none other than a duplicate version of himself.

But it wasn't quite himself. The person who had so suddenly appeared might have been his identical twin but for the fact that his face was older, perhaps around fortyish, and was scarred by more than the usual depredations of the passing years.

Linde was still sobbing, her eyes covered by her hands, oblivious to the appearance of this newcomer on the scene. He promptly crossed the clearing and ignoring a totally stunned Hartmann, knelt in front of her. Drawing a handkerchief from his pocket he ever so gently dabbed at the tears streaming down Linde's face. She uncovered her tear-filled eyes and taking the kerchief, wiped her cheeks as she gazed into his eyes, not seeming to notice the apparent aging of the man kneeling before her.

She pleaded with him softly.

"Please don't leave me Karl. Please don't go."

On hearing this, Hartmann's duplicate sprang to his feet in a fury and turning, angrily railed at the younger man.

"You fool Hartmann! You would trade the love of this beautiful young woman for an empty lost cause? Are you mad?"

Hartmann had up to this moment been but a speechless observer of the scene being played out before him. But now, having recovered his composure and suddenly discovering anger at being addressed in this highly offensive manner he was stirred out of inaction. He leapt to his feet, his movement making Linde look up. She rose unsteadily from the ledge, instantly alarmed and frightened by the spectacle of two furious Hartmanns confronting each other, not more than a few paces in front of her.

She looked from one to the other, not knowing which one to address and wailed in anguish.

"Oh Karl, what is happening. There are two of you. I don't understand. Am I seeing things or perhaps I'm going insane?"

Hartmann's duplicate turned to her and wrapping his arms around Linde, who had resumed her sobbing, gently held her to him, burying her face in his chest. He glared at Hartmann who in turn, scowled back at him, and angrily berated his younger self.

"You fool. You and your damned Führer just don't get it, do you? Have you completely forgotten Fuchs' warning about trying to change the past? I now know for certain that what you yourself have seen written in the historical record is indeed what will eventually happen to Hitler, and nothing you or he can do, even with all the wealth he hopes to accumulate, can ever change the outcome written there. You and your misguided loyalty to the Reich have cost me dearly … and it's going to cost you dearly too, as you will eventually discover when you follow in my footsteps.

"Go! Go back to your own time. History dictates there is nothing I can say or do to save you from suffering the consequences of your folly."

Hartmann stared at his older self in disbelief, trying to reconcile what had been said against the strategy that Hitler would be pursuing. If, as was planned, he ensured the Führer was safely transported to the future, how could his leader's demise in the Berlin bunker, as recorded in the history books, ever come to pass? Whilst recognising that this older man, by his appearance and intimate knowledge, certainly must be a future version of himself, he still found it impossible to accept that his own future was necessarily inextricably linked to this duplicate's past. Whatever his future self might have experienced in *his* past he now disregarded in the certainty of his ability to carve out a completely different future for himself. He glared at his duplicate and then, as his gaze fell on Linde weeping in the older man's arms, he simultaneously experienced heartbreak, guilt, and regret. He was somewhat consoled by the knowledge that Linde was now in the care of this older version of himself, and thereby felt relief at not abandoning her in her hour of need without having someone trustworthy to care for her. However, knowing she would be safe with his duplicate did nothing to lessen the ache in his heart at leaving forever the woman he loved … but at least it did help assuage his feelings of guilt.

Nothing his future self had said had diminished his determination to assist Hitler in escaping to the future, and stung into action by his powerlessness to alter the situation in which he now found himself, and still infuriated by his older self's censure, he snatched up the rucksack, and without another word, turned on his heel and strode back into the cave.

CHAPTER 22

Hartmann clambered into the Zeitmaschine fuming and slammed the access panel shut behind him. He gripped the control console to stop his hands from trembling with rage, and gritting his teeth, willed himself to calm down. After his turmoil had settled to the point where he felt sufficiently able to think rationally, and had managed to dismiss from his mind the confrontation outside the cave, he turned to the task of addressing exactly where he currently stood in relation to his time of departure from the chamber in 1944. He reasoned that, as he had just returned Linde to her own time, this being the day after they had first met, he was now located fifteen years and a day into his future. He also remembered glancing at his watch just before entering the Zeitmaschine – Ten thirty. Hartmann adjusted the time duration dials accordingly, subtracting, as usual, a few hours from the total to again ensure he arrived in the chamber well after his time of departure. The red lever was drawn back, in the correct position to return him to the past, and now, with nothing left to hold him here in this world of the future, he depressed the red button. As the time speed meter needle commenced its rotation backward around the dial, he shut out all thoughts of Linde in a determined effort to put his romance with her well behind him, and instead concentrate on the future he would be facing on his return to the past.

As the time speed meter needle slowed, the dark void outside the glass panel was once again supplanted by the familiar blur of light as the Zeitmaschine returned to the time when festoon lights brightly lit the chamber.

When the green lamp informed him it was safe to exit, Hartmann slid the access panel aside and climbing out, looked around the chamber. As anticipated, with both access doors locked, no one could have entered the chamber in the short space of time he'd been away, with the result that everything around the machine appeared exactly as it had been before he left, down to his discarded cigarette which had left a short trail of ash on the floor in burning away to the butt. His neatly folded clothes lay on top of the electrical cabinets where he had left them, and quickly stripping off his 1969 attire, he donned his Obersturmführer uniform, hiding his civilian clothes inside the electrical cabinets along with the rucksack.

Hartmann unlocked the door leading to the Berghof and strode down the tunnel. The two sentries guarding the Berghof end had been replaced in their regular duty roster cycle, and their replacements stood stiffly to attention as he locked the door behind him and marched away. Neither the guards at the door, nor the supervisors and labourers working on the new tunnel, nor Hitler himself, could have been aware of, or could even have begun to imagine his recent adventure in the future.

In his determination to set aside all thoughts of Linde Engel, Hartmann drowned his sorrow by immediately throwing his full energy back into the tasks entailed in Hitler's plan, partly because it would help relieve the pain he felt in leaving the woman he loved, and partly because it was his sworn duty to do so, but also very much due to the fact that, having abandoned Linde to make good his oath to the Führer, he desperately needed to prove his future duplicate self wrong about changing the past. Once the Führer had succeeded in escaping to the future, it was simply beyond Hartmann's comprehension how Hitler could possibly end up committing suicide in the Berlin bunker in 1945. The historians would simply have to re-write their history books.

CHAPTER 23

Later that afternoon there was a knock on Hartmann's office door and Ober leutnant Engel entered and saluted, ready to present his daily progress report on the tunnelling works. Hartmann inspected Engel's face with an interest he had not previously exercised, this time taking note of the man's wavy chestnut hair and hazel eyes. He also recalled Engel's earlier comment about living in Berchtesgaden with his wife and young daughter.

He invited Engel to take a seat.

"Tell me Ober leutnant Engel, I am informed the scenery around the Königssee is quite spectacular at this time of year. Speaking as a local, would you recommend a visit?"

Engel was taken aback by the question, Hartmann having previously strictly adhered to matters of engineering and scheduling the tunnel works to the exclusion of all else. Engel responded it certainly warranted a look.

"I also understand one can visit the church of Saint Bartholomew across the lake. Have you perchance taken the opportunity to venture there with your family?"

"I'm afraid not, Obersturmführer Hartmann. My wife cannot swim and having a great fear of the water, won't countenance the required ferry crossing. We consequently usually opt to have our picnic lunch in the village park, even though my daughter longs to visit the church across the lake."

Hartmann thanked him for his advice and asked for his report.

On Engel's departure, Hartmann paced the floor of his office in a quandary, wondering how to resolve the predicament in which he now found himself. Because of the love he still nurtured in his heart for Linde, how could he possibly be instrumental in her father's demise? And yet, all the participants in construction of the tunnel, including Engel, were after its completion, necessarily condemned to a fate which would guarantee their silence in order to preserve the secret of the Zeitmaschine. After agonising over the situation without coming up with a satisfactory solution, Hartmann finally decided to let matters run their course, during which time he hoped to find a viable answer to this new dilemma.

Three weeks after Hitler had ordered Hartmann to drive the project faster, Ober leutnant Engel reported that the tunnel was near completion and ready for inspection. Hartmann unlocked and opened the steel door in the North wall and strode up the tunnel to the cave at the far end. He noted with satisfaction the workmanship evident in the brickwork lining the tunnel walls, and was amused to see lamps had been installed in the arched ceiling at ten metre intervals. Hartmann had allowed Engel to include lighting in his plans, not wishing to let it be widely known that in the future, when the tunnel was being used by the Führer, there would be no electricity available from the ruins of the Berghof to power them. As he passed the middle of the tunnel, muffled thumping noises above informed him the labourers were now filling in the access well through which building materials, machinery and labour had been delivered.

At the far end of the tunnel, work was still in progress on the steel door opening out into the secret cave. Its hinges had been bolted into the rock walls, but the narrow steel door itself lay flat on the floor of the cave whilst a mason deftly cemented rock fragments to its exterior surface to provide the camouflaged outer face with which Hartmann was by now so very familiar.

So far, all three elements of the Führer's plan over which he had control had progressed satisfactorily. He retraced his steps through the tunnel and made his way to Hitler's office in the Berghof to report.

The secretary in the outer office was busily filing documents, and looked up enquiringly as Hartmann entered the room. Hartmann gave the seated junior Schutzstaffel officer a scornful glance with the thought that, when Hitler finally made his exit to the future, this young man would have no real purpose here and would have to trade his cushy job for active service on the battle front.

After informing the secretary that preparations in the bunker complex were now complete and ready for the Führer's inspection, Hartmann made his way to the temporary office set up in the meadow to house the tunnelling construction supervisors.

Ober leutnant Engel and one of his officers were preparing for their immanent departure, packing away project drawings and notebooks when Hartmann pushed aside the tent flap and entered. They stood to attention, their faces betraying the forlorn hope this young SS-Obersturmführer might yet compliment them on a well-executed project. This was not to be the case. He strode past them to the rear wall of the tent with open hands clasped behind his back surveying the tent's contents right and left before wheeling around to face them. He pointed in the direction of the Berghof.

"I have one more assignment for you. You will access explosives and in three days' time you shall, on my command, destroy the tunnel linking the secret chamber to the Berghof. In accomplishing this task, you shall close the doors at both ends of the tunnel and buttress them with sand bags to withstand the force of the detonation. It is imperative that after this operation has been completed, the tunnel must be completely blocked from one end to the other."

The two men glanced at each other in surprise, but knowing better than to question this Obersturmführer with his direct connections to the Führer himself, assured him the tunnel would be destroyed in accordance with his instructions. He gave them a Hitlergruiß salute which they were obliged to return, and pushing aside the tent flap, departed, leaving them gaping after him in astonishment.

Hitler's secretary had arranged an inspection meeting for the next evening, and Hartmann met the Führer at the entrance to the bunkers. They walked the length of the new tunnel to where the near-complete rock faceted door lay in the cave and on their return to the chamber, Hartmann briefed Hitler on the forthcoming demolition of the old tunnel and the remaining task of loading the stored treasure into the Zeitmaschine.

"When you give me the order, every available space in the machine's cabin will be filled with valuables to maximise your success in the future, and only sufficient space will be left for two persons to make the journey in comfort."

Hitler glanced at the young Obersturmführer striding beside him and congratulated him on his efforts.

"You have done well Hartmann."

The three scientists had been barred from entry since the day Hartmann ordered them out and now he and the Führer were assured of being undisturbed as they returned to the chamber. Hartmann walked up to the Zeitmaschine and peered inside the cabin, thoughtfully eyeing the control console.

"Perhaps, this might be an opportune moment to practice operation of the Zeitmaschine's controls, should Mein Führer wish to do so."

Hitler agreed and Hartmann locked both doors to the chamber as an added precaution against interruption. The Führer took his seat behind the Zeitmaschine's control console, and Hartmann climbed in after him, taking a seat on the opposite bench.

"For his first time at the Zeitmaschine's controls, perhaps Mein Führer might wish to travel to this day next week? This would place his arrival a few days after he and Fräulein Braun have departed to take up residence in the future. The support cradle on which the Zeitmaschine is presently sitting would therefore be lying vacant and consequently there would be no danger of our machine colliding with another version of itself. This of course would be in accordance with the warning scientist Fuchs imparted on our initial induction, and is of vital importance for the Führer to remember when planning future journeys."

In response, Hitler set up the week duration dial while Hartmann looked on. After thrusting the red lever forward and checking battery power, he raised the glass cover and depressed the red button. The chamber outside the portal disappeared in a blur and when the speed meter needle came to a standstill a few seconds later, Hartmann slid the door panel aside and followed Hitler out into the chamber. Its festoon lamps still shone brightly, but a layer of dust lay on the floor and the upper surfaces of the electrical panels. Sandbags were stacked against the wall alongside the door leading back to the Berghof, and the air was heavy with the smell of recently detonated explosive. Hartmann strode over to the closed steel door leading back to the Berghof and heaved at the handle. It opened a few inches with a rasping sound emanating from its hinges, and a small cloud of dust drifted into the room. He glanced at Hitler who was still standing by the side of the Zeitmaschine, contemplating the changes in the chamber's appearance.

"The tunnel is now completely blocked Mein Führer, in accordance with the demolition planned to take place after you left for the future a few days ago."

Hitler walked over to join Hartmann who stepped aside respectfully to allow him a better view of the confusion behind the door. As they both had already observed on their earlier voyage to the distant future, the tunnel was now completely blocked by rubble. Hartmann gave voice to his satisfaction.

"My engineers will have carried out their function well after you left. If Mein Führer would now care to inspect the door at the end of the tunnel which was found to be incomplete only a few minutes ago ... ?"

The two men strode up the tunnel to the far end where camouflaging of the exit door had indeed been completed and it now sat securely on its hinges. Hartmann inspected the rock-faceted outer surface for a third time and clucked his tongue with satisfaction. As he had observed previously, when the door was closed it was nigh impossible to tell where the rocks on its outer face ended and the rocks on the surrounding cave walls began. Hartmann brushed the foliage at the cave entrance aside and they stepped out into the clearing. It was evening and the first stars were making their debut in the night sky. Behind them and further down the hill, the Berghof's windows glowed brightly whilst further up the slope the Zum Türken's windows also blazed with light. For a while they stood in silence listening to the distant sounds of laughter and activity as Schutzstaffel officers working in the surrounding chalets returned to their billet in the Türken and the nearby barracks after completing their daily work routines.

Hitler turned to his aide.

"You have carried out your tasks to perfection, Hartmann. I will immediately summon Fräulein Braun to the Berghof and we leave for the future the day after tomorrow. You may now start loading the Zeitmaschine's cabin with the stored valuables."

He led the way back to the Zeitmaschine and after depressing the green button, Hitler turned to Hartmann.

"I feel quite comfortable in handling these controls, Hartmann. The machine is, as you have previously observed, quite simple to operate and I'm entirely confident all will go well when Fräulein Braun and I travel to the future to fulfil our historic quest."

CHAPTER 24

The chamber was a hive of activity the following day. Hartmann had taken the precaution of hiding the Zeitmaschine from view by covering it with a tarpaulin before slave labourers from the Konzentrationslager were brought in to remove the partitioning around the shrouded machine.

Under the watchful eye of Oberschütze troopers, the labourers were then tasked with bringing in the boxes from the valuables vault and placing them in a stack adjacent to the tarpaulin cover. On completion of the transfer, Hartmann cleared the chamber of all personnel and marched down the corridor following the last of them out.

He gave orders to the two troopers on duty that absolutely no one apart from the Führer and himself – not even Herman Göring, Hitler's deputy – was allowed to pass through the doorway they were guarding. At the supply depot he withdrew a bundle of hessian sacks from stores and returning to the chamber, laid them alongside the valuables boxes. Then, squatting beside them, he reached for the nearest box and one by one upended each of the metal containers, pouring the riches they held into sack after sack, finally discarding the emptied boxes in a heap alongside the Zeitmaschine.

During his early teenage years, Hartmann had read with fascination fictional novels about treasure trove – Dumas' '*Count of Monte Christo*'had been his favourite – but never had he dreamed that in real life such wealth could actually exist in such abundance. Diamonds, gold bullion, silver coins, bejewelled amulets, pearl necklaces and all manner of precious gemstones set in bracelets and rings sparkled and danced before his eyes as they tumbled into the sacks. A lesser man might have succumbed to the temptation to pocket a few of the valuables, but the thought never entered Hartmann's head. Finally, when the last sack had been filled and the last empty box cast aside, he secured each of them with a short length of cord, and commenced loading the sacks into the Zeitmaschine's cabin.

After jamming the last of them in place, Hartmann stood back, swept dust off his uniform's sleeves and with hands on hips, surveyed the cabin interior. The floor and bench opposite the control station were stacked with the bulging sacks, but he had nevertheless managed to leave ample room for the Führer and Fräulein Braun in order that they might travel in comfort to their future destination, whilst also allowing space for the suitcase the Führer had indicated would be accompanying him.

He turned his attention to survey the chamber which had been swept spotless in preparation for the Führer's departure. The previously piled sandbags lay to one side of the doorway leading back to the Berghof, in anticipation of being stacked against the door to buttress it against the forthcoming detonation. Hartmann considered the pile of empty discarded treasure boxes and debated whether to clear them away, but saw little point in taking the trouble to remove them and besides, he knew from his previous voyages to the future that they had indeed been left in the chamber. The cable running from the electrical panels to the power port at the rear of the Zeitmaschine had given the batteries their final boost and now lay disconnected and neatly coiled on the floor, whilst the charge meter inside the cabin when last checked, had assured him the batteries were fully charged. The chamber was well lit and the lamps in the new tunnel leading to the cave were ready to light the way in for the labourers who would be relocating the sandbags. When Hitler reached his destination he would have to rely on torch light to find his way out, and to this end the two powerful torches Hartmann had secured for the Führer's use were now secreted under the controller's bench. All was ready for his departure and with no further details in the chamber requiring his attention, Hartmann returned to the Berghof to report.

Early the next day, Hartmann rendezvoused with the Führer and Fräulein Braun at the entrance to the bunker complex. He was shocked to see that Hitler had shaved off his signature moustache and had parted his hair in the centre of his head instead of having it swept to the left as had always been the case. Hitler was also wearing sunglasses, was attired in casual civilian clothes, and wore a bemused smile on observing the surprised expression on his aide's face.

"I have made a thorough study of your earlier report Hartmann, and you yourself have seen the adverse reaction to my appearance by the American in the Türken's carpark. My countenance would not, in all probability, be readily acceptable amongst the citizens of the future, who undoubtedly have been persuaded by malicious anti-Nazi propaganda to be ashamed of their wartime leader. It will do me well to hide my true identity unless or until time dictates otherwise."

Fräulein Braun had brought a small basket overlaid with a sprightly coloured checked cloth which, she informed Hartmann, contained a sandwich lunch, thermos of coffee and fruit for a journey which, unbeknownst to her, would in fact only take a couple of minutes. She smiled her appreciation and thanked Hartmann when he offered to carry it. The suitcase Hitler had brought with him was quite small but judging by the Führer's posture as he clutched the handle tightly, it was weighed down by contents considerably heavier than mere spare clothing. Hartmann motioned his free hand meaningfully toward the case and looked enquiringly to the Führer who shook his head.

"Thank you Hartmann, but I am quite content to carry this case myself."

They made their way past the two SS Oberschütze troopers, locked the door behind them and proceeded down the passage into the chamber, whereupon Hartmann shut and locked the second door. Fräulein Braun's eyes widened when she saw the Zeitmaschine gleaming in the lamplight and Hartmann thought he saw a touch of fear in her face. Whilst he was hoisting the suitcase into the cabin and laying it on top of the hessian sacks, Hitler informed him of a change in plans.

"Fräulein Braun and I will travel to the future as you and I have done previously, but I have reconsidered and decided to go forward by only fifty five years."

Hartmann glanced at him quizzically.

"I do this for good reason, Hartmann. After considering your report, I believe sixty years in the future would be an excellent time to launch my crusade to resurrect Germany's dominance over Europe. Therefore, if I arrive five years earlier, I can begin the process of building up my fortune and network of political allies. Then, after five years have elapsed, I will have accumulated the wealth and political connections necessary to enable my push for leadership to commence sixty years from now."

Hartmann was about to agree to Hitler's revised plan when Fuchs' warning regarding collisions came to mind, and he immediately voiced his concern.

"There's a major problem in doing as you propose Mein Führer, and I am most certainly glad you mentioned your intention to me. If you were to travel forward by only fifty five years, then in a further five years' time after your arrival, your Zeitmaschine will be sitting in its cradle when you and I arrive on our previous sixty year voyage into the future. The two machines would vie with each other to occupy the same space on the cradle, the result being a terrible collision in which the Zeitmaschine in which we travelled previously would be destroyed with us inside it."

Hitler was taken aback by this and stared at his aide, puzzled.

"I see what you mean Hartmann, but when you and I travelled previously there was no collision, so surely we must have taken — that is, *must now take* — some sort of action to ensure such a collision cannot occur."

"A good point, Mein Führer, and I believe I have the answer. You will recall when we arrived in the future on our first journey, we found a Zeitmaschine parked adjacent to our own on the second cradle? I now see where the other machine came from. It was in fact the machine in which you and Fräulein Braun are now intending to travel.

"Therefore, in order to avoid collision, we must now do exactly as Fuchs did in his introductory presentation, and that is to swap cradle locations."

"Excellent Hartmann! Excellent. Your foresight has not only saved the Zeitmaschine and my ability to use it in the future, but in all probability you have also saved our lives. Your explanation also solves the presence of the second Zeitmaschine which has troubled me ever since our earlier journey."

Hartmann undertook to swap cradle locations and withdrew to reposition the Zeitmaschine. It was heavy work and the cradle was inching along slowly on its rail due to the considerable weight of treasure trove in the Zeitmaschine's cabin when Hitler appeared at his side to assist him. Hartmann felt deeply honoured that the Führer should condescend to help in such a menial task, and expressed his appreciation as the Zeitmaschine finally slipped into position.

"You have done much for me Hartmann. I am afraid this small expenditure of effort on my part today is little repayment for your invaluable contribution to my quest."

With relocation completed, they returned to the access portal where Hartmann assisted Fräulein Braun as she climbed gingerly inside and slid along to the far side of the bench beside the control station. Hartmann handed her the picnic basket, and she thanked him, perching it on her lap.

"When we arrive in the future, Fräulein Braun and I will first make our way to the Zum Türken, where we will register as tourists and rest there while I prepare my agenda. But Hartmann, there remains one further critical task to which you must attend after my departure. Insurmountable problems would be created for me, and our cause would be fatally jeopardised if the technology underpinning this incredible machine ever came to the attention of others who might yet be considering the possibility of time travel. It would be a calamity should this machine ever be duplicated Hartmann. A calamity. A replica of this machine would open up the doors to all manner of possibilities, perhaps even allowing my enemies to follow me into the future and ultimately force my return. If this were to happen I would be condemned to oversee the War to its bitter conclusion and, as your report would have it, meet my end in the Berlin bunker. Therefore, after Fräulein Braun and I have left for the future, it becomes critically important that you follow the instructions I now leave you – instructions which will, so to speak, burn my bridges behind me and eliminate the possibility of such a situation ever occurring."

Hitler's countenance darkened.

"You have obeyed my orders up to this day with distinction, Hartmann. You must not fail me in carrying out this, my final command."

Hartmann snapped to rigid attention.

"Your orders whatever they may be shall be carried out to the letter, Mein Führer."

"Very well. As soon as we have departed, you will have the three scientists responsible for creating this machine arrested, charged with plotting against me and have them held in detention before facing the firing squad. To this end, I have left you documentary 'evidence' of their complicity to back up your charges. You will also investigate to ensure no other persons have been involved in the Zeitmaschine's development or have had access to any of the scientists' documentation, and you will complete this task by destroying all their notes, drawings, journals and any other records that might indicate this time travel project ever existed. Do I make myself perfectly clear?"

Many had already been scheduled for elimination to preserve the secrecy of the Zeitmaschine project and three more would certainly make little difference. Hartmann was quick to respond.

"It shall be exactly as you have commanded."

He hailed the Führer with a salute and received one in return.

With that, Hitler climbed aboard the Zeitmaschine and taking his seat at the controls beside Fräulein Braun, slid the glass panelled door closed behind him. He set the time duration dials, checked the remaining controls and raised the glass lid covering the red button. Giving one last glance at Hartmann standing stiffly to attention outside, the heel of his palm came down firmly on the button.

Hartmann witnessed the Zeitmaschine blurring out of sight in front of him and then it was gone, leaving the two steel framed cradles lying empty in the middle of the chamber. For a few seconds he gloomily reflected that, with the departure of the Zeitmaschine there remained not the slightest possibility of ever visiting his beloved Linde again.

In a determined effort not to think of such matters, and reminding himself there was still much work to be done, he immediately occupied himself with the remaining tasks in accordance with the Führer's final instructions.

Hartmann gave orders for the arrest of the scientists and had Schutzstaffel investigators raid their quarters looking for any remaining documentation linked to the Time Extension Project. The bulk of technical information related to the project turned out to be stored right there in the chamber, in the form of engineering diaries, technical notes, specifications and detail drawings secreted in drawers inside the cabinets along the far wall of the chamber. He had them removed, packed into cardboard cartons and taken under armed guard to a convenient location behind the Berghof where they were doused with petrol and set alight. For a few minutes Hartmann watched the flames licking around the pile of charred papers spilling out as the blaze consumed the cartons. Then, satisfied that every last scrap of information they contained would be totally consumed in the inferno, he returned to his office and radioed the engineers in the meadow with orders to prepare for demolition of the access passage to the chamber.

Over the next twenty four hours, Hartmann paced up and down the passage watching as work progressed toward final destruction of the tunnel. Holes were drilled in the roof and walls at three metre intervals after which explosive handlers busied themselves packing them with sticks of Dynamite. Hartmann instructed their supervisor that when the task of wiring the detonators together had been completed, they were to shut the door at the Berghof end of the passage to allow a large consignment of sandbags awaiting placement to be stacked against it to buttress against the forthcoming explosion. He glanced at his watch. Estimating that the team of labourers inside the chamber stacking bags against the door at the other end of the Berghof tunnel should have finished by now, he decided to enter via the cave to inspect their work.

On arrival at the entrance, the labourers were already spilling out of the cave's fringing foliage into the fresh air, covered in sweat and dust and carrying their depleted water canteens. Hartmann waited impatiently until the works supervisor and guards had herded the last of them down the slope and out of sight before brushing the foliage aside and entering.

Inside the chamber, the steel door to the Berghof tunnel was now completely hidden behind the sandbags stacked against the door, through which he could make out the muffled voices of the explosive handlers on the other side.

He had just finished inspecting the piled sandbags and was about to light a cigarette when a soft rustling sound behind him made him spin around.

The air blurred in front of him and the Zeitmaschine rematerialized on its support cradle.

Its glass panel door slid open and a figure stepped out.

It was not the Führer.

CHAPTER 25

The woman who climbed out of the machine was probably in her mid-forties and wore a dress that would not have met with approval in the fashion houses of 1944. She looked around the chamber taking stock of her surroundings before finally focussing her attention on Hartmann. Instinctively responding to this unexpected situation, he drew his pistol from its holster as a precaution. Both parties were eyeing each other warily when a second occupant of the Zeitmaschine appeared in the access opening and proceeded to climb out. He too was strangely dressed, but was very much older than his companion, probably in his eighties. Hartmann stared into his face. There was something vaguely familiar and unsettling about this man's countenance, and Hartmann was instantly aware he had known him for a long, long time. But when? Where? At this moment, he couldn't recall.

The woman was the first to speak.

"Please put down your gun, Hartmann. We have come from a long way into the future to assist and guide you because from today onward your activities are going to be of vital importance not only to Germany, but indeed to all of humanity."

Hartmann lowered the gun to his side, opting not to holster it, and continued to maintain a suspiciously watchful eye on the new arrivals.

"First of all Hartmann, may I introduce you to a man who knows you extremely well."

The woman indicated her fellow traveller with a wave of her hand and the old man stepped forward at her invitation, smiling broadly.

"Do you recognise my companion?"

Hartmann searched the man's face again. Yes, he definitely knew this person whom he immediately took, because of his strikingly familiar features, to be one of his relatives – perhaps an uncle he had visited with his parents when he was very young – and yet somehow he felt he had seen this person quite recently, perhaps as recently as the previous day.

The man at the woman's side put an end to his confusion.

"Hartmann, I am in fact who you will become in sixty years' time. I am an older version of yourself."

Hartmann was stunned and stared at the stranger in disbelief.

"I can confirm this is indeed the case Hartmann. Ask me any questions pertaining to your past life and I will provide you with answers."

Hartmann was nonplussed and couldn't find his tongue.

"If you can't think of any particular incidents to test my claim, perhaps I can remind you of a few of your childhood experiences which although of no real consequence, are nevertheless known to none other than ourselves. For instance, do you remember crying in the boy's toilet block on your first day at primary school, or your secret hiding place in Aunt Babette's laundry cupboard? Perhaps I might remind you about your crush on Greta Klein at the tender age of nine or the time you exploded fire crackers in Herr Goldschmidt's letter box leaving scorch marks all over his letters?"

"Stop! Stop!"

Hartmann was acutely embarrassed at having his childhood secrets revealed in the presence of this female stranger, and momentarily forgetting the doors to the chamber were closed to outsiders, he cast a hurried eye around the room to reassure himself that no-one else might have been party to these mortifying revelations. He scrutinised the old man's face more closely and on seeing there the truth, holstered his pistol and sat down heavily on the pile of sandbags.

The two time travellers strolled over.

"We cannot stay long, Hartmann. Please listen carefully to what we have to say because the information we're giving you will not only help you survive the turmoil of the next few days, but will also be vital in determining the destiny of all humankind.

"You will, of course, succeed in blocking the tunnel, a fact already known to you because you've travelled to the future three times and have looked behind the door on each occasion. You will also be successful in eliminating all those who have worked on the Time Extension and tunnelling projects to keep the secret that lies within this chamber – by now you will have organised the elimination of the three scientists and the destruction of their records, is that not so?"

Hartmann nodded acknowledgement, and feeling somewhat uncomfortable about this disclosure, cast his eyes down to the chamber floor to avoid the time-traveller's gaze.

"Now comes the difficult part. The Führer and Eva Braun will be returning to this chamber in two days' time. The Zeitmaschine will drop them off before travelling to another temporal destination. Both of them will of course, be distressed and angry, and it wouldn't be particularly beneficial for anyone's health to be present in this chamber when they arrive. You must therefore ensure that at the time, all personnel are kept well clear of the cave and its immediate surrounds. You yourself must maintain the lowest possible profile in the days ahead, and avoid visiting the Berghof until Hitler has calmed down and summons you. When he does, you will mention nothing of this meeting or any matters we have discussed – your life depends on your silence in this regard. Do you understand?"

Only two days ago, Hitler had departed from the chamber in the Zeitmaschine, determined to use the fortune he carried with him to further his ambitious quest. Hartmann couldn't envisage any circumstances the Führer might have encountered in the future which might then have persuaded him to abandon his wealth and political ambitions, and instead return to an uncertain future in the present time, nor could he imagine why, after all the precautions they had exercised to keep the existence of the Zeitmaschine and its location a secret up to the present time, the Führer would then allow these two time travellers to return to 1944 without himself having oversight over them and the machine in which they travelled.

However, given the information he was now receiving was coming from no less a person than his future self, the only sensible course of action was to accept what they had so far imparted and, nodding his understanding, he agreed to act in accordance with their instruction.

Elder Hartmann gazed sympathetically at his younger self and offered him words of comfort.

"The information we are revealing is no doubt difficult to comprehend, but please be assured that, as your older self, I have lived through and witnessed everything that has happened, and will ever happen to you. Indescribably bad times are coming your way, but good times will eventually follow. Happily, you will live to a ripe old age because this octogenarian standing before you is living proof of this simple fact."

His female companion looked down solemnly on the seated Obersturmführer.

"Please stand Hartmann. I have an item of the utmost importance to leave with you before we leave."

Hartmann rose unsteadily from the sandbags, and still dazed after the preceding revelations, watched mute as the woman from the future reached into her pocket and withdrew a business card.

"Take this card Hartmann and memorise the information it contains. It is of vital importance for the future of the world from which we have come that you remember our visit and the details on this card, as it will allow you to find me in the years to come."

Hartmann took the card and turned it over a few times. Amongst the small print, larger bold letters proclaimed:

'Morgen Schreiber
Senior Editor
Die Welt'

He looked up, enquiringly, puzzled.

Morgen Schreiber answered his unasked question.

"Die Welt is a newspaper which doesn't exist yet in your time, but will come into being after the War has come to an end. Commit my name, position and other details to your memory and do not forget them. One day in the future when you are very much older, you will read an article in my newspaper about a man who has the appearance of Hitler. After conducting further research you'll discover he is in fact your wartime Führer masquerading under an assumed name. You must come to my office, tell me your story and show me the newspaper article together with photos of the Führer and Fräulein Braun after you have told me your tale. You will find me extremely sceptical at first, but you must persist in getting me to listen to your story, which I will finally and reluctantly be forced to accept as the truth."

Schreiber turned to her companion and asked if there was more he wanted to add. The elder Hartmann nodded and reaching forward gripped Hartmann's shoulder with a fatherly hand, gazing wistfully into his eyes.

"Although you are no doubt very much disturbed by what you have experienced today, we know from our own experience of the future that you have understood what we have told you. You must give us your oath that you will do as we have asked, and in so doing, guard the secret of today's meeting until you make contact with Frau Schreiber again many years from now. We cannot impress upon you strongly enough the importance of the role you are destined to play in determining the peace and stability of the world from which we have come."

Hartmann looked from each of his visitors to the other, still very much overwhelmed by the peculiarity of this exchange, and shook his head in an attempt to clear his mind.

"It is most difficult for me to understand. But because you know so much about my personal life and have my resemblance, I must necessarily conclude you are most definitely my future self."

His bewildered countenance gave way to a wry smile.

"Also, as you yourself must be fully aware from our shared upbringing, I was brought up by my parents to always obey my elders. It would therefore be foolish of me to now disregard what my future self tells me, especially when one considers that you are most definitely my elder.

"I therefore pledge that I will follow your instructions."

CHAPTER 26

I interrupted Hartmann's narrative to compliment him on how skilfully he had woven me into the fabric of his story. Although intrigued by his tale, my scepticism remained undiminished and leaning forward, feigning mock belief in his tale, I asked,

"Where is this Zeitmaschine parked and when can I have a ride in it?"

Hartmann admonished me with the trace of a smile.

"Be patient. There is so much more to be told."

I looked up at the office clock. Although my colleagues had taken over much of my workload there were still pressing matters requiring my personal attention.

"I regret my time is limited Herr Hartmann – Die Welt has deadlines to be met and I've spent considerably more time with you than I originally intended. However, despite not believing for a moment in your Zeitmaschine, I have found your story strangely compelling and would certainly like to hear the rest of it. With your agreement perhaps we might adjourn at this juncture and meet again when I have a little more free time available."

Hartmann searched my face uncertainly.

"Would ten o'clock tomorrow morning be Ok?"

His face lightened.

"Yes, thank you. That would be satisfactory."

He rose from his seat and reached across the desk to retrieve the envelope he had laid there earlier. I raised a hand in protest.

"Perhaps you can leave your evidence with me so that I can study the proof you claim for your story?"

Hartmann shook his head.

"I'm afraid, without completing my narrative, the documents inside this envelope would be meaningless to you. I will hold onto it until I have finished my story tomorrow."

I nodded acceptance despite my disappointment at not being able to view them, and coming around the desk, shook the hand he held out to me. Then, without another word, he turned and strode out of the office.

I was about to log onto my desk computer to see if I could find a reference in last week's paper which might have had some bearing on Hartmann's story, when Freda buzzed to remind me of the editorial meeting scheduled for that evening. The meeting dragged on covering many outstanding issues and in the end, because it finished at a rather late hour, I chose a good night's sleep rather than search for Hartmann's supposed 'proof'.

He was there in our offices precisely at ten, and Freda ushered him in, asking if we would like coffee. We discussed a few pleasantries about the weather and the soccer for a few minutes until she reappeared with a tray of coffee and biscuits and we helped ourselves. I took a sip from my cup and asked Hartmann to resume his story when he was ready.

He thanked me and promptly returned to his narrative.

CHAPTER 27

Hartmann's older self acknowledged Hartmann's pledge and warned him of the danger he would face over the following days.

"You will find Hitler more emotional, erratic and introspective than he has been previously, and his tactical decisions will become increasingly questionable. His forced return from the future coupled with memories of the July plot to assassinate him will have him convinced no one is to be trusted. He will be seeing enemies at every turn and many of his unfounded suspicions will lead to the elimination of some of his closest associates and confidants. It is during this dangerous period that you must keep a low profile, whilst wherever possible, still demonstrating your fervent loyalty to both him and the Reich.

"My presence here before you young Hartmann, is living proof you will survive, but you will have to endure and suffer much to ensure the future to which I belong comes to pass."

Hartmann's head swirled with these insights. The person predicting his future was neither clairvoyant nor fortune teller, but rather, an older and presumably more knowledgeable version of himself, and his familiarity with matters related to Hartmann's future was therefore beyond question. Never before in the history of humankind had any person received such accurate insights into their future circumstances and indeed, Hartmann would be the only person who would ever be so well informed.

Schreiber checked her watch as her companion finished, and turned to Hartmann.

"We are leaving you now. This will be the last time we'll travel to the past in the Zeitmaschine, Hartmann. You will only understand what has transpired here today when you are much older. But between the three of us, we have ensured the past as it appears in the history books will not have been violated. Remember us, and do as we have instructed – your role is of vital importance in preserving the peace and stability of the future world."

With that, the two visitors returned to the Zeitmaschine. Schreiber shot a parting comment as she climbed into the cabin.

"You will be doing an excellent job of blocking the access tunnel tomorrow. The chamber has remained a secret up until the time from which we have come."

Moments later the Zeitmaschine blurred out of sight and Hartmann was once again alone in the chamber with nothing at all in his immediate vicinity to suggest anything out of the ordinary had taken place in the preceding minutes. The entire affair could easily have been but a fanciful dream, except for the fact that in Hartmann's hand he held Morgen Schreiber's business card. He looked at it closely, turning it over and over thoughtfully, memorising every minute detail it contained. Then he slipped it into his pocket.

Resolutely turning his attention to the practicalities of the day, he made his way to the engineer's tent in the meadow, arriving just in time to hear the explosives supervisor informing Engel all would be in readiness by evening to collapse the tunnel. Hartmann ordered them to detonate the explosives the next morning at seven, and follow up by setting aside the sandbags in the chamber directly afterwards to allow assessment of the destruction that had taken place inside the tunnel. Engel confirmed this would be carried out exactly as instructed and enquired whether Hartmann wanted to be called when the resultant blockage was ready for inspection.

Hartmann had already inspected the rubble-filled passage behind the door three times in the future and what he had seen had been quite satisfactory, besides which, Morgen Schreiber, the woman from the future, had also agreed it had been a job well done. He shook his head.

"That won't be necessary. I am entirely confident your work in the tunnel will achieve the outcome I require."

Engel and the supervisor looked at each other, hardly believing they were receiving what appeared to be a compliment from this officious young Schutzstaffel officer.

The next morning the explosives team cleared all personnel from the meadow directly above the tunnel route, and after a final inspection of the sandbagged buttressing of the doors at either end, gave instruction to the explosives handlers to detonate the charges.

When the dust had cleared sufficiently, labourers were brought in to set aside the sandbags and on final completion of all works necessary to give the chamber the appearance matching its disposition during his visits to the future, Hartmann returned to his office to make arrangements for all the supervisors and labourers involved in the tunnelling project to be *'taken care of'*.

With one exception.

In his determination to safeguard Linde's father from sharing their fate, and for want of a better solution, he had finally come to the conclusion that the only way to save Ober leutnant Engel's life was to swear him to secrecy on all matters related to the tunnelling project and keep him employed on ongoing bunker maintenance on the Obersalzberg. In this way, Hartmann could keep a watchful eye on the man to ensure Engel kept to the agreement.

Every now and then as he went about his duties, the memory of those golden days spent in the future with Linde would drift back into Hartmann's consciousness, and he wondered whether fate would ever be generous enough to allow their paths to cross again. He reflected that at this very moment she was down there in Berchtesgaden only a mere five kilometres from where he was currently stationed. But it was now 1944, and she would only be nine years old, and consequently any thought of visiting her was completely out of the question. Often during his preoccupation with the tunnelling works he had reflected with a smile that, whilst he was attending to his duties in and around the Berghof, she was probably attending primary school in Berchtesgaden, and he would conjure up an image of her with plaited hair and perhaps a missing tooth, sucking the end of a pencil whilst she pondered over some elementary arithmetic problems.

CHAPTER 28

Hauptsturmführer Wolff frowned down at the documents on his desk.

The number of Wehrmacht Heer officers who had participated in Hartmann's highly secretive tunnelling project failed to match the number of men scheduled for transfer to the bloody battle front at Dukla Pass in Poland. The Berghof's chief Gestapo security officer pored over the documents again until he finally found the discrepancy. Ober leutnant Engel's name was missing from the list.

Wolff's duties embraced oversight of every activity in and around the Berghof and he was consequently particularly peeved that the Führer had not seen fit to enlighten him on details of Hartmann's tunnelling project. He had been personally instructed by the Führer not to interfere with the highly secretive delivery and storage of the boxes with their mysterious contents, and had been barred from visiting the chamber in which the three scientists had been engaged on their so-called top secret project, as well as being banned from any contact with the scientists themselves. Wolff had subsequently felt a vicarious pleasure when the job of organising their elimination had fallen to him. He also despised Hartmann for refusing to divulge the nature of this project – a project which was continuing to have a major impact on the affairs of the Berghof establishment and therefore on his own workload, and he resented the young Obersturmführer's easy access to the Führer – access to which he, by his rank and status, should have enjoyed more frequently than Hartmann, but which, so far, had been doled out to him on a strictly limited basis.

Wolff marched into Hartmann's office without bothering to knock and confronted him with his findings.

"I see you are responsible for removing this man from the list of those scheduled for transfer to our forces in Poland."

He glowered at Hartmann.

"It is not for you Obersturmführer Hartmann to pick and choose who stays or goes. I have been charged directly by the Führer to ensure that every last person working on your tunnelling project will either be sent to the Konzentrationslager for elimination, or despatched to the fiercest of battles on our front lines, and I intend to follow his explicit command to the letter. You have been briefed and are well aware of my commission and I suggest you follow my example in following orders. I am warning you, Obersturmführer Hartmann, do not stand in the way of the Gestapo when one of its officers fulfils directives received directly from the Führer."

Hartmann protested, claiming Engel was of critical importance to his ongoing work in the bunkers, and argued he would be of far greater advantage to the Reich here on the Obersalzberg than in Poland. But Wolff would not be moved.

"Are you questioning, and would you countermand the Führer's explicit orders?" he hissed. "Then perhaps you might wish to challenge the Führer regarding his decision upon his return."

Hartmann immediately saw the futility in trying to save Engel. If, as his future self had predicted, the Führer was forced to return the next day, he would certainly have greater considerations on his mind than being bothered about Engel's future. To challenge the Gestapo without the Führer's protection in such circumstances could very well lead to his own arrest and incarceration. On the other hand, if his future self was wrong and Hitler didn't return, Hartmann would then have altogether lost the protection the Führer previously provided and would suffer the fate of all those who defied the Gestapo. When it came down to the crunch, if he persisted in trying to save Engel, he faced the prospect of having his own career severely curtailed – or worse – and Engel would still in the end be transferred to face the Russian onslaught at Dukla Pass. Hartmann was not at all consoled by the fact he had at least tried his best to save Linde's father, knowing only too well from her story that, in reluctantly acquiescing to Wolff's demand, he was effectively participating in an arrangement which would result in Engel's demise.

After Hauptsturmführer Wolff had stormed out of the room leaving him to wrestle with his conscience, Hartmann wondered if the Führer really would return the following day as had been foretold by his time-travelling visitors.

His viewpoint was now challenged by two mutually contradictory but nevertheless both equally desirable outcomes. On the one hand, he wished for the success of Hitler's quest to stay and prosper in the future because of his loyalty to the Führer and the Reich, and yet at the same time he hoped for the Führer's return, as this would certainly confirm the bona fides of his future self and all that had been communicated to him in the chamber.

Later that afternoon, following a directive from Hauptsturmführer Wolff demanding Hartmann's attendance in his office, he was confronted by the Gestapo chief flanked by two of his grim-faced officers. Wolff pointed an accusing finger at Hartmann.

"We have been conducting further investigations into your clandestine activities in the bunkers, Obersturmführer Hartmann. Three days ago you were observed entering the tunnel leading to this secret chamber of yours accompanying the Führer and Fräulein Braun, and an hour later you emerged from the chamber alone. Sentries guarding access to the chamber around the clock report that at no time did the Führer and Fräulein Braun subsequently reappear. Two days later you not only oversaw the demolition of the access tunnel to the chamber, but also ordered the destruction of documents which no doubt might have borne insights into your nefarious activities."

Wolff's eyes glinted with pleasure on noting Hartmann's discomfort at these observations and he sneered.

"Perhaps you might be able to ease our concerns, Obersturmführer Hartmann, by informing us as to the exact whereabouts of our beloved Führer?"

Hartmann responded coolly without hesitation.

"The Führer is quite safe and will be reappearing at some stage in the future, and this is all I am able to divulge at this point in time."

Wolff jerked back his chair and sprang to his feet, his face flushed with anger at being dismissed so casually by this young upstart Obersturmführer, well below him in rank. Bending forward over the desk he again waved an accusing finger at Hartmann.

"That is not a satisfactory response Obersturmführer Hartmann. You stand accused of involvement in a criminal conspiracy aimed at deposing our Führer, and are presently inextricably linked to his disappearance by your own covert activities."

He nodded to his officers who stepped forward to assume a stance on either side of Hartmann.

"You have blocked off the Berghof approach to this secret chamber with your pyrotechnics, so you will now kindly lead us to the portal at the far end of the tunnel you've been constructing in order that we may examine the chamber's contents."

Hartmann glanced either side at the two hefty Gestapo officers sandwiching him and considering his parlous situation, concluded there was little option but to comply with Wolff's demand. The Führer was by now safely ensconced in the future and apart from the two support frames and the electrical cabinets which had since been disconnected from their power supply, there was very little else in the chamber that would throw light on what had recently transpired within its walls.

Hartmann shrugged and after giving Hauptsturmführer Wolff a look of utter contempt, led the trio to the secret cave. Wolff looked on in fascination as the camouflaged door swung open, and he stepped forward to inspect its rock encrusted surface. He ordered the door be shut again and commanding guidance from Hartmann, worked at the catch mechanism until he had mastered the ability to open it without assistance.

Wolff and his two officers inspected every inch of the chamber. One of them pushed the second support cradle aside during his search, moving it along its track by a couple of metres. Hartmann, watching their every move, made a mental note of the fact on the realisation that, when he was free to return, he would have to bring it back to its original position to ensure that the many versions of the Zeitmaschine he knew of currently whirling about in the future would need to have the platform back in its original location upon which they could safely settle.

Wolff picked up one of the treasure boxes and inspected its SS insignia.

"My staff observed the delivery of these boxes. What did they contain?"

"That, I'm afraid, is confidential information which must remain known only to the Führer and myself."

Wolff slammed the box to the floor and hands on hips, glared at Hartmann.

"I warn you once again Obersturmführer Hartmann, do not think you can trifle with the Gestapo. You will answer my questions!"

"I answer only to the Führer."

Wolff fumed, but instead of tackling Hartmann's obstinacy head on, turned his attention to the electrical cabinets, all but one of which had been opened by his cohorts and found to be empty, having had their contents stripped out two days earlier under Hartmann's orders, and subsequently consumed in the flames behind the Berghof. He eyed the remaining locked cabinet.

"You no doubt possess a key?"

He extended a hand.

Hartmann shrugged again, reached into the leather pouch on his belt and dropped the key into Wolff's upturned palm.

One of Wolff's associates retrieved the rucksack and civilian clothing Hartmann had brought back from the future, and as the others looked on, he upended the rucksack, spilling its contents onto the floor. Wolff stooped to examine them, sifting through item by item. He straightened to unwrap the small bundle of valuables and after doing so, confronted Hartmann with a triumphant malevolent smile.

"Civilian clothes: foreign currency: contraband jewellery and coins: a map of the Obersalzberg: hiking apparel and equipment – you weren't perhaps planning to travel abroad?"

He held out his hand.

"Your pistol if you please Obersturmführer Hartmann."

Hartmann glared at him as he unbuttoned his holster and handed over the weapon.

Hauptsturmführer Wolff snarled.

"You are under arrest and shall henceforth be confined to your quarters under guard whilst we conduct further investigations into the Führer's mysterious disappearance."

CHAPTER 29

What Hartmann's future self had predicted did indeed turn out to be the case.

Just before noon on the following day Hitler stormed into the Berghof with a much distressed Eva Braun trailing close behind. He was attired in civilian clothes, had his hair parted in the centre of his head and was sporting a full moustache and neatly trimmed beard. He was soaked from head to foot and his expensive-looking shoes were covered in mud from stamping across the meadow after emerging from the cave during a brief thunder storm.

Three unfortunate Oberschütze troopers who had challenged him after failing to recognise their rain-sodden Führer in his new guise, had already been arrested and sentenced to be shot, and a word of warning was quickly spreading throughout the Berghof complex to save any other un-informed staff from suffering a similar fate.

On receiving word of the Führer's return, Hauptsturmführer Wolff realised there was no basis on which he could continue to hold Hartmann in detention and considering the close relationship which seemed to exist between Hitler and his aide, it was clearly in his best interests to immediately remove the guard outside Hartmann's quarters.

The following day Hartmann received the summons to Hitler's office that he'd been dreading, and by the time he was ushered in by an extremely nervous secretary, Hitler had already traded the civilian apparel he had been wearing for his regular uniform, trimmed his moustache to its short signature style, parted his hair to the side and shaved off his beard. The Führer was fuming, pacing up and down the office cursing and swearing as Hartmann entered. He wheeled around and glared at his aide.

"My Zeitmaschine has been stolen, Hartmann. Stolen!"

Hitler stomped around the room muttering curses while Hartmann, following the good advice he had received from his future self, said nothing but stiffened to full height and standing to rigid attention, stared fixedly at the wall in front of him.

Eventually, the Führer tired of his pacing and throwing himself into an armchair, and without deigning to look in Hartmann's direction, spat out an account of his return from the future.

"Fräulein Braun and I were enjoying a short stay in the Zum Türken, when a pair of brigands descended upon us, forced us at gunpoint into the Zeitmaschine and transported us back to 1944. I cannot understand how they knew such things, but they seemed to be totally familiar with the machine and its controls. When we returned to the present day, they bundled us out of the Zeitmaschine's cabin."

He raised his voice to a roar.

"I, Adolph Hitler, Führer of the Third Reich, and they dealt with us as if we were trash!"

Hitler angrily thumped the armrests of his chair with clenched fists.

"They left us there in the chamber, Hartmann, and disappeared, taking my Zeitmaschine with them. They stole it, Hartmann. They stole my Zeitmaschine and have left me stranded here in 1944."

Hitler sat for a long time seething, whilst Hartmann remained silent, standing stiffly to attention, daring to neither move nor respond in any way.

Abruptly, Hitler jumped to his feet and smacking fist into palm, turned to his aide, his face suddenly transformed and glowing with a look of triumph.

"I have it, Hartmann! I shall overcome this little setback and will return to the future after all. We must summon the scientists and have them build me another Zeitmaschine."

Hartmann's blood ran cold. The probability he would be facing a firing squad today was a one hundred percent certainty. He swallowed hard before responding.

"I am afraid that will not be possible, Mein Führer."

Hitler glared at him, stunned by his negative response, and Hartmann felt perspiration gathering on his forehead. He swallowed hard again and kept staring fixedly at the wall in front of him as he spoke.

"Following the Führer's earlier orders, I had the three scientists eliminated and their scientific notes destroyed. I regret to inform Mein Führer, there is not one shred of information remaining anywhere on this planet which would assist anyone who might have intentions of re-creating the scientists' Zeitmaschine."

Hitler stared at him in shocked disbelief. Then he buried his face in his hands. Hartmann stood rigid, sweating, waiting for the explosion of rage that would seal his fate.

It didn't come.

Hitler's muffled, cracked voice escaped from between his fingers, bitter and tired, as he slumped back into his chair.

"Leave me now, Hartmann."

Hartmann didn't hesitate a second, but acting on this very welcome command, hurried out of the office with wings on his feet before the Führer had a chance to change his mind.

Hitler was nowhere to be seen for the next two days. When he did reappear, he again summoned Hartmann to his office. The Führer invited him to take a seat as he entered, waving him toward the armchair at the coffee table. Hartmann sat, very much relieved to see the Führer had calmed down considerably, but was still apprehensive as to what might now follow. Hitler joined him in the chair opposite and contemplated his young aide for a few seconds.

"We have had quite an adventure and much disappointment with the Zeitmaschine, have we not, Hartmann?"

Without waiting for a response, he continued.

"It would not be of benefit to our cause if this matter should become widely known, especially if it came to the attention of our enemies who might at this very moment be thinking about the possibility of similar projects."

Hartmann nodded agreement.

"Hartmann, two days ago I might have had you shot for destroying the only means we had of ever duplicating the Zeitmaschine. However, I am very thankful I was able to control my anger and feelings of outrage at what you had done because after all, you were merely following my orders, as you have done dutifully so many times in the past. Of all my staff and associates, you are the one I have come to trust with complete confidence knowing you will always be there, ready to obey my commands without question.

"We are living through very dangerous and troubling times, Hartmann. Many of my compatriots do not share my vision for the Reich. Some would sue for a peace treaty with our enemies when victory is still within our grasp. Many are disloyal and some would even see me deposed as Führer, as you are well aware from the numerous assassination attempts on my life.

"For these reasons, I require a person who is totally loyal and committed to our cause, to keep a close watch on my staff and associates, including all visitors with whom I come into close contact. I want you, Hartmann, to be that person, responsible for my personal security. You shall be given the power to detain, search and question anyone who might enter my immediate vicinity, irrespective of their rank or importance. Do I make myself clear?"

Hartmann was very much relieved to hear Hitler's proposal and agreed immediately to the suggested office with much enthusiasm. Since the July assassination attempt on Hitler's life, a number of Schutzstaffel officers had been arrested and shot for suspected complicity in one or another of these assassination plots, irrespective of whether they turned out to be real or were later found to have been imagined. Being Hitler's body guard was not only a great personal honour, but was also an insurance policy against suffering a similar fate. He also relished the fact that, given his new role, he now enjoyed absolute protection from any scheme that Hauptsturmführer Wolff might be hatching to diminish his standing in the Berghof and indeed, his new responsibilities would in fact allow him to limit the Gestapo chief's personal access to the Führer.

In his assessment of the new relationship he shared with Wolff a disturbing thought came to mind. Knowing the secret of the camouflaged door, Wolff now possessed unfettered access to the chamber. If he should interfere with the disposition of the cradles or worse, place solid objects on them, surely this would introduce the possibility of a collision when the Zeitmaschine in one of its many incarnations materialised on reaching its destination in the future. Although Hartmann and the Führer had already travelled to the future without their Zeitmaschine being involved in such a collision, he wondered whether this had been due to Wolff simply refraining from such actions, or was it because steps had been taken to permanently bar him from entry into the chamber.

Troubled by uncertainty and in his determination not to leave such a critical state of affairs for chance alone to decide, Hartmann voiced his concern to the Führer whose face clouded as he too considered the situation and its possible ramifications.

"This is a matter which I alone must resolve, Hartmann. You need take no further action in this regard."

Hitler rose from his chair and Hartmann followed suit snapping to attention.

"I will be leaving the Berghof shortly Hartmann, and will not be returning until our enemies have been defeated. Our military intelligence have advised that the Allied air forces intend turning their attention to the Obersalzberg, with the Berghof consequently becoming a prime target for their bombers. You shall be ready to leave at a moment's notice to accompany me in the role I have just described. Our main base will be the Chancellery in Berlin, but in addition to my public appearances, we will also be regularly visiting our command bases in other locations."

Hartmann returned to the Zum Türken and sitting on the edge of his bed went over all that had transpired over the last three days. From what had already occurred he knew that in the future, the Zeitmaschine would be weaving through the fabric of time to find its way to the growing number of temporal destinations he already knew of, and he speculated on what might happen if anyone else over the intervening years should discover the secret of the camouflaged door and find the chamber. If they should then interfere with the cradles would this endanger him, the Führer, or his later self and Frau Morgen Schreiber in having to deal with the possibility of collisions? Obviously from what he had already experienced himself during his own travels, and also from the visit the pair from the future had paid him in the chamber, he knew its secret must have been maintained throughout the passing years. However, it struck him that this could very well have been because he had taken additional steps to protect the secret inside the chamber. Hartmann recalled the message he had read on the chamber door after travelling fifteen years into the future to meet Linde, and deciding there was indeed more that could be done, he returned to the chamber the following morning carrying a large sheet of plywood which he affixed to the inner side of the door in the North wall. On the board he inscribed the following text:

> *Rocks have been placed in the cave entrance*
> *to assist in hiding its presence.*
> *Simply push out to exit.*
> *Best wishes,*
> *Hartmann.*

He stepped back a pace to inspect the sign, and deciding it was exactly as he remembered from his previous voyage, closed the door and made his way to the clearing outside the cave entrance. He gathered rocks from a pile the tunnelling masons had left behind, and carefully built up a wall in the cave's narrow entrance. It was stable enough to endure, but could be pushed out easily by anyone inside the cave seeking to exit. He scooped up young ferns sprouting nearby and pressed handfuls of moist earth around their roots as he planted them in crevices in the rock wall he had created.

Hartmann stood back and ran a critical eye over his handiwork.

The cave was already well hidden and in time the ferns would grow, and as they established themselves, they would completely cover the wall he had built.

* * *

On his return to the Zum Türken later that afternoon he found the lobby buzzing with excitement over the latest news. During his absence, Hauptsturmführer Wolff and two of his officers had been arrested after being accused of plotting the Führer's assassination and had faced the firing squad that very same day.

CHAPTER 30

In mid-January 1945, Hitler moved into the Berlin Führerbunker with Eva Braun, Joseph Goebbels and his family. Karl Hartmann took up residence in the nearby as-yet undamaged wing of the Reich Chancellery, and was ever close at hand whilst the Führer oversaw the War from this last bastion of command.

By the end of January, the Russian Army had crossed the River Oder into Germany, only eighty kilometres from Berlin and consequently from the Chancellery.

During the next two months, defeat followed defeat as Germany's armies were pushed back from the Eastern and Western fronts. The historic city of Dresden was destroyed in a massive fire-bombing raid, Western forces crossed the Rhine into Germany and the Russians captured the heavily defended city of Budapest. Previously non-aligned countries as far flung as Egypt, Venezuela, Turkey and Syria were now joining the Allies with declarations of war against Germany.

In April the end was in sight and Hitler's government was rapidly beginning to unravel.

Hitler commanded arms minister Speer to destroy all industrial infrastructure before it could fall into Allied hands, but Speer disobeyed his orders and left them intact. Hitler commanded Waffen SS General Steiner to mount a pincer attack on the Russians in combination with the Ninth Army only to discover the attack hadn't taken place, allowing the Russians to enter Berlin. Herman Göring, located in the South at Berchtesgaden, suggested he should assume leadership, to which Hitler responded by having him arrested. In late April, Reichsführer-SS *Heinrich Himmler*, who had left Berlin on the twentieth, was attempting to discuss surrender terms with the Western Allies. Hitler ordered Himmler's arrest and had his representative at headquarters shot.

By now, the Russian army had completely surrounded the city of Berlin and their front line was only several city blocks from the Chancellery.

It was stuffy and somewhat uncomfortable in the bunkers and Hitler invited Hartmann to accompany him on his evening walk through the ruined Chancellery gardens, accompanied by Blondi on her leash. The sound of cannonfire was constant and much closer now, and the acrid smell of exploding munitions smoke filled the night air. As they strolled through the gardens, Hartmann mused if one could but ignore the explosions that rent the night air, the pervasive smoke, the ash that rained down on them from nearby burning buildings, and the moonlit ruins of the Chancellery, then the image of this man walking by his side with his dog on a leash could have been a scene played out in a million peaceful locations around the globe that evening.

They strolled in thoughtful silence for a while before coming to a fallen concrete column. Hitler stopped, sat down and patted the space on the column beside him, inviting Hartmann to do likewise. The Führer looked up through streamers of smoke at an otherwise clear starry sky and reflected on how unaffected were the heavens by humankind's theatre of destruction below. He peered sideways at Hartmann who was looking distantly into the night sky, lit up by the flash of explosions, and thinking about Linde whilst he gently fondled Blondi's velvety ears.

"It is the end for me and the Reich, Hartmann.

"At midnight tonight Fräulein Braun and I will be having a little celebration in the bunker that I would be pleased to have you attend. Then tomorrow, I wish to have your assistance with a difficult task I have in mind."

Hartmann turned to him, deeply affected by Hitler's invitation.

"I would be honoured to be in attendance, Mein Führer."

After a brief pause he added with a wry smile.

"I believe I don't have any important engagements requiring my attention at that time."

Hitler smiled disconsolately at his aide's attempt at humour and rose from the column. Hartmann followed and they completed their circumnavigation of the grounds in silence, with Blondi padding along between them.

CHAPTER 31

Just after midnight on the twenty-ninth of April 1945, Adolph Hitler married his long-time mistress, Eva Braun, in a modest civil ceremony. Hartmann felt proud and honoured to be witness to the proceedings and was especially elated to find himself in the presence of Generals Burgdorf and Krebs, his long-admired heroes, who were also in attendance at the ceremony.

After a simple wedding breakfast with his wife, Hitler dictated his will and held meetings with Goebbels and the Generals. Hartmann left the bunker and took up a position in the Chancellery gardens from whence he could more readily hear what was occurring in the immediate neighbourhood. The sound of cannonfire was considerably louder and closer than it had been on the previous night and after a fruitless walk around the perimeter during which he tried to glimpse some of the action beyond the barricades, he retired for the night.

In the morning he received a summons to the Führer's quarters. Hitler was waiting for him, and after acknowledging Hartmann's salute, directed him to open a canvas kit bag sitting on the table. Inside were a soldier's uniform and papers.

"Hartmann, you have served me faithfully and well and I wish to reward you for your loyalty. You are young, but most importantly, you bear the seed of the Aryan race with which I have strived to purify the German people. I had the contents of this bag prepared some time ago to give to you in the event we should ever find ourselves in the current regrettable circumstances. As you can see, it contains the uniform of an Oberschütze foot soldier, together with matching identification papers and money. At such a time, these things are far more practical than medals and citations. When the time comes, you must make your escape from the Chancellery wearing these clothes and may they preserve you in the days ahead."

Hartmann stood stiffly to attention and stared defiantly at the Führer.

"I have certainly had no thought of escaping. You are still our Führer and I will stay to defend you whilst breath remains in my body."

The muffled thud of a cannon shell exploding in the gardens outside penetrated through the thick walls of the bunker and a wisp of dust floated down from the ceiling. Hitler glanced forlornly at his aide. If only he had had armies comprised of youths of this calibre, he lamented, Germany would have won the War years ago.

Hitler's face was strained as he motioned Hartmann to follow him into his apartment. On the floor, Hitler's beloved Blondi lay dead. On the bed, Eva Hitler also lay dead, dressed in the frock she had worn during her wedding ceremony the previous night. Hartmann bowed his head in silence and stared fixedly at the floor, whilst Hitler looked blankly at her lifeless form for a few seconds before turning back to him.

He extended his hand.

"Your pistol if you please Hartmann."

Hartmann hesitated and stared at Hitler's upturned palm, before looking up to the Führer's face with a puzzled frown.

Hitler scowled.

"This is not the time to question your Führer's commands, Hartmann. Your pistol, if you please."

Hartmann stood to attention, drew his pistol from its holster and handed it to the Führer. Hitler looked down with revulsion at the gun cradled in his palm before returning Hartmann's gaze, his face a study of grim determination.

"I have made certain arrangements with Goebbels this morning. Please ask him to come to my quarters after you leave this apartment. Also, on your way out you will take with you the kit bag I showed you earlier – I command you use its contents when the time comes to make your escape. After you have spoken with Goebbels you are by my order, dismissed from all duties to myself and the Reich."

Hitler noted the look of renewed defiance on Hartmann's countenance.

"That is my final command, Hartmann. You shall obey my orders."

Hartmann reluctantly acceded to Hitler's direction, clicked his heels and gave the Führer a parting Hitlergruiß salute. He wheeled about and strode out of the apartment, picking up the bag of clothing and documents as he left. On his way to find Goebbels the sound of a single gunshot coming from the rooms behind him brought him to a standstill. He debated for a second or two whether to return, but decided against it, and after finding and conferring with Goebbels, he left the bunkers.

Shortly afterwards, whilst he paced around the Chancellery garden, an orderly approached him and confirmed what Hartmann already knew.

He returned to the bunkers to report to General Weidling who was now in command of the small detachment of military personnel remaining in the Chancellery complex, and later in the day, Weidling informed his assembled personnel that a breakout would be attempted at midnight that very night.

CHAPTER 32

When the time came to leave, Hartmann donned his Oberschütze uniform as the Führer had commanded, and fled the Chancellery with a small group of officers and officials. They scattered in different directions, each determining what he imagined might be the safest escape route option.

Two city blocks from the Chancellery Hartman ran into a cluster of terrified young women clutching babes in arms, accompanying a few elderly couples clinging to each other and a troop of limping, injured teenage Hitlerjugend defenders retreating from the fighting front, now no more than three city blocks to their rear. They stopped in their tracks on seeing Hartmann in his army uniform and a bloodstained, dirt-smeared youth who seemed to be in charge pushed forward, and looking hopefully up to him, asked for direction. From his time pacing around the Chancellery gardens, Hartmann knew the Russians were also advancing toward them from several city blocks in the opposite direction and he shook his head.

There was nowhere to run – no avenue of escape left to evade the pincer tactics of the advancing enemy forces. After a hurried consultation, he led the bedraggled group of defenders and their accompanying cohort of refugees through the shattered doorway of a badly damaged apartment building. Inside the foyer, he instructed them to sit quietly on the floor in the hallway and await the arrival of the enemy's forces, reassuring them that as civilians they would be safe from harm. The exhausted young fighters sank to the floor and Hartmann moved slowly through their ranks, addressing their wounds as best he could, whilst striving to assure them that bearing arms would literally be a death sentence when the Russians finally arrived. He collected the motley assortment of weapons they had scavenged from the dead and soldiers too badly wounded to continue the struggle, and threw them behind a pile of rubble in the damaged section of the building. Hartmann knew this was the end for him as well and defiant to the last, would not countenance abandoning his military uniform.

When the Russians finally came upon them, Hartmann, being the only one in the group in military garb, was roughly handled and immediately hauled away at gunpoint.

The following morning, along with a sizeable contingent of captured German troopers, he was incarcerated in a temporary encampment for disarmed enemy forces in a nearby football field the Russians had set up expressly for that purpose.

Hartmann was questioned repeatedly over the next few days regarding his rank and previous movements. Between interviews he wandered around the barbed wire perimeter of the camp endeavouring to avoid interaction with other captives lest one of them recognise him and attempt to ingratiate himself to his captors by revealing Hartmann's true Obersturmführer rank and identity.

The Russian commandant in charge of the camp showed little regard for the welfare of its inhabitants. Sanitation and sewerage for the prisoners of war were practically non-existent, food was meagre and rationed, and trucks brought in water of highly questionable quality. No medical aid was available and apart from some hastily erected tarpaulin shelters, there was little protection from the weather. Many of the Wehrmacht soldiers who had been wounded in the battle for Berlin eventually succumbed to gangrene or blood poisoning, whilst over the coming weeks of incarceration, dysentery and starvation accounted for many of the rest.

Every day as his fellow camp inmates sickened, suffered and died around him, Hartmann tried to make sense of the inhumane treatment meted out to himself and his fellow internees. Why, he asked himself, were they being punished so cruelly when their only crime had been to follow orders from their superiors – were his counterparts in the enemy ranks not equally culpable for doing likewise and inflicting cruel inhuman suffering on his comrades? He reflected on the past when it was he who had been on the other side of the barbed wire – when it was he who had accepted the brutality, the concentration camps, the ghettos and the purges as being necessary evils in Hitler's drive to purify the German people. And now, thrust into similar circumstances on the prisoners' side of the wire, he finally found himself at one with all those who had experienced the nightmare of the concentration camp – the Jews; the Gypsies; the Communists; the dissidents.

Hartmann also reflected on the future.

Now, at this pivotal moment in history, Germany had been devastated beyond comprehension, its infrastructure destroyed;

the flower of its youth decimated; its government subject to the whim of foreign powers; its population starving and universally despised by countless millions around the globe, and yet Hartmann knew, as no other person yet knew, that this country, this Germany, would rise from the ashes of war, and in sixty years' time, would once again be a thriving prosperous leader in the European Union.

Hitler and his Nazi government had sent the cream of German youth to an early grave, murdered millions in gas chambers, bankrupted the nation, invoked the censure of its neighbours, and left the country in ruins in his maniacal drive to exert German dominance over Europe and yet, by the sheer strength and determination of its people, Germany would once again attain in the future, the prosperity and dominance that Hitler had failed to achieve – *without* having to inflict the suffering and loss which had accompanied his quest for power.

Several weeks after Hartmann's internment, the Russian high command gave orders for the camp to be disbanded. The bodies of those soldiers who had recently died were dumped in a heap in a distant corner of the field, but due to the shortage of petrol, rather than being set alight and burnt, they were left there to rot under the blazing sun.

Word passed through the survivors' ranks that the Russians intended loading those who had managed to cling to life into trucks bound for forced labour camps in Russia. Hartmann knew from what he had read about the War's aftermath in the future Türken's internet cafe that transportation meant certain death through ill-treatment, starvation and disease and on the night before the trucks were due to remove the camp's inhabitants, he crawled across the field under cover of darkness to the pile of dead and decomposing bodies and burrowed in amongst the corpses.

The pressing closeness of rotting flesh around him and the sweet putrid smell of death in his hiding place caused him to dry retch repeatedly, but he closed his eyes tightly and only just managed to cling to his sanity whilst he waited for a night which seemed to have no end to be over.

Early the next morning, three Russian guards accompanied by two large vicious-looking dogs that drooled saliva and strained and panted at the extremity of their leashes, searched the perimeter of the camp for any inmates who might have thought to evade transportation by hiding in the long grassy verges surrounding the field.

Hartmann looked on in dismay from his hiding place amongst the corpses as a young soldier he had befriended, alarmed by the approaching search party, sprang up from the ditch in which he had lain hidden and backing against the barbed wire perimeter fence raised his hands high above his head.

He heard the soldier cry out.

"Don't shoot. Please. Please don't shoot."

Two of the Russian guards turned inquisitively to the third who, by his response to the soldier's plea, showed he evidently understood German. With a sneer, he translated for the others.

"*On skazal, 'ne strelitzye'.*"

The trio laughed heartily whilst the dogs snarled and strained at their leashes only inches away from the cowering, terrified soldier. The dog handler nudged the guard on his right with his elbow and winking an eye at his companions, released his grip on the dogs' leashes.

Hartmann clamped his eyes shut and murmured a prayer over and over to any god who might be listening, in an attempt to blot out the soldier's screams, until they finally ended in a gurgling groan. He tentatively opened his eyes to ascertain what was happening only to be a horrified witness to one of the guards bringing down his rifle butt on the bloodied soldier's head. The groaning immediately stopped and there was silence.

The dog handler kicked the soldier's corpse, reined in his dogs and the three guards resumed their inspection walk around the perimeter, laughing and joking with each other over the murderous savagery they had left behind in their wake. As they approached his hiding place, Hartmann frantically wriggled his body backwards pushing his feet back against the corpses further inside the pile in a desperate attempt to burrow deeper into the heap. But the Russian soldiers pinched their noses as they approached and keeping their distance, gave the heap of rotting flesh in which he lay hidden a very wide berth.

Later that morning, a truck backed up to the pile of corpses, its rear wheels grinding to a halt barely a metre from Hartmann's head. Two Russian soldiers wearing masks of torn wet rags wrapped around their mouth and nose, climbed out of the cab. They plodded to the rear of the truck and dropped the back board. Hartmann took in short quick breaths to limit the movement of his chest and through near-closed eyes watched the men as they hauled a corpse out of the truck's dark interior. It fell with a thud, sprawled at the soldiers' feet. They bent down, grasped it by the wrists and ankles, and because the corpse was so thin and emaciated, they swung it effortlessly onto the pile. It slithered down over the bodies already lying there and a limp leg came to rest over Hartmann's exposed shoulder. The Russians reached into the truck again and withdrew two more corpses which they tossed close to where he lay hidden. As they raised and locked the backboard, one turned to address his companion in a voice muffled by his mask.

"Slava bohrhoo etor poslednyi. Ya boodoo rad kagda myi vyber-emsia is etovo oojasnovo myesta."

Since arriving in the camp, Hartmann had learned a little Russian while being interrogated and afterwards, in seeking translation from a fellow inmate who understood the language, in an attempt to gain advantage from being aware of their plans. On this occasion, from the very few words he now understood and the obvious relief in the men's voices, Hartmann guessed they would not be returning. The soldiers clambered back into the cab and with a crunch of gears, the truck rumbled back across the field to join a convoy of transport vehicles gathering near the perimeter gate. As he watched, Russian guards herded a shambolic mob of camp inmates toward the waiting trucks, yelling insults at them and slapping stragglers with their rifle butts. The starved skeletons that passed for survivors were barely able to clamber into the trucks, and two unfortunates who fell repeatedly whilst trying to do so were shot by the guards, their bodies left sprawled in the dust as a warning to the others.

Although the grotesque experience of his hiding place would haunt him with nightmares for the rest of his life, and though every fibre of his being urged him to scream with protest and revulsion at his horrific circumstances, Hartmann managed to remain still and silent, hidden under the foul smelling corpses until the last of the trucks rumbled out of the camp.

When he finally felt confident not another soul remained in the grounds, Hartmann hastily scrambled out of his hiding place and sitting beside the pile of rotting bodies, clasped his wasted shins with his hands, bowed his head until it rested on his knees, and in this foetalesque bearing he wept bitter tears as he rocked back and forth.

Back and forth.

Back and forth.

Toward noon, Hartmann was finally able to regain some semblance of control over his anguish and rising painfully, he cast fearful glances around the deserted football ground before tottering toward the open gate. Although he had witnessed the departure of the truck convoy, he nevertheless cautiously swept the area through tear-blurred eyes, dreading the possibility he might yet be bailed up by a Russian patrol. But the area around the gate was as quiet and devoid of life as a graveyard, and he staggered into the adjacent guard house looking for food and water.

The Russians had stripped the building of every useful piece of furnishing and utensil, and had certainly not left any food stocks behind. However, his keen eye caught sight of a pile of abandoned breakfast scraps the cook had spilled on the kitchen floor. Part of it bore the imprint of a boot that had squashed some of the remnants against the floorboards, but he brushed away blowflies hovering over the remaining spillage and scraping up as much as he could salvage, devoured the first real food he had eaten in days. Outside the building where the guards had washed their meal utensils, a small pool of waste water lay in a shallow depression and falling to his knees, he scooped up handfuls of the turbid liquid and drank until only mud remained as testimony to a pool having once existed there.

Hartmann rose unsteadily to his feet and ventured out into the devastation that lay beyond the gates. He stumbled down rubble strewn streets lined on either side by the skeletal remains of burnt out buildings, where battles between the city's defenders and advancing Russian forces had left little that was recognisable in the city he had known and loved since childhood.

There was an uncanny silence and an absence of military personnel throughout the immediate vicinity. The last remnant pockets of German defenders had been rounded up in camps similar to the one from which he had just emerged, prior to their transport to Russian labour camps, whilst enemy forces had been re-deployed to other areas of action where entrenched German troops still battled in their futile stand against the Russian onslaught.

In the place of the military he now saw gaunt faced women and skinny young children dressed in rags, scavenging for food, whilst shrivelled old men sheltered under tattered awnings, trying to keep warm under dirt soiled blankets.

CHAPTER 33

Hartmann's narrative trailed off into silence and his eyes dropped to the floor. His anguish in recalling these bitter memories was palpable and I struggled to express some words which might have been of comfort.

"I was born a few years after the War, and can't even begin to imagine the horror you must have faced in that detention camp and then later on, out on the streets."

Hartmann slowly lifted his gaze from the floor. His eyes again glistened with incipient tears.

"I roamed through abandoned houses searching for food. There were rats in the streets feeding off the corpses of dead soldiers – I managed to catch and kill a few of them and cooked them in the embers of a burnt-out building."

He looked down at the floor again, pausing for a moment before looking up, shaking his head.

"You would be surprised to know how good they tasted to a starving man."

His gaze wandered around the office for a few seconds, not focussing on anything in particular. Then once again gathering his thoughts, he returned his attention back to me with that characteristic look of intensity with which by this time I had become so familiar.

"But please, allow me to finish my story. I was twenty five years old at the end of the War, and look at me now – an old man in his eighties. As you can imagine, I have many, many interesting stories that could be told after having lived such a long and eventful life. But I will spare you the catalogue of my adventures during the years that followed because they are mostly not pertinent to my narrative. There remains however, one last important episode in my association with the Zeitmaschine that I wish to share with you before I finally show you the evidence I promised earlier – evidence that I know will finally convince you beyond reasonable doubt regarding the truth of my tale."

Despite the fact I felt no proof would ever convince me that a contraption such as Hitler's Zeitmaschine could ever exist outside the pages of a science fiction novel, I nevertheless leaned forward in my seat with eager anticipation.

"Please continue then with your narrative, Herr Hartmann. Your incredible story continues to intrigue me and I can assure you of my absolute and undivided attention in finishing your tale."

CHAPTER 34

The first few months were hard. Very, very hard. Food and protection from the weather were always difficult to come by. In the Berlin quarter under their control, the American administration was initially reluctant to address the humanitarian catastrophe posed by the starving population. However, they eventually underwent a change of heart and Hartmann found work in one of the street gangs they organised, tasked with clearing the roads of rubble, and building temporary shelters for civilian survivors. For his efforts, he was rewarded with food rations which over the following months enabled him to regain his former strength and health, together with a modest feeling of well-being.

Over the next few years, memories of his internment in the Russian concentration camp, and now the experience of assisting his fellow countrymen in finding their feet, significantly altered his attitude toward the Nazi regime under which he had previously vouchsafed allegiance. As he assisted in addressing the problems of rehabilitation and rebuilding Berlin's infrastructure he found amongst the ruins and suffering the qualities of hope, kindness and understanding amongst the people he had formerly regarded as being impure. Day after day he was confronted by former inmates of Hitler's concentration camps – many of them walking skeletons and barely alive – who nevertheless shared their food and cared for one another, and over time, he came to realise that these altruistic and good qualities in human beings were far more important than skin colour or religious and ethnic backgrounds.

Hartmann's enthusiastic efforts to raise the standards of his fellow citizens were soon recognised by his supervisors, and eventually the administration placed him in charge of one of their local relief and rehabilitation programs.

As conditions in Germany improved and normalised around him, Hartmann became aware of one of the less obvious consequences of war – the shortage of men in a nation that had lost up to ten percent of its male youth in casualties. Hartmann was tall, well proportioned, blond, blue-eyed and handsome, but most importantly of all, unmarried. Now approaching forty years of age, he was viewed as a prime catch by many a hopeful maiden, and he consequently ran the gauntlet of suggestive flirtations nearly every day. But although many of his female admirers were quite charming, intelligent and pretty, if Hartmann thought of them at all, it was only to compare them unfavourably with Linde Engel. Throughout his journey, from the Berlin bunker to the present time, he had not forgotten her love for him, and he longed to see her once again.

In the early years after the War, he had found amusement in constantly calculating her age whilst trying to picture what she might look like at that very moment, and wondered what she might be doing so very far away to the South in Berchtesgaden.

When he had first met her in 1959 she had been twenty four, so that in 1949 he calculated she would be fourteen, and going to high school. At that time, Hartmann tried to imagine what she looked like – perhaps she wore her hair in a ponytail and had a face full of freckles – and he would chortle aloud just at the thought.

In 1954 she would have been nineteen. When he thought about her that year, Hartmann imagined Linde as a pretty university student in Munich with the boys buzzing around her and her friend Mitzi Bayer like bees around a honey pot. If he had dared to visit Linde then, he could have warned that her mother was about to become ill, and soon Linde would have to quit her studies and return to Berchtesgaden to look after her.

The years had rolled by and now it was 1959. Linde would now be twenty four years old and happily at work in Herr Kaufmann's jewellery shop. Possibly, he imagined, at this very moment she might well be in the act of serving his younger self who had just entered into her life, intent on converting his diamond to cash. He smiled inwardly as he recalled his nervousness on that occasion, and felt so glad he had been brave enough to return to the shop to initiate the first steps leading to their romance.

Yes, 1959, the year when they had begun to share those golden days in the future which, now that the years had run their course, had become the present. Right at this very moment, whilst he was here at work in Berlin, his younger self and Linde were on the threshold of falling in love down there in Kaufmann's jewellery shop.

Suddenly a shiver of excitement ran down his spine as Hartmann recalled their last moments together outside the cave

– the moment when his older self had unexpectedly appeared out of the forest to censure him for insisting on returning to 1944. How foolish he had been not to heed his older self's good advice to stay with Linde in 1959 instead of returning to fulfil his promise to Hitler.

His mind raced.

Would it be possible, he wondered, to return to the same scene and change things, now that he was acquainted with the horrendous future lying ahead for his younger self? Surely he could persuade his younger self to remain with Linde instead of returning to 1944. If this could be achieved, his earlier self could then marry Linde and spend the rest of his days in loving bliss, never to know the awful circumstances to which he himself had been subjected at the conclusion of the War.

In his excitement, he failed to take into account the dictum laid down by scientist Fuchs regarding the immutability of past actions, but instead became obsessed with the possibility of changing the course of events which had occurred on that fateful day.

With every good intention, he resolved there and then to revisit Berchtesgaden in order to persuade young Hartmann to abandon his intended return to 1944. However in truth, his decision was not entirely derived out of altruism for although motivated by consideration for his younger self's happiness, his heart still ached at having lost Linde and he longed to see her if only just this one last time.

Hartmann immediately made arrangements for his work to be handled by colleagues over the next few days, and returning to his apartment, he hurriedly packed a few items of clothing and toiletries in a small port for the journey.

The next morning he walked out of Berchtesgaden station and looking around, experienced an overwhelming feeling of nostalgia that tempted him to visit Kaufmann's jewellery shop, the Gasthof Neuhaus or Frau *Krüger's* boarding house, all of which evoked fond memories from his past. But instead, anxious in his desire to see Linde once again, he made his way to the car hire counter and rented an economy Volkswagen.

Hartmann pulled to a stop in the Zum Türken's car park and strolled up the path leading to the hotel entrance, casting an eye around his familiar surroundings, enjoying once again being in an environment he remembered only too well. On entering the lobby he strode up to the reception desk and recalling the incident with Herman Wirth on his scooter some fifteen years ago, immediately recognised Herman's mother behind the counter. Frau Wirth looked up as he approached and stared at him wide-eyed with concern.

"I beg your pardon Sir, but what has happened to you? Your face is … is very much changed since you left a few hours ago."

Hartmann stared at her not comprehending.

"My face? A few hours ago? What on earth are you talking about?"

"Well, please forgive me for saying so, but you are looking very different and a good deal older than you were when I apologised to you this morning about my son's misadventure on his scooter."

Hartmann's mind raced as he quickly pieced together what was happening. Fifteen years ago he had nearly been run down by young Herman Wirth on his scooter after which Frau Wirth had come from behind the reception desk to give the boy a good hiding. To Hartmann, fifteen long years had elapsed since this incident had taken place, but to Frau Wirth it had happened only that very morning. A few hours ago she had looked into young Hartmann's face – a face which now seemed to her to have suddenly not only aged by fifteen years, but also bore the reminders of the ordeals he suffered during and after the War.

But the scooter incident had occurred only shortly before young Hartmann and Linde left in the Zeitmaschine to travel ten years into the future … And after their four day romance in the future, young Hartmann had returned with Linde to her own time.

Which was now.

Today – Sunday!

He glanced at his watch – it was half past eleven.

Young Hartmann would be bringing Linde back in the Zeitmaschine within the hour. Hartmann cursed under his breath for not realising the time of their arrival and young Hartmann's subsequent departure back to 1944 left him with a critically narrow window of opportunity to persuade his younger self not to return to the past. He left Frau Wirth staring after him in astonishment as he rushed from the lobby.

Hartmann ran as fast as he could across the meadow, and entering the forest of trees at the far end, headed for the clearing in front of the cave. He could hear raised voices up ahead, followed immediately afterward as he neared the clearing, by the sound of Linde sobbing. Hearing his beloved Linde in tears enraged him and as he entered the clearing he called out harshly.

"Hartmann!"

He advanced toward Linde with swift strides and ignoring his younger self sitting at her side making a vain attempt to console her, he dropped down on his knees at her feet. Drawing a handkerchief from his pocket, he gently dabbed the tears streaming down her face. Linde uncovered her eyes, took the kerchief from his hands and wiped the remaining tears from her cheeks. She looked straight into his eyes, her tear-filled eyes obscuring his apparent aging and begged softly.

"Please don't leave me Karl. Please don't go."

Her words stung him to such an extent that he completely forgot his original intent. Instead, he rose to his feet and turned on the younger man in a blind rage.

"You fool young Hartmann! You would trade the love of this beautiful young woman for an empty, lost cause? Are you mad?"

His younger self, snapping out of his astonishment, jumped to his feet and stared back at him angrily, whilst Linde, startled by the sudden movement at her side, rose unsteadily to her feet, frightened by the confrontation between the two Hartmanns now glaring at each other a few paces in front of her. She looked from Hartmann to his younger duplicate, her tear-filled eyes wide with anxiety and began to wail in anguish.

"Oh Karl, what is happening? There are two of you! I don't understand. Am I seeing things or am I going insane?"

Hartmann wrapped his arms around Linde who had covered her face with her hands and had resumed her sobbing. He pulled her close to his chest and as he did so, he was suddenly struck by the fact this entire scenario was being played out exactly as he remembered it from fifteen years ago, albeit now he was seeing it from the perspective of the older Hartmann in the drama. He had come to this place to give his younger self guidance necessary to prevent him from suffering as he had suffered, and yet the situation had not played out as he had intended. Hartmann's mind whirled as memories came flooding back – the episode many years ago when he had attempted to prevent Linde's father from being sent to Dukla Pass only to be thwarted by Hauptsturmführer Wolff. At last, here confronting him was again incontestable proof of scientist Fuchs' dictum regarding the past – whatever was known to have occurred previously was truly immutable and could never be altered. However, having this insight forced upon him did nothing to quell the frustration he felt at being powerless to change the present situation, and he glared at the younger man in a fury.

"You fool. You and your damned Führer just don't get it, do you? Have you completely forgotten Fuchs' warning about trying to change the past? I now know for certain that what you yourself have seen written in the historical record is indeed what will eventually happen to Hitler, and nothing you or he can do, even with all the wealth he hopes to accumulate, can ever change the outcome written there. You and your misguided loyalty to the Reich have cost me dearly … and it's going to cost you dearly too, as you will eventually discover when you follow in my footsteps.

"Go! Go back to your own time. History dictates there is nothing I can say or do to save you from suffering the consequences of your folly."

The younger man stared at him for a few seconds, anger and sullen determination written across his face, before his gaze returned to Linde still locked in Hartmann's arms, and his expression seemed to soften a little. With Hartmann still glaring at him, the younger man snatched up his rucksack and without another word, turned and marched the short distance to the cave, disappearing behind the overhanging ferns.

Hartmann still clasped Linde tightly to his chest with one hand, relinquishing the hold of the other to stroke her hair, whilst he whispered soothingly in her ear.

"It's all right, Linde. It's all right. I am with you at last and promise I will never leave you again."

She gently pushed away from his chest, and lifting her head to gaze up into his glistening eyes hoarsely whispered.

"I love you Karl."

As she took in more of the man who held her so tightly and yet so tenderly, her expression changed to one of concern. She raised a hand to his cheek and traced her finger tips across the lines etched deeply across his face.

"But you look so much older, Karl. I don't understand. What has happened here today?"

"Yes, I am older now Linde but I am so very much wiser. I'm still the Karl Hartmann you have known and loved, but I have aged in a way I will tell you about on the way back to the Türken. But my dear, dearest Linde, please just believe me when I tell you that I have loved you from the moment I first laid eyes on you in Kaufmann's jewellery shop and intend spending the rest of my days proving my love for you."

Linde searched Hartmann's eyes, and in them she found the truth. With a cry of joy she threw her arms around his neck and instead of tears of sorrow, now wept tears of happiness as she kissed him passionately again and again.

They walked hand in hand across the grassy meadow back to the hotel rejoicing that now they would be together at last, and Hartmann commenced telling Linde the story of his life after he had disappeared into the cave that day. He continued the story in the Türken's lobby where they settled on a couch facing away and some distance from Frau Wirth lest she pursue him with awkward questions about his apparent aging.

Linde sat wide-eyed, listening to his tale. He told her he had known her father and described how they had worked together to create the tunnel leading from the cave to the Zeitmaschine chamber. Linde's eyes welled with tears when he declared that Engel had been a fine soldier with a strong work ethic and she hugged him when he revealed his endeavours to prevent her father's transfer to Dukla Pass, only to have his efforts thwarted by the cold and heartless Hauptsturmführer Wolff. She wrung her hands and wept when he described his ordeals after escaping the Berlin bunker, and again interrupted his tale with hugs and kisses when he spoke of his decision to return to Berchtesgaden that same day on the night train.

After his story had been told, they packed Linde's bundle of belongings into Hartmann's car and drove down to the little town in the valley. Once again in Berchtesgaden's familiar surroundings, Hartmann recalled from his visit to the town fifteen years ago that the inns would be fully occupied with billeted American soldiers. Not being overly enchanted at the prospect of spending another night sleeping on Frau *Krüger*'s old mattress, he decided to return to Berlin on the afternoon train.

Linde was at first quite uneasy at the thought of losing Hartmann yet again, even though it might only be for a few days, but he kissed and hugged her, and gave his assurance that nothing would keep them apart a minute longer than was absolutely necessary. He pointed out being left to their own devices during the next week would give her all the time she needed to settle her affairs in Berchtesgaden, whilst it would also give him the time he required to prepare his apartment for her arrival in Berlin.

The next day, Monday, Linde returned to the jewellery shop to inform Herr Kaufmann of her decision to move to Berlin at the end of the week. The old man was shocked at the news and begged her to stay on, insisting he would be unable to continue running his business without her assistance. But although she felt rather guilty and sorry for him, she was adamant, and thanking him for all his past kindnesses, apologised for only being able to give such short notice. That same evening Linde broke the news to Frau *Krüger*, who simply shrugged, and after grumbling about the capriciousness of youth these days, went about her daily routine unmoved.

During the following week Linde received regular telephone calls from Hartmann in addition to two of his letters which arrived from Berlin later in the week. Thereafter in the evenings, she sat on the edge of her bed in the boarding house, reading and re-reading his words of love and descriptions of the life that would soon be theirs in the capital.

The following weekend, Linde was farewelled at Berchtesgaden station by a small cluster of her closest friends, and after a ten hour train journey which seemed to take forever, she was re-united with Hartmann at Berlin Central Station.

CHAPTER 35

And you married Linde?"

"Yes. That wonderful woman blessed me with the happiest years of my life. Although I had long ago renounced my earlier belief in a German master race and was doing much good work among homeless and disadvantaged people, my life would have been unfulfilled without her by my side. After our marriage I travelled widely and achieved many things. We raised four children and they now all have children of their own, and I could talk for hours about these things. But I have come to see you here at your newspaper office for one very good reason.

"I am here because *you told me to come.*"

I shook my head in protest, yesterday having been the first time I had ever laid eyes on him, and argued that although his fascinating tale might have deemed it otherwise, in reality his meeting with me back in 1944 was clearly an impossibility. But he waited patiently until I had finished.

"You will recall from my account that when the two time-travellers delivered their message to my younger self in the chamber, it was you Morgen Schreiber, who gave him your business card."

He reached into his jacket pocket, withdrawing a wallet from which he extracted a small weathered business card, and passed it to me across the desk. Its edges were ragged and the card was heavily creased and stained with age, but I could just make out my name in the faded printing.

"Your older companion visiting young Hartmann that day was of course myself, and of a very similar age to what I am now. Although in my story we apparently travelled together in the Zeitmaschine to visit young Hartmann, I too am at a complete loss to explain how this could have happened because I never saw the Zeitmaschine again after the day you visited me back in 1944, nor did I lay eyes on you again until I walked into your office yesterday.

"During our encounter in the chamber back then, you instructed me to search for signs of Hitler's arrival in the world of the future, but due to the exigencies of war and the trauma I experienced following Germany's defeat, your message was temporarily forgotten. And when I married Linde and soon afterwards had a house full of children to care for, the message remained buried in the backwaters of my mind. It was only after Linde passed away a few years ago that I found the time and inclination to once more seriously consider what had transpired in the Zeitmaschine chamber. Hitler had, after all, travelled to the future and that being the case, surely there would be references in the media to a man who possessed the wealth he planned to accumulate through his misuse of the Zeitmaschine's powers. As you will recall from my story, he set the controls of the Zeitmaschine to travel fifty five years into the future. That was back in 1944 and he therefore would have arrived in 1999, that is, five years ago. This would have given him plenty of time to adopt a new identity, gain a grasp of the prevailing political order and start making useful contacts, whilst at the same time, using the Zeitmaschine to amass the fortune he thought necessary to launch himself into the forefront of German politics.

"I therefore became an assiduous reader of Die Welt and have been scanning its pages from 1999 onward, looking for articles which might reveal clues relevant to his arrival in the present time. My research showed he had done quite a remarkable job of keeping out of the newspapers whilst secretly amassing his fortune. During these five years he was also exceedingly active in building up a network of powerful sympathisers who have used his money to bribe their way into key positions in unions, industry, the media and political circles. It is only now he has achieved these things that he has taken to the media to start peddling his noxious propaganda about a new world order.

"Obviously with a different identity, it was difficult at first to fathom which of the many personages making the news each day might have been this new incarnation of Hitler, but one name which kept cropping up with increasing frequency in the financial and political pages of your paper finally led me to identify my quarry – Hitler now goes by the name of Dietrich Kaiser."

As editor of Die Welt I was well acquainted with Kaiser's rise to power – his activities were being reported in our paper on a near-daily basis these days. From the articles I had read about him, his agenda certainly seemed well aligned with what one might have expected from a clone of Germany's wartime leader. Hartmann waved his hand toward the envelope lying on my desk.

"In there you will find archive photos of Adolph Hitler and Eva Braun, together with a recent article from your own newspaper. I invite you to compare the photos with the picture in the article."

I picked up the envelope and shook out its contents. There were two black and white photos – one of Hitler and one of his mistress. I was well acquainted with their faces from documentaries and newspaper articles, and picking up the accompanying page I unfolded it whilst Hartmann looked on intently. The article pertaining to Kaiser included a large photo of the couple smiling to a crowded hall from their platform on the stage, and took up half the page. Picking up the photos I held each close to their corresponding images in the news item. Kaiser sported a full moustache and a neatly trimmed beard and his hair was parted in the middle of his head. His face, as shown in the article, compared very well with the photo I held alongside, but if that facial hair was intended to disguise his true identity it was doing an excellent job. For Eva Braun, or Frau Kaiser as the article would have it, there was not the shadow of a doubt. Her hairstyle had changed to match current fashions, but her face was a perfect match with the photo. I looked at Hartmann in amazement. He was smiling indulgently, and nodding toward the newspaper extract, invited me to read the article aloud.

I read out the headline at the top of the page:

"*BILLIONAIRE INDUSTRIAL MAGNATE TO LEAD NEW PARTY*"

I looked up at Hartmann. He waved a hand, encouraging me to read on.

"*Dietrich Kaiser, billionaire industrialist, today announced he would lead the newly formed Homelands Party to the forthcoming elections. Pictured here with his wife, Herr Kaiser, in a fiery speech to a packed town hall meeting of right wing union leaders last night, mounted a blistering attack on the growing number of countries in the*

European Union who were dependant on German loans which, he claimed, were in effect an anchor dragging the nation backward, preventing it from achieving the prosperity and prominence that was its due.

He signalled that his Party would legislate to return foreign immigrant workers and refugees to their countries of origin, and would introduce new laws to confiscate assets of ethnic and religious undesirables who challenged the authority of the state. The assembled delegates gave him a standing ovation at the end of his rousing oratory"

There was more, much more, but I had read enough.

"With his new hairstyle and that beard covering his face, it might be a little difficult confirming this man is indeed a reincarnated Hitler, but what he is reported to have said in the article certainly rings true to form. Despite the fact I am still totally unconvinced your Zeitmaschine could achieve what you have described in your tale, I somehow sense we have in the narrative the makings of a newsworthy story. Before I delve any further into your story, is there any positive substantial evidence you could provide which might assist in making references to a time machine more acceptable to our readership?"

Hartmann cradled his chin between thumb and forefinger and knitted his brow, considering my question.

"Well, perhaps a visit to the Zeitmaschine and a demonstration of its powers might suffice?"

I was staggered by his response.

"What! … Do you mean to persist with the claim that this machine really does exist?"

"Well of course, it's only a guess on my part, but you've read the newspaper article. All the facts stack up. Kaiser and his wife are clearly a perfect match for Hitler and Eva Braun; He espouses the same agenda as did Hitler, and he's rich beyond comprehension. I have no doubt he uses the Zeitmaschine in the manner I described earlier to create his great wealth – it must still exist."

He pointed a forefinger at my chest.

"Would you kill the goose that lays the golden egg?"

"Well, where do you think he has hidden it?"

"I very much doubt it has moved – not physically at least. Sure, it's probably moved a lot through time, but the machine was far too large to transport through the tunnel and the narrow door in the cave. Kaiser would never risk dismantling and reconstructing it elsewhere for fear it might cease working, and anyway to do so he would need assistance, which would reveal his secret to others. I mean to say, Kaiser wouldn't be able to dispose of accomplices as he had me do with the three scientists back in 1944. This would be difficult in Germany nowadays, even for a wealthy man. No, it is my considered opinion that the Zeitmaschine still sits in that chamber, as it did in 1944."

I rose from my chair, trying to keep a lid on my excitement, and bent over the desk toward him.

"I have to see this Zeitmaschine, Herr Hartmann! I must see it"

"I anticipated you would, and can make myself available for the next few days. You know from my story where we would be heading, so may I suggest you book flights to Munich, and from there it's about a two hour drive to Berchtesgaden."

"Fine. I'll make the necessary travel arrangements. How do I contact you to advise details?"

"That won't be necessary. There's an early flight to Munich tomorrow morning at nine – I propose meeting you here in your office at seven o'clock to take advantage of it. Can you make the necessary bookings in time?"

I confirmed this would not be a problem and as I reached for the phone, Hartmann wheeled about and strode out of the office.

Whilst Freda was attending to our travel details, I contacted several members of the editorial staff asking them to stand in for me over the next week while I followed up on what I told them could prove to be the most astounding story of the century.

I had very little sleep that night. I kept turning Hartmann's story over and over in my mind. It all held together incredibly well apart from two troublesome aspects. First of all, the Zeitmaschine itself. How could such an extraordinary invention remain hidden from and unknown to the general scientific community for over half a century? And secondly, how could I have played the part of visiting young Hartmann in the Zeitmaschine in the company of his older self, when up until yesterday I had never even heard of Hartmann nor had I known about the existence of Hitler's time machine? Even Hartmann himself was unable to explain our presence in the chamber in 1944. Then again, the photographic evidence of Hitler and Eva Braun being here in the present time was compelling, and would have been inexplicable without the assistance of a time machine to carry them to the future. It all led to the same conclusion – I had to discover whether such a machine really existed and if it did, witness a demonstration of its time transcending powers for myself.

Hartmann was in my office the next day precisely at seven with an attention to punctuality I had rather expected of him.

"Our flight to Munich is confirmed; it leaves at nine thirty this morning. Freda has organised a hire car at Munich airport for our trip to Berchtesgaden, and accommodation is arranged in the Zum Türken lodge for the next three nights."

"Good. I have a small port in the outer office with the clothing and necessaries I might require over the next few days, and as we'll require lighting at the end of our journey, I have also packed a couple of powerful torches."

I picked up my valise.

"Well Herr Hartmann, I am very much looking forward to our little adventure. There's a staff car waiting for us downstairs so if you're ready, we'll be off."

As I moved toward the door he placed a restraining hand on my arm.

"If we are going to share this adventure together, I would prefer not to be so formal. Would you call me by my first name, '*Karl*', and with your permission I will call you '*Morgen*'."

Through the telling of Hartmann's story I now somehow felt I had known him intimately for a long, long time and not to be on first name terms during our quest seemed unthinkable. I acquiesced wholeheartedly with the suggestion, and as I watched him march out of the office ahead of me, shook my head in near-disbelief. Two days ago he had walked into my office with yet another '*old gentleman's*' story and today I would be flying from one end of the country to the other with him, chasing a story which, if it could be confirmed, would turn the history books upside down.

I stopped in the outer office to pick up our tickets and reservation voucher from Freda who wished us a safe journey, and I mused that our arrival in Berchtesgaden would only be the beginning.

Indeed, our real journey would only be starting when we finally reached our destination.

CHAPTER 36

The drive to Berchtesgaden was uneventful and around mid-afternoon our hire car rounded the bend leading into the Zum Türken's car park. As the car turned, two men came into view, one wearing a World War Two SS officer's uniform, the other outfitted as, and looking the spitting image of Adolph Hitler. They glanced our way and as we entered the car park they took off, beating a hasty retreat across the meadow. As wearing of Nazi uniforms and parading as doppelganger of Hitler were generally met with hostile public disapproval, I sensed a news-worthy story and quickly parking the car, jumped out with the intention of interviewing them. But by the time I had done so, the two were already well on their way across the meadow heading for a line of trees in the distance. Hartmann exited the vehicle and joined me on the curb. He shook his head, staring at the dwindling figures with a distant look on his face.

"I remember this very incident from the past, Morgen. I believe we have just been witness to my younger self's visit to this carpark accompanying Hitler who was intent on determining the truth of Hartmann's report for himself … as was told in my story."

I stared at him flabbergasted, before returning to watch as the two distant figures finally reached the other side of the meadow and disappeared into the fringing forest.

We trudged up the path to the hotel entrance in silence, my mind wrestling with what we had just seen, and entering the lobby, made our way to reception where we found the desk clerk embroiled in conversation with an American tourist dressed in navy blue blazer, tan trousers and gaudy orange tie.

I turned to Hartmann shocked, and whispered my astonishment.

"My God Karl! He's the character straight out of your story."

Edging closer to eavesdrop on their conversation I was astonished to hear yet more corroboration of Hartmann's narrative.

"… But I'm telling ya, these guys down in the car park said they was going to some sort of masquerade shindig here at the Türken tonight. One of them was dressed as Adolph Hitler and his offsider was wearing a Schutzstaffel outfit. They sure as hell went to a lot of trouble with their uniforms, so there must be some kind of party somewhere on the mountain if it ain't gonna be here in the Türken."

The desk clerk smiled pleasantly in diplomatic response to the American's suggestion.

"I'm afraid there will be no such event held here at the Türken tonight or indeed any other night, and we certainly would discourage visitors from wearing attire that might upset the sensibilities of our other guests."

Hartmann drew my attention to the window behind the desk clerk, through which I could see a portly gentleman, sitting on a sofa reading a newspaper. He sported a large moustache and wore a white carnation in the lapel of his dark blue jacket. I shot a quick glance at Hartmann and saw he was grinning from ear to ear.

The man on the sofa looked up and seeing us waiting for attention, slapped his newspaper down on the table, arose with difficulty and ambled out to the counter where he looked from Hartmann to myself to determine who was in charge. I informed him of our booking and he turned to extract a key from a nest of pigeon holes on the wall whilst inviting us to enter our details in the hotel register on the desk.

Planting elbow on the desk, he dangled the key above the ledger while Hartmann signed in. Hartmann relieved him of the key and turning to me, his face lit up by excitement, jabbed the pen at the ledger to draw my attention to a signature higher up on the page. I inspected the entry he had indicated whilst signing myself in, and endeavouring to hide my own excitement, queried the manager.

"I see you have Herr Dietrich Kaiser staying with you. I'm impressed you have such important clientele staying in your hotel. Isn't he the leader of the new Homelands Political Party?"

The manager's face broke into a broad smile at my compliment and he looked down briefly to adjust the carnation in his lapel. Glancing left and right to ensure no one was within earshot, he leaned forward across the counter, answering in a confidential manner, his voice lowered to a whisper.

"Herr Kaiser likes to keep a low profile when he stays with us, and prefers I didn't bring his presence to the attention of our other guests. He is probably our best customer, visiting the Zum Türken with his wife every two weeks."

"I can understand people coming here that often Herr Wirth. The views you have of the mountains are spectacular. I'm sure he and his wife enjoy taking advantage of the hiking trails around these hills?"

"This is the strangest part of his visits, Frau Schreiber. The Kaisers are unusually punctual, arriving every second Friday, right on lunch time. But after a quick meal, Herr Kaiser leaves his wife in the hotel on each occasion and goes for a walk by himself precisely at two, returning to the hotel precisely at six. Every time, Frau Schreiber, every time, every two weeks. Such punctuality and such very strange behaviour. His wife on the other hand doesn't seem the outdoors type and invariably keeps to herself in their suite. She never goes for walks."

I agreed this was indeed odd behaviour and was about to join Hartmann standing behind me, impatiently waiting to go upstairs to discuss the bizarre circumstances we had experienced since arriving, when another feature of his story crossed my mind.

"Do you have internet facilities in your hotel?"

"Certainly, Frau Schreiber."

He pointed to the door on the right hand side of the staircase.

"We have an excellent internet café facility right over there. We have five machines and a printer should you require it, and tea and coffee facilities are available free for guests using the facility. Unfortunately, the café doesn't seem to get used quite as much as I thought it might when I first had it installed. But only a couple of days ago we had a young travel writer researching the Obersalzberg, and he made very extensive use of the facility. He actually used up over two reams of paper in copying out his research notes and left the waste paper baskets overflowing with his printing errors."

The manager stared distantly across the lobby to the hotel entrance as he recalled the travel writer's visit.

"Strange fellow. Oddly dressed in old-fashioned hiking gear. He didn't have any money on him, but instead paid for the use of the internet and his overnight stay by selling some gold coins to another patron. But the most peculiar thing about him was, for a travel writer, he didn't seem to have much of a handle on computers."

I glanced over my shoulder at Hartmann. His eyes were glistening and although he was trying to maintain a straight face, I could see he was hard at work suppressing outright laughter.

I turned to the manager.

"We might have use for your internet café later on, thanks, but after we've been shown our suite, I think we might go for a walk to enjoy the views of the mountains we admired on our way in from Berchtesgaden."

Once the porter had left our room, Hartmann couldn't contain his mirth any longer.

"Could a person ask for any better corroboration of one's story than that which the Türken's manager has just given us?"

"The deeper I go into this Karl, the harder it becomes to disbelieve any part of your tale, even though I hasten to add, it still seems totally preposterous. Come on, I must see this Zeitmaschine for myself and only then will I finally know once and for all if your story has been an ingenious fabrication accompanied by a string of the most highly improbable coincidences or, if this proves not to be the case, what you are about to show me is going to turn the scientific community on its head and force a re-write of the historical record."

We pocketed our torches and set out for the cave. As we crossed the meadow I marvelled that although this entire area had once been a main operations base for Hitler and his coterie of Nazi commanders, there remained not the slightest evidence of the barracks which had housed hundreds of Schutzstaffel officers and soldiers in 1944. Instead, small trees and bushes now hid what remained of crumbling foundations of buildings which had either been obliterated in bombing raids or had been demolished over the following decades.

At the far end of the meadow we followed a narrow, barely visible track between the trees, and on peering closely at the ground, I could just discern the impression of shoe prints in the soft earth, and the evidence of broken fern fronds confirmed its recent use.

If I had not had Hartmann guiding me, I might easily have walked right past the cave without being aware of it having been there. Its entrance was overgrown with foliage which, after raising a commanding hand to bring me to a halt, Hartmann swept aside, and on entering the cave, beckoned me follow. I could see by our torch light that everything was exactly as he had described, and any doubt about Hartmann's story which might have still lingered in my mind completely slipped away as Hartmann tugged at a rock causing the camouflaged door to swing open. Behind it, the entrance to the tunnel leading to the secret chamber was revealed in the sweep of our torches.

With growing excitement I followed Hartmann along the downward sloping passageway. We played our torches upon walls of brickwork which had, unlike the ruins above ground, remained undetected, undisturbed, and therefore able to testify to the skill of the tradesmen who had worked on this tunnel so many years ago. On the concrete floor we could make out multiple shoe prints in the dust, heading in both directions. We passed through the door at the end of the tunnel and were finally in the secret chamber.

But disappointment awaited me there.

Sweeping my torch back and forth, I could find nothing in the chamber to suggest a Zeitmaschine had once dominated the centre of the room. True, the chamber housed the two large support cradles central to Hartmann's story, but the absence of the Zeitmaschine itself rekindled a doubt which crept back into my mind. I wandered around the room picking out its contents by the light of my torch. Dusty electrical panels stood lifeless and silent against the wall and a pile of empty rusting steel boxes bearing the circular SS-Runen insignia of the Schutzstaffel lay near one of the cradles. The door opposite our entry point stood slightly ajar with sandbags piled to one side spilling out their contents, and a small petrol generator sat behind one of the cradles, its exhaust connected via a hose to a vent in the ceiling. All was exactly as Hartmann had described except for the missing Zeitmaschine.

Hartmann strode over to the generator, and turned to me smiling.

"This machine was something very new to me sixty years ago, but now I see it's simply a very ordinary modern portable generator that Kaiser has brought into the chamber to ensure the Zeitmaschine's batteries always remain fully charged."

He bent over to examine it.

"My God, this machine is warm! It must have been in use not so long ago."

He turned to me with a look of alarm.

"We must leave the chamber immediately. Follow me at once!"

I stared after Hartmann perplexed, as he rushed for the door.

"Come quickly! I will explain later, Morgen. We must get out here fast and please, as we exit, make sure the door is closed behind you exactly as we found it."

I did as instructed and hurried after Hartmann through the tunnel. He closed the camouflaged door carefully and we retraced our steps along the track until the trees started to thin out, at which point he stopped suddenly holding up his commanding hand.

"This is far enough. Now we must hide."

We left the track and took cover behind a nearby thicket. Dropping behind the bushes and bidding me do likewise he explained his concern.

"The generator was warm to my touch, and therefore must have been running a few hours earlier. Kaiser no doubt used it to recharge the Zeitmaschine's batteries before leaving for his regular visit to the future, a fact I should have realised from the Türken manager's commentary about his movements. Allowing for the time it takes to walk to and from the chamber, recharge the batteries and spend around three hours in the future gathering the information he uses to increase his wealth, would account for the time he is absent from the Türken.

"Interestingly, although the Zeitmaschine has the capacity to return him back to the chamber an instant after he previously left by pressing the green button, I believe the reason he doesn't avail himself of this facility lies in his desire to keep his day, as he experiences it, twenty four hours long. You see, if he spends three hours in the future and then returns just after he left, he would be adding an extra three hours to the length of his day, which he might find upsets his body clock. He obviously is avoiding this by resetting the duration dials and pressing the red button rather than simply using the green button to return."

Hartmann checked his watch.

"It's now past five thirty and just as well we left the chamber when we did as Kaiser will be returning any moment now. It would have been most unfortunate if he had discovered us in the chamber on his arrival."

I understood and nodded.

"What now?"

"If we wait here, we should be able to observe him on his way back to the Türken."

We waited in silence and after another five minutes our patience was rewarded as the swish of ferns underfoot heralded the approach of the person who emerged from the forest heading for the path across the meadow. He had dark black hair, a neatly trimmed beard and moustache, and was carrying a bulging satchel under one arm.

I glanced at Hartmann, and whispered my astonishment.

"It's Dietrich Kaiser. It's the man who featured in the newspaper article."

"Yes. And there before your very eyes you are also looking at none other than Adolph Hitler, Germany's wartime leader, who supposedly died some sixty years ago."

We watched from our hide as he passed by on the track, and as he disappeared from view, Hartmann rose and beckoning me to follow, struck out across the meadow. But just in case someone had been watching for Kaiser's return, he led me some distance away from the track before redirecting his steps back toward the hotel, presumably in order not to appear we had been following in Kaiser's footsteps.

The lobby was teeming with a confusion of tourists when we strolled in. Porters were trundling baggage to their rooms, and the young clerk at reception was attending to a large party of new arrivals whilst the manager engaged in discussion with their tour guide. Through the window wall between lobby and dining room I saw that Kaiser had joined a woman, whom I easily identified as Eva Braun, and three bulky strongmen at the bar.

Hartmann indicated he wanted to rest for a while after our walk and left for our room upstairs, but I waited until the manager finished conversing with the guide before venturing over to question him about Kaiser.

He was writing in the register and looked up as I approached.

"Ahh, Frau Schreiber. You have had a pleasant walk?"

"Yes, very pleasant, thank you. But tell me, on my way through the lobby just now I observed a man in the bar whom I believe to be Kaiser, am I correct?"

"Yes, I noticed his return from walking. He's very regular in his habits, you know. After he returns he always re-joins his party at the bar before seating himself for dinner."

"His party?"

"His wife, their chauffeur and two other large gentlemen."

He leaned forward across the counter and again lowering his voice to a whisper took me into his confidence with another snippet of gossip.

"I believe all three of those gentlemen are body guards, and wouldn't be at all surprised to find they had guns hidden on their persons."

He glanced across the lobby toward the dining room.

"We reserve the table with the best view of the Obersalzberg for Herr Kaiser and his wife because he is very generous in tipping the staff. But the other three usually remain at the bar a while longer drinking lager before joining the Kaisers at a nearby table."

I thanked him for sharing this information and asked, out of politeness, his recommendation for dinner before taking my leave.

On the way back to our suite, elements of Hartmann's story tumbled about in my mind. I was trying to make sense of it all, when all of a sudden I was struck by the historical absurdity of having just observed Adolph Hitler and his mistress, who had both died some sixty years previously, and who were now at this very moment sitting in the Türken's dining room preparing to have dinner.

Earlier, my sole purpose in coming to Berchtesgaden had been to view the Zeitmaschine in order to either confirm or quash Hartmann's story. But a realisation was taking hold in my mind that Hartmann and I had arrived here at the Türken at precisely this particular point in the course of human affairs not just destined to be passive onlookers, out for a scoop for my newspaper. I sensed we had somehow been cast as the main protagonists in a far more momentous set of circumstances than I could ever have previously imagined, and concluded that being here on this day to bear witness to Kaiser's visit was no mere coincidence. Destiny had brought us to the Zum Türken on the very same day Kaiser had visited, and destiny was now demanding we take an active part in thwarting his evil intent.

I recalled how messianic Hartmann had sounded in my office when he claimed his secret would be pivotal in changing the course of human history, but now my own thoughts were proving equally so. At last I could see how it could have been that Hartmann and I had indeed visited his younger self in 1944, and there was not a doubt in my mind that in some way we had been the principal players in returning Hitler to his rightful place in the historical narrative – as Hartmann's story had foretold.

It now seemed entirely obvious to me that we had been charged by fate with the mission of ensuring this monster did not succeed in his goal which, if given half a chance of success, would have once again seen the world plunged into darkness.

CHAPTER 37

Hartmann was reclining on his bed reading the newspaper when I entered the room, but he swung around to sit on the edge when he observed my agitated state of excitement.

"What has happened?"

I sank into the easy chair beside his bed.

"Karl, I think I know what must be done about this unbelievably improbable state of affairs in which we now find ourselves.

"Do you recall, on the day you accompanied Hitler to the chamber for your induction in 1944, how Fuchs explained the time paradox? He told you the past and present could exist side by side, and perhaps even overlap. Well, by that very same token, the Zeitmaschine allows us to visit ourselves in the past or the future. But the point I really want to get across, and scientist Fuchs knew this only too well, is that no matter how hard one might try to evade what history has shown will eventually happen, the past remains immutable and cannot be altered. You yourself have established this fact when you tried to persuade your younger self not to return to assist Hitler by confronting him outside the cave in 1959, and again earlier when your younger self tried to prevent Engel from being sent to Dukla Pass. In both cases, despite your best efforts to the contrary, you were unable to alter what history had already determined was to be the case.

"If an event has happened in the past, then it has happened for all time, and if we travel back in time with the intention of changing things in order to achieve a more desirable outcome in the present, we will only fail in our endeavour. There is nothing we can do in the past that will change an outcome whose consequences have already been observed in the present. For similar reasons, any attempt to evade a past occurrence that has already been recorded in the history books by escaping to the future, as Hitler tried to do, would also be futile and again, would only end in failure.

"However, and this is the really interesting and important thing Karl, if we know an event has taken place in the past, but there is no apparent reason why it should have happened at all, what then? Well, in such a case there would be nothing to stop a person from travelling back to the past in the Zeitmaschine, and doing whatever is required to ensure that that event actually *does*, or should I say, *did* take place."

Hartmann's perplexed face in response to my rambling alerted me to the fact that in my growing excitement, I was not explaining myself clearly enough to carry him with me.

"Don't you understand what I'm saying, Karl?"

He shook his head and stared at me with a puzzled frown.

"What I'm getting at is, in your story, the two of us visited young Hartmann to advise him of Hitler and Eva Braun's impending return in two days' time – and return they did, just as you related in your story."

Hartmann nodded, but his frown persisted.

"So, Morgen. What are you trying to say?"

"Well, this is an example of what I've been getting at, Karl. Those events didn't just happen by themselves – we, *you and I*, were involved, and I'm sure those events would not have happened if we hadn't made them happen."

At last I could see understanding lighting up his face and as the words tumbled out of my mouth, I felt an uneasy excitement at the prospect of tampering with the past to ensure the outcome recorded in the history books would eventually be realised.

"No one is ever going to believe our story about Hitler's escape from 1944 in a time machine, and until we've safely transferred him back to where he belongs, back into the annals of History, I believe we should keep the secret of the Zeitmaschine to ourselves.

"But without revealing all we know, we cannot expect that the police or any other authority would be willing to become involved in this matter. It is we, Karl, *you and I*, who must command the power of this machine to make sure the events which occurred in your story actually *do*, or rather, *did* take place.

"At last I have come to realise how your story could be entirely true when it came to the two of us travelling through time in the Zeitmaschine to visit your younger self in the secret chamber. I also believe we were the '*brigands*' responsible for returning Hitler to the chamber in 1944, two days after visiting your younger self, although at this point in time I am at a complete loss to see how we could possibly accomplish such a task."

I paused as Hartmann brought a hand to his forehead to focus his thoughts.

"I can see where your logic is leading us Morgen. But surely the execution of such a mission would involve a great number of risks in tampering with events of the past, not to mention posing some considerable difficulties for us in the present. For instance, how do we go about convincing Kaiser and his wife they should accompany us to the past in the Zeitmaschine? Surely they would realise that once transported back to 1944, they would be facing a very unwelcome future – the one described in the history books."

I frowned. It was a detail I hadn't yet been able to explore, and to which I therefore had no answer.

"A good question Karl and my immediate response is that I don't envisage our methods of persuasion would be entirely restricted to logical arguments. Somewhere along the line I foresee an element of coercion. But before we get too bogged down in details such as this, let us think this whole concept through very carefully. We must ensure there are no unintended consequences arising out of our activities, because meddling around with the past will undoubtedly be quite tricky, and could result in us creating bigger problems for ourselves in the present and the future if we are not careful.

"But I must say we have one very big factor indicating that whatever we do, we will be successful in actually shipping Hitler back to the past."

Hartmann raised an enquiring eyebrow.

"And that factor would be … ?"

"The obvious, Karl. *All these things have already happened.* Hitler was returned to his own time without any of his Nazi cronies becoming aware of his sojourn into the future, and he ended up committing suicide in the Berlin bunker. These are all indisputable historical facts. All we have to do is devise a plan that ensures Hitler's return to the past where he belongs, whilst still keeping within the parameters of what we know to be the historical record. As difficult as this may sound at first, our success in carrying out this mission is, as I've pointed out, absolutely guaranteed."

"This is incredible, Morgen. When I first approached you in your Die Welt offices, I had no purpose other than to fulfil the promise I made to you back in 1944. I was only driven by the fear that Hitler's presence in the present time would impact adversely on my children and their families. I hadn't considered for a moment the possibility of anyone actually returning Hitler back to 1944, let alone of myself becoming involved as one of the central protagonists in the affair. As you say, we will have to be very careful in tampering with the past, but we must also be mindful of avoiding trouble with the authorities in the present if it turns out we are compelled to use force in persuading him to board the Zeitmaschine."

Hartmann rose from the bed and paced around the room deep in thought, whilst I sat in my chair wrestling with a string of ideas, trying to mould them into a cohesive plan which would effectively deal with events we knew from the historical record had already occurred, in combination with steps Karl and I would have to take in the future in order to return Hitler to the past.

I looked up to see Hartmann had stopped pacing and was now staring at the wall, deep in thought. He returned to his seat on the bed, leaned forward facing me with a grin and gave the top of the bedside table a rap with his knuckle.

"If we're going to take action starting this very day, our first step should be to find out when Hitler no longer exists as Dietrich Kaiser in our present time. When we learn this we will know exactly when we'll be taking him back to 1944.

"We can gain this knowledge by time travelling to the future to find out when Kaiser has disappeared. Newspapers will be sure to carry headline articles about a person of his importance and standing suddenly vanishing without a trace, and knowing when he and his wife disappeared will indicate when we_took, or rather, *will be taking* action in this regard.

"Now, the manager of the Türken informs us Kaiser comes here with his entourage as regularly as clockwork every two weeks. He arrived today, Friday, and leaves tomorrow, Saturday morning. Two weeks from now he will be here again, and again in four weeks' time and so on, unless we take steps to stop his cycle of visits from recurring. It also makes sense that whatever action we take in this matter, it should be sooner rather than later. So I suggest we base our plans on taking Kaiser and his wife back to 1944 when he visits again in two weeks' time."

This all made good sense and I agreed with what he had proposed so far.

"Should we be successful in our endeavour, Morgen, and as you say, there is no doubt we will be, then as a consequence, by Sunday fortnight the Kaisers will have been missing for two days and the story of their disappearance will be well established in the press and the public arena, and no doubt a police manhunt might also be under way in an attempt to find them.

"In other words, if we visit the Türken in sixteen days' time, we will not only discover he and his wife have disappeared, but we can obtain confirmation of the fact from a number of different sources, including the Türken's gossiping manager who will, I'm sure, have a lot to say about the disappearance of one of his best customers. I suggest we start on our mission as soon as possible. In fact, why don't we start right away? What do you think, Morgen?"

I stared at Hartmann for a moment, impressed by his cool clear logic, before rising from my seat.

"I'm right with you, Karl. Let's not waste a second – Let's get started right away."

Hartmann jumped to his feet and headed for the door, and I followed after him confessing I had been very much looking forward to the possibility of travelling in the Zeitmaschine at least just once. So far only five people on this planet had journeyed through time, and I was looking forward to coming in as traveller number six.

He smiled indulgently at my enthusiasm.

"Travelling on a train is far more interesting, Morgen. There's always something to do – view the scenery through the window; talk to your fellow passengers; chat with the conductor; read the newspaper. When travelling in the Zeitmaschine, you enter; you sit down; you watch a meter needle spin around for a minute or two, and all the while there is nothing to see outside apart from either a fleeting blur of light or more likely, total darkness. You stand and you exit – it's not very interesting."

I shook my head at his blasé dismissal of this technological triumph as I followed him out of the room. On our way through the lobby we observed Dietrich Kaiser and his wife through the glass window wall enjoying pre-dinner drinks at their table while their three '*assistants*' sat drinking beer nearby.

We made our way to the cave and this time the Zeitmaschine was there, seated on its cradle exactly as he had described. As I hurried forward to look inside the cabin, Hartmann cautioned me.

"Hold on, Morgen. Before we travel through time we must always ask ourselves one vital question – 'will there be anything already sitting on this cradle when my machine is due to rematerialize on arrival at its temporal destination?'"

I stared at him blankly, not comprehending.

"This is why scientist Fuchs created the two cradle supports you see in this chamber. Both were fitted with wheels to allow their positions to be interchanged if it was felt that there was a possibility of the Zeitmaschine colliding with another version of itself."

When one stopped to think about it, the scenario he outlined seemed perfectly rational, even though my mind still recoiled at the notion of two identical Zeitmaschines colliding into each other, each of them being the only one of its kind ever made. I nodded my understanding and Hartmann proceeded to apply his logic to our present situation.

"In two weeks' time, after Kaiser has returned from his regular Friday trip to the future, he'll leave the Zeitmaschine sitting on its cradle. If we arrive two days later on the Sunday, our Zeitmaschine would crash into the one he has left parked there between visits. So, in order to avoid this unwelcome eventuality, we must now exchange cradles. Do you now understand the importance of pausing to consider the situation at the end of one's journey?"

I agreed and thanked my lucky stars I had him with me to ensure my very first voyage in the Zeitmaschine wasn't also destined to be my last.

I gave him a hand in exchanging cradle locations and in so doing was surprised at how easily the one loaded with the Zeitmaschine moved considering the weight it must have been carrying. Hartmann swung onto the command bench and commenced adjusting the controls, whilst I wandered around the machine inspecting it closely, hoping to gain some inkling as to its mode of operation. However, I was disappointed to find little of interest visible to the naked eye. Its outer shell was fashioned out of smooth polished panels of stainless steel, some of which were held in place by screwed fasteners which I surmised, would allow their removal for maintenance access to its inner workings. At the rear of the machine I found a recessed electrical port containing a plug which obviously would be a match for the socket on the generator supply cable Kaiser had left neatly coiled on the floor of the chamber.

Hartmann leaned out of the portal to advise the machine was ready and I hurried back. He waited until I had slid the access panel door shut behind me whereupon he raised the lid of the glass enclosure and depressed the red mushroom button inside. Despite Hartmann's observation regarding the monotony of time travel, I had nevertheless expected some sort of indication that the machine was actually performing its intended function, perhaps in the form of an accompanying soft humming noise or a slight vibration. But I could detect no change at all in the cabin's environment and of course, I had to remind myself, we were not actually travelling anywhere. Why indeed would this machine give any such clues to its change of state when it was only travelling through time? I peered through the access door's glass panel. The chamber outside was steeped in darkness without our torches to light it up, and with nothing out there to indicate the passing hours and days, the thought entered my head that perhaps the machine had malfunctioned and we were consequently sitting expectantly like crash dummies awaiting a momentous outcome which would never eventuate. Hartmann, observing my concern, pointed to the time speed meter in which the needle was rotating at a moderate speed around the dial, and laughed.

"There in that small dial is the only indication to advise us the Zeitmaschine is actually doing its job. Did I not tell you? Time travel is not very interesting."

I glanced again at the meter and noticed the needle's rotation was already slowing to a standstill, and after the green light alongside it showed it was safe to disembark, Hartmann invited me to open the access door and exit. On climbing out of the cabin and just as he had predicted, we were confronted by another version of our Zeitmaschine on the second cradle. I swept the chamber with my torch and found that, apart from the presence of the second machine, nothing else had changed. The dark, dusty electrical consoles against the wall, the pile of empty treasure boxes alongside the cradle, the steel doors to the tunnels, the sandbags, and the small generator behind the other Zeitmaschine were all still there, just as they had been when we boarded the machine fourteen days ago. We were walking past the second Zeitmaschine toward the North door when its access portal made a slight hissing sound as it slid open. I stood transfixed, rooted to the spot, and gaped in astonishment as a duplicate of myself peered out from the cabin's interior to address us.

"Please don't be alarmed. As you can see, I am a future version of yourself, and have some important information you are going to require if you are to successfully negotiate the situation ahead of you this evening."

Hartmann and I drew closer to the portal and to our added astonishment a duplicate of Hartmann came into view sitting at the Zeitmaschine's controls. I glanced at Hartmann looking for answers, but his face showed he too was just as mystified as myself at this surprising turn of events. My duplicate continued.

"You will not yet understand the import of what I have to tell you, but you must commit the following facts to your memory before you venture any further.

"Frau Kaiser received your note and joined you in the Türken's lobby. You asked her to accompany you outside onto the Türken's veranda where you talked for about five minutes until your conversation was interrupted by one of the Kaiser bodyguards coming out to check on her. She dismissed him after which she left you on the veranda to rendezvous with her husband in the car park. That was the last you saw of her and immediately after her departure you returned inside the hotel to join your friend at the bar.

"You may embroider the story with as much detail as you see fit, but these are the main elements you must be clear upon. I know you will remember what I have just been telling you because I was in your shoes not so long ago."

I was somewhat nonplussed but managed to show my understanding with an affirming nod. I had a host of questions to put to her, but my duplicate glanced at her watch and cut me short.

"I'm sorry, but we must fly. There's much work Hartmann and I have yet to deal with today. Good luck!"

So saying, she withdrew inside the cabin, shut the panel door and a moment later the air blurred around the second Zeitmaschine and it disappeared.

For a moment or two, Hartmann and I gawked at the vacant cradle, somewhat stunned by what had just occurred, before I managed to put voice to my astonishment.

"Well Karl that certainly was an intriguing encounter – I guess sometime in the future I am destined to become the duplicate who has just given us this advice, and hopefully by then I might understand what my message was all about. But right now we'd better press on to the Türken and see whether or not the Kaisers did in fact disappear two days ago. If this proves to be the case, it will confirm we succeeded, or maybe I should say, *will succeed* in transporting the Kaisers back to the past where they belong."

CHAPTER 38

The Zum Türken's lobby was a scene of absolute chaos on our arrival. TV cameramen were setting up equipment in preparation for the evening news; reporters were targeting individuals from the crowd of curious hotel patrons, hoping to find someone with newsworthy recollections; uniformed police were rolling out barrier tape, isolating areas of interest in the lounge and dining room, and to the right of the stairs, the internet café was crammed full of journalists sending emails or engaged in heated argument with one another over cups of coffee at the urn. I spotted a Die Welt journalist and cameraman in the throng and was pleased to see my newspaper was on the spot to report on the situation, which we had immediately presumed was all about the Kaisers.

"Ahh, Frau Schreiber, Herr Hartmann."

Herman Wirth had wended his way through the throng to greet us, mopping his forehead with a handkerchief.

"There has been much excitement and upset to the hotel's routine since you left us two days ago."

Two days ago? At first I didn't comprehend as, after all, we had just travelled fourteen days into the future, but I quickly realised how matters must have unfolded over the past few days. If Kaiser and his wife were indeed missing, Hartmann and I must have been here at the Türken two days ago to ensure their disappearance actually did take place. Wirth promptly obliged by confirming my thoughts on the matter.

"As you know gentlemen, Herr Kaiser and his wife are not only our most important guests but are major figures in the world of finance and politics, and consequently very much in the public eye these days. Their disappearance has set off an intensive police investigation and raised a storm of interest in the media. My hotel has been thrown into utter confusion over the last two days by these reporters and television crews sniffing around for a story, and the police have severely disrupted our ability to run the hotel in an orderly manner. Their detectives have been pestering our guests and staff in their hunt for leads in the Kaiser disappearance case, and they've taken copy of our guest register with the intention of interviewing all patrons who were here in the period a day prior to Kaiser's arrival to the day after he was due to leave. Now that the two of you are here I will introduce you to one of them so you can make your statements and be done with this unpleasant business."

Before we could persuade him otherwise, Wirth trundled off to announce our presence to the police and I watched apprehensively as he spoke to a balding, middle-aged man with a thin pencil moustache, who glanced at us suspiciously when Wirth pointed in our direction. He pocketed the notebook in which he had been making notes and made his way briskly through the crowd toward us. I glanced at Hartmann and noted that he looked as uncomfortable as I felt. It appeared we were about to experience one of those tricky unintended consequences of time travelling

I had cautioned him about earlier in the evening. The detective fished out his notebook on arrival and scanned our faces with a penetrating look which made me feel particularly vulnerable.

"Good evening. Otto Jaeger, detective leading the investigation into the Kaisers' disappearance. I believe I have the pleasure of addressing Frau Schreiber and Herr Hartmann?"

Jaeger looked us up and down with a thin diplomatic smile which was probably intended to put us at our ease, but in fact had the totally opposite effect.

"I understand you were both amongst the Türken's guests on the night Herr Kaiser and his wife disappeared?"

I immediately recognised this as the confrontation my future self had primed us for back in the chamber, and in so doing he had given me the information I would require to answer the detective's questions. For a moment I felt concern that Jaeger might ask me awkward questions that my duplicate hadn't thought to tell us about, but quickly dismissed this absurd notion, recalling that this interview had already taken place with my duplicate and there was of course no possible *other different question* she hadn't been aware of.

Jaeger was looking at me intently waiting for my response and I answered in the affirmative. He opened his notebook and read from notes made previously.

"The hotel porter informs me you asked him to deliver an envelope to Frau Kaiser in her suite. Shortly thereafter she was seen coming downstairs to meet you in the hotel lobby. One of Kaiser's bodyguards seated at table in the dining room saw you and Frau Kaiser going out together onto the veranda."

Jaeger fished a pen out of his pocket and scribbled something in the notebook.

"The bodyguard who came out on the veranda is also missing and his disappearance has been included in our overall investigation."

He looked me up and down again, suspicion clearly written across his face.

"Exactly what happened after you and Frau Kaiser went out onto the veranda?"

The facts as presented in the chamber by my future self now seemed rather bare under the circumstances, so I added a little context to make our movements that evening appear more credible.

"You are no doubt aware from the hotel register that I work for Die Welt newspaper. My colleague and I came to the Türken to arrange a meeting with Herr Kaiser and his wife for a feature article we intended presenting to our readership, and the note I sent up to the Kaisers' suite was a request for an interview. Unfortunately, Herr Kaiser wasn't available at that moment, but his wife was gracious enough to grant me a few minutes of her time. As it was a pleasant evening, I suggested we talk outside on the veranda, offering as it did a little more privacy."

I paused, wondering how much the detective needed to know. Jaeger looked up from his note-taking.

"Yes, please go on."

Again recalling my duplicate's earlier advice, I continued to elaborate on a conversation I presumably would be having with Frau Kaiser two days ago and about which I had no knowledge whatsoever apart from the scant details my duplicate self had provided.

"We had been talking outside for about five minutes when one of Frau Kaiser's bodyguards came out onto the veranda to check she was not overly inconvenienced by my questions. She allayed his concerns and sent him back inside."

"And then what happened?"

"Nothing to speak of. Frau Kaiser expressed concern that her husband was late in returning from his walk and intended going down to the carpark to meet him. I offered to accompany her, but she declined and left. There was no point in my remaining outside, so I went back inside the hotel to join my colleague at the bar. I'm afraid that was the last I saw of Frau Kaiser, and there's no further information I could offer which might assist in explaining her disappearance."

Jaeger finished writing and pocketed his notebook.

"I will be questioning other staff about this affair and they will no doubt be able to corroborate your statement?"

I nodded.

He searched my face with another of his penetrating glances, his countenance continuing to betray an uncomfortably suspicious bent.

"That will be all for the moment, Frau Schreiber. We have your addresses from the register and if necessary, may be asking you to assist with our enquiries at a later stage".

He stroked his chin and cast an eye around the crowded lobby.

"This has been a most puzzling affair. Our police search and rescue teams will be sweeping the locality around the Zum Türken over the next few days, looking for clues – people just don't vanish like this."

'*How wrong he was*', I thought, as this was exactly the outcome we were aiming to achieve.

Jaeger looked from me to Hartmann and concluded the interview with a curt, "Thank you for your cooperation", and turning on his heel, left us to interview another guest he had singled out across the lobby.

Herman Wirth noticed his departure and ambled over.

"A terrible affair. A terrible affair. Kaiser was one of our most valued guests and his disappearance is a great loss for the hotel. I fear this incident is bound to have quite a damaging impact on the Zum Türken's reputation."

I made an effort to console him by pointing out that any exposure in the media, whether good or bad, was usually good for business.

"You will probably have a host of customers in the foreseeable future looking to satisfy their curiosity about the missing billionaire and his lady."

"Yes, perhaps you are right. After all, the hotel is already fully booked out for the next few days … which reminds me, I must apologise, but with all these news people and detectives staying here we are unable to offer you accommodation tonight. Perhaps you can find a place to stay in Berchtesgaden?"

Hartmann and I returned to the Zeitmaschine and travelled back to the moment immediately after our departure sixteen days ago with a press of the green mushroom button. I was eager to return to the hotel to plan our next move and started toward the chamber door when Hartmann brought me to a halt.

"Aren't you forgetting something, Morgen?"

I looked back at him, not comprehending.

"Morgen, what is going to happen when Kaiser returns to this chamber in two weeks' time to find his Zeitmaschine has miraculously migrated from one cradle to the other all by itself?"

I slapped my forehead for not having thought of this for myself.

"Of course – we need to swap cradles back to their original locations."

Hartmann nodded.

"We have to be extremely careful in everything we do from now on to ensure Kaiser doesn't suspect for a moment that someone else is using his machine … and we certainly don't want any more awkward situations like the one we have just experienced with Detective Jaeger. I'll now reset the duration dials to Kaiser's last input configuration, we'll swap the two cradle around and he'll never be any the wiser regarding our use of his machine."

CHAPTER 39

In the evening, we discussed our findings over dinner.

"Not only have we confirmed the Kaisers disappeared during their visit to the Zum Türken next Friday fortnight, but we also know whilst I was accompanying Frau Kaiser onto the veranda, Kaiser was presumably visiting the future in the Zeitmaschine. We also know that while the Kaisers and I were outside the hotel, their bodyguards were inside drinking in the dining room and you, if my future duplicate's information was correct, were having a drink at the bar. This would then have been the most opportune time for me to corral Kaiser and his wife into the Zeitmaschine without interference from hotel staff or their bodyguards. But the conundrum that now bedevils us is, if I returned inside to join you at the bar, how did we get outside again without arousing suspicion, to make the most of this golden opportunity?

"Another important question we need to answer is what could possibly have been in the note I sent up to Frau Kaiser's room inducing her to come downstairs to meet me? From my experience in journalism, public figures, especially the rich and famous, are pretty difficult to access and rarely consent to interviews with strangers who manage to bypass their security net. If we could just work out how we overcame these hurdles, I think we might be well on the way to working out an effective plan to return Kaiser to 1944."

Hartmann set down his stein and shook his head.

"You've got me there Morgen. How you, a total stranger, could have convinced Frau Kaiser to accompany you to an unknown destination in the middle of the night is beyond me. You must have written something pretty damn compelling to even get her out of her room."

We both brooded over the problem for a few minutes until, in a moment of clarity the obvious answer came to me in a flash. I thumped the table.

"Of course!"

Hartmann cast a quick nervous glance around the dining room, anxious that my enthusiasm might have aroused the attention of other diners, but seeing at this late hour we were the only ones still at table, he relaxed and leaned forward expectantly.

"You have guessed what was in the envelope?"

"Yes indeed. I'm certain of it. Think in terms of blackmail, Karl. What's the last thing the Kaisers would want the public to know?"

Hartmann nodded sagely at the thought.

"Yes, you're right. Just a hint of their past at this point in time would be enough to destroy his political future. What do you propose putting in the envelope?"

"I can't think of anything better than exactly what you handed me after finishing your story in my office – photos of Hitler and Eva accompanied by the news article and a brief note of my own informing her I would be waiting downstairs in the lobby. Then when she comes down, it shouldn't be too difficult to convince Frau Kaiser that it would be in her best interest to accompany me to the chamber to participate in the deal I make with her husband. Somewhere along the way, we will join up with you, and the three of us will go on to the chamber to await Kaiser's return from the future."

"That all sounds very well, Morgen, but haven't you forgotten what your future self told you to say to Detective Jaeger? After Frau Kaiser left you on the veranda, you returned inside to join me at the bar. Whatever would possess her to hang around outside alone in the dark waiting for you to return, while you're inside with me enjoying drinks at the bar?"

"Good point Karl. Perhaps we can find an answer to the riddle by using the Zeitmaschine. We just need to work out how."

"And when Kaiser returns to the chamber after his visit to the future? You don't think he's just going to accept being bundled back into the Zeitmaschine and returned to 1944 without putting up a fight?"

"Yes, I know, Karl. As I pointed out previously, a little old fashioned coercion is sure to be involved. You know him better than I. Perhaps you can suggest some way of ensuring his compliance?"

Hartmann sat back in his chair and staring down at the tablecloth, stroked his chin.

"Well, I do know of a certain shady character in Berchtesgaden who collects Second World War militaria. I should be able to persuade him to lend me a pistol for a day or two. Would that do the trick?"

"Very nicely indeed."

I looked at my watch.

"It's getting a little late now. Why don't we get a good night's sleep and organise our next move in the morning?"

Hartmann frowned.

"Morgen, the Kaisers will be leaving in the morning. Shouldn't we be working on our plan right now while we have the chance and while they're still here in the hotel?"

"There's no need to rush Karl. We could take a week, a month or a year to work out a plan, but it wouldn't make any difference to the outcome. All we need to do when we are finally ready to take action is to time travel to next Friday fortnight from *whenever* we happen to be at that particular moment in time, and then execute our plan. It's as simple as that. However, I think we're already pretty close to having worked out all the necessary details. When we finally feel comfortable with what we've come up with, we'll time travel forward to put our plan into effect."

"I'm happy to hear you wanting to call it a day Morgen. I'm pretty well done in and that's hardly surprising considering since leaving your office early this morning we've been chasing after this story for over sixteen hours – not to mention a further three hours spent in the future Türken being interviewed by that detective. After all we've been through today I could do with a little rest."

"Agreed, Karl. We'll get a bit of shut-eye now and tomorrow, we'll finalise our plan."

CHAPTER 40

As we ate breakfast the next morning, I couldn't rid myself of a troubling feeling that had caused me a night of restless and broken sleep – I couldn't shake the lingering thought we had somehow missed something important. I glanced across the table at Hartmann who was absent-mindedly tumbling food around his plate with his fork.

"The questions Detective Jaeger was asking in the Türken lobby next Sunday fortnight and his overly-suspicious attitude toward us have been playing on my mind. I have the feeling we've slipped up somewhere along the way, but I just can't seem to nail what we might have done wrong."

Hartmann looked up from his plate.

"I feel it too, Morgen. We seem to have become embroiled in a very complex and disturbing affair."

We continued our breakfast in silence, each of us sifting through yesterday's experience in the future Türken until, with a shiver, I realised what was bothering me.

"Karl, in two weeks' time I arranged with the Türken's porter to take my note up to Frau Kaiser. I was seen with her in the lobby and on the veranda by her bodyguard. I told Detective Jaeger I returned to the lobby after Frau Kaiser left the veranda, but I only claimed this based on my duplicate self's information. At this point in time I have no proof that I did actually go back inside, and even if I did, were there any witnesses to corroborate my story? I have no idea what I was supposed to have done inside the lobby or the bar because I haven't done it yet, and for all I know, I might have returned to our suite upstairs without anyone even noticing I had come in from the veranda.

"Put all of that together and one might easily conclude that, as the last person to have been seen with Frau Kaiser before she disappeared, our friend Detective Jaeger will be considering me as number one suspect in her disappearance. No wonder he was looking at me so suspiciously. We also don't know if there were there any witnesses to confirm your presence at the bar and if there weren't, then due to our association, the investigation will no doubt be looking on you as being complicit as well."

Hartmann laid down his fork and looked at me in dismay.

"This is intolerable Morgen. We've landed ourselves right in the middle of this mess by becoming involved with that damned detective. It's all Manager Wirth's fault – insisting on introducing us. We can't leave this situation for fate alone to resolve, and we'll have to come up with some sort of fix to ensure we're not on his list of suspects, because if we don't, we could end up in serious trouble with the police. What do you think we can do to raise ourselves above suspicion?"

"Well, one thing's for sure, Karl. We know Kaiser and his wife will disappear in two weeks' time, so we can deduce that we somehow succeeded in carrying out our plan. The question now is, how can we use the Zeitmaschine to arrange things on the evening they disappeared in order to end up with a rock solid alibi that guarantees our removal from Jaeger's list of suspects?"

I gazed into space, racking my brain for answers whilst Hartmann returned to poking at the food on his plate, deep in thought.

He set down his fork again and looked up at me grinning.

"If we want to know how we'll be accomplishing this, why don't we just take a look and see?"

"What do you mean? Be serious Karl."

"The Zeitmaschine, Morgen. We can travel forward to the time when you came out onto the veranda with Frau Kaiser, and watch from a respectable distance to see how you handled – that is to say – *will handle* the situation."

I stared at Hartmann.

"Spying on our future selves. What a strange and interesting concept, Karl … and what an excellent idea."

We quickly finished our breakfast and hurried off to the chamber. Hartmann set the dials to take us to ten o'clock in the morning on Friday fortnight to allow us to witness the sequence of events that would unfold that day. Kaiser and his party would arrive at noon for lunch at the Türken. Then two hours later he'd be making his way to the chamber for his fortnightly excursion to the future in the Zeitmaschine in which we had just arrived, and finally there would be a three hour wait before Frau Kaiser made her appearance on the veranda with my duplicate.

Close to the Türken's veranda we settled behind a copse of bushes that gave excellent cover whilst still providing a commanding view of the events to be played out on and around the veranda.

Around noon, in keeping with their regular schedule, Kaiser's entourage emerged from the path to the carpark and disappeared into the hotel. Two hours later, Kaiser reappeared on the veranda carrying a slim satchel under his arm, and hurried away down the path across the meadow. We now settled in for the three hour wait before Frau Kaiser and my duplicate were due to appear on the veranda. It was nearing five o'clock when a voice coming from directly behind made us jump to our feet in alarm.

"Good evening."

Whirling around to confront the owner of the voice, I was astonished to find we were once again being addressed by duplicate versions of ourselves grinning broadly. They looked at each other and laughed.

"Please do not be disturbed by our presence here. We have come from the future to assist you, and together we'll resolve the difficult situation in which you presently find yourselves. But first of all, I must point out that you have unwittingly fallen into another of time travelling's many traps."

I glanced at Hartmann. He looked back and shrugged, obviously equally puzzled and unaware of any such glitch. My duplicate smiled at our surprise.

"You planned to return Hitler and his mistress to 1944 this evening, is that not so?"

I agreed, nodding.

"Well, would this not entail future versions of yourselves taking them back to 1944 in the very same Zeitmaschine you left in the chamber earlier today and which Kaiser is presently using?"

I was still puzzled and yet to understand the nature of the problem. My duplicate put an end to our bewilderment.

"After you witness your future selves returning to the chamber to take the Kaisers back to 1944 in that machine, how are the two of you going to return to your own time two weeks ago without a Zeitmaschine at your disposal?"

I was stunned. Why hadn't we thought of this simple fact for ourselves?

"Fortunately, your future self – not I, but the one you and I will become at the end of this sequence of events – has devised a way out of this mess, and this is our purpose in coming back here to assist you in remedying the situation. What I'm about to put to you is rather complicated so please listen carefully. Then when we are done you will no longer need be concerned about Detective Jaeger's suspicions.

"After my companion and I have left this spot, you are both to return to the chamber. There you will be met by future duplicates of yourselves. Don't be concerned by anything you see there because it will all be sorted out further down the track. Your future selves will be waiting in the Zeitmaschine, ready to ferry you back to the past by two hours. After they do this, you will return to this very same location, where you'll see your earlier selves seated behind these bushes waiting for Frau Kaiser to appear, because at that moment in time you will have become us – the Hartmann and Schreiber you presently see standing before you. You will address your earlier selves who'll be standing where you are presently standing and you will communicate to them all I have imparted to you.

"Even though the situation I am presently experiencing is yet to be experienced by you in your future, it is now becoming a part of my past, and because what has already happened in the past is immutable, you are henceforth committed to performing this entire episode again, but necessarily from our point of view."

She paused to ensure we were following. My head was spinning but I managed to acknowledge I understood everything she had said so far.

"Good. Now, before another duplicate Schreiber appears on the Türken's veranda with Frau Kaiser, my companion Hartmann will leave us, enter the Türken, and order a drink at the bar. After a while he will be joined by me and we'll strike up conversations with the bar staff, and endeavour to be as conspicuous as possible. Later, during dinner we'll take every opportunity to engage the waiters in conversation and after dinner we'll read newspapers in the lobby in full sight of the hotel staff and guests before retiring upstairs. All of these interactions will convince Detective Jaeger, when he later interrogates staff, that neither of us was outside when Frau Kaiser disappeared – and there you have the alibi we've all been seeking."

She glanced at her watch, turned to duplicate Hartmann and indicating the Türken's veranda with a jerk of her thumb, advised it was time to go. Duplicate Hartmann left the cover of the bushes and strode up to the veranda. After watching him disappear inside the hotel, my duplicate turned to us.

"In a few minutes another duplicate Schreiber will appear on the veranda with Frau Kaiser. As you'll recall from what you've been previously told, they'll chat for about five minutes before her bodyguard ventures onto the veranda to check on her. After she sends him inside, our duplicate will accompany Frau Kaiser to the chamber at which stage I'll leave this hide and take her place inside the hotel. As I pass the dining room I'll inform the bodyguard who came outside that Frau Kaiser decided to go down to the carpark to wait for her husband. I'll then join my companion Hartmann at the bar, and do all those things previously described, before we retire for the night. Tomorrow after breakfast, Karl and I will return to the chamber where we'll await the return of the Zeitmaschine. Our future selves will then transport us back in time to the Zeitmaschine in which you arrived at ten o'clock this morning, and we'll travel back in that machine to the moment after you left to come here this morning."

My head was still in a spin with the complexity of it all but I nevertheless fully appreciated what was required of us. My duplicate abruptly hushed us with a finger to her lips and with a frown of concentration, fixed her gaze on the veranda where a third Schreiber had just emerged from the hotel, accompanying Frau Kaiser. The pair on the veranda engaged in conversation for about five minutes until joined by Kaiser's bodyguard who had come out to check on her. There followed a brief exchange between Frau Kaiser and the bodyguard before she dismissed him and he returned inside to re-join his comrades. On his departure, our duplicate and Frau Kaiser stepped off the veranda to make their way across the meadow.

My duplicate turned to us.

"It's time for me to go, and for both of you to return to the chamber. Go now."

So saying, she darted across the short stretch of turf to the veranda and disappeared inside, presumably taking up her next role in this merry-go-round of events which we hoped, would create the alibi we were seeking.

On our way back to the cave I glanced behind and saw that Kaiser's body guard had reappeared on the veranda. He was looking our way, and just before the trees hid the hotel from view I saw him step off, heading in our direction. However, he was far off in the distance and I was confident of gaining the shelter of the cave before he would even reach the woods.

On arrival at the cave, we found the camouflaged door open. I deliberated over this, wondering whether we should close it behind us, but on reflection I figured after travelling back two hours in time, we too would be sending our earlier duplicates to the cave and they would need to open the door if we closed it now. This being the case, and having found the door open ourselves, we left it as we found it.

In the chamber we were greeted by duplicates of myself and Hartmann, his face masked by a black balaclava. The Zeitmaschine stood on its cradle and Frau Kaiser, who had been cowering against the electrical cabinets, stared at us as we entered before burying her face in her hands to weep. I asked my duplicate what was wrong with her, at which she shrugged.

"She's just a bit frightened, but it's nothing for you to be concerned about."

My attention was attracted to the Zeitmaschine where another of my duplicates was leaning out of the cabin, waving his hand, beckoning us.

"Hurry! There's no time to waste with explanations. Kaiser will be arriving shortly and we must be gone before he arrives. We are now returning you by two hours to the past, where you will find your earlier duplicates hiding near the hotel's veranda. You will send them back to this chamber, and on entering the Türken will do all those things described to you earlier. I know you've probably got a host of questions you'd like answered, but please believe that to give you some idea of what is to come would not be in the least enlightening, and would only add to your confusion. Be content that if you act as instructed all will be fine and your alibis in the Kaiser Disappearance case will be successfully established."

Our duplicates dropped us off in the chamber two hours back in time and seconds later their machine disappeared in a blur. Close to the hotel, we came upon our earlier selves seated behind the bushes, intently watching the Türken's veranda. Coming up behind them, I winked at Hartmann before addressing their backs.

"Good evening."

The two seated figures whirled around and jumped to their feet. I turned to Hartmann and together we laughed at the comical situation in which we had been the other two participants only two hours ago.

After explaining what was required of them, I turned to Hartmann and jerked a thumb in the direction of the Türken.

"It's time for you to go."

Hartmann nodded and strode off to the Türken's veranda.

Soon after, in keeping with what had occurred previously, another duplicate of myself accompanied Frau Kaiser onto the veranda. They conversed for five minutes until interrupted by her bodyguard. Frau Kaiser sent him back inside and after a hurried conversation, she accompanied my duplicate, leaving the veranda and making their way to the cave.

I turned to our earlier selves grinning.

"It's time for me to go, and for both of you to return to the Zeitmaschine. Go now."

I darted across the short stretch of turf to the veranda and in the Türken's lobby, sought out the three body guards seated at table having dinner. Singling out the man who had appeared on the veranda a few minutes ago, I bent low beside him.

"Frau Kaiser asked me to inform you she's gone down to the car park to wait for her husband."

The bodyguard laid down his knife and fork and after eyeing me suspiciously, his displeasure quite evident, he turned to snarl at his two companions.

"She shouldn't have done that without telling us first. I'd better chase after her before the boss finds we've let her go walking around alone in the night."

He scowled at me as I backed away from his chair, and wiping his face with a serviette, jerked it aside and rose from the table. I retreated to the bar to join Hartmann whilst out of the corner of my eye, I watched the bodyguard lumbering out of the room toward the veranda in what I anticipated would be a futile attempt to catch up with Frau Kaiser.

"So far so good, Karl. Everything appears to be going according to plan."

We relaxed with our drinks, making a point of engaging the bartender in lengthy conversation at every possible opportunity. Hartmann kept an eye on the two bodyguards still at table, and after finishing our drinks, we took up nearby seating in the dining room to observe what they might do when their companion returned after his failed attempt to find Frau Kaiser.

During dinner, Hartmann and I mulled over our experiences and the inherent complexities of time travel, and I asked whether in all those years since the War he had ever thought of revisiting the secret chamber.

"Yes. I did visit it several times at the very outset, but there was never any indication the Zeitmaschine might have returned during my absence. Hitler had taken it into the distant future and I didn't think I would ever see the damned thing again. I replaced the rocks at the mouth of the cave each time I visited to preserve its secret. But with the passing years, I had more or less lost interest in the whole affair until one day in 1999 I suddenly realised Hitler must have arrived in the present time according to his plan. With rekindled interest in following up the saga, I eventually spied a photo of Kaiser in your newspaper, and knew him to be the man I had assisted in escaping from 1944."

During dinner we engaged the waiter in a lengthy discussion about the weather, enquiring about the suitability of the following day for hiking, and after our meal, rewarded him with a very generous tip he was sure to remember when interviewed by the detective two days later. We were just taking our seats in the lounge to read newspapers when the two body guards passed us on their way outside to search for their companion, mystified by the fact that neither he nor the Kaisers had returned.

I turned to Hartmann and winked. He responded with a suppressed laugh, and I grinned back at him, imagining the three bodyguards searching around in the darkness for their lost mistress, their anxiety soon to be compounded by Kaiser himself failing to appear.

We chatted with some of the other guests for good measure as we read our newspapers before finally calling it a day and retiring to our suite.

I slept soundly and in the morning after breakfast, we gathered our things together and finalised the hotel account. As we passed through the lobby on our way to the chamber, we observed the two Kaiser bodyguards from the previous evening arguing with one another near the staircase, and with some amusement guessed at their topic of conversation.

Both cradles were empty when we entered the chamber and taking a seat on the sandbags, I waited patiently according to instructions for the arrival of the Zeitmaschine. Neither of us felt particularly conversational, but I guessed Hartmann's mind was as busy as my own, trying to comprehend what our duplicate selves might be doing at every stage of this undertaking, and tried to visualise where and when they were at this moment. A few hours later the air blurred over the cradles, and the Zeitmaschine materialised with our duplicate selves inside beaming at us as we drew near. The access door slid open and my future self invited us inside.

A short time journey brought us to a temporal halt alongside the machine we had left in the chamber at ten o'clock yesterday, whereupon we and our duplicate hosts exchanged best wishes for the future – a curiously ironic expression at which we all laughed – after which we alighted from their Zeitmaschine and clambered into our own. As Hartmann lifted the glass cover above the green button, I peered through the panel and gave our duplicates in the other machine a parting wave. They smiled and waved in return. There was a blur where their machine had been, and then they and their Zeitmaschine were gone, leaving us once again the sole occupants of the chamber. I turned to Hartmann.

"We now have the perfect alibi Karl, and I believe we have also learned all we need to know about the future. On our return to the Türken we'll finalise our plan on the basis of what we have learnt in the last twenty four hours."

Hartmann nodded and pressed the green button.

CHAPTER 41

I was looking forward to a hearty lunch, not having eaten since breakfast many hours ago in two weeks' time. The waiter who had brought us breakfast before we set out on our trip to the future looked up from the table he was clearing and hurried over.

"Yes, can I help you?"

He stared at us in consternation when I requested the lunch menu.

"But Frau Schreiber has only just finished breakfast less than an hour ago, and chef has not yet begun to prepare the food platters for lunch."

His response caught me by surprise. I looked at my watch which read a few minutes after three and snatched a quick glance at the clock above the door to the kitchen. It read five past nine. I cast an eye around the room where a scattering of hotel guests still lingered at table, chatting or reading newspapers over the remnants of their breakfast, and immediately recognised another of time-travelling's unexpected anomalies. During our travels, our watches had all the while been faithfully registering the passage of time whilst we sojourned in the future and went about our business. These faithful little timepieces, unaffected by our temporal adventures, just kept ticking away the hours and minutes regardless of whether they were spent in the past, present or future. In fact, the hour hand on my watch had made two and a half circuits around the dial since we finished our breakfast in this room less than an hour ago. I made a mental note to inspect our watches more frequently and adjust them accordingly after each voyage we made in the Zeitmaschine, before responding to the waiter whose face was beginning to cloud with concern. I endeavoured to make sense of our request.

"This mountain air certainly gives one an appetite, hey? Perhaps a platter of butterbrot, cold sausage and cheese if it is not too much trouble for the chef?"

The waiter retreated to the kitchen shaking his head as we settled in at the table.

"Unintended consequences and the quirks of time travel, Karl. We certainly don't want a repeat of what we've just been through in creating our alibi, and now find we also have to adjust our watches every time we travel in the Zeitmaschine. We really need to think more carefully about the problems we might encounter before we go time travelling."

"That's for sure Morgen – every time we get into that machine, it just seems to land us in a totally new and unexpected predicament."

"Perhaps we've been rushing things unnecessarily, Karl. After all, we always have all the time in the world to get things right before we travel – as I pointed out previously, no matter how long it takes and no matter *whenever* we happen to be, we can always navigate the Zeitmaschine back to next fortnight."

That afternoon we consolidated our ideas into a cohesive plan and agreed that what we had formulated left nothing to chance. The next morning, while Hartmann drove down to Berchtesgaden to obtain a pistol from his 'associate', I took to the internet café to type out the note intended for Frau Kaiser. In keeping with the manager's forlorn observation regarding the café's infrequent use, I found the facility bereft of patrons and took the opportunity to reproduce, unobserved, copies of Hartmann's photos and newspaper article. I slipped them into an envelope, and followed this by typing out the following Word document at one of the computer stations:

> *'I know the secret of the Zeitmaschine and know who you are. Please refer to the enclosed photos as evidence. This information is also held in the hands of a third party for my personal protection. If you wish to avoid disclosure of your secret to the media, you will come down to the lobby where I shall introduce myself in order that we may discuss this matter further.'*

I printed out two copies, sealed one of them in the envelope with the photos and news clipping, and pocketed the second copy to show Hartmann.

It was well after six o'clock when he returned from Berchtesgaden. I folded the newspaper I was reading as he entered our suite, and looked on with mild amusement as he cast furtive glances up and down the corridor outside our room before entering and locking the door behind him. His eyes swept our suite in an unnecessary, but obviously comforting act to reassure himself we were indeed alone, after which he strolled over to where I was waiting patiently for an update.

"Well?"

"Not a problem. My associate was only too happy to be of assistance when I enquired about his illegal possession of military grade firearms."

Hartmann reached into his inner vest pocket and withdrew an object wrapped in a faded oil-stained tea towel, which he proffered for my inspection. He watched intently as I unwrapped the folds of cloth to reveal the gun he had borrowed.

"It's a Luger P08 pistol, standard issue, as used by the Waffen SS during the Second World War. I had one in my holster when you visited me in the chamber sixty years ago."

I looked down at the gun cradled in the palm of my hand, and then up at Hartmann.

"Is it loaded?"

He nodded.

"The safety catch is on but all the same, please handle it with care."

"Ok, but I certainly hope we don't have to use it. There's nothing in the historical record to suggest Hitler turned up in the Berghof one day sporting unexplained bullet holes in his torso."

I re-wrapped the Luger, handed it back to Hartmann and looked on as it disappeared into his vest pocket. He reached into his trouser pocket and pulled out a small wad of black cloth which he threw onto the bed.

"I also borrowed that off him."

"What is it?"

"A balaclava.

"I'm much older now than the young Obersturmführer whom Hitler knew so well, but all the same I think it would be prudent to take precautions. The idea of using a balaclava came to me when I saw my duplicate in the chamber wearing one. By hiding my face in the presence of the Kaisers, I can prevent them from noticing similarities between myself and the young Hartmann they left behind in 1944. It would put my earlier self's life in great danger if on his return to the past, Hitler saw the resemblance between me and his aide, and putting two and two together, decided to foil our plan by murdering young Hartmann, calculating that in doing so, he would be eliminating me from his future."

It was a detail that hadn't entered my head and I complimented Hartmann on his foresight. I picked up the copy of message intended for Frau Kaiser, and handed it to him for endorsement.

He read it and looked at me dubiously.

"Do you think it's going to work?"

"Of course it's going to work, Karl. Heavens man! You've seen the evidence of its effectiveness for yourself when we visited the Türken next fortnight. Didn't you see Frau Kaiser coming out onto the veranda with me?"

Hartmann nodded and handed back the note.

"Yes, that's true. I guess I didn't give it sufficient thought."

He stared abstractly through the window.

"You know Morgen, everyone out there in the world at large is saddled, and has to deal with the consequences of what they have done in their past, but in our case, we find ourselves committed to doing things in the present because of what we know has happened in the future. It's all very strange and confronting."

I thought about it for a moment, captivated by the notion.

"It is indeed, Karl. But hopefully we will soon be done with our foray into the future and after we've delivered Hitler back to 1944, everything will finally settle down to become a thing of the past."

CHAPTER 42

The next morning we relaxed over breakfast, having finally come to the realisation that, using the Zeitmaschine's capabilities, we could be *whenever* we wanted to be by adjusting the duration dials, and after our meal, we booked a suite for Friday fortnight to cover our stay in the future.

Whilst Hartmann went to work setting the time duration dials I checked the battery charge meter behind me and marvelled that, despite all the travelling it had done for both Kaiser and ourselves, the needle had moved very little, if at all, from the fully-charged position. Of course, we had Kaiser to thank for that. No doubt he had been exercising extreme caution in his approach to time travel and recharged the batteries at every opportunity, because the one thing on which scientist Fuchs hadn't been able to assure the Führer was the possible consequence should the Zeitmaschine run out of power in *'mid-flight'*. Simply stopping at a point somewhere between commencement and completion of a journey wasn't the only possible outcome. The machine and its occupants could very well become trapped in an indeterminate state, never to reach any point in time at all.

Hartmann set the controls to deliver us to twelve noon next Friday fortnight, one hour before Kaiser's party would be arriving at the Türken and two hours after we had set ourselves up in the bushes near the Türken's veranda. But with all the comings and goings of the Zeitmaschine on this day, I was feeling a little apprehensive and asked whether there was any possibility our machine might collide with another version of itself on arrival. Hartmann had already considered the circumstances at our intended destination and shook his head.

"It's true that on our previous visit we parked our machine in next fortnight's chamber at ten o'clock in the morning, two hours before we will now be arriving, but as you'll recall, our future selves returned us to the machine and we returned it to the past, so the cradle will be empty when we arrive at twelve."

His hand came down on the red button.

As we signed in at the Zum Türken's reception desk for the suite we had booked two weeks ago that morning, Herman Wirth sitting in his office looked up from his newspaper and seeing us at the desk, shuffled out to greet us.

"Ahh! Frau Schreiber, you and your friend have returned after such a short time to enjoy a little more of our fresh mountain air, eh?"

"Yes indeed, Herr Wirth. Whilst we're still here in the area, we thought we might return to try a couple more of walking trails we missed on our first visit. But tell me, do you have any other interesting guests staying with you this weekend?"

"I'm afraid there's no one of consequence coming, apart from Herr Kaiser who of course will be arriving shortly with his entourage for their usual fortnightly visit to the hotel. We're also hosting a hiking party and some English tourists sightseeing amongst the ruins of buildings and bunker tunnels built during the War. This hillside is riddled with their remnants and even here at the Türken we sit on part of an underground tunnel complex beneath the hotel. It's usually open for inspection for a small fee if you have the time to have a look."

"They certainly sound interesting. Perhaps we might explore the possibility a little later."

"And were you able to sort out things with your secretary? She seemed rather anxious to get in touch with you."

"My secretary?"

"Yes, she phoned the hotel last Thursday week asking to speak with you. I told her you and Herr Hartmann checked out of the hotel the previous Sunday, but because you had booked accommodation for today in advance, I advised her that I would get you to give her a call when you returned."

I responded as calmly as possible, thanking him for the message whilst hiding my concern at this unexpected development which now threatened to unhinge our plans.

After the porter had shown us to our suite, Hartmann enquired about Freda's call.

"I wasn't aware you had spoken to your secretary. What was that all about?"

"No Karl, I haven't spoken to her, but I had to say something in response to Wirth's question. Freda's phone call is a glitch I hadn't anticipated, and will have to be dealt with immediately before we can proceed any further. As a matter of routine, when I go chasing news stories, if she hasn't heard from me within a week of my departure, she becomes concerned, as some of the leads I follow up are not without an element of danger. In this particular instance she might very well have initiated enquiries with the police, and that would definitely be the last thing we need with Detective Jaeger about to interview our earlier selves in two days' time. Despite all the good work we have done in creating an alibi, it would only serve to renew his suspicions. The fact she tried to contact me threatens to derail our entire plan and therefore, before doing anything else, I need to prevent her from getting in touch with the police last week."

"Yes, I see the problem now, but what can you do about it? Could you phone her right away and tell her everything is all right?"

"No Karl. Calling her now wouldn't help. She phoned well over a week ago and by this time would have phoned the police for assistance. However, judging by the conversation we've just had with Wirth, it appears the police haven't made enquiries yet, which in turn suggests I must have done something in the past to calm her concerns."

"And that something would be … ?"

"The obvious, Karl. There's only one course of action available to me now and that is to time travel back to last Friday week in the Zeitmaschine, call Freda on my phone, and re-assure her I'm all right. She's probably tried to ring me on my phone earlier but because we've been leapfrogging backwards and forwards over the last two weeks without spending any actual time actually *being* within that interval of time, I wasn't in a position to receive her call."

Hartmann mulled over my words for a moment and looked up at me with a wry smile.

"Well, if we haven't spent any time actually living within those two weeks I guess in the future we'll live another two weeks longer than we might have lived to make up for the days we missed."

Again, I couldn't fault Hartmann's logic and happily agreed as I picked up my torch.

"I must dash. A quick trip to last Friday; a phone call to Freda, and then I'll return to today to join you in completing our mission."

Hartmann frowned.

"Just make sure you do make it a quick trip. Kaiser will be taking off on his regular trip to the future at two o'clock this afternoon and he'll want to use the machine you're using to talk to your secretary last week. You'll have to be out of the chamber before he turns up and it's almost one o'clock now – it's going to be a close call."

I hurried from our suite, fortunately having the presence of mind to realise that by this time our earlier selves would have set themselves up in their hide opposite the Türken's veranda. To avoid making their situation even more confusing, I took the longer route through the beer garden at the rear of the Türken which, although necessary under the circumstances, unfortunately wasted precious minutes from the time available to make my call to Freda.

On my arrival at last Friday I hurriedly dialled her number and anxious minutes passed before it dawned on me that deep down in this chamber with the access steel doors closed behind me, there was little hope of connection. With Kaiser soon to be on his way to use the Zeitmaschine in a weeks' time, I simply had to call Freda to prevent a sequence of events that threatened to unravel all of our good work to date. In despair, I made a dash from the chamber to the clearing outside the cave and finally met with success in making the call. Returning to the Zeitmaschine I pressed the green button, desperately hoping to be out of the chamber before Kaiser arrived.

But I had run out of time.

As I was just about to leave the cave the swish of ferns underfoot heralded Kaiser's approach. I retreated back down the tunnel, shutting doors behind me, and frantically looked around the chamber for a place to hide. Behind the sandbags or the electrical cabinets butted up against the walls were both out of the question and I dared not hide behind the Zeitmaschine with the realisation that, given Kaiser's concern about running out of battery charge whilst time travelling, there was every likelihood he would be venturing behind the machine to recharge them. This left only one possible place to hide – behind the pile of empty treasure boxes.

I dived behind them just as the door to the chamber opened, and pressed my body hard against the floor, lying as flat as possible. Had he seen me? Had I unwittingly left any indication of having used the machine in his absence? My mind raced and I realised with horror that although the red lever was still in the correct '*travel to the past*' position, I had set the duration dials to take me back by a week to call Freda, whereas Kaiser had set them to take him back from the future by *two* weeks on his previous fortnightly excursion. Would he suspect my tampering with the controls or would he assume that he himself had inadvertently changed the setting?

The generator gave a grunt as it surged into life and suddenly the chamber was awash with light from the flashing red warning and interior cabin lamps as he energised the main switch to check the battery charge meter. I cringed as illumination flooded the area around me, but apparently Kaiser must have been far too preoccupied with his fortnightly ritual to venture a glance behind the pile of boxes.

Footsteps. The generator gave one last chug and was silent. More footsteps. A swish as the door panel closed and the red light ceased to flash. Would he now discover the discrepancy on the duration dial and investigate?

There was a soft sighing sound as the Zeitmaschine dematerialised and then it was gone, taking its cabin lights with it and leaving me drained and thanking my guardian angel for the darkness which now enshrouded the chamber.

Hartmann laid down his newspaper and looked up anxiously as I burst into the room, breathless and in a state of high excitement.

"I was starting to worry about you when Kaiser left the hotel and you still hadn't returned. Where were you? What happened?"

I told him about my close shave, and he shook his head.

"Please, Morgen. No more close calls. How did your phone call go with Freda? Were you able to address her concerns?"

"Yes. She was just a little worried on not hearing from me and had already phoned the hotel the day before. I told her we were still chasing after our story in Berchtesgaden."

I looked at my watch and comparing it to Hartmann's saw there was a thirty minute difference between them which told me exactly how long I had just spent in the past. I pointed out the curious time difference to Hartmann and observed that in one respect, time travel was very much like travelling East-West in a plane, where adjustment of watches became necessary as one crossed time zones and, by the same token, pointed out that time travellers would, if away from the present long enough, experience symptoms of jetlag.

"Speaking of time, we have two hours to while away before you are due in the chamber and I'm committed to handing Frau

Kaiser's envelope to the porter. After what I've just been through in the chamber, I need a little distraction to settle my jangled nerves.

I glanced uncertainly around the room.

"I'm not too keen on sweating it out here in our suite, and certainly don't fancy drinking in the bar with Kaiser's bodyguards looking over my shoulder. Perhaps there's something else we could do to while away an hour or so?"

Hartmann pondered for a moment.

"If you like, I could show you around the bunker tunnels underneath the Türken that Wirth mentioned earlier. Back in 1944 I sometimes used them on rainy afternoons to get from my billet to the Berghof without getting drenched. Wirth mentioned they've become something of a tourist attraction, and I saw what looks like the entrance near the Türken's veranda."

We purchased admission tickets from an old woman sitting under a sunshade and in return received a pamphlet comprising map of the bunker complex and summary of their historical significance. A steep flight of stairs led us down to a corridor Hartmann remembered well, and as we passed by, he pointed out a closed section branching off the main passage.

"That short tunnel is dead-ended. In 1944 it was furnished with a lockable grille facing this corridor, and was used to hold political prisoners and other '*undesirables*'."

He shuddered as he recalled the past.

"I regret to say that on my orders, scientists Fuchs, Jung and Kluge spent a day in there before being sent to Konzentrationslager Flossenbürg for elimination."

We walked on in reflective silence. In some places the tunnel walls were pock marked by bullet scars testifying to the last stand of the Oberschütze defenders who were trapped in the bunkers when the allied armies swept through the area. The tunnel we were negotiating ended abruptly in a barricade and Hartmann waved a hand indicating the shadowy gloom beyond the barrier.

"The tunnel continues past this point to the Berghof. I walked this route a few times in 1944, but it's no doubt blocked off at the far end because the Berghof no longer exists."

He stood, gazing into the darkness for a minute or two, and I waited patiently while Hartmann reflected on memories of a past life. He turned to me with a wan smile.

"That was such a long time ago."

We retraced our steps to the entrance where the old woman under the sunshade also sold ice-creams. I bought two, handed one to Hartmann, and we stood enjoying the tranquil beauty of the Obersalzberg hills rolling off into the distance, the warm sunshine on our face and this simplest of pleasures, our ice-cold confections, before returning to a mission that would alter the course of human destiny.

In our suite, Hartmann pocketed the balaclava and picking up the Luger, brushed off imagined dust before slipping it into his vest pocket. I retrieved the envelope and stared at it for a few seconds before raising my eye to see that Hartmann was staring back at me reflecting my own mood of resolute determination.

"This is it, Morgen. Let's go downstairs and make history happen."

CHAPTER 43

We parted company in the lobby. Hartmann left the hotel through the rear beer garden exit whilst I returned to the bar for a drink to brace myself against what was about to unfold. The dining room was empty apart from Kaiser's three bodyguards sitting at table in their unshakeable practice of drinking to while away the hours. The minute hand on the clock over the kitchen door crept around the dial at an agonisingly slow pace, until it eventually told me the time for action had arrived.

I sought out the hotel porter and handed him the envelope, with instruction it was to be delivered without delay. He left promptly after being given a handsome tip, and I didn't have long to wait before Frau Kaiser appeared at the top of the staircase looking deeply troubled. She paused, casting her eyes around the lobby before descending. I moved forward to meet her at the bottom of the stair and introduced myself under an assumed name.

Her worried eyes were full of questions and I glanced around the lobby.

"This is not the place to discuss such sensitive matters. I suggest we go out onto the veranda where we can command a little more privacy."

She nodded agreement, and in making our way to the entrance, I cast a fleeting glance toward the dining room where the Kaiser bodyguards had done with drinking and were now seating themselves at table for dinner, and noticed one of them staring back at us through the window wall.

On the veranda I told Frau Kaiser I knew everything there was to know about her husband. She looked shocked as I revealed detail upon detail regarding her husband's political ambitions and his gaining wealth by abusing the Zeitmaschine's powers. Her eyes widened with every new revelation, and she finally begged me to stop and tell of my intent. I gave her a concocted story about wanting to negotiate with Kaiser in order to receive a large slice of his wealth to buy my silence, and followed this by asking her to accompany me to the secret chamber to be a party to the deal I proposed making with her husband upon his return from the future.

Our conversation was interrupted at this juncture by the bodyguard who had observed us passing through the lobby, and had followed us onto the veranda. On noting Frau Kaiser's troubled countenance, he looked me up and down distrustfully.

"Is everything all right out here, Frau Kaiser?"

I momentarily forgot that this very scene had already been concluded satisfactorily, and now with her bodyguard regarding me in a disturbingly aggressive manner, I felt alarm that matters might well get out of hand at this point in time.

But Frau Kaiser glanced back at me before drawing herself up in a dignified stance and turned to address her bodyguard.

"Yes, Hans. Everything is quite all right. You may return to the others. Thank you for your concern."

Hans gave me one last suspicious glance.

"As you wish Frau Kaiser."

He turned on his heel and after watching him disappear inside to join his companions, I pressed Frau Kaiser.

"Come. We must leave for the chamber at once. Your husband will be returning in the Zeitmaschine very soon."

She stepped off the veranda with me and as we made for the track across the meadow, I glanced behind just in time to catch a glimpse of a figure darting out from behind a nearby copse of bushes, sprinting toward the veranda, and had to stop myself from chuckling aloud as the children's' party game of *musical chairs* came to mind.

CHAPTER 44

On reaching the cave I found the camouflaged door open as expected from my earlier journey, and ushered Frau Kaiser into the tunnel ahead of me, guiding her by the light of my torch. In the chamber the Zeitmaschine lay seated on its cradle and nearby, Hartmann waited in the shadows, his face masked by the balaclava.

Frau Kaiser gasped on seeing him and backed against the wall in fright. Her eyes swept the room in panic and with a fearful cry, she made a dash for the Zeitmaschine only to be confronted by duplicates of Hartmann and myself seated inside.

Her eyes darted back and forth between me and my duplicate Schreiber in the machine and she cried out in terror.

"Who are you? What have you done with my husband? Where is he?"

"Please calm yourself Frau Kaiser, you are quite safe and Herr Kaiser should be returning to the chamber shortly."

Despite my assurances, she backed away against the electrical cabinets, burying her face in her hands, and started to weep.

Footsteps could be heard issuing from the tunnel and seconds later, another pair of Schreiber and Hartmann duplicates entered the chamber. Frau Kaiser was still sobbing, and the duplicate who had just arrived asked what was wrong with her.

I shrugged.

"She's just a bit frightened, but it's nothing for you to be concerned about."

Our duplicates in the Zeitmaschine called out to the new arrivals, urging them to hurry aboard for their two hour journey to the past. They scrambled into the cabin and in a few seconds the Zeitmaschine had vanished with the four of them on board.

I was very much relieved to see them go, anxious to see their cradle vacated, with Kaiser soon to arrive from the future. For a while I tried to console Frau Kaiser, reassuring her the next time the Zeitmaschine appeared, it would be carrying her husband, but she wouldn't be comforted and I finally gave up, leaving her to weep.

In due course the air blurred and the Zeitmaschine re-materialised on its cradle. Frau Kaiser rushed to its side as the access panel slid sideways and Kaiser appeared in the opening. He leaned out of the doorway, very much startled to find his wife inside the chamber.

"My God! What are you doing in here, Eva?"

She sobbed and grabbed hold of his trouser leg. As he reached out a hand to comfort her, Hartmann stepped out of the shadows shrouded in his balaclava, aiming the Luger directly at Kaiser's head.

"Please step down from the Zeitmaschine Herr Kaiser."

Kaiser's head jerked up in surprise and he froze at the sight of Hartmann's gun, no more than a metre away, pointing at him. In an instant he recovered from his momentary shock and releasing Frau Kaiser's shoulder, demanded.

"What is the meaning of this outrage? Who are you?"

Hartmann paid no heed and waved the gun menacingly in front of Kaiser's face.

"You will step down immediately from the Zeitmaschine or I will shoot to kill."

In the light issuing from the cabin's lamp, Kaiser recognised the weapon, and fully aware of its capabilities, climbed out of the access doorway without further hesitation.

His wife threw her arms around him, weeping profusely, but he brushed her roughly aside and blustered.

"Do you know who I am? I am Dietrich Kaiser, a man of immense importance and power in this country and I'll not be treated in this outrageous manner. I demand that you tell me who you are and what this is all about!"

I walked toward them out of the darkness and he whirled around to see who else was there in the chamber's recesses.

"We wish to do a little time travelling with you and your wife, Herr Kaiser."

Kaiser stared at me, feigning ignorance.

"Time travelling? What in heaven's name are you talking about?"

I patted the side of the Zeitmaschine.

"We know everything there is to know about this little machine Herr Kaiser, and are fully aware of its capabilities. We know how it operates and we know how you employ its powers to accumulate the wealth you then use to pollute this country with your corruption."

Kaiser scowled and was about to take a step toward me when Hartmann jerked the Luger menacingly in his face to remind him who was in charge.

"Herr Kaiser, you will now kindly face the Zeitmaschine and hold your hands behind your back."

Hartmann emphasised my request by waving the Luger in a circle from Kaiser's face to the side of the machine and he did as was bidden, protesting angrily.

"You will be sorry for committing this outrage. Believe me, you will suffer immensely for the mistake you are making."

Ignoring his outbursts, I produced a length of stout cord from my pocket and warning Kaiser my associate still had the gun trained on his head ready to shoot if he moved, commenced binding his wrists together.

Frau Kaiser took a step forward, and looking over my shoulder, I growled a warning at her to keep her distance. She stood there helplessly, tears streaming down her face whilst her shoulders sagged in despair. As she wiped the tears from her eyes, I had to remind myself forcefully who she really was and what she knew about her husband, and all he had done before and during the War, to ward off any feelings of sympathy I might have had for her.

I tested my handiwork with the cord and was satisfied Kaiser wouldn't be a nuisance during our journey to the past.

"You may turn around now, Herr Kaiser."

His eyes blazed with a look of hatred that could have killed, whilst he spat out words of fury and vengeance.

"You will not get away with this! My bodyguards are already looking for me, and if they have difficulty in finding us, the police will be called in to hunt you down like the dogs you are."

I studied his face thoughtfully, very much surprised at how unflustered I felt during this momentous encounter.

"Then we'll have to take you to a time when the authorities and your bodyguards will never be able to find you, won't we?"

I beckoned Frau Kaiser.

"Would you please climb aboard the Zeitmaschine Frau Kaiser?"

I gave her a hand to climb into the cabin and after seating her on the bench opposite the control station, turned to Kaiser who stood glaring at the gun Hartmann held inches from his face. Producing a small roll of duct tape I had brought along especially for the occasion, I tore off a strip, and although he ducked and weaved to avoid it, managed to plaster the tape across his mouth.

"We do wish to have a pleasant journey, and we wouldn't want to hear abusive language in front of Frau Kaiser whilst travelling back to the past, would we?"

I took a firm hold of his arm and turned him toward the access opening.

"Please take the seat next to your wife."

I offered a helping hand as he struggled to climb into the cabin but he shrugged me off with a thrust of his body and with great difficulty and to my surprise, managed to clamber aboard unaided.

I turned to Hartmann.

"Have you done the calculations for the time duration dials?"

"Yes, I know exactly the date and time of Hitler's original departure in 1944 because it is emblazoned on my memory. We also know the time and date where we happen to be at this very moment. Taking one from the other is rather simple arithmetic and gives me the exact years, weeks, days and hours since he left the chamber in 1944. And if I take three days away from the total and set the dials accordingly, we will be arriving in the chamber exactly three days after he originally departed."

"Very well. Hand me the gun. I'll watch the Kaisers whilst you reset the dials."

Hartmann handed over the Luger and climbed aboard whilst I waved it at the seated couple.

"Please remain quiet and still, and no one will get hurt."

Hartmann finished setting the duration controls and called out to me, his voice still somewhat muffled by the balaclava.

"All set, Morgen. Jump in and we'll be off."

I was about to comply when the door to the chamber gave a loud clang as it crashed into the wall. I swung my torch around and stood rooted to the spot at the sight of Kaiser's bodyguard Hans, standing in the doorway. I now recalled him walking out onto the Türken's veranda and looking in our direction as we entered the woods. He must have seen us and following in our footsteps, discovered the cave and found the camouflaged door open.

Snapping out of my mental inertia, I whirled about and scrambled into the cabin, frantically calling for Hartmann to press the red button. But before I could shut the door panel behind me, Hans had advanced in swift strides to the Zeitmaschine and had leapt into the cabin, pushing me roughly along the bench, squeezing me up against Hartmann.

As he did so, and in response to my desperate plea, Hartmann's fist was already descending on the red button, and as I grappled with the bodyguard, the Zeitmaschine commenced its journey back to the past.

I was no match for the powerfully built Hans, who quickly overcame my struggles and wrenched the Luger from my grip. All eyes in the cabin were fixed on his face, glowing with triumph and looking fiendish in the light cast by the flashing red warning lamp. He waved the Luger first at me and then at Hartmann, and smirking evilly, sneered at us.

"I regret having to interrupt your little party game, but wonder if you'd care to follow me outside and explain just what you think you're doing; abducting Herr Kaiser and his wife and holding them in this stupid contraption."

I glanced past him at the dark void swirling outside the cabin portal and shuddered as scientist Fuch's warning flashed through my mind.

"We can't go out there, it's …"

Hans cut me off, his evil smile spreading a little further across his face.

"Oh, but you're forgetting this little item here."

He patted the Luger and waved it menacingly in my face.

"I think it's telling us you will do exactly as I say. Now, if you want to live just a little longer you'll get up off your behind and follow me outside."

He rose from the bench and backed out of the access portal with the Luger pointing at my head.

There was no scream.

No sound at all.

The momentum of his backward movement carried the rest of his body into the oblivion that swirled outside, and just before his arm followed his body in dissolving into the void, his hand opened, releasing the Luger, dropping it to the floor.

I grabbed at the pistol and slamming the door panel shut, swung around to prevent the Kaisers from taking advantage of the situation.

But I needn't have been concerned. They were, just as I had been, in a state of shock at having witnessed Hans' exit and sat frozen in their seats. Frau Kaiser still had a hand over her mouth after stifling a scream on seeing her bodyguard's bulky frame dissolving before her eyes, and Kaiser was staring in horror, gaping at the darkness on the other side of the closed glass panel.

Hartmann was shaking his head, staring vacantly at the dials, murmuring in an unemotional monotone, more I think to himself than to any of us.

"Scientist Fuchs cautioned me against doing this very thing. Hans' body will have been rendered down to the minutest of atoms, all of which will be scattered throughout the days and weeks through which the Zeitmaschine travelled during his exit. In the future from which we have come, the floor will be littered with the dust which once comprised his body."

He continued to gaze fixedly at the speed meter as the needle sped around backwards, and it was some time before I managed to recover my senses sufficiently enough to comment on our recent experience.

"… And you said travelling by train was far more interesting …"

The speed meter needle began slowing down and just before it stopped completely, the darkness outside the window gave way to the bright haze of the chamber's festoon lamps.

I slid the door panel open, climbed out, and turning to Kaiser, invited him to do likewise, keeping the Luger trained on him all the while. He clambered out with difficulty, followed by his wife who clung to his arm, her tear-stained eyes roaming fearfully around the chamber.

I turned to Hartmann.

"Set the duration dial to go back in time by exactly two days."

Whilst he was thus occupied, I addressed the Kaisers.

"We have returned you to a moment three days after you left this chamber in 1944. From this point onward, perhaps you can find some way to challenge the destiny history has decreed for you. But knowing that the past is fixed and cannot be altered, I doubt very much whether you will be able to avoid what we have all come to know from the historical record."

I motioned the pistol to direct the Kaisers toward the wall behind them.

Kaiser shuffled backward glowering at me, his wife still clutching his arm. I stepped forward and ripped the tape from his lips and he immediately erupted with vitriol. I merely smiled through his curses and threats, his outpouring of hatred and venom, and eventually, seeing his rage was having no effect on me at all, he turned to pleading.

"But what will happen to Germany once I am no longer the architect of our country's future? Do you mean to deny me everything I have worked so fervently for these last few years? Are you content to see your country decay under a tsunami wave of worthless immigrants, and let the other European states suck us dry like parasites? My wealth could have brought this nation the greatness and power that was its due. Would you deny this future to your Fatherland? What will happen now to the great wealth I have accumulated?"

"Your money can rot in the banks for all I care. It will buy you no favours from now on."

But Kaiser wasn't about to give up that easily and his face twisted itself into what he might have considered was a winning smile.

"Yes, it does me no favours where we happen to be at the moment, but my wealth still awaits you in the future. If you agree to return us there, I can offer you and your friend riches beyond your wildest dreams."

I stared at him with disgust shaking my head and called out to Hartmann.

"Ready, Karl?"

He replied in the affirmative and I stepped back to the Zeitmaschine still aiming the Luger at Kaiser's head.

"We are leaving you now. Frau Kaiser can untie your bonds after we've left."

I climbed into the Zeitmaschine, the pistol all the while pointed at Kaiser, and before sliding the door closed, threw his satchel full of now-worthless documents out onto the chamber floor. Hartmann's fist came down on the red button and the last thing I saw through the panel before the scene outside dissolved was Kaiser, hands still tied behind his back, clumsily rushing forward toward our machine.

The speed dial needle had hardly started to move upscale when it was on its way down again marking our voyage back to the past by a further two days. I slid the panel door open and stepped out into the chamber.

Gazing around the brightly lit room, my eyes came to rest on the young Obersturmführer who was in turn gazing back at me with a look of astonishment. As I watched, he drew his pistol from its holster and pointed it in my direction. There was a movement behind me as Hartmann stepped out of the Zeitmaschine and joined me at my side.

The young Obersturmführer looked from each of us to the other, puzzled and uncertain, not knowing what to make of our presence in the chamber, but I addressed him before he could take any further action.

"Please put down your gun, Hartmann. We have come from a long way into the future to assist and guide you because from today onward your activities are going to be of vital importance not only to Germany, but indeed to all of humanity."

He lowered his gun but didn't re-holster it.

I asked him whether he recognised my companion and on seeing he was suffering a bout of speechlessness, Hartmann stepped forward to establish his credentials by relating childhood secrets which no other than he and a younger Hartmann could have known. Young Hartmann holstered his pistol and visibly shaken, sat down heavily on the pile of sandbags. We strolled over to where he sat and described the events that would unfold over the coming days, with particular reference to Hitler's return in two days' time.

I reached into my wallet and handed him one of my business cards, asking that he memorise its details and explained that one day in the distant future he would visit me in my office to tell the story of Hitler's escape to the future in the Zeitmaschine.

The young Obersturmführer glanced from me to Hartmann agreeing that my companion must be his future self, and thereupon vowed to do as we asked.

Having secured his promise, Hartmann and I boarded the Zeitmaschine. He adjusted the duration dials to return us to the Monday morning immediately after we had returned from establishing our alibi and through the access window I took one last look at the bewildered, shaken young man before his image blurred and we were again travelling forward in time. Hartmann reflected on the encounter we just had in the chamber, gazing abstractly at the time speed meter.

"My younger self looked so totally confounded by our visit, and will be suffering so much hardship after the War that I'm tempted to say I feel sorry for him, but I would be saying that I feel sorry for myself, wouldn't I?"

He gave me a wan smile before returning to gaze at the meter.

When the needle finally came to a standstill and we were once again back to the Monday of our original departure, I rejoiced in our achievement and was thankful at last to be relieved of the burden of our mission. I offered Hartmann congratulations on what we had accomplished together.

"From being a mere pawn in Hitler's grand plan to spread evil across the face of Europe, you have redeemed yourself Karl, by becoming the prime protagonist in removing this monster from our future. When our story is eventually revealed in my newspaper, you will be revered as the saviour of the free world."

Hartmann did not respond immediately, but instead, stared morosely down at the control panel. I waited, puzzled by his unresponsiveness, not fully understanding his failure to share my exuberance.

After an overly lengthy pause he looked up at me.

"I'm not really convinced that revealing what we have done would be a very wise thing."

"What do you mean, Karl? Are you disturbed at the thought of becoming famous?"

"No, notoriety wouldn't disturb me. The fact is, I am not entirely happy with our adventure becoming known to the general public. Please give me your promise you won't reveal what we know about this affair to anyone until I have had time to settle my troubled mind regarding Hitler and his time machine."

I looked at Hartmann, worried and wondering where his thoughts were taking him.

"This adventure belongs as much to you as it does to me, Karl – probably more so. I'll give you all the time in the world to sort out your thinking and promise not to reveal any details of this affair to another soul until you give me the word. But of course, in return you too mustn't mention anything of our adventures – naturally, I want this biggest scoop of all time to be an exclusive for my newspaper alone, Ok?"

"Ok. I give you my word, and thank you Morgen."

We were about to disembark from the Zeitmaschine when the situation that would face us on return to the Türken came to mind, and I gave vent to frustration as yet another time paradox revealed itself.

"Karl, we've been dashing about in the past and future without a meal break and now, ready for a hunger-busting lunch, the waiters will once again only just be clearing away our breakfast dishes. They're sure to look on us as absolute gluttons when we request more food, having already just finished our breakfast in the dining room for a second time."

Hartmann frowned and contemplated our predicament before offering a practical solution.

"Well Morgen, we have to return the Luger and balaclava to my associate in Berchtesgaden. Perhaps we can get some brunch at one of the cafés in town whilst we're there and avoid the difficulty involved in returning to the Türken for a meal."

I was about to agree when I was arrested by a disturbing thought.

"Wait a moment Karl. Today is Monday but it was tomorrow, Tuesday, when you visited Berchtesgaden to borrow the Luger. If we call on your associate this morning you would be returning the pistol a day before he actually loaned it to you. This might not only rather surprise him, but could possibly transgress some incomprehensible law governing time travel that I wouldn't particularly wish to explore at present. Instead, why don't we travel to tomorrow afternoon a few hours after he gave it to you?"

Hartmann stared at me for a second or two, contemplating the absurdity of the situation we might easily have created for ourselves, and shaking his head turned to the controls to reset the duration dials.

CHAPTER 45

I remained behind the wheel of our car and watched Hartmann stride up a short path through a rather untidy garden overgrown with weeds, to knock on the front door of a house that had known better times. A face appeared briefly between the curtains facing the street and moments later, the front door opened only sufficiently for the occupant to get a better view of whoever had knocked. On recognising Hartmann, a bald-headed young man with heavily tattooed arms opened the door wider, stepped out, and after hurrying Hartmann inside, looked furtively up and down the street before shutting the door behind him.

Hartmann re-appeared five minutes later and we drove on to the Café Forstner to enjoy a lavish lunch accompanied by a magnum of champagne to celebrate the successful conclusion of our mission. As we ate, we re-lived our temporal voyages and toasted our future selves, who of course, we had by now become, and who had always been there to advise and guide us in negotiating the tortuous path to success. My glass was half-raised in yet another toast when I was arrested by a very disquieting thought. Hartmann lowered his glass on observing my look of concern and, after apprehensively glancing around the surrounding tables, leaned forward in his chair to ask what was wrong.

"Karl, the morning after we consolidated our alibi we had breakfast in the Türken and returned to the chamber to wait as instructed for our future selves to pick us up."

"Yes, that's right. So?"

He eyed me uneasily, waiting for me to make my point, whilst I wrestled with recollections of our recent exploits, trying to get my thoughts in order.

"Well, Karl, at this very moment in time we just happen to be those future selves who picked us up, and as far as I can recall, we haven't done any such thing."

Hartmann sat back in his chair and stared at me in shock.

"And also, thinking along similar lines, I'm reminded of two other occasions for which there is no accounting. Think back to when we first sought to discover when Kaiser was due to disappear. On arrival on that Sunday we found our future selves there in the duplicate Zeitmaschine waiting to tell us how to respond to Detective Jaeger's questions. Without my duplicate's advice, we would have been in a right pickle, wouldn't we? Well, there again I don't recall time travelling to give my earlier self that advice.

"And again, after watching the Türken's veranda, and then returning to the chamber to be ferried back to the past by two hours, our future selves were there in their Zeitmaschine waiting to give us a lift. In each of these three instances, our future selves were involved and yet here we sit, celebrating our success with champagne, we – those very same future selves – and yet I have no recollection of participating in any part of what I have just outlined as a necessary role for a future self."

Hartmann slapped his forehead.

"My God, how could we have failed to appreciate that these important interactions with our earlier selves have yet to take place? Come, Morgen. We have to take immediate steps to ensure these things actually do occur as we remember them."

He jerked his chair back and rose from the table, and I was about to follow suit when anxiety gave way to calm, and rational thought prevailed. I eyed the half full magnum of champagne on the table and sitting down again signalled Hartmann, who was staring at me anxiously, to do likewise.

"Well, perhaps we don't have to return immediately to the chamber, Karl. Again we are forgetting the Zeitmaschine can carry us to any time at any time. We can leave this table any time we please and still arrive at the correct moment in the past to do whatever needs to be done. Why not relax for a change and enjoy the rest of our lunch and this excellent champagne in this fine restaurant instead of dashing off to do what can readily be achieved once we are done here."

Hartmann's look of alarm melted into a sheepish smile and he sank back into his chair.

"Yes, you are right, Morgen. I keep overlooking this fact."

I topped up our glasses, and after finishing off our meal at a leisurely pace we returned to the chamber to play out the roles dictated by our recollections of the past. Before setting out, Hartmann once again considered the possibility of Zeitmaschine collisions.

"We know in two of the three situations, there will be another version of the Zeitmaschine sitting on its cradle. So first we must exchange cradle locations."

I agreed, again thankful he was ever there to remind me of this danger, and we pushed the cradle to its alternative location.

Hartmann calculated the necessary time duration settings to pick up our earlier selves waiting in the chamber, and pressed the red button.

As the speed meter needle came to a standstill, the shadowy chamber revealed by our earlier selves' torches emerged out of the darkness. I slid open the access panel and welcomed them as they clambered aboard, whilst Hartmann reset the duration dials to take them back to ten o'clock on the Friday after they had set out to execute their mission.

On arrival they thanked us and climbed into the machine parked alongside. I smiled and returned the wave our duplicates gave us from the other Zeitmaschine while Hartmann re-set the duration dials. On my affirming nod he again depressed the red button taking us to the Sunday evening when our earlier selves would be arriving to face their disturbing encounter with Detective Jaeger. After a short wait, the air beside our machine shimmered and another Zeitmaschine materialised alongside. We heard our earlier selves leaving their machine, and as they came into view I slid aside the access panel to give them the information they would require to satisfy Detective Jaeger's questions. Hartmann meanwhile was resetting the time duration dials for a third time to take us to our final appointment with our earlier selves in ferrying them back to the past by two hours.

As the darkness gave way to reveal the chamber lit by their torches, our duplicates came into view whilst near the electrical cabinets we could see Frau Kaiser in tears.

As I opened the door panel, she rushed towards our machine, but seeing me inside the cabin instead of the husband she had been expecting, she gave a shriek of terror and recoiled from our machine. Moments later the pair of duplicates who had been keeping watch on the Türken's veranda entered the chamber. They climbed aboard at my urging, and after transporting them back in time by the requisite two hours, we had finally tied up all the loose ends to finally bring closure to our epic adventure.

Back in the Türken, on informing Herman Wirth we would be leaving the following morning he wished us a safe return to Berlin and hoped we had had a pleasant and satisfying stay.

I gave Hartmann a wink before responding to the manager's parting words.

"Thank you Herr Wirth. Herr Hartmann and I have indeed had a very fulfilling time here at the Türken."

CHAPTER 46

That evening, Hartmann and I had a heated exchange of views over the dinner table.

It began when I launched into an exposé proposing how our story was to be revealed in Die Welt on our return to Berlin.

"First of all, I will take a group of scientific experts on a short time journey, just like the one when scientist Fuchs demonstrated the Zeitmaschine's powers, sending Jung forward in time to the following day. We'll arrange to have photographers and a few selected notables, perhaps from the judiciary, to witness the event. Then once we've demonstrated the machine's capabilities, we'll reveal the truth about Kaiser – that he was really Hitler in another guise, and we'll describe how he had time-travelled from 1944 with the intention of once again throwing Europe into chaos with his hateful thirst for world domination. We'll then reveal the rest of our story – how we corralled Kaiser and his wife in the chamber and transported them back to the past where they belonged ..."

Hartmann was staring at me aghast, and I broke off my enthusiastic narrative when I finally took note of the horrified look on his face.

"What's wrong, Karl? Is it something I said?"

"You can't be serious, Morgen. You should just hear yourself talking! Surely you must realise that in revealing our story you will be plunging yourself into a very complex and dangerous situation. By informing the authorities we forced the Kaisers into the Zeitmaschine and then abandoned them where they can never be found again, you will be admitting to the crime of kidnap, and I might add, you were armed with a loaded illegal firearm to gain their compliance. The fact that Kaiser happened to be a time-travelling Hitler would be of little consequence as far as the police are concerned, even if you could get them to believe your story about the Zeitmaschine. Their job is to pursue criminals, and armed kidnap must be about one of the most heinous crimes in their calendar. In two weeks' time they'll be investigating a crime scene – the disappearance of Kaiser and his wife – and will no doubt also be on the lookout for Hans, the bodyguard who perished on our journey back to 1944. Then when you come out in the press and state you were the one who kidnapped them at gunpoint, you will be exposing yourself as the perpetrator of a very serious crime, a triple kidnap in fact if one includes Hans, which would undoubtedly result in your being prosecuted before the courts.

"As the law currently stands, it makes no difference who they actually were. Kidnapping is the crime with which you would be charged and by your own admission you would be found guilty as charged. The legal system, as you very well know, doesn't judge whether an action is morally right or wrong. Its sole responsibility is to prosecute transgressions defined by the laws of the land, and unless you can convince the government to pass special laws to cover your own particular circumstances, you will face the same fate as any other criminal who goes around dispensing justice and disposing of people they don't like."

He paused momentarily to study the shocked expression on my face.

"I might also add, the kidnapping charge would most probably be followed by a charge of murder when you prove unwilling to bring Kaiser and his wife back to the present time. The police would also no doubt treat me as an accomplice, and I would therefore be charged as an accessory after the fact, or worse."

I sat back in my seat, my earlier enthusiasm quashed only to be replaced by troubling doubt. Hartmann had a point.

"But Karl, surely when the police compare photographs of Kaiser and his wife with those of Hitler and Eva Braun, they will be able to see that the two couples were one and the same. We should be celebrated for exposing Hitler's plan, and for sending him back where he rightfully belongs."

Hartmann shook his head gravely.

"I believe you are still getting morality confused with legality. There would be some people out there who might want to lay a laurel wreath on your head and perhaps nominate you for the Nobel peace prize. But countering this, you must take into account the many criminal union, industrial and political officials who have been corrupted by Kaiser's massive wealth. They won't be happy about the loss of their benefactor and the money they will no longer be receiving, and they'll be baying for your blood. '*The law is the law*', they'll shout, and won't keep quiet, but will keep petitioning the authorities until you are prosecuted."

"Karl, this is the most fantastic story of all time and would be the biggest scoop my paper has ever had. Are you just going to sit there in that chair and calmly tell me to drop a story of this magnitude and remain silent about this entire saga that we've just battled our way through?"

Hartmann leaned forward over the table and slowly nodded.

"I am afraid so. Yes."

"There's printer's ink running through my veins Karl – I haven't given up on any of the major stories I've covered in the past, and without exception they've finally made the headlines because of my sheer persistence. Not one of my previous scoops was anywhere near as important as this saga and I'll be damned if I'm about to give up on the Zeitmaschine story until convinced there's no other option. There must be some way to present our tale to the world without necessarily incriminating ourselves. Give me a little time to think things over and I'm sure to come up with a way out of this dilemma."

Hartmann shrugged and returned to his meal in silence. He knew I needed space to think the matter over and quietly set about dispatching the remainder of his meal, leaving me to wrestle with my thoughts. However, I had lost my appetite and after poking at the food on my plate, I made my apology and left the table to go for a long walk outside in the cool night air.

I wandered about the meadow for quite some time considering Karl's arguments and found I couldn't fault his logic. There was no escaping the fact that if I persisted in owning up to my part in Kaiser's disappearance there was a very real possibility I would face legal proceedings, most probably followed by a lengthy jail term or, I mused ruefully, a long spell in a mental institution for the criminally insane.

And, I wondered, what evidence did I have to prove Kaiser was in fact a time-travelling Adolph Hitler? Of course, he and his wife did bear a striking resemblance to photos of the wartime German dictator and his mistress, but across the world at large wasn't it quite commonplace to find people who shared similar facial characteristics? Would my only defence in a kidnapping, and a probable murder trial, rely solely on the fact the Kaisers just happened to look like Hitler and Eva Braun? My fairly extensive experience in reporting court cases told me the prosecution would tear me to shreds.

In the end, and with great reluctance, I had to admit Hartmann was probably right, and consequently, it would be futile and dangerous to reveal the story of Hitler's forced return to the past.

But I still had the scoop of the century for my newspaper. We still had the Zeitmaschine! We would reveal to the world through the pages of Die Welt, the ability of this incredible machine to transcend time. I would trade the secret of the Zeitmaschine in exchange for exclusive rights to follow up on research into its workings, its history and ongoing experiments in time travel. It would be our gift to the world, and of course, it would benefit my paper enormously as we drip fed our readership with the latest exclusive news from the scientists.

I hurried back to the hotel to acquaint Hartmann with my new line of thinking which, I now felt confident, would stand on its own and would bypass the complications inherent in bringing Kaiser into the picture, whilst still allowing us to take centre stage in revealing this technological triumph to the world.

I found him in our suite in the easy chair, quietly reading the newspaper. He looked up, startled by my exuberant change of mood as I hurried into the room, breathless and excited.

"I have carefully considered your arguments at the dinner table this evening, Karl, and must admit you are absolutely right in your summation of the situation. It would be folly in the extreme to expose myself to probable criminal charges. The whole story about returning Hitler to 1944 will unfortunately have to remain a secret shared by the two of us and no other."

Hartmann observed me closely for a moment, puzzled by my display of cheerfulness in the face of abandonment of the Kaiser story, instead of the disappointment which should have accompanied my decision. He nevertheless responded sympathetically.

"You have made the right decision, Morgen. I realise as a newsperson, coming to this conclusion must be extremely distressing for you, but you must think of self-preservation foremost. Comfort yourself with the knowledge that between us, we have prevented a tragedy of titanic proportions, which would have ensued if we had not intervened."

"That part of our story will indeed have to remain under wraps, Karl – but we still have the Zeitmaschine."

He looked at me blankly.

"I'm not with you Morgen. What do you mean?"

"The Zeitmaschine, Karl. Imagine the furore we'll create when we reveal the time transcending properties of this incredible machine to the world."

Hartmann stared at me, his face a picture of incredulity. He spoke slowly, stressing each word.

"*You … would … reveal … the … secret … of … the … Zeitmaschine … to … the … world?*"

I was staggered by his unenthusiastic response.

"Of course, Karl. This will be the biggest story to ever hit the newsstands. You and I will become famous as the discoverers of this marvellous machine."

Hartmann was again looking at me with face aghast and I stopped short, my enthusiasm giving way to growing annoyance and impatience at his failure to appreciate our unique situation.

"For heaven's sake, what's the matter this time, Karl?"

"You cannot reveal the secret of the Zeitmaschine to the world. I simply won't allow it."

I was beginning to feel more than just a little annoyed at his negativity and retorted angrily.

"And why not?"

"For God's sake Morgen, think it through. Think! We have been in command of this Zeitmaschine for two weeks now and what have we done with it?"

Before I could respond that we had just saved the world from disaster, Hartmann answered the question he posed.

"In the last two weeks we have encroached on people's privacy to spy on what they were up to and have then taken action to thwart their plans. We have used this machine to kidnap people without leaving a trace. We have used our ability to time travel to create a perfect alibi for a crime we actually did commit. We have done all these things with the best of intentions. Surely you can imagine how these very same acts could be duplicated by criminals whose intentions aren't quite as honourable as our own?"

I was about to protest, but Hartmann pressed on with his argument.

"And what about Hitler? He used this machine to create unimagined wealth in his quest for power. Think of the people he corrupted with his bribery. Consider how he derived his wealth because for every single Euro he gained unfairly in trading shares on the Deutsche Börse someone else had to suffer an equivalent loss. And what might he have achieved in carrying out his quest for world domination if we hadn't intervened to disrupt his plans?

"And what about me? Yes, me! I am forever ashamed and filled with remorse on recalling the number of people who were sent to their death on my orders when as that young Obersturmführer I enthusiastically carried out Hitler's wishes to safeguard the secret of the Zeitmaschine. If I was prepared to kill just to keep it a secret, consider what criminals might do to gain access to a machine that would reward them with wealth that defies imagination. These criminals would stop at nothing, and would be prepared to despatch anyone who tried to prevent them from getting their hands on such a machine.

"And when knowledge of the time machine is finally revealed and the details of its workings become known, other machines will be constructed. Do you really think when all of this comes about that humankind will be able to prevent greedy, corrupt and criminal individuals from commandeering time travelling powers to further their own ambitions? Their selfish striving to command great wealth would see the collapse of the world's financial institutions, governments would lose control, and civilization as we know it would descend into chaos.

"I'm afraid that, based on what I have experienced in this long life, you would not be able to stop this technology from falling into the wrong hands. All these bad things would come to pass because I have witnessed the dark side of human nature and I know the leopard does not change its spots."

I stared at Hartmann. There was truth in his words, but my mind would just not accept abandoning disclosure of the Zeitmaschine's existence.

"I understand your arguments Karl and everything you say does indeed make sense. But you must give me time to think this through. Let me work on it for a while and perhaps after a good night's sleep I can come up with some sort of compromise solution. There simply has to be some way of revealing what we know about the Zeitmaschine without its disclosure turning the world upside down."

CHAPTER 47

I slept fitfully that night and in the morning was tired and dispirited coming downstairs for Sunday breakfast – still without any idea on how to reveal the existence of the time machine without ultimately causing the chaos Hartmann had prophesied.

We ate in silence, but after a few minutes when I looked up from my plate I caught a glimpse of Hartmann considering me with a very strange look on his face. His countenance quickly changed when he saw me looking in his direction.

"What is it, Karl?"

He shook his head.

"Nothing. Nothing really, Morgen. I was just wondering what we should do next after we leave the Türken, now that it's all over."

"Well, our work here is done here. We could stick around for a couple of weeks to see what happens, but then we already know what is going to happen, don't we? On Sunday night in two weeks' time after having delivered Hitler to the past, our earlier selves will be here in the hotel being interviewed by Detective

Otto Jaeger, and I can't see we'd be able to learn any more about the Kaiser affair by sticking around than we have already discovered in visiting the future …"

I stopped mid-sentence. Hartmann had dropped his fork on his plate and was now staring at the wall behind me, his face contorted with a look of horror. I turned to follow his gaze, and seeing nothing untoward behind me, turned back.

"What's wrong, Karl?"

"The Zeitmaschine is sitting in the chamber right at this very moment, Morgen."

"Yes? That's right. So what's the problem?"

"And it will still be sitting there for the next two weeks unless we move it. Don't you see Morgen, we already know there are going to be multiple comings and goings of the Zeitmaschine over the coming two weeks, with landings on both cradles. With our machine sitting there in the chamber the whole time, a collision is inevitable when another version of itself tries to occupy the same cradle space. This is another factor we have failed to take into account. We'll have to do something pretty damn quickly to stop a collision from occurring."

I stared at Hartmann. He was right. Again we had stumbled into another time paradox which now demanded our immediate intervention to avert disaster.

"Well, we are here and alive today Karl, so obviously we must have moved, or rather *will have to move,* the Zeitmaschine to another time to avoid any chance of this happening."

"Yes, and I think I have quite a simple remedy to the problem. After we check out of the Zum Türken, we'll set the controls to take us forward by two weeks and a day or two – let's say to the Monday following the Sunday evening when we were interviewed by Detective Jaeger. Doing this will ensure our Zeitmaschine isn't sitting in its cradle for the next two weeks and incidentally, this will also give us the opportunity to see how the police are going with their investigation."

"Good thinking, Karl – I think you might have nailed it. Although we'll be leapfrogging over two weeks that we'll never have the opportunity of living through, nothing will be lost because, as you have observed previously, our life expectancy will merely be advanced by another fifteen calendar days."

After checking out of the Türken, I stashed our bags onto the bench opposite the control station whilst Hartmann set the duration dials to carry us through to Monday fortnight, and soon we were once again walking the path across the meadow back to the Türken, keen to hear the latest news. As we neared the hotel we were stopped in our tracks by the sound of barking dogs. I glanced at Hartmann and saw he was as puzzled as myself – the Türken didn't accommodate pets, and wild dogs were unknown in the area. Cautiously venturing forward, the presence of the dogs was quickly explained on observing a crowd of police, hotel guests and newspaper reporters who had gathered on the Türken's veranda to watch a pair of dog handlers as they offered items of Frau Kaiser's clothing to two Alsatian trackers to familiarise them with her scent.

I looked at Hartmann with alarm. If traces of Frau Kaiser's scent were still present on the track across the meadow, the dogs would almost certainly lead the police directly to the cave with every chance the tunnel to the chamber, and therefore the Zeitmaschine, would be discovered.

"We can't let this happen Karl – we have to move fast. What can we do to stop them?"

Hartmann shook his head.

"We probably can't, Morgen. But what I can do is navigate the Zeitmaschine forward in time so that even if they do discover the chamber they won't find our machine inside it."

Hartmann's idea seemed to be such a simple solution to our immediate predicament that I enthusiastically embraced it on the spot without giving his suggestion the consideration it warranted.

"OK Karl, go ahead and do that. I'll press on to the Türken and join the search party. Who knows? I might even be able to slow them down a bit to buy you a little more time to get away."

I reached out to Hartmann to wish him luck. As I gripped his hand firmly and warmly, I recall him looking at me once again with the same strange expression I had observed in the Türken's dining room.

The world stood still as we shook hands, and I was suddenly imbued with the feeling that the axis of our very existence ran through that singular handshake.

Hartmann nodded as if to confirm my thoughts, then turned and hurried back down the track toward the cave. I watched his dwindling figure for a minute or so before making my way to the hotel to join the crowd on the veranda.

The police were handing Frau Kaiser's clothes back to Herman Wirth as I arrived, cautioning him to preserve her belongings as evidence, and Detective Jaeger seemed to be in charge of the police presence. I also noticed the Die Welt reporter and cameraman I had seen in the lobby on Sunday who were also on the spot, preparing to report on the unfolding situation, and made my way over to them.

The reporter was pleased to see that I was taking an interest in the affair they were covering, and brought me up to speed on the investigation so far with facts I already knew only too well, but adding the handlers and their dogs were part of a German army unit, recently returned from Afghanistan where they had been helping to locate hidden roadside explosive devices.

The handlers announced readiness to move forward and the crowd of onlookers parted to allow their charges sufficient room to pick up Frau Kaiser's scent. No sooner had the dogs left the environs of the veranda, then it became immediately apparent that her scent lingered on, as the dogs headed straight for the track across the meadow. Most of the hotel guests crowding the veranda remained behind, but I joined the small detachment of newsmen and police who followed in their tracks. Earlier I had thought to catch up with the lead and somehow slow their search to give Hartmann more time, but now it occurred that Frau Kaiser's scent wasn't the only one on the track. Mine would be there as well, having accompanied her to the chamber, and I hesitated, fearing the dogs might take an interest in me, rather than continuing to follow Frau Kaiser's scent. I decided not to risk resurrecting Detective Jaeger's suspicions and trailed a little way behind the pack as they passed from the meadow to the track between the trees and thence on to the cave.

The party came to a halt with the dogs baying outside the cave entrance, whereupon one of the handlers swept aside the ferns and peered inside. He called for someone to fetch a torch and whilst one of the police detached himself from the group to oblige, the handler produced a pack of matches and bending low ventured inside. A couple of minutes later he emerged shaking his head.

"The cave's narrow, leads nowhere and doesn't show any sign of previous occupation. Perhaps Frau Kaiser took shelter in here for some reason, but she must have retraced her steps back to the hotel, because the trail stops here."

On hearing this, some of the newsmen left the group, shaking their heads at the unresolved mystery, and returned to the Türken. The remainder stood around waiting for the police officer to return with the torch, filling in time trading theories about Frau Kaiser's mysterious disappearance.

When the torch arrived, Detective Jaeger took possession and disappeared under the overhanging ferns. Just as the dog handler had determined earlier, he too was unable to find any evidence to indicate previous occupation apart from the scattering of spent matches on the floor.

I watched relieved, as Jaeger emerged from the cave and handed the torch back. Struggling to explain the dead end to which the search had come, he raised the possibility that Frau Kaiser may have retraced her steps along the track for part of the way before diverging from the inbound path, and ordered the handlers and their dogs to take up positions three metres on either side of the track on their return to the Türken in order to detect whether this may have been the case.

The police handlers and dogs returned to the Türken in this formation without further incident, whilst I listened with interest and amusement to the reporters trailing behind as they continued their exchange of theories about the ongoing mystery.

Upon reaching the Türken's veranda without gaining further insight, the police stood in a cluster debating what to do next, whilst the handlers tossed tennis balls to reward the dogs for their efforts. I watched as Detective Jaeger scratched his head and asked the others if they had any suggestions. They all shook their heads to show they too were completely stumped, and after a few minutes of debate the group broke up. Some amongst their number headed for vehicles in the car park, whilst others, including the detective, retired to the hotel to seek liquid consolation in the Türken's bar.

CHAPTER 48

That evening I dined with the Die Welt reporter and photographer. Most of the conversation centred on Frau Kaiser and her husband's disappearance, interspersed with the usual gossip currently circulating around Berlin office. The waiter who served us at table enquired whether Herr Hartmann would be re-joining me later and I responded he was pursuing another story but would be returning at some stage in the future.

Later in the evening, when most of the hotel's patrons had drifted off to their rooms and the conversation at our table had lapsed into long thoughtful silences, I left my colleagues, with the pretext of going for a walk before retiring.

With torch at the ready and a near full moon lighting up the landscape, I made my way along the track to the cave. It was to the credit of the masons who had camouflaged the door so many years ago that the secret it concealed remained undetected, even when the cave's internals were being inspected by the dog handler and Detective Jaeger. I strolled down the tunnel to the chamber where, as expected, I found the Zeitmaschine no longer seated on its support cradle.

But *when* would Hartmann have taken it? No doubt he would have assumed the worst possible scenario – the police discovering the secret hidden behind the camouflaged door and the dogs leading the searchers through the tunnel to the chamber. For Hartmann to travel back to the past would be madness. In contemplating whether to do so he certainly would have been aware that this would certainly result in his machine colliding with an earlier version of itself, and anyway, there was nothing we had encountered in any of our past adventures to indicate this might have happened.

He must have travelled forward to a time when he thought the Zeitmaschine would be safe from falling into the hands of the authorities in the event of the chamber finally being discovered. Knowing as I did of his antipathy toward the existence of this machine ever being disclosed to the public, reappearing on the cradle in the middle of a police search would definitely be the last thing he would have wanted.

But then, when would he return? Next week? Next month? Longer? Would he indeed return at all or would he travel forward and remain forever in a distant future?

I stood there in a quandary wondering what to do next. I doubted Hartmann would be re-appearing any time soon. Should I stay at the Türken for a few more days or return to Berlin? Recalling that Herman Wirth had informed us the hotel was booked out by the police, the press and his regular visitors, I decided to drive our hire car to Berchtesgaden where I might stand a better chance of finding accommodation for the night.

I now also remembered leaving my valise containing spare clothing in the Zeitmaschine and casting an eye around and not seeing it anywhere in the chamber, realised Hartmann must have departed taking it with him. However, I suspected that rather than his doing this as an act of thoughtlessness, it had most likely been quite the opposite and for my benefit. If the police had indeed discovered the camouflaged door and subsequently found the valise in the chamber with my name embossed on its leather flap, it would have led to my being implicated in the Kaisers' disappearance despite all of our previous good efforts to fabricate our alibi. It was no doubt for the best reason he had taken it with him.

I pulled out a note pad and pen from my jacket pocket and wrote:

Karl,
Urgent!
When you return please
contact me at my office

I extracted a few of the empty treasure boxes from the pile on the floor and used them to build a small cairn in front of the door to the tunnel, finishing it off by clipping the note I had written to the top box and trusting Hartmann would see it in the light of his torch when he at last emerged from his time journey.

I left the chamber and inspecting the camouflaged door after closing it behind me, was reassured not the slightest clue remained in its outward appearance to claim the attention of future police searches of the cave. I swept the ferns aside, made my way along the track to the Türken's car park, and drove down to Berchtesgaden.

CHAPTER 49

Freda was glad to see me on my return to Berlin. Although she had managed to redirect much of my workload to colleagues, the accumulation of paperwork on my desk was nevertheless nothing short of breathtaking. I called her into my office.

"Freda, the story I've been pursuing in Berchtesgaden is still on the boil. Would you book me flights to Munich on a fortnightly basis, leaving here early Friday morning, returning Saturday afternoon, hire car from Munich, and an overnight stay at the Zum Türken in Berchtesgaden."

She asked whether Herr Hartmann would be accompanying me to which I replied he was still down in Berchtesgaden and I hoped to catch up with him at some stage in the future.

And so began my search for Karl Hartmann.

Once every two weeks I would travel down to Berchtesgaden, check into the Türken, go for a walk across the meadow when no one was around, and finally end up in the chamber. But the Zeitmaschine cradle lay empty on every such occasion and never did I detect anything to indicate Hartmann might have returned between my visits. I replaced the small note with a much larger sign fixed to the internal face of the chamber door to ensure when he did finally reappear, he would be sure to see it. I also recalled how, in Hartmann's story, he had built up a wall of rocks in the mouth of the cave and, as an added precaution against passers-by discovering the secret within the cave, when I was quite sure the police search for the Kaisers had finally been abandoned, I fashioned a similar stone wall that could be easily pushed out by anyone coming from within, and camouflaged it with clumps of budding ferns and grass roots. In my future visits to the site all I needed do to establish whether Hartmann had returned, was to check whether the wall had been breached.

Over time, through my regular visits to the Türken, Herman Wirth and I became the best of friends and occasionally he would reminisce with me about times gone by over a shared stein of pilsner.

"It's very disappointing when one loses such regular guests as was Herr Kaiser and his entourage. I could always count on him, his wife and the three bodyguards to boost the number of guests staying here in the hotel, even in the off season, not to mention the generous tips he gave my staff. But Morgen, at least your regular visits make up in some small measure for at least one of my lost customers."

However, after many months of fortnightly visits I reassessed the situation, and decided when Hartmann finally returned he would be sure to contact me. I reflected on our conversation at the dinner table in which he had opposed the idea of revealing to the world what we knew about the Zeitmaschine. But to what time in the future did he think he could take it and still remain confident its existence would remain forever unknown? Would he resort to destroying it to achieve this end? No, surely not. The thought once crossed my mind that Hartmann might do what Hitler had done in using the Zeitmaschine to accumulate great wealth, but I quickly rejected the notion. This had been one of his main arguments against bringing knowledge of the machine to the public domain, and the man was no hypocrite. Anyway, what good would such wealth do for a person of his age?

In the end, and much to the disappointment of the Türken's manager, I decided to limit my visits to the secret cave, and therefore the Türken, to once a year.

Back in the Die Welt office, my colleagues queried me about the story I had told them was brewing in Berchtesgaden and I responded that it had failed to materialise into a worthwhile printable story, which of course was unfortunately so very, very true. It had become a dead issue I told them, and consequently I wouldn't be pursuing the matter any further. To reinforce my position on this, I cancelled my visits to Berchtesgaden on the newspaper's account.

But secretly, at my own expense, I continued my visits.

At first I returned once a year, only to find the wall I had built in the cave entrance intact and increasingly overgrown with ferns, moss and grasses. Later, with a growing sense of futility, I reduced the frequency of my visits to once every five years, with the same disappointment awaiting me at the entrance to the cave on every subsequent visit.

CHAPTER 50

I retired from my post at Die Welt many years ago and these days find travelling by plane quite arduous, especially when my titanium hip replacements set off those damned security metal detectors at the airports. Once I get through their initial screening, the security guards make me remove my shoes and ask me to perform all manner of gymnastics as they wave their silly metal detector wands around my person.

Herman Wirth, the manager of the Türken, passed away a few years ago. Through Hartmann's story, I had come to know of him as a young boy on a scooter, later as a youthful desk clerk behind the Türken's reception counter, then as manager of the Türken and finally, as my friend. And of course, because I had stayed at the Zum Türken on so many occasions and shared the local gossip with him in his later years, he had become such a large part of my life that with great sorrow I attended his funeral in Berchtesgaden.

The walk from the Türken to the secret cave would be quite difficult for me now due to my arthritis, and for all these reasons and the fear of yet another disappointment in finding the wall at the entrance to the cave still intact, I haven't visited the area for .. well, I can't remember how many years. On my last visit there I decided to break down the wall at the entrance to inspect the chamber just one more time. But after doing so, found the rusting cradles empty without the slightest hint to suggest the Zeitmaschine might have returned to occupy either of them. I removed the note to Hartmann affixed to the door. The message I had prepared in anticipation of Hartmann's homecoming seemed totally meaningless once I realised that, considering my advanced years, when Hartmann reached his destination in the future, and when and if he finally read my message, I would most probably not be around to welcome him back. I rebuilt the wall at the cave entrance with a great deal of difficulty and much regret, to give this incredible saga some sort of closure and have never again returned to visit Berchtesgaden, the Türken or the cave in the forest.

The story I have told here could never be presented as being newsworthy because of the lack of any evidence to contradict the historical record and the fact that the main protagonist in my story is no longer with us. I have decided instead to reveal it to the public as the fictional novel you are presently reading because the police will be sure to take it as a fantasy – a tale made up by an old woman as she slowly slips into senility. There is therefore, no danger of my being arrested over the disappearance of the Kaisers.

The thought repeatedly goes through my mind that once upon a time I had the greatest scoop of the age right there in the palm of my hand, and I still cannot reconcile myself to losing control of it. But now the Zeitmaschine no longer exists in our present time and there is no hard evidence to back up my story's veracity. That is, of course, unless one wished to present a recently discovered war-time bunker chamber containing a pile of rusty steel boxes, two large rusting metal frames on wheels, rotting sandbags spilling their contents onto the floor, an old generator, and some ancient dust-laden electrical panels as evidence to corroborate a tale which would stretch anyone's credulity beyond all reasonable limits.

Besides this, the story the historical record tells us is quite clear. Hitler presided over the Third Reich with not a shred of evidence one could find in researching the archives to suggest he travelled to the future for a few years before returning to finally commit suicide in the Berlin bunker at the end of the War.

As I grow older, I suffer ever-declining health and fear I do not have much time left if I am ever to reveal my story.

Several days ago I dreamt I was having dinner in the Türken with Karl Hartmann. When I awoke the next morning, I remembered the dream, but more importantly, I remembered his arguments against handing the gift of time travel to humankind. I have pondered over this so very many times since that discussion, and must admit I long ago came around to agreeing wholeheartedly with the thrust of his argument. The ability to travel through time would eventually find its way into the hands of the worst elements in our society, and the civilised world as we know it would descend into absolute chaos.

I have written this novel with the forlorn hope that some of my readers in government circles will take it seriously enough to heed my warning and will, thus alerted to the danger time travel poses for civilized society, legislate against anyone with ambitions of emulating the success of Hitler's three scientists in producing another version of this incredible machine.

But my main purpose in going into print with this story is my fervent prayer that copies of this book – just as time capsules are intended to do – will survive into the future world to which Karl Hartmann has travelled in the Zeitmaschine. I also hope and pray, whilst he is still alive in that future, that Hartmann might come across a copy of this book with a title that is certain to capture his interest.

And finally, I hope he will read what I have set down in this novel, because I want you, Karl Hartmann, and indeed I want the whole world to know what an incredibly important, heroic and magnificent deed you have performed for the benefit of all humankind.

I also want you to know how proud I am to have known you, and to have travelled alongside you as your partner in this, our glorious and noble quest.

EPILOGUE

Hartmann recalled the thoughts that crossed his mind whilst sharing their last supper in the Türken, and he knew what had to be done. He looked down at her proffered hand and returning her gaze with a mixture of great sadness and determination, accepted her good wishes with a nod whilst they shook hands warmly.

Then he turned and hurried away down the track toward the cave, leaving the commotion on the Türken's veranda and the sound of the barking tracker dogs far behind.

Hartmann took one last look around the chamber illuminated in the sweep of his torch before scrambling into the Zeitmaschine's cabin and settling in front of the control station. Glancing around the cabin his eyes alighted on Morgen's valise lying on the opposite bench. He debated whether he should leave his colleague's bag behind or take it with him, but was troubled by the possibility that the police might finally discover the chamber and find the valise bearing Morgen's name, thus implicating his friend in the Kaiser investigation. He decided it would simply have to accompany him in the Zeitmaschine to his ultimate destination.

Hartmann slid the access panel door shut and turned to check the battery charge indicator. It showed batteries were nearly fully charged, and he felt a strange gratitude toward Kaiser for being so meticulous in always keeping them topped up. He next turned his attention to the time duration dials. Ignoring the hour, day and week dials he focussed his attention on the larger year meter dial. He noted the years from one to ten took up about one quarter of the dial's circumferential scale and therefore, recalling Fuchs' advice about the scale being logarithmic, he deduced the numbers from ten to one hundred would take up the next quarter. This appeared to be correct, borne out by the fact that seventy, the last number actually inscribed on the dial, was about three quarters of the way through the second quadrant. The rest of the dial wasn't inscribed with numbers because, as Fuchs had explained, it became increasingly difficult with the values becoming ever closer to each other to set them down on the dial with any accuracy. Hartmann figured the third quarter would consequently cover the years from one hundred to a thousand, and by extension, the fourth quarter of the scale would cover the years from one thousand to ten thousand.

Hartmann drew a deep breath and leaning forward over the console, rotated the time duration knob all the way around until the needle pointer was set on the maximum setting – nominally ten thousand years. He pushed the red direction lever to the forward travel position, and raising the glass cover over the red button, paused with hand poised over it.

Hartmann had no idea whether the Zeitmaschine's batteries could support such a long journey through time. He hoped they would, but somehow he knew that even if they were able to do so, should he afterwards experience a change of heart, they would never have sufficient charge to return him back to the present time.

He shook his head to clear any doubts from his mind and his fist came down firmly on the red button. Hartmann watched the needle of the speed meter as it started to rotate around the dial, all the while gaining speed, until it was finally spinning around at a dizzying rate. The darkness outside the panel door window pane was at first challenged a number of times by a flicker of light, and he wondered whether this might have been due to Morgen or perhaps the police casting around the chamber with their torches, looking for the Zeitmaschine. But very soon thereafter, all flickering ceased and outside the door panel the chamber remained shrouded in total darkness. Hartmann leaned back in his seat, folded his arms and wondered how long his journey would take.

Although he could see the time speed meter needle spinning around the dial, he had no inkling as to how fast he was actually travelling toward the future. A minute per second? An hour per second? Faster? He had no idea. The frightening thought entered his head that if it took too long to travel ten thousand years, he might end up dying from lack of water and starvation before reaching his destination, or perhaps the batteries might fail, leaving him stranded inside the Zeitmaschine with an incomprehensible void swirling outside, threatening to extinguish him should he attempt to disembark. He took another look at the battery charge indicator on the wall behind him and felt somewhat comforted by the fact it hadn't moved by any amount he could discern, and he prayed the batteries held enough power to take him to journey's end.

As the hours passed, he tired of the perpetual darkness outside and the unvarying rapid rotation of the speed meter. His eyelids had begun to droop a little and he decided to use this opportunity to catch up on some much needed sleep. Hartmann extracted a few items of clothing from his port, bundled them together to make a pillow, and lay out along the length of the bench to get some rest.

He must have dozed off because he was awoken a little later by a sudden jolt. He sat bolt upright and looked at his watch. He had actually slept for about three hours. The jolt worried him. In all of his previous travels there had never been any sound or vibration issuing from the machine nor had he experienced the sensation of motion of any kind. The speed meter needle was still racing around the dial at the same hectic rate and he turned to examine the battery charge meter. It had dropped significantly to around half-way down the dial. As he turned away from it, the Zeitmaschine shuddered after which followed another disturbing jolt.

Just then, through the portal glass a tiny flickering glimmer of light captured his attention. The shuddering recurred at infrequent intervals accompanied by an occasional jolt, whilst the flickering light outside gradually grew stronger. Hartmann tried to make sense of what he was seeing and feeling, but in the end he shrugged, accepting perhaps the answer might be revealed at the end of his journey, and then again, perhaps the answer might never be known to him.

A few hours later there was another series of shudders during which the Zeitmaschine tilted at an alarming angle, and it remained in this new orientation without righting itself again. The battery charge meter needle stood on the edge of the lower quarter red zone, and Hartmann again prayed the batteries would last to journey's end.

He felt hungry and ransacked his port and Morgen's valise hoping to find something to eat, and was rewarded with a muesli bar from the valise. He sat back contentedly munching it whilst watching the flickering light show outside the portal glass.

After another hour, he noticed that the speed meter needle was slowing and at the same time the flickering light outside was separating out into increasing periods of light and darkness.

'*Of course*' he twigged. The flickering light must have been caused by the passage of days and nights as the Zeitmaschine sped through time, and was only now starting to resolve itself into its two separate components, now that the machine's rapid progress through the ages was slowing down. But how could this be? After all, the Zeitmaschine was located in an underground chamber with no openings to the world of sunlight outside.

He glanced again at the battery charge meter. The needle was well into the red zone and he now knew for certain there would be no returning to the world he had left behind.

The speed meter needle crawled around the dial for another minute before finally coming to a standstill. As it did so, the Zeitmaschine was subjected to violent heaving and lurching accompanied by a terrifying explosive grinding noise which rose up through the floor. Hartmann was flung against the cabin wall and then onto the floor. As he struggled to rise, the floor became too hot to touch and started to buckle with the heat. The Zeitmaschine remained tilted at its previous angle, but he managed to clamber over the spilled contents of the port and valise onto the bench and peered out through the access panel window. It was daylight outside – but what daylight! The radiance entering the cabin was so brilliant it nearly blinded him.

The soles of his shoes began to smoke as he found his feet, and he desperately struggled to open the access door which had jammed due to the intense heat now rapidly spreading throughout and deforming the upper structure of the machine. At last, with a mighty heave, he managed to slide the panel aside. It jerked and ground its way through the guides, and Hartmann cast himself out of the doorway, landing in a patch of slushy snow melting at the edge of an expanding pool of water which steamed and bubbled around the base of the Zeitmaschine. A cloud of steam rose from his charred shoes as they came into contact with the snow, providing thankful relief for his tortured feet, and he stood shakily, taking stock of his surroundings.

Immediately in front of him, the base of the Zeitmaschine was visible through the surrounding pool of turbulently bubbling water. The previously shiny smooth panels of stainless steel below floor level now presented themselves as a matrix of molten metal and rock fragments, some of which still glowed red hot under the water.

Hartmann immediately guessed what had happened. The height of rock material here must have been higher than the original floor level in the chamber and consequently, on re-materialising in this future world, the base of the Zeitmaschine had tried to occupy the same space as the protruding rocks. In the ensuing collision, both rocks and machine base had fused together to form this confused molten conglomerate. Hartmann was struck by the terrifying thought that, had the Zeitmaschine not possessed its tall base structure, his body would have been closer to the ground, and he shuddered with horror realising if not for this, his legs would have been destroyed along with this mass of molten rock and metal.

He turned away from the crippled machine to survey the surrounding countryside. There was nothing in the immediate vicinity to indicate the chamber housing the Zeitmaschine had ever existed. Together with the access bunker tunnels, it must have completely collapsed over the centuries and afterwards, the brickwork and stones would have been eroded and washed away over the ensuing millennia.

The entire mountainside on which he stood was now covered in ice and snow. There was neither sign of buildings nor evidence of any other human presence to be seen. No trees; no birds; no animals; nothing but snow, ice and rocks. The distant mountains that in 1944 only bore summer snow on their peaks were now completely covered in a white blanket extending from their summit all the way down to the winding valley at their base, and the valley itself was filled with a wide streamer of ice which he immediately recognised to be a glacier.

Ten thousand years had carried Hartmann forward through time into the middle of the next ice age.

His feet, having previously roasted on the floor of the cabin, were now numbing with cold as his wet shoes turned to ice. Even the pool of water around the Zeitmaschine had stopped steaming and thin shards of ice were beginning to form at the edges of its outer rim. Hartmann made a circuit inspection of the badly damaged Zeitmaschine. It leaned to one side in concert with the slope of the hillside on which it stood. The steel cradle upon which it had once rested had disappeared, having corroded away thousands of years ago, whilst the concrete base of the chamber would also have disintegrated and been eroded away over the millennia. No doubt the roof had collapsed over time to yield the pale flickering of days and nights he had witnessed previously. All the rubble from the chamber roof, the tunnel, the Zum Türken, in fact everything on the mountain, would have eroded and been washed away over the centuries, leaving only the residual layer of rubble that had destroyed the base of the Zeitmaschine.

The machine itself had escaped these ravages of time during its journey through the passing ages because it had never suffered exposure to the weather as it travelled through time. But now, here on this hillside, it was laid bare and vulnerable to the elements which had destroyed all these other man-made structures.

Here, undisturbed by any humans who might still exist elsewhere, far away in this cold forbidding corner of the planet, subject to the severest of winters, its stainless steel panels would slowly begin to rust away and its internal components would disintegrate, leaving no evidence in the millennia to come that it had ever existed.

Hartmann felt content in the knowledge that the Zeitmaschine was at last far removed from the world of man, its powers to remain forever a secret, safely out of the hands of those who would employ it to humankind's detriment.

He began to shiver as the icy air penetrated his thin clothing and climbing back into the Zeitmaschine's cabin, he emptied out the remaining contents of his port to dress in as many layers of clothing as he could salvage from them. Because the floor underfoot was still hot, he slipped the empty valise case under his shoes to avoid direct contact, thus allowing his feet to thaw without being scorched again. The cabin had already cooled down appreciably but in his multi-layered clothing he was temporarily safe from the creeping cold.

Hartmann mulled over his present situation.

Apart from mild hunger pains and a general feeling of fatigue, he felt surprisingly well and began to reflect on his earlier life. Admittedly it had started off badly with his allegiance to Hitler, but in the years following the War he felt he had somewhat atoned for his wartime misdeeds by working for the charitable institutions which had given aid and comfort to the displaced and suffering masses.

And now, in this, his final act of removing this abomination, this Zeitmaschine, from the hands of those who would use it selfishly to bring about the collapse of civilised society, he had finally redeemed himself and freed his conscience from the last vestiges of guilt that had dogged him since the end of the War.

Tendrils of cold were beginning to find their way through the layers of clothing wrapped about his body, and Hartmann gained distraction from growing discomfort by reminiscing on the past.

He wondered whether any man could ever have had a more turbulent and interesting life. Perhaps if events had turned out otherwise and his hasty departure had not been forced upon them by circumstances, he might have been able to give Morgen Schreiber the media sensation she craved, before taking the Zeitmaschine on this, its final journey.

He reminisced on their adventures in the Zeitmaschine, travelling back and forth through the fabric of time, guided for the most part by their future selves. The whole concept of being thus guided seemed, and inevitably had proved, logically possible. But how in the first place did his future self obtain the knowledge he passed down to his earlier self? Obviously, he construed, from his future self's future self. But where did it all begin? Surely, he concluded, the knowledge passed down from one self to another must somehow have been circular in nature. But his brain was becoming increasingly clouded by fatigue and drowsiness, and he was unable to pursue the matter any further to make sense of it.

Instead, his thoughts drifted back to Linde. In his mind he conjured up the image of Herr Kaufmann's little jewellery shop in

Berchtesgaden where, so many years ago, Linde's smile had been the key that had unlocked his heart. He closed his eyes and folding arms across his chest, settled back on the bench to luxuriate in thoughts of the young maiden behind the shop counter. He could clearly visualise the scene in that 1959 jewellery shop as if it had been only yesterday, when Linde had smiled at him with eyes that sparkled with life and vitality. He recalled the shyness and embarrassment which had beset him at the time forcing him to flee from the shop after their first encounter.

Cameo images of their whirlwind romance now flooded back – their first meal together in the Gasthof Neuhaus; the picnic by the Königssee with the little white church nearby; his arm around her shoulders in the movie theatre. He recalled with great affection the first time they had made love in his bed at the Türken and smiled on remembering that, due to their preoccupation with more pressing matters, they never did get around to eating their Prinzregententorte dessert.

In his mind, Linde seemed so very real that Hartmann didn't dare open his eyes lest her image vanish in this freezing reality. Perhaps if he reached out he could touch her, and he ached to hold her in his arms once more. He murmured to challenge the moaning wind outside the portal.

"I love you Linde, I have always loved you."

Her presence in the cabin was so strong now, so strong and so close.

An icy zephyr blew into the cabin and he shivered.

"I'm cold Linde, so very cold."

It seemed through the fog which was slowly and relentlessly overwhelming his brain that she was looking at him sadly, bidding him rest and promising to watch over him while he slept.

He awoke with a start an hour later, shivering violently. Any warmth remaining in the cabin had long since been dissipated into the icy wastes outside. The crippled Zeitmaschine lay locked in a lake of ice, and icicles were forming around the top of the access doorway. Hartmann was unable to move his legs, and his hands, face, nose and ears were numbed and totally without feeling. After a while, as needles of freezing air stabbed at his innards with every breath he took, and fingers of ice found their way through his clothing, steadily penetrating deep inside his flesh, the shivering finally subsided.

His breathing had become overly laboured and difficult, and short painful gasps were all he could manage. Hartmann was experiencing a curious detachment from his body whereby it seemed all these afflictions were happening not to himself, but to another person whom he had once known. He felt totally confused and so very, very drowsy as he tried to recollect what he had been thinking about before falling asleep. After dumbly sifting through the thick fog which now befuddled his brain, and finding no answer there, he grudgingly gave up, content to passively watch the gentle drift of snowflakes falling outside the access portal.

* * *

Some hours later, a few glittering snowflakes swirled into the cabin on a playful breeze and drifting past Hartmann's lifeless eyes, settled on the panel in front of him, next to the red button. Tiny atoms of oxygen in the frozen water began to bond sluggishly with atoms of iron in the panel's surface, initiating the long, slow process of corrosion which over the coming centuries would eventually rust away and destroy the cold metal heart of Hitler's Zeitmaschine.

About the Author

Brian Farber is a retired construction engineer who has travelled widely from his home in Queensland, Australia, to work in many remote and interesting places. He is an avid reader of, and found inspiration, in stories written during the Golden Age of Sci-fi. He has now taken the opportunity to write, a pursuit not previously afforded him in his erstwhile busy professional life.

Insights into the development of Hitler's Zeitmaschine can be found on the blog site 'Farblog'.

www.ingramcontent.com/pod-product-compliance
Lightning Source LLC
Chambersburg PA
CBHW071735110726
47908CB00006B/1593